LOST AT L3

A Sci-Fi Comedy Adventure

Douglas Phillips

Bryant Phillips

CONTENTS

Foreword

Science fiction is a mismatched genre.

Science is the pursuit of a pure, unadulterated understanding of our universe. Not only is it serious and factual, it demands independent verification in the form of peer review. Over the past five hundred years, science has split into various specialties such as physics, chemistry and biology, but they all share the same process—the same rigor.

Fiction, on the other hand, is make-believe. It's the imagination unbridled and allowed to roam free. Fiction is the antithesis of science and yet somehow science and fiction combine to form an exciting, enjoyable, and thought-provoking genre within literature. Science fiction entertains us while building upon known science. It can even inspire new science. Technology that once seemed fanciful is now commonplace. In 1945, Arthur C. Clarke championed the idea of satellites in a geostationary orbit being used for communication. At the close of the Second World War, such an idea seemed absurd, bordering on outlandish. Now, geosynchronous satellites are the mainstay of concepts like GPS. In the 1960s, the crew of the Starship *Enterprise* used handheld communicators to talk to orbiting spacecraft. *Star Trek* also introduced us to the idea of noninvasive body scans. These days, we have cell phones and MRIs. The Taser used by law enforcement is an acronym formed from the science fiction novel in which it first appeared—Thomas A. Swift's *Electric Rifle*.

Within science fiction, there are a bunch of subgenres that range from hard (plausible) science fiction all the way through to quasi-fantasy, but hey, who doesn't love space wizards like the Jedi? Somewhere in this mix comes another perplexing idea—science fiction comedy. Sometimes, the best way to understand the world is to laugh at it. And although it's lighthearted, sci-fi comedy is no joke. In 1978, Douglas Adams's *The Hitchhiker's Guide to the Galaxy* proposed the idea of the Babel Fish—a small electronic device that could translate instantly between languages, just like Google Translate on my phone over forty years later.

As much as I love hard science fiction, sci-fi comedy is my secret addiction. Whether it's *Galaxy Quest, Red Dwarf, The Hitchhiker's Guide* or Netflix's *Don't Look Up*, comedy gets us to relax and see the world in a fresh light. Laughter isn't the best medicine in a pandemic. That honor goes to vaccines, but laughter comes pretty damn close. Whether you enjoy *Star Wars* or the Russian equivalent *Czar Wars*—whether you like *Doctor Who* or the more accurate *Doctor Whom*—I hope you'll enjoy *Lost at L3*. It's a lighthearted romp through the endless possibilities of science, fiction, and comedy.

Peter Cawdron

PART ONE

Lost in Space

1 ADVENTURES IN SPACE

PRISHA DHALIWAL STEPPED off a municipal tram and squinted against central Florida's famous sunshine. She tucked a lock of dark hair under the brim of her cap, smoothed her navy-blue jacket, and brushed away traces of lint from the two gold stripes on each sleeve.

A sign spanned the entrance to a large plaza bustling with people: *Orlando Space Park, Your Gateway to the Stars.*

She'd be flying right seat today, proving her new skills to a captain she'd never met. Megalodon corporate rules required all new hires to fly at least three times with a captain, then wait on pins and needles for an official signoff. If all went well, she'd soon have a third stripe on her sleeve along with the pride of being a full-fledged first officer.

Perhaps next year, with persistence and hard work, she'd make captain and get to command her own spaceplane. Forever a distant dream but getting closer each day.

Prisha hurried across the plaza. She'd been given a name, Captain Larry Mohs, but Megalodon HR hadn't provided a photo. No matter, Prisha had already filled in the missing information. Captain Mohs would be valiant. Educated and refined. Blond, with a chiseled jaw like the prow of a ship. She'd salute him, and he'd snap a practiced salute back.

Prisha quickened her pace in anticipation.

A woman in the same Megalodon uniform but with four stripes gave a friendly wave as she passed going in the other direction. She seemed nice. Perhaps they'd fly together tomorrow? Of course, she couldn't possibly outshine that legend of space exploration, Captain Larry Mohs. No one could.

What an epic day this will be!

Zap! "Oops!"

Prisha had walked right through one of the floating 3-D ads that populated the spaceport plaza, this one for a nearby beach resort. A phantom bikinied woman spreading branded lotion across her shoulders paused, put hands on hips, and furrowed her brow at Prisha. For an apparition, she looked realistically pissed.

"Sorry!"

The apparition gesticulated like an incensed Italian movie star whose big scene had just been interrupted. Two other pilots from a competing company walked by. One gave Prisha a sideways glance and a this-must-be-your-first-day kind of leer.

Prisha cringed. Humanity had made so many advances in science, and yet still no invisibility button when you most needed it. The 3-D phantom went back to her lotion. The leering pilots moved on. Prisha took a deep breath.

You can do this.

Those guys were no better. She was trained. Eight flights! Besides, stalwart Captain Mohs would provide further guidance in her apprenticeship, with methods that were meticulous but kind.

She set off once more, taking care to weave between the mix of people and floating ads. Just ahead, a chain-link fence separated the public plaza from flight operations. Beyond it, several spaceplanes were parked in a row, their gleaming white noses pointed to the sky.

A small dog wiggled through a break in the fence and ran off toward the row of rockets like he owned the place. In these days of competitive spaceflight, security was limited to whatever spare change was left in the corporate safety budget. It certainly made for an interesting preflight walkaround. Nesting pelicans, a raccoon looking for a shady place to spend a hot afternoon—who knew what sabotage of nature she might discover? No matter, she'd been trained for any adversity and with an exacting captain providing leadership…

And there he was.

Prisha stopped and twisted her head. He wore a Megalodon uniform, lopsided, with a tropical shirt peeking from under the jacket. An aging party-boy gut, skin like rotisserie chicken, and eyebrows so wiry they could nest a songbird. The man held a sign on a stick.

"Step right up, folks, trip of a lifetime, with the best prices anywhere! Why pay extra when you'll get the same views for a discount no one else can match, they know it, and you know it too, so c'mon over and let's get those boots into orbit, am I right?"

The name tag made Prisha's heart sink: *Cpt Larry Mohs.*

"Unparalleled views with less than a ten percent vomit rate! Folks, what goes up must come down, so step right up and get down!"

My captain is a TV pitchman?

Mohs paused, scanning her uniform. Prisha started a halfhearted salute, then extended her hand. Her stomach churned like a washing machine. "Captain Mohs, so nice to meet you. I'm Prisha Dhaliwal, your first officer junior grade for today."

He gave her the once-over, head to foot. "Super-duper. I could use an extra hand. Hold this."

He passed a sign that displayed a teenage girl whose open mouth and wide-eyed expression was somewhere between abject shock and I've-got-a-wasp-down-my-shirt. Bold letters proclaimed: QUIXOTIC ADVENTURES. SPACE FLIGHT FOR EVERYONE*.

Fine print provided a long list of exceptions: children under seven, people with heart conditions, asthma, high blood pressure, or RSD (rabid squirrel disorder). Realistically, the fine print was probably only for the lawyers. Except for the squirrel thing—nobody wanted to get near that.

"I've got to piss like a race llama," Captain Mohs stated loudly. "Just give 'em a pitch that'll fill that last seat for the ten-thirty flight."

"Shouldn't passengers be using the Megalodon booking system?" Prisha protested.

"Prish—can I call you Prish? I'm calling you Prish. Prish, Quixotic Adventures is not exactly front-page material, know what I mean? Yeah, technically we're part of Megalodon now, but the acquisition is still in progress. A few t's to cross and i's to dot, plus one or two deposits in a Cayman Islands account if you get my drift." Captain Mohs scratched himself nonchalantly. "Until then, this is how we do things. Plus, I get Mega-points for every seat I fill."

He pushed the sign over her head. "Hold it high and let 'er rip."

He waited. Prisha stared at the sign and back to the captain.

Mohs rotated both hands in circles. "Go ahead, do your shtick."

Prisha didn't really have a shtick. She was sociable enough but no extrovert. Something of a dreamer if she was being honest (which was every waking minute), and she'd always had a passion for sharing.

While training, she'd taken a part-time job at a nursing home, often bringing an astronomy book for adult story time. With wheelchairs gathered round, she'd wax on about the mysteries of the universe and the glory of a dark night sky. The old-timers loved it—at least, they looked happy enough—but it might have been good meds.

Captain Mohs leaned close. "I can tell you're digging deep. Use it, shape it. Pretend I'm a prospective customer—get me on that flight!"

Prisha set her jaw, taking care with each word. "Um... hur-ry hur-ry, step right up, ladies and gentlemen, boys and girls, for the thrill of a lifetime. You won't believe your eyes."

"Good! Okay, not actually that good. Less circus-is-in-town, more vibrato."

Prisha nodded, then cleared her throat. "Hey, wow. Everyone. Listen up. You've never seen Florida until you've seen it from fifty miles up!"

"Fantastic. Now go full oomph and I'll be back in a nanosecond." With that, Captain Mohs dashed off through the gate.

Prisha stood alone, holding the sign. Other flight crews passed by, some with customers in tow. She tried several sales pitches to unaccompanied tourists but with no success, and no sign of Captain Mohs either.

Twenty minutes? What's he doing in there?

A stocky woman wearing a Yankees Suck baseball cap and dark aviator sunglasses walked up. She glanced at the Quixotic Adventures sign, then back at Prisha. "See Florida from space, huh?"

She had a Jersey accent with a touch of superiority. Possibly a celebrity the way she wore the aviators, though by the looks of her waistline maybe one of those TV cooks on the Food Network.

"Yes!" Prisha beamed at her prospect. "See the stars... I mean the twinkly kind of stars, not the... you know, movie stars, ha, ha." Prisha tried to get a fix on the eyes behind those dense sunglasses. Reality show contestant? Women's wrestling, maybe?

Prisha remembered her shtick. "Fifty miles high at our apex. You can see the whole state end to end."

"That sounds like something any normal person would want... which I definitely am," the mystery woman said mechanically. She glanced at other tourists passing by, mimicking one woman's stance, then showing her teeth in an awkward smile.

"To be honest, Florida isn't what it used to be with all the coastal flooding down south. It's shrunk a bit."

"There's a pill for that."

Prisha laughed uncomfortably. "Anyway, maybe you could sign up for our ten-thirty flight and see for yourself?"

The woman tapped her lip. "Ten thirty. Quixotic Adventures. Yeah, this just might work." She straightened up, her eyes fixed on Prisha. "Your flight sounds like just the thing for an average American tourist. Like me. A tourist. Who likes space."

"Full disclosure, it's actually Megalodon now, not Quixotic, and even that name probably should have been Exotic Adventures, but the captain... oh, never mind. We board in ten minutes. At least I think we do." Prisha glanced around, but Captain Mohs was still indisposed.

"Sign me up."

"Great! It's just you, right? No... entourage?"

The woman scowled, her eyes barely visible over the frames of the aviators. "You ask a lot of questions."

"Of course, sorry." Prisha was going to place this woman eventually. Olympic weightlifter? Famous dog whisperer? "This way, please!"

She guided the mystery woman to the security gate and flashed her Megalodon employee badge to the guard with a casual flair. He yawned and waved them through to the tarmac.

Prisha extended a hand as they walked. "I'm Prisha Dhaliwal. First Officer. But I'm hoping to get my own spaceplane someday."

The woman spoke in a rapid clip. "Bouchet, Claire Bouchet. Uh… United States Foreign Service, yeah, that's it."

"Oh, government! I thought you might be a celebrity."

"Good idea, I'll have to remember that one."

"What countries were you assigned to?"

"That's classified."

"Oh. Of course."

They crossed the tarmac toward a line of towering rockets, each with a sleek white spaceplane at the top. Several bore the shark logo of Megalodon Industries on the tail—*Acquire, Control, Dominate*™.

"First time?" Prisha asked, studying Claire Bouchet, US Foreign Service Officer, as discreetly as possible.

"No, I've neutralized lots of—oh, you mean in space?"

Prisha forced a smile.

"Yeah, first time in space. Why would anyone subject themselves to this twice?"

"Suborbital flights are a lot of fun, you'll see! I've got eight under my belt." Claire would find out soon enough that spaceflight was unquestionably humanity's finest achievement. Prisha would see that she did.

Their captain was nowhere to be seen among the gleaming spacecraft, but further down, another rocket stood ready. Scorch marks blackened its base and the spaceplane perched atop was streaked with rust.

"Ah, there he is." Prisha pointed to a metal gangway where Captain Larry Mohs dragged a large duffel bag up its steps. His combover waved like tall grass in the wind.

"Looks a little beat-up," Claire noted, without clarifying whether she was referring to the rocket ship or the captain.

Prisha scrunched her nose. "A bit, yeah. But I'm sure it flies well. You don't get those scorch marks for sitting around like a lazy showroom model, right? Spaceplanes don't get any better than…"

She searched for a tail number but could only make out *N6A*, with nothing but tattered remnants of additional numbers. A faded corporate symbol on the tail was thankfully not the image of the panicked teenager, though it was either a coconut or a bowling ball with excess body hair depending on how you looked at it.

"Good old November Six Alpha *Whatever* will be our trusty steed to the stars today. And lucky passenger Claire Bouchet snagged the last seat!"

Prisha guided Claire up the steps, stopping at a platform where the rocket joined the spaceplane. Captain Mohs was headfirst into an open hatch, cramming the duffel bag into a storage hold, the waistline of his pants sliding precipitously. Prisha hastily looked away.

Mohs pulled his head out, examining Claire. His face split into a flash of pearly whites—and one gold.

"Got another customer," Prisha announced with pride, handing back the Quixotic sign. She introduced Claire, who struggled with a weak smile.

Captain Mohs shook her hand like the piston of a steam train. "It takes two to tango and five to fly!" Mohs pulled a card reader from his jacket pocket and Claire produced a credit card. "Prish, why don't you take care of the preflight while I get our last guest checked in."

Prisha made her way down the gangway and strolled around the base of the rocket, inspecting every nook and cranny and finding nothing to note. These workhorses were reliable, plus the ground crew would have already handled refueling and mating to the spaceplane.

Prisha slapped one of the rocket fins. "Ready to fly."

"So exciting!" A young woman in pastel colors with long blond hair and an ear-to-ear smile scampered up to Prisha and began shaking her hand. "I'm Amanda Summer, how are you today?"

She had a slight Texas drawl. The sun seemed to shine a little brighter as Amanda made a half-spin and her flowered dress danced in the breeze.

"Nice to meet you, Amanda, I'm First Officer Junior Grade Prisha Dhaliwal. You're on this flight?"

"I am! Wow, I can't wait to get up there! And oh my, Prisha, you wear that uniform well. Very sharp. You could easily be on page six of *InSpace Holographic*. Maybe even on the cover!"

Prisha instantly liked everything about Amanda. The smile was genuine, the eyes truthful. Not a hint of pretension in the voice, and with a natural charm that put her in the lead for best passenger of the day.

Amanda leaned in close like she was telling a secret. "Just so you know, I'm a flight attendant with Megalodon Airlines, so you and I are like coworkers even though this is my first trip to space."

"You're in for a treat." Prisha waved a hand toward the gangway and Amanda breezed gaily past, practically fluttering up the steps. At the platform, the spaceplane's oval hatch stood open, and Amanda peered inside.

"Spaceplanes are more vertical than what you're used to," Prisha explained as they climbed inside. The cabin extended overhead with ladder rungs embedded into what would normally be considered the floor. Seats hung on swivel mounts at either side, making access from the ladder easy. Four of the five passenger seats were already filled.

"Looks like you'll be right behind me," Prisha said, pointing to the empty passenger seat near the top. This was a Mark 4 spaceplane that had no bulkhead separating pilots from passengers, a design that Prisha preferred—more room for weightless tumbling once they were flying. The much newer Mark 7s had their own advantages: heads-up displays that actually worked, integrated entertainment/tracking consoles on every seatback, and a lavatory design that didn't reek of whatever the last passengers had eaten for lunch.

A distinctive aroma filled the entryway. "I'll just flip on the ground ventilation system," Prisha said apologetically as Amanda started her climb up the rungs.

Prisha closed and locked the hatch, then followed up the ladder, saying a quick hello to each passenger as she went. Claire had already buckled up in the first seat opposite the hatch. In the next row, a dark-skinned, middle-aged guy sat on the left side. His eyes were half-closed in a dreamlike stupor.

Does he understand we're about to launch into space?

On the right side—whoa! Unquestionably the best-looking man she'd seen in… forever. Wavy blond hair was accented by attractive darker streaks and swept above green eyes peering from beneath lightly tinted shades. His impish smile produced attractive laugh lines around his eyes. He wore a stylish suit with a narrow tie perfectly positioned for grabbing and pulling him close.

Prisha gave an awkward wave that turned out more like a squeeze of some invisible baby toy. Mr. GQ returned a disarming laugh.

Real smooth, Prisha. No wonder it had been four weeks since her last date. She hurried on.

In the top passenger row, an unkempt bearded man wearing head-to-foot camouflage sat on the left. The scent of a well-used compost bin accompanied his quick glance. Prisha smiled. He didn't.

Amanda was buckling up in the right seat. "If it helps you, Prisha, I'd be happy to handle the in-flight service once we're airborne."

"You are so sweet, but absolutely not! Today you get to sit back and let someone else serve the cocktails. Just kidding. We don't have cocktails. Or coffee, for that matter. Or tea. But we do have water! At least, I think we do."

Reaching the top rung, Prisha slid into the right-hand copilot seat. Captain Mohs filled the left, his pilot's jacket slung over the seatback. Bulging buttons struggled to keep his brightly colored tropical shirt from bursting. "All set?"

"Sure." Prisha's heartbeat picked up now that launch was moments away. She slipped her own jacket over the back of her seat and gave a quick polish to the two gold bars that decorated each shoulder epaulet on her crisp white shirt. "Captain, this is my first competency assessment, so let me know what part of the flight you want me to handle."

Would they take turns? Was she supposed to watch? "Captain's prerogative," was all her instructor had told her.

Mohs locked his seat into the reclining position. "You've got it from here. Now that we have paying customers on board, I'm just along for the ride."

Prisha blinked.

Eight instruction flights were one thing, but this would be her first with a cabin full of passengers. Mohs leaned back and tilted his cap over his eyes. He probably would have put his feet up if there was any place in the cramped cockpit.

Prisha slipped on a headset, then switched the microphone to the passenger address system. "Hi, everyone, I'm Prisha Dhaliwal, First Officer JG. Welcome aboard this Quixotic flight to the stars—or possibly Megalodon—there's an acquisition thing going on. No matter, it's a ten-thirty flight and that's all that counts. Who's ready to soar?"

Silence.

"Well, I know you're as excited to go as I am, but first, a few safety pointers. Watch your hands and feet as I put your seats back."

She pushed a button and each seat rotated into the reclined position, including her own. No screams from pinched fingers. Good so far. "Oh yeah, I forgot... and if you haven't already, buckle up."

From behind, Amanda spoke up. "Place the flat metal fitting into the buckle and adjust the strap to fit low and tight around your hips. To release, lift the face plate of the buckle."

Prisha twisted and mouthed a quiet "thanks." Her flight instructor hadn't rehearsed the passenger briefing stuff—probably to be expected with Dr. Don's School of Dentistry and Aviation. You get what you pay for.

With a toggle of the intercom, Prisha contacted the Orlando Space Park tower for launch clearance, then flipped a switch to start a holographic countdown clock that hovered just above her shoulder where everyone in the cabin could see it. As the numbers clicked down, her heart pounded exponentially faster.

... 3... 2... 1...

The automated launch system kicked in, and the rocket beneath spaceplane November Six Alpha *Whatever* roared to life. The cabin shook; there were a few gasps from behind and one enthusiastic cheer (Amanda).

"And we're off," Captain Mohs muttered from under his cap. At least he hadn't fallen asleep.

They rose slowly at first but soon passed through a layer of scattered clouds as their thundering climb accelerated. The blue sky darkened with a few stars already beginning to show.

Prisha kept her voice loud enough to be heard over rattling seats and groaning metal. "Off to our left is the city of Jacksonville with Georgia beyond. On our right, the sunken remains of south Florida, recently designated as our fourth national underwater park. If you haven't snorkeled around the Miami Beach skyscrapers, you should try it sometime!"

Am I supposed to be the tour guide? Captain Mohs hadn't objected to her announcement or even shifted in his seat. He might even be snoring, though it was hard to tell over the roar of the rocket.

Fupple truck him. It's my flight now.

Prisha could hardly suppress the proud smile that might be a permanent fixture on her face from here on out. She could almost feel that third bar on her shoulder with each tick of the altimeter.

At seventy kilometers, the curving horizon proved the fragility of Earth's true nature—an immense sphere separated from the infinite void of space by a thin layer of air. Oohs and aahs from passengers began in earnest. No vomits yet. Still early, though. Prisha announced the location of the airsick bags just in case.

At ninety kilometers, a loud clang rang through the cabin and the booster shut down. "Not to worry, folks. That's just the rocket attachment arms releasing. You're going to like this next part."

Captain Mohs snorted a laugh from under his cap, proving he wasn't asleep. The bottom fell out as their roller-coaster ride began a weightless glide.

"Woo-hoo!" Amanda squealed.

"That's a helluva thing!" someone further back hollered.

Now weightless, Prisha stowed her headset, unbuckled, and floated down the cabin aisle. "We'll be coasting through our apex for the next twelve minutes. Feel free to move about the cabin, as they say, which is a lot more fun when you literally weigh nothing!"

The two passengers she'd met earlier were both out of their seats. Claire hung upside down, still with her mirrored shades on. Amanda bumped off the ceiling, then coasted over to the lethargic black man, who was still buckled in his seat. The man had a finely sculpted beard and spectacles that made him appear well educated, maybe a professor, though an absentminded one.

Reginald was his name, he said. He looked confused. "Is this the bus to Tulsa? I don't think we're on the ground anymore." Amanda transformed into her flight attendant role, helped him unbuckle, and pointed the disoriented man to the stars outside.

Bearded camouflage guy was up too, floating next to a pen that had drifted out of his pocket. He stared as it slowly tumbled, then performed his own somersault.

Prisha felt a tap on her shoulder and spun around—too quickly. She collided with the remaining passenger: *that* guy, Mr. GQ. Their arms tangled, which only transferred her momentum, and they spun together like ice dancers in a tandem jump until finally hitting the aft bulkhead.

"Sorry!"

"My fault!"

He released her, but their faces remained inches apart. He had a strong nose with a slight uplift at the tip. Square jaw, lightly stubbled. Polished white teeth showed beneath lips that twisted into a confident smile.

Her heartbeat spiked. "Hi... um, welcome to me. To us! To space! I'm Prisha."

Idiot!

His smile crept sideways across his lips. "Thanks for the dance, Prisha. I'm Chase Livingston." His voice was like silk. Piercing green eyes bored right through her.

She steeled herself. "You... um, tapped me?"

"I need you."

"You do?"

"Yes. You see, I'm a scientist, but it's my first time in space. A capable first officer like yourself probably knows a lot, so I thought you could show me the ropes."

He pointed out the window. The glory of Planet Earth spread below. Florida, the Gulf of Mexico, the Atlantic Ocean, even as far out as the Bahamas. Haze and clouds made it difficult to see much farther, but it was a better view than any rooftop restaurant.

Prisha's mind drifted. "My port side is better... the plane, I mean! Sorry."

They drifted to the opposite side—slowly—while Prisha regained her composure. "On a clear day you can see all the way to Atlanta." They pressed together at the window. He smelled of sea salt mixed with a touch of granite. She pointed into the haze on the horizon. "Over there."

Chase smiled. "Ah yes, I can just make out the new Golden Spire building at Peachtree Center." He couldn't, no one could—he was just being nice. Or snarky.

"You're smarter than you pretend to be, Mr. Livingston." *Best line yet!*

"It's Chase. And I think you're new at your job."

Best comeback ever. Prisha's whole face was on fire. "Um. Yeah. First day."

He laughed, but with kindness. "I remember my first day. Princeton Plasma Physics Lab. I accidentally knocked over a lithium-ion generator and shut down the whole tokamak fusion reactor. Crazy stuff."

Prisha had no idea what he'd just said and was pretty sure that Chase lived on an entirely different plane of existence, but at least he was nice about it.

Chase studied the horizon. "It's a beautiful view, thanks for showing me. But what's that over there?"

A moving light was slightly above them, bright, and getting brighter by the second. Prisha stared without recognition. The light outshone every star and had a glowing orange halo around it. "A good question. Another spaceplane?"

"If it is, it's coming this way. And fast."

Prisha's eyes widened. The thing took on an oblong shape as it got closer. Much closer.

"Back to your seats, everyone! Quickly, please!"

With practiced efficiency, Prisha launched herself forward and glided into her seat just as the searing light blasted past at a speed too ridiculous to estimate. The spaceplane shook violently and suddenly surged ahead, accelerating as if a large wave in the ocean surf had caught them.

Prisha buckled up just as she was pressed into her seat. Shouts from behind made it clear that any passenger who hadn't made it back to their seat had just been thrown against the aft bulkhead—maybe everyone.

Wide awake, Captain Mohs scanned the gauges on the HUD hovering between them. Velocity had jumped to fifteen kilometers per second and was accelerating rapidly. "What in the Sam Hill flapdoodle was that?"

"A meteor?" Prisha answered. "I'm not sure, but we seem to be caught up in its wake!"

An unidentified meteor streaking through precleared suborbital space seemed about as likely as a semitruck barreling through a children's playground, but it was the only explanation she could come up with.

They did not cover this in training!

2   UP, UP, AND AWAY

SQUISHED LIKE A BUG on a windshield. The g-forces were bad enough in a padded spaceplane seat. Prisha could only imagine what it was like for the unlucky passengers who were plastered across the aft bulkhead.

We'll probably have to give them a discount once we get back to Florida!

A glance backward blew that idea out of the water. The vast globe of Earth had noticeably shrunk and receded further as their speed increased.

"Seventy-five kps," Prisha called out. Max velocity for any suborbital flight was eight kilometers per second, and that was after they'd reached their apex and were heading back down. The digits on the velocity indicator were still spinning with no end in sight.

The blazing light oblong *thing* had left a trail of glowing sparks like a comet's tail. Maybe it was a comet, but that didn't explain why it had lassoed them and flung them across space like a skipping stone.

There aren't waves in space, are there?

"Mr. Livingston. Um, Chase," Prisha called over her shoulder. "Any idea what just happened?" He'd said he was a scientist.

"Unexplained aberration of solar system dynamics," he managed with a strained voice that seemed unusually far away. Probably one of the people stuck to the back wall.

"Got any brakes?" someone shouted. They'd probably noticed that Earth was rapidly becoming nothing more than a blue-white dinner plate in a star-filled sky.

Captain Mohs yelled back, "Stand by, folks, we'll get this plane turned around and have you back on the ground just as soon as we can."

A tall order. No brakes. Not even a rocket anymore; their booster had detached and returned to Earth. It had probably already landed back at the Orlando Space Park and was being refueled for their two-p.m. flight.

Mohs glanced at Prisha. "Any ideas, Junior Grade?"

Prisha's brow was contorted like an overused twist tie. She lifted a heavy arm high enough to slip on her headset, then toggled the transmit button on her arm rest. "Orlando Space Park, this is Megalodon November Six Alpha..." She paused, still having no idea what their tail number might be. "Never mind. Um... say, guys... we've had an encounter, maybe a comet, we don't really know. And we're accelerating away from Earth. Could really use your help on this."

There were a few clicks, then a voice: "*Please remain on the line, we'll be right with you.*"

"Oh no."

Mohs was wearing his own headset. "Blast it all."

A few more clicks and a cheery voice came on. "*Welcome to Megalodon Customer Service! Please say or enter your customer ID.*"

"God help us." Mohs wiped a hand across his brow, then stated forcefully, "Representative!"

"Good idea," Prisha said.

The cheery voice returned with a hint of apology. "*Sorry, I didn't get that. Please say or enter your customer ID. If you don't have one, remain on the line and a customer service agent will be right with you!*" Music started playing.

"Ugh."

"We're experiencing a high call volume right now. Your wait time is... nineteen... minutes." Back to music, a soaring instrumental piece that ungraciously started over every twenty seconds.

Prisha took another glance behind. Earth had shrunk to the size of a teacup saucer while the music was getting scratchier. Death by Call Center was a distinct possibility.

"Emergency frequency?" Prisha asked. The captain nodded.

She reached to the head-up display and air-dialed a new radio frequency. The irritating music ended with a final *"<scratches> Your call is important to us. <scratches> Goodbye!"*

Mohs held an index finger firmly in the air. "By Jove, I'll disconnect my Megalodon internet service! That'll show 'em. Just as soon as I, uh... get home."

Prisha pressed the transmit switch. "Orlando Space Park, anyone there?" Surely the emergency frequency would be staffed by a real human being.

She waited. More scratches, then a broken reply, unintelligible.

"Say again, Orlando?"

Scratches were mixed with a faint voice. Their spaceplane was probably halfway to the Moon by now. The velocity indicator ticked through two hundred kps.

"Not looking good, Captain."

Understatement of the year. That third bar on her shoulder was disappearing as fast as the Earth behind them.

"Hmm," was the captain's diagnosis. She waited, but no words of wisdom were offered.

While Mohs pondered their predicament, Prisha wasn't going to let the passengers continue to suffer. "I'm going back to help."

She unbuckled and pried her head from the seatback. The acceleration wasn't getting any worse, but it felt like being dragged on a rope behind a speeding hydroplane, not that Prisha had ever done anything like that. Well, actually, she had. There was that ski boat thing with Jimmy back when she was young and stupid. Who allows herself to be slung behind an out-of-control powerboat while the driver literally cheers for a wipeout? A teenager whose idiot-soaked skull bones hadn't yet fused together, that's who.

Modern-day Prisha (with exactly 206 perfectly breakable bones) squeezed herself around the seat and hooked a foot into the top of the ladder. Carefully, one rung at a time, she descended.

Amanda was buckled up and so was the guy in camouflage fatigues (probably the owner of the duffel bag the captain had stuffed into the baggage compartment—he looked like a duffel-bag kind of guy).

In the next row down, Claire was speaking into one of those fancy HoloWatches on her wrist. A holographic antenna popped up and she adjusted a floating dial, stopping when she noticed Prisha staring.

"Secured channel to Washington," Claire explained. "Forget you ever saw this."

"Classified?"

"Tighter than an Area 51 autopsy."

"But if you're getting a connection, it's kind of important—"

Claire cut her off. "I'm not."

"But if you do."

"I won't."

"But you'd tell me?"

"If you're on my need-to-know list."

"Am I?"

Claire stared darkly, then went back to adjusting holographic antenna settings. Prisha was a little disturbed by their shadowy passenger's behavior but needed to focus on more immediate concerns—the groans coming from the back of the cabin. She continued down the ladder to the bottom rung.

A few feet below, Chase and a very disoriented Reginald were pinned against the aft bulkhead. Chase nursed a bruise on his forehead. He made it look good, though.

Prisha hung tight with one hand and reached down with the other. She forced an award-winning service smile. "Could I help you gentlemen back to your seats?"

"Best idea I've heard in a while," Chase managed. He pried Reginald's arm from the bulkhead and pushed him toward the ladder. With Prisha's help, the confused man was able to squirm his way into the lowest seat.

"Can we pull over?" Reginald asked. "I need to get off this ride."

"Sure, give us a few minutes to work on that." Prisha was proud that at least one employee of Megalodon was providing good customer service. "Just one more rescue to work out."

Prisha kept one foot on the lowest rung and reached out for Chase's hand. They touched fingers and, with a lunge, grasped wrists. Both groaned, and Chase eventually got a foot on the rung to pull level with her.

His chagrined, somewhat mischievous smile could have melted a block of ice. "Just thought I'd keep Reg company on the back wall. Thanks for your help."

She inspected his bruise, touching lightly as he winced. "You should be okay, but I'll take a better look once we slow down."

If we slow down.

Chase started up the ladder to his seat, and Prisha followed. Going up felt like an eternity, with biceps shaking from the strain of multiple g's, but she finally got there and dropped back into her seat.

Note to self: more time in the gym!

"Just passed through one thousand kps," Captain Mohs stated without emotion. The rightmost velocity digit was still spinning though no longer a blur. But like a hockey puck sliding across ice, turning this ship around was already beyond their control.

Minutes ticked by. The pressure on their seats reduced, eventually bringing them back to weightlessness. The display finally settled on 1,216 kps, a good number to list on the Megalodon corporate report they'd probably need to file. Whatever had dragged them away from Earth had disappeared into the starry background and left them coasting. Behind, home had become nothing but a blue-white marble.

Captain Mohs announced in a slow cowboy drawl, "Well, folks, it looks like the worst is over. Not expecting more turbulence, so I'll turn off the fasten seat belts light. You're free to unbuckle and move about the cabin. There's a lavatory in the rear, and I'll ask Prish to provide each of you with a bottle of water, no charge."

Prisha unbuckled. He probably saw the stink eye she flashed at him because he amended his announcement. "Yeah, folks, I know this isn't quite the flight that any of us expected. But on the plus side, we've probably broken at least a dozen records for propulsion, top speed, whatever, and I'm sure we'll all be famous when we get home. My dad always told me if life gives you lemons, put them in your mouth and suck it up. Sure, he was terrible at fathering, but the man was a master at metaphors. So just sit back and relax while we study our options for getting turned around."

He switched off the passenger address system and turned to Prisha, his eyebrows lifted in question.

"Um… hitch a ride on the next comet going in the other direction?" Prisha offered—not seriously, but somebody had to throw out the first bad idea.

Mohs pointed a finger. "Good idea." It wasn't.

Prisha squinted.

"Yeah, you're right. Bad idea. But we'll find something. Hey, it's a great training exercise for you, Prish."

Prisha fumbled her response. "Well, I'll try, but—"

"All I can think about right now is a good stiff drink. Whiskey if we had it. Bourbon would work."

"Right," Prisha mumbled. "I'll take a look while I'm getting the water."

As Prisha floated into the aisle, the camouflaged duffel guy blocked her path. "Pretty damn clear what's going on," the man grumbled in a baritone voice with a Cockney accent.

"I'm really sorry, sir, we're doing the best we can," Prisha answered. "Would you like some water?" Bottles were stored in the back. He'd have to let her pass, which might also defuse any confrontation.

Unsavory stains dotted his shirt. His matted dark hair was pulled back in a ponytail, and he had a grizzled beard like steel wool. Two slits of diamond were set into darkened eye sockets. What age was he anyway? Ninety? Forty? He looked like he'd just returned from a decade of self-isolation on Baffin Island sledgehammering rocks at a quarry.

The man twisted his beard with a gnarled hand. "Razor."

"Sorry, sir, we don't have any shaving accessories on board. Just water."

"My name is Razor. Not *sir*." He spat out the last word with contempt.

Prisha swallowed hard, furiously flipping through her best customer service ideas. It was either that or an arm-wrestling match and she was pretty sure who'd win that conflict.

"Oh, I love unusual names. Mine's unusual too, at least for an American. Over in India, Prisha is rather common. Is it Mr. Razor?"

"Just Razor." His stare could curdle dairy. "We're stuck out here, aren't we?" His fists balled up. He looked strong enough to break a window, and spaceplane windows were bulletproof.

"Stuck is such a strong word."

"Not really." Claire floated up the aisle to join the blockade. "Trapped, entombed, squashed, lifeless… as in, dead. Those words are stronger." She folded her arms, slowly twisting in the air like the hand on a clock.

Amanda chimed in, lifting from her seat. "Prisha, you're doing such a great job, the stars outside are pretty, and floating around is really fun, but…" Amanda winced.

Reginald finished. "We're not going home, are we? The captain is just saying he'll turn us around to make us feel better." The man still seemed pretty calm, all things considered.

Prisha looked helplessly around the circle of passengers and to the pale blue dot vanishing into a sea of stars.

Ideas. Come on, brain!

Chase answered before Prisha could. "I'd estimate we're twenty million miles from home, give or take. And since this spaceplane probably only has attitude thrusters, returning home from out here is… unlikely."

Silence. Razor's jaw clenched. He looked like he was contemplating who to punch first.

"Hang on, everyone." Prisha flung herself forward and huddled close to Captain Mohs. "Um, Captain, we're going to need a plan, or we'll have a mutiny on our hands." She admitted she had no solution, but surely deep-space emergencies didn't count as training exercises, did they?

The captain had set his imagined glass of whiskey aside to study a chart that was now displayed on the HUD. Ellipses of various sizes encircled the Earth. Mohs pointed to the fine print on the chart. "Says here that Earth orbits can exist at almost any distance. We might start turning the corner any minute."

"That sounds good," Prisha answered. She actually had no idea, but it was a better idea than hitching a ride on a comet.

"Highly unlikely." It was Chase again. He whipped off his shades, which he had apparently put back on for this very purpose. "What's our velocity?"

Prisha pointed to the velocity indicator, which still read 1,216 kps.

"Is it dropping?"

"No, it's been steady."

"Then we're not on an elliptical orbit around Earth. Johannes Kepler figured this out back in 1609 with his three laws of planetary motion. Later, Isaac Newton computed the motion of any object subject to a gravitational field. If we were on an elliptical path, our velocity would be slowing as we approached apogee, the furthest point in the ellipse."

Damn. Prisha and the captain both stared at Chase.

"Then where are we heading?"

"Probably there." Chase pointed to a thin crescent of light that hung in the very center of the windshield. With the glare of the sun off to the right, it wasn't easy to see, but it looked like a crescent moon.

"It's Venus," Chase clarified.

"We're heading to Venus?" Captain Mohs asked incredulously.

"Looks like it."

The crescent was growing larger by the minute. Prisha called over her shoulder. "Hey, everyone… you might want to take your seats again."

"If you don't mind, I'd kind of like to watch from here," Chase said. "You guys have the best view, and if we're going to crash on Venus at this speed, buckling up isn't going to make the slightest difference."

"Kind of fatalistic?" Prisha responded.

"Hey, we live, we die, we ferment a little and are reborn as new cells in some other creature."

"Circle of life?"

"Yeah, pretty much."

"But on Venus?"

"Yeah, probably not. Surface temperatures are nearly a thousand degrees."

Prisha thought for a moment. "Fahrenheit?"

"Does it matter?"

"Good point."

At their ridiculous speed, the crescent soon filled half the sky. There was nothing to do but watch. Chase had guessed right about the thrusters. Small jets were positioned around the outside but were designed only to orient the wings prior to descent into Earth's atmosphere. They might attempt a landing on Venus, but even if it were successful, they'd be stranded like clay figurines inside a kiln, quickly becoming crispy around the edges.

Captain Mohs settled back in his seat like a truck driver cruising down the interstate and announced over the passenger address, "Well, folks, we might be making an unscheduled stop at Venus today.

Which reminds me of a funny limerick. There once was a lady named Venus, whose thumb looked just like a—"

"Velocity is increasing again." Chase pointed to the HUD. "Venus is pulling us in, but that might be good. This might end up being a gravity assist."

Captain Mohs pulled off his headset and put it over the head of a bemused Chase. "You take it. You're doing better than me."

"A gravity assist?" Prisha asked.

"It's like a slingshot," Chase said, his voice now going out over the passenger address. "We get pulled in and slung out the other side going even faster. Standard NASA maneuver for interplanetary missions."

Better than crashing—if he was right. The narrow Venus crescent loomed ahead, brilliant white, but it *was* drifting to the right side of the windshield. Of course, there would be solid ground on its dark side too, but as they closed in, the planet revealed its full shape. Dark cloud tops formed a distinct horizon with stars peeking out from behind. There was a slight chance they might graze its edge. One percent chance… maybe two.

"Fascinating." Chase gripped Prisha's seatback.

Prisha gritted her teeth. "Eeee… this is going to be close."

They watched half in horror, yet strangely captivated, as their spaceplane skimmed the upper reaches of the Venusian atmosphere, then whipped around the planet's night side and into brilliant sunshine.

Now, bright white clouds spread beneath them as far as they could see. They hadn't smacked into anything yet and might not. Even as the velocity crept up, there wasn't any feeling of acceleration. More like falling.

"Passing fourteen hundred kps," Prisha announced. More records shattered, plus a flyby of a distant planet.

Epic first day on the job. Of course, it might be my first and last day.

The spaceplane shot into open space as the veiled planet slid past the starboard windows. They hadn't splatted, but now that they were on the sunlit side, the downside of their maneuver had become obvious.

The sun, brighter than any human had ever seen it, lay directly ahead.

3   FUN IN THE SUN

"WELL, THAT LOOKS… hot." Reginald floated just behind Prisha's seat. In fact, a crowd had gathered. So much for seat belt rules.

"Always knew I'd end this way," muttered Razor.

Amanda gave him a quizzical look. "You knew you'd be on a spaceplane zipping past Venus, then plunging into the sun?"

Razor nodded. "Pretty much. Yeah." He picked something out of his teeth and wiped it across his already-dirty camo shirt. He looked like the kind of guy who spat a lot. Probably fought off wild boars on the weekend and showered every June.

As the sun filled the windshield, the temperature in the cabin crept up. Captain Mohs had already turned the ventilation to full.

Chase shrugged. "Hey, we got past Venus. Of course, the sun is a million times more massive, and gravity quadruples with each halving of distance."

"I didn't need to hear that," Claire said from further back.

A tense minute later, Chase pointed to a band of fire that jumped out from the sun's edge. "Funny thing about solar prominences—"

Claire interrupted. "Do you mind? Some of us are preparing to die here."

Chase was quiet, but only for a moment. "We seem to be heading more towards the right side this time."

"Is right better than left?" Amanda asked.

"Not really—either edge could fling us around to the other side."

"All the way around? Maybe it could fling us back to Earth?" Amanda seemed interested in the science, though it might have been a desire to avoid becoming part of a melted spaceplane.

"Comets do it all the time. The Parker Solar Probe too."

"Which is?"

"A NASA spacecraft that was sent to the sun. But now that I think about it, on its tenth pass, the Parker probe burned up. So…"

Amanda bowed her head. Razor nodded with conviction, apparently sure of their coming demise.

"Oh, I almost forgot!" Prisha flipped a switch on the pilot's control panel and a metal cover slid across the outside of the windows, suddenly making the cabin darker. "We have reentry shielding."

Captain Mohs gave her the thumbs-up. "Good idea, Number One."

Prisha beamed. Not only had the captain addressed her with the pilots' slang for a full-fledged first officer, but with their shields down, they might survive this solar flyby after all. Unless, of course, the sun decided to drag them into the innards of its nuclear furnace, in which case the captain, his junior grade first officer, and everyone else would become equally molten.

Intense heat still radiated from window glass and walls, making it perfectly clear you wouldn't want to be outside. With no view forward, they were flying blind—probably just as well since there wasn't anything to control.

A flash of light through the side windows accompanied a strong jolt that rattled the spaceplane's frame like a race car hitting a twenty-mph speedbump. Razor slammed against the ceiling. Chase slammed into Razor.

"What was that?"

"We may have flown through the solar prominence." Chase always seemed to have an answer. "A prominence is hot plasma ejected from the sun's surface like a tornado that's a million degrees."

"Still not helpful," Claire called out from the back.

Their spacecraft hadn't yet shredded into splinters like one of those barns that are always exactly in the path of a tornado in the movies. Nothing had melted either, though the cabin was beginning to feel more like an oven than a shelter from the sun. Prisha loosened her tie. She'd been in worse heat—Rajasthan in summer, where people literally used the sidewalks to cook eggs.

"Fifteen hundred kps," Prisha announced, wiping the sweat off her brow. She would have provided a report on cabin temperature too, but the Mark 4 spaceplanes had neglected that little detail in their design. Some engineer had probably thrown out the thermometer, proudly showing his boss that excess weight had decreased by 0.7 grams.

Minutes ticked by. They were still alive. No more jolts or flashes of burning plasma. The cabin even felt somewhat cooler. Tensions cooled too.

"Dare I pull up the shields?" Prisha asked. The captain nodded.

She flipped a switch and the covers slid up, revealing a dark sky filled with stars. The sun was now behind them, and their speed was trending down. Either they were nearing that orbital apogee that Chase had mentioned, or the mighty sun was exerting a backwards pull.

Chase asked the captain, "I don't suppose you have location tracking on your control panel?"

"Relative to Earth, sure," Mohs answered. "But the inertial navigation numbers are off the charts." He pointed to a digital readout stuck on four nines.

Chase rubbed his chin. "Getting our bearings would give more information about our chances. I wonder, can you spin us around in a circle?"

Prisha glanced at the captain, who gave his approval for the maneuver. She lifted a plastic cover over a joystick and flicked the stick left. Thrusters momentarily thrusted, and the spaceplane pivoted. Stars drifted by, then the sun, then more stars. No sign of a blue marble out there. Chase studied as they turned. Prisha stopped their pirouette after they'd made a full circle.

"Nice tour, Science Guy." Claire's voice dripped with sarcasm. She and Reginald hovered just behind Chase. Amanda and Razor were further back, looking out the side windows.

"Give him a chance," the captain said. "He might be on to something."

Chase pointed. "That's Procyon there, and Pollux above it. Regulus is directly ahead. It's September back on Earth, which means the sun is in Leo, and since Leo is still ahead of us, that means Earth is directly behind us."

The captain pushed his cap over his eyes and settled back into his seat. "Or maybe not."

Claire threw up her hands in exasperation. "Fantastic. We're still going in exactly the wrong direction."

"We're going to die out here, aren't we?" Reginald asked.

"Yup," Claire answered. "Dead. Expired. Lifeless. Deceased. Passed on and gone. Not going to be a pretty sight."

Mohs lifted his cap and stared into space. "Why do these things always happen to me? Been at this gig for nine years. I try. I work hard. Just when I get the fuel bill paid, a pump goes out. Or the insurance guy is after me for past-due premiums. When Megalodon bought me out, I thought I had a shot at retiring. Now…"

Prisha forced a smile, but she didn't have much to work with. "Don't worry, Captain, we'll figure something out. With the sun behind us, our speed is dropping. At least that's something."

"I like your attitude," Razor said from the back of the floating group.

Prisha swiveled around. "Who, me?"

"Yeah, you. Never give up. There's always a way. Sure, you might have to eat crickets and slugs for breakfast, maybe gut a moose and climb inside its hollowed-out rib cage to survive a cold night. But once you've learned to bite the heads off fish or create a signal flag with your own blood as paint, you learn what life is about."

"And what is life about?" Reginald asked, looking squeamish.

"Survival," Razor said with a flourish. "Day-to-day survival. Pure and simple." Razor seemed sure of himself, but then this was a man who wore camouflage for a tourist spaceflight.

Prisha scrunched up her nose. "Not exactly what I was thinking."

"I think the first officer was trying to figure out how to get us back to Earth," Chase added helpfully.

"Same thing," Razor countered.

Chase confronted Razor face-to-face. "Explain how biting the heads off fish is the same thing as finding a navigational solution through interplanetary space?"

"You want to survive? You plan, prepare. You do whatever you have to do. You never give up. Me? I've already got a plan." Razor pointed roughly to Prisha. "But it's her job to turn this ship around."

"Why isn't it his job?" Reginald pointed to Captain Mohs, who continued his stare into space, unperturbed by the dark conversation around him.

"That bloke? Yeah, right." Razor's eyes shot daggers at the hapless Mohs as if the captain were a strong candidate to become the nourishment in Razor's survival plan. Razor returned to the back of the cabin, either to sulk or to plot further.

Like Mohs, Claire looked beat as she stared out the windshield. "Okay, Space Genius, you got your bearings. So, where are we going to end up? After we're all dead, that is." She turned to Chase and shrugged. "Just curious."

Chase pointed straight ahead. "Assuming we're at or above solar escape velocity, somewhere in Leo. Maybe Regulus, or some other star. Thousands of years from now, of course."

"Of course," Claire answered, finally satisfied knowing her fate. She floated away. The rest did the same, leaving the captain staring at the nothingness ahead, and Prisha alone with her thoughts.

Things weren't all bad. Their unalterable trajectory would make them the first interstellar space travelers. Maybe a thousand years from now, their frozen, dead spaceplane would arrive at a planet orbiting Regulus. They'd be picked up by an alien race who would use advanced technology to resuscitate their desiccated bodies. Once restored to health, they'd be made honorary citizens of a nebula-spanning civilization, and they'd tour between worlds like rock stars. Prisha would get her own alien house in a city floating in clouds of pink-and-green nebula gas, just like one of those Hubble space telescope photos.

Yeah, I could do that.

"Who's thirsty?" Amanda floated up behind Prisha and the captain. "Our round-the-sun adventure parched my throat."

"Sorry, I never got around to that water," Prisha answered, unbuckling.

"No, sit! I can get it. You and the captain have to keep us flying. The water is in the aft bulkhead locker, right?"

"Aw, thanks, Amanda. You didn't have to become the flight attendant." Amanda was definitely on the invitation list for a wine-and-cheese party once Prisha settled into her alien nebula house.

Their newly hired but unpaid flight attendant was gone for several minutes. Prisha was just about to go help when Amanda floated back. In one hand, she held out bottles of water for the captain and Prisha. In the other arm, she cradled a small dog.

"Who does this little guy belong to?" Amanda stroked the dog's head. It had curly fur, white with a few black spots, and eyes as big as saucers. The poor thing was shivering.

"Oh my!" Prisha unbuckled.

"Now wait just a second, young lady, pets aren't allowed on space flights," Captain Mohs announced. "Not after that incident with the governor and his emotional support rat. Holy guacamole, nobody wants to clean up after that kind of mess."

It was an odd factoid of spaceflight history that might be worth hearing about over a few glasses at the wine-and-cheese party, but not now. Prisha floated close, giving a gentle pet to the nervous dog.

Amanda said, "I found him in the crawlway to the baggage area. I heard him yipping. Did you know there's a duffel bag back there too?"

"Mine," Razor announced.

Amanda swiveled around. "So, is this doggy yours too?"

Razor shook his head. "Never seen it before."

The other passengers gathered around to check out the newest addition to their troupe. None made any claim to the dog, and the dog made no move to choose any of them.

Prisha looked into the dog's large cherub eyes. "You're a stowaway?"

The dog whimpered. Amanda checked under the hood. A he. "There, there, little guy, everything is okay. We'll take care of you."

His coloring looked familiar, possibly the same dog Prisha had seen slipping through the hole in the fence back in Orlando. But there was something else about him. The gleam in his eye made it clear this was no ordinary stray. There was a deep intelligence in there. Pride, even. This little canine had a story to tell, even if they might never hear it.

"He must be thirsty." Prisha flipped up the squeeze tube on her water bottle, took a sip, then squirted some in the dog's mouth. A few globules floated away, but the pup slurped down most of it. He wagged his tail, then vigorously scratched behind one ear, a maneuver not easily accomplished in zero-g.

Amanda helped the dog resolve the itchy spot. "I think we'll call you Itchy Boy."

If dogs could sigh in abject dismay, this one did. He hooked his hind leg behind the same ear, scratched more forcefully, then looked up.

"You're so adorable! How about Earlobe? Do you like that name better?" Amanda was probably only half-kidding. The dog seemed to think so too. He scratched again with fierce determination.

"Maybe we should call you Scratch?" Amanda asked. The dog licked Amanda's chin repeatedly. "Then Scratch it is. What a sweetie you are!"

Prisha asked the captain, "Any idea how stowaway Scratch got on board?"

"Probably while we were loading. Doesn't much matter, he's as marooned out here as we are now. Which brings up the question of our supplies."

"Thirty-two water bottles and forty-one pretzel packs," Amanda announced.

Mohs shrugged. "More than I thought we had. Enough for five or six flights."

"*Suborbital* flights," Prisha corrected.

"Right. This one is looking to be somewhat longer." He poked a few air buttons on the heads-up display floating between the pilot seats. It brought up the graphic he'd been studying earlier: multiple ellipses of varying distances from Earth. Except for the odd historical factoid or bawdy limerick, the ellipse graphic seemed to be all the man had. Mohs sighed deeply and returned to his silent coma of self-pity.

She couldn't blame him. Cute dogs and alien fantasies aside, things were looking bleak. The sun was now behind them, looking much like it did from Earth. It would shrink further with every passing hour until it was just another star in the sky. By then they'd have run out of supplies, oxygen, and patience. Razor's plan for survival of the fittest would probably kick in.

Prisha caressed the two gold bars on her epaulet and let out a sigh at least as big as those from Mohs and the dog. Two bars would be all she'd ever get. A commission of her own was an impossible dream now, left far behind on a planet where she'd once lived. The rest of her days would be spent flying across empty space—days that could probably be counted on one hand. It wasn't anyone's fault, not even the captain's. Just a freak accident of nature. A passing comet, or asteroid—or *something*—that had somehow dragged them halfway across the solar system and flung them out to certain death in the dark wasteland of space.

Back on Earth, there would be an inquiry. A Megalodon corporate rep would step up to a stack of microphones. With a heavy heart and a resigned shrug, the results of the inquiry would be announced:

FUN IN THE SUN

Spaceplane November Six Alpha *Whatever*, piloted by the brave and capable Captain Larry Mohs, along with an unnamed rookie copilot, had been "lost to the cosmos."

Prisha's wallow in despair was interrupted when a curiously bright dot appeared in the center of the windshield. The dot rapidly expanded to a sphere, green, turquoise, and white. It wasn't Venus. It wasn't Mercury either, and it certainly didn't look like any picture of Jupiter, its moons, or any of the other planets.

What the… ?

The multicolored sphere was rushing right toward them.

"Seat belts!" Prisha screamed.

Within seconds the sphere filled the windshield. The spaceplane dove through a layer of white into green, followed by a strong jolt that slammed Prisha and Captain Mohs forward into their seat harnesses. "Uhhhg!" they both wheezed in unison.

The spaceplane erupted in the noise of ripping metal, screaming passengers, and one yipping dog. They spun in circles with a bewildering blur of colors whipping by the windows.

Just as quickly, they blasted through the white once more and out into the blackness of space, twisting and turning in a gut-wrenching roller coaster from hell.

Captain Mohs caught his breath and yelled, "What was that?"

Caps, water bottles, and anything else that wasn't bolted down bounced around the cabin. Prisha yelled back, "I don't know! A planet of some kind? I think we hit it!"

Straining against the lurches, Prisha twisted around half-expecting to see the cabin in shreds and bodies flying out into space. Though the passengers were flopping around like rag dolls, everyone was seat-belted. No broken windows, no gaping holes. Even the dog was secured in Amanda's lap with a purse strap.

The portside wing hadn't fared as well. Through one window, Prisha could make out shredded metal with dangling cables that whipped about as the plane continued to wobble. Above the tattered wing, the green-and-white globe slid past each window, eventually reappearing in the forward windshield.

Just as a baseball fouled straight up by the bat slows before its fall into the catcher's mitt, their speed had dropped to zero but was now picking up again. Like road rage on a California freeway, whatever they'd hit didn't seem satisfied with just one crash.

"It's coming around again!" Prisha yelled. "Hold on!"

"It sure looks like a planet!" the captain yelled.

"Too small, has to be an asteroid," Chase called out.

"Killer Death Rock!" Reginald screamed.

The dog barked.

Whatever it was, the sphere's size grew dramatically once again. This second smashup wasn't going to be a glancing blow.

The planet-asteroid-deathrock filled the forward view, this time lit by sunlight from one side, giving better contrast. The white patches were scattered clouds floating in a thick atmosphere with a distinct top edge. Where the clouds parted, green landforms came into view. The place looked Earthlike, but greener and much smaller.

The spaceplane's nose hit the atmosphere like a rock thrown into mud, slamming them forward in their seats. This time Prisha lowered the reentry shields. Intense vibrations confirmed the shield was doing its job both to protect the glass and to alter airflow dynamics to slow them down.

Flying blind, Prisha gripped the control wheel with a fierce determination that this crash would have a pilot in command to the end. Another loud bang twisted the plane to the right, accompanied by sounds of shearing metal. The jolts became furious and rapid. The plane bounced up, then slammed down. Cracks, rips, and screams echoed through the cabin.

With a final gut punch that knocked the wind out of Prisha's chest, the crash ended with a sudden deceleration to a dead stop.

…

Calm replaced chaos. The cabin was still and quiet.

…

Prisha opened one eyelid.

I'm still alive.

She opened her other eye. No smoke in the air. No fire. No blood splatters across the instrument panel.

With a trembling hand, she raised the reentry shield to reveal green—not a color any pilot expects to see out a spaceplane windshield. Shredded green plants covered the glass. Broad green leaves tangled with twisted vines. It was as if they'd just crashed into the back of a landscaper's truck.

Captain Mohs had a vise grip on his own control wheel. He stared out at the greenery, blinking. Behind them, the cabin was still in one piece. All five passengers were buckled in their seats, each seat remarkably still bolted to the cabin floor.

"Everyone okay?" she called groggily. Grunts and other unintelligible noises were followed by a yip. *Amanda ought to patent that purse strap idea.*

Prisha unbuckled and stood up, startled to find that the spaceplane aisle had become a floor and gravity had returned to normal. She tottered down the aisle, checking passengers as she passed. Claire's sunglasses hung lopsided across her stunned face, one lens broken out. Reginald held both hands against his cheeks like Edvard Munch's "The Scream." Razor was already out of his seat and giving himself a physical inspection.

Captain Mohs followed closely behind, shaking each passenger's hand. "Fine job, outstanding work," he told them.

By the time Prisha had made it to the aft bulkhead, the passengers had unbuckled and followed in a line. The aft hatch was badly bent with a gap on one side. Air streamed through the gap, warm and humid, carrying a scent of rich compost.

"Are we back on Earth?" Claire asked, just behind Prisha.

"No way this is Earth," Chase said.

"Maybe it's not real," Amanda said. "I've seen stuff like that on TV." She held the dog in her arms. His tail was like a windshield wiper on full as his nose strained to sample the earthy smells wafting in.

"Open it," Razor suggested.

Prisha lifted the lock handle and pushed. Nothing. Clearly jammed in its frame. Razor offered his shoulder and pushed hard. On his second try, the hatch swung open, banging against the outside.

Razor stepped out onto sand. One by one, they each followed.

Surrounding them, tropical vegetation grew from sandy soil that was soft and dry. Behind the spaceplane, a swath of torn plants and sheared palms marked the path of their crash landing. Overhead, the sun shone bright, just as it did on Earth.

"Oh, look, Scratch!" Amanda pointed the dog to the other side of their now-wingless spaceplane.

The view opened dramatically to a white sand beach framed by palms. Small waves broke along the shoreline of a turquoise sea. Colorful sparkles danced across the water where shafts of sunlight broke through puffy clouds.

A small bird passed overhead and darted into the jungle. A breeze followed, rustling the leaves of tropical trees that reached up to the blue sky where miniature cottony puffs floated. The clouds seemed close enough to touch.

Claire whispered, "It's Earth, but… it's not Earth."

"It's definitely not Earth," Chase said with authority. He glanced up to the sun, then peered to the horizon, which also seemed impossibly close. "Ladies and gentlemen, welcome to L3."

4   SHIPWRECKED

TWO PILOTS, FIVE passengers and one dog stood in a clearing gouged out of a jungle, disoriented but mostly unhurt. No broken bones, no gushing blood, though the passengers were probably questioning their decision to buy a ticket on this flight to nowhere.

L3, it was called. At least, that was where Chase claimed they had landed.

Crash-landed. Their spaceplane lay in ruins with both wingtips sheared off and wires dangling out. Vines and other jungle debris tangled around the twin tails. For a quarter mile behind the plane, a long stripe of shredded plants and broken branches marked the path of their crash. It looked like a clear-cut if lumberjacks got drunk and went joyriding in a bulldozer.

On one side, the jungle was thick with broad-leaved plants and alive with the sounds of bugs, chirps, and dripping water. On the other side, gaps between palms revealed a tranquil blue-green sea. Gentle waves broke in a soothing rhythm. Prisha could almost imagine an air freshener commercial being filmed here.

Chase's wavy brown hair was tousled either from the crash or the breeze coming off the sea. Magical either way. The scientist continued his explanation.

"L3 is not so much a planet as a location in space," he said. "Technically it's the third Earth-Sun Lagrange point, a point of gravitational equilibrium on the opposite side of the sun."

"So, we couldn't be further from home?" Claire Bouchet asked. Her mirrored sunglasses sat askew at the end of her nose, one lens missing. It was the first time the eyes of their most mysterious passenger had been revealed. Grayish blue.

Chase shook his head. "Not at all. We're lucky we crashed here. Otherwise we'd be sailing off into interstellar space." He sniffed. "Breathable air. Goldilocks warm. The chances of randomly bumping into that are one in a billion."

"But we're on the far side of the sun?" Captain Mohs had pushed his pilot's cap to the back of his head, revealing a bald pate where a few strands of combover hair hung on for dear life.

Chase extended an arm and held his thumb up to the sun, which was just peeking through palm fronds in a late-afternoon position. "Half a thumb, the same apparent size as we see from Earth. So, yes, we're on the exact opposite side of the sun. Here, let me show you."

Chase picked up a broken stick and kicked away shredded leaves to expose white sand. He put a round rock in the center—"Here's the sun"—then drew a circle around it and placed a pebble at the six o'clock position. "And here's Earth."

He drew a second circle with its own pebble. "Here's Venus. We whipped around Venus, then the sun, and on to L3." He placed a smaller pebble at the twelve o'clock position, then drew a curving flight path from six to twelve.

Claire pointed to the completed map. "Where's Mercury?"

"Doesn't matter."

"But it's a planet."

"Yes, but we didn't whip around Mercury, so I didn't draw it."

Claire scowled, clearly miffed about losing an entire planet from a solar system that only had seven more to spare. Chase made two dimples in the sand at the four and eight o'clock positions.

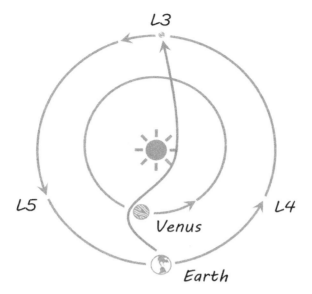

"The point is that Earth has three distinct Lagrange points along its orbit where the gravitational pull from Earth and the sun are in a delicate balance. L3, L4, and L5."

"What about L1 and L2?" Claire asked.

"They also exist, but not on Earth's orbit. Lagrange points are like dimples in space. Things tend to gather there."

"Things?" Still Claire. Still pedantic.

"Asteroids, rocks, that kind of stuff."

She pointed. "But you only put a pebble at L3. What about the other two?" Some people were natural art critics.

"There's nothing there. Well… a European weather satellite was positioned at L5 a few years ago. They noticed a small asteroid there, more of a boulder really."

Claire crossed her arms, waiting. Chase shrugged and placed a pinprick of a pebble into the L5 dimple. Claire seemed satisfied with the addition to the map.

Chase continued. "Of course, if you'd asked me yesterday if L3 had a planet, I would have said no. L3 is less stable than the other Lagrange points, and we can't see L3 from Earth because the sun is always in the way, so we've only checked once—the Parker Solar Probe a few years back."

"The probe that burned up in the sun?" Claire again. If she was becoming an irritant, Chase didn't show it. Some people were natural explainers.

"Yes, that one." Chase shrugged. "But now that we're here, I guess the Parker camera didn't have enough resolution to spot such a small object. This place must be really tiny. Just look how close the horizon is."

A few puffy clouds floated over a curving beach that reached to the horizon. You could probably walk the entire length of the beach in less than five minutes.

"The clouds are weird too," Prisha said, pointing to a cotton puff overhead that seemed to hover not far above the treetops. "That's not right, is it?"

Chase rubbed his chin. "Working theory... this place is the size of an asteroid but with a super-dense core capable of producing Earthlike gravity." For proof, Chase jumped, landing with a thump. "But only near the core. Newton's inverse square law answers the question of why L3's gravity doesn't affect the trajectory of space probes or produce measurable tugs on nearby planets like Venus."

"Or Mercury," Claire insisted.

"Or Mercury," Chase agreed. "Who knows? This little planetoid may have been here for millions of years. It *does* have a diverse biosphere."

"Bugs, too." Captain Mohs swatted at a fly.

"Then we've discovered a new planet!" Reginald exclaimed. "Do we get to name it?"

"Planet Scratch," suggested Amanda. She looked at the stowaway dog still cradled in her arms. "Would you like that?"

Scratch yipped happily.

Mohs cleared his throat. "British explorers named places after their most valiant sea captains." He looked around, brows raised, waiting. No one else seemed to share his logic.

"Until we can file with the International Astronomical Union, L3 will do," Chase said, bringing an ignominious end to Planet Mohs much like an anvil squashes a cartoon coyote.

Thankfully, Amanda changed the subject. "So, L3 is going around the sun just like Earth?"

"Exactly," Chase confirmed. "It also has a three-hundred-and-sixty-five-day year, so it's always chasing Earth but can never catch up."

Amanda swiveled in a circle as she explained their predicament to the dog. "So, you see, Scratch, we're on a tiny planet that is always hidden from Earth. Isn't that amazing?"

Reginald sighed. "Lost at L3."

"Afraid so," Chase said.

A rough voice came from the jungle. "Better than being dead." Razor held a hunting knife in one hand and was sharpening it against a fist-sized rock. Where he'd gotten the knife was anyone's guess. He slipped it into a scabbard tied around his thigh.

"So how do we get home?" Reginald was sitting on what was left of the spaceplane's wing.

Captain Mohs patted the fuselage, badly scraped but in one piece. Shredded wings were another matter. "Not in this old gal. Her flying days are over."

Prisha held up a finger. "Her flying days might be over, but…" As Razor had pointed out—crudely but accurately—they weren't dead yet. Even poor old N6A *Whatever* had some life left in her: a working radio.

Leaving the others, Prisha climbed back into the broken spaceplane. A few water bottles were scattered about, but otherwise its interior looked remarkably intact. She switched on the radio, then fumbled with the microphone, her voice jittery.

"Um, hi there. This is Megalodon spaceplane November Six Alpha… and a few more numbers that aren't important right now. We're lost at a place called L3. Anyone out there?"

Chase appeared at the open hatch, listening as the radio speaker scratched out static. A green LED on the control panel gave visual proof that the radio was working, but being on solid ground hadn't improved the reception.

Chase winced. "Unfortunately, Earth is now about sixteen light minutes away, so even if the signal makes it past the sun and reaches someone, you'll need to wait thirty-two minutes for a response."

Prisha scowled.

"Sorry, science sucks sometimes," Chase said with a shrug. "Well, not suction per se since that implies a near vacuum, which—"

Prisha kicked the control panel. "It's not science. *I* suck. I should have done more. I should have kept calling, or tried more frequencies, or… I don't know."

She lowered her head. Tears came without warning. "I'm the freakin' first officer! I'm supposed to know what I'm doing!" She wiped her eyes, but it was a losing battle.

Chase put a hand on her shoulder. It felt reassuring, with a healthy dose of prom date awkwardness thrown in. "You did the best you could," he said.

Between sniffs, Prisha managed a "thanks." She *had* tried. She'd remembered to lower the reentry shields, ordered the passengers back to their seats—twice.

Prisha waved a hand at Chase. "Go. The radio is my job. I'll stay here and see if anyone answers."

Chase left but came back a minute later, waggling his eyebrows in an adorable kind of way. "I have an idea."

Prisha couldn't help but smile. "Ideas are good, I'm listening."

"The sun is big. So big it bends electromagnetic waves, which makes Earth out of reach for our radio transmissions."

"That's your idea?"

"It gets better."

"Of course it does."

"There's more than just Earth out there. Remember the European weather satellite I mentioned, the one stationed at Lagrange point 5? L5 is on a direct line of sight from L3. No solar interference."

"Ohhh-kay."

"So, we communicate to the European satellite instead, and maybe it will relay our message to Earth."

Prisha bent her brow. "How do we do that? Sorry, I'm just a pilot. They didn't teach us anything about interplanetary radio relays."

"And you're a great pilot. What kind of antenna does your radio have? High-gain, or low-gain?"

Prisha blinked. This conversation was turning toward the kind of technobabble she remembered from Spaceplane Systems class, which always required at least two cups of coffee to survive. "Low-gain? I think?"

"Good."

"Good?"

"Yes, that means we could adjust it to a high-gain antenna."

"And that's better?"

"Absolutely. High gain narrows the energy to a line that can be pointed in a specific direction. Better for communicating with a dot in the sky."

"Like the European satellite at L5?"

Chase winked. "You got it."

Prisha stood up, extending both arms. "Do you mind?" Chase did the same and they embraced in a warm hug. "Thank you."

"For what, explaining antenna gain?"

"For existing. I was getting worried I was alone in this 'save our butts' gig. Captain Mohs—"

"Say no more."

"I only met him this morning. He seems nice enough, but—"

"He has all the leadership of a fair-weather politician. None." Chase flashed a smile. "I for one think First Officer Prisha Dhaliwal did a superb job getting us this far."

If Prisha had a mirror, she'd no doubt find twinkly stars in place of her irises. "I… um…" She took a deep breath. "Where do we start?"

"Point me to the radio's antenna."

They went outside and clambered onto the wing. Prisha identified a nub along the fuselage spine that she vaguely recalled from the same training class.

Chase examined it. "Give me a few minutes."

Prisha returned to the cockpit to monitor the radio just in case the low-gain version of this antenna had managed to reach someone. Twenty minutes passed with nothing but static.

Chase came back highly animated. "Cool, so I fashioned a screwdriver out of a chip of palm tree bark, pulled the existing antenna off, then lengthened its electric coil using some copper wire I found dangling out of the wing—Scratch's tail was the perfect-sized dowel, and he didn't seem to mind. Then I hammered a broken piece of aluminum into a parabolic shape—coconuts helped. After that, it was just a matter of hooking things up."

Prisha's eyes widened. "You did all that in twenty minutes?"

Chase shrugged. "Locating L5 in the sky was the hard part. Luckily, the astronomy app on my phone works off-line. I adjusted for our position being one hundred and eighty degrees opposite Earth, then computed the azimuth and declination angles and pointed our new high-gain antenna at L5. Give it a shot."

Prisha stared. "Are you real?"

Chase grinned. "Chase Livingston, scientist. At your service, ma'am."

With wary eyes on the superhuman standing before her, Prisha lifted the mic and pressed transmit. "Um, yeah. European satellite people? Hi. This is Prisha Dhaliwal. I hope things are going well back in Paris. Oh, I bet you don't speak English. *Bonjour?*"

She looked up. Chase was shaking his head no.

"Oh right, you probably have automatic translators. Anyway, if you get this message, could you tell someone at Megalodon Industries that their missing spaceplane is at L3? That's a place... well, you probably know where it is since you're space people. Anyway, it's not just the spaceplane, there's seven of us stranded here. Oh, plus a dog. His name is Scratch."

Chase stared up, tapping his fingers on his chin.

"Right, so anyway, please send help because we really need it. Like, a lot. Thank you. *Merci.* Prisha Dhaliwal signing off from L3."

"Nice message," Chase said.

"Will it work?"

"Well, I'm confident your words are winging their way to L5 right now, but what happens after that depends on the Europeans. They might take days to process it, plus I can't be sure of their antenna design. Sorry, I don't have the specs."

"I'd say you did pretty well with coconuts and palm bark."

He smiled. "I enjoy making things. I built a scale model of the Space Shuttle when I was a kid. From scratch. With fuel and a parachute recovery system. Got that baby up to ten thousand feet before some guy from the Federal Aviation Administration knocked on our door."

Prisha laughed, not at him but with him. Her own childhood had a few stories like that—the awkward part, not the science. She switched the radio to Passive Monitor mode. It would beep at them if a transmission was received.

Outside the plane, Prisha and Chase found themselves alone, with voices coming from the nearby beach. They followed a path between palms to a lovely strip of white sand that formed a curving shoreline. A cool breeze blew in from the shallow sea. Not far away, a neighboring island straddled the ridiculously close horizon—just a quick swim away. They might even be able to wade across.

The others were already exploring the beach. Amanda was making a sand angel next to Scratch. Mohs was sprawled under a palm, his cap covering his eyes. Reginald had already spelled out SOS with rocks, but Prisha couldn't bring herself to point out the obvious flaw with that plan. Razor was taste-testing the water (salty, by his reaction), and Claire stood not far away, arms folded, rigid as a fence post, monitoring Razor's every move.

What is it with Claire and Razor? Sure, the man was a walking garbage dump with sociopathic tendencies, but it was hard to imagine why Claire thought it was her job to supervise.

Regardless, the sand was soft and the breeze delightful. Chase took off his shirt and shoes. Prisha tried not to stare at his muscular chest, though her attempt at prim behavior was entirely unsuccessful. Eventually, she gave in and took off her own shoes, rolled up her pant legs, and loosened her tie.

L3 was as beautiful as any South Pacific tourist brochure, no question. Yet Prisha felt a knot in her stomach. This planet was alien. Who knew what lurked in those azure waters? Sure, the sea *looked* tranquil, and the mesmerizing lapping of gentle waves upon soft sand was so, so pleasing, perfectly complementing an exquisitely cool breeze that carried delicious scents of tropical flowers…

Yeah, okay, it's a paradise.

Razor barked suddenly, "When you've all had enough of dipping your toes and napping, there's the small business of survival. What do you rookies plan on eating?"

There's always a catch. "Well, we still have water and pretzels."

"I gave Scratch some of the pretzels," Amanda admitted, giving the dog a tummy rub. "He seemed hungry. It was just a few."

Razor glared.

"Maybe three or four. Packs."

The glare intensified.

"Okay… six," Amanda confessed.

Razor rolled his eyes and gave a callous laugh. "Greenhorns, all of you!"

"We're not limited to pretzels," Chase offered. "I found a broken coconut by the spaceplane. Mostly a shell, but we might find others with a thicker endosperm."

"I beg your pardon," said Mohs, who had roused himself and joined the group.

"Endosperm. It's the edible part of any shelled nut," Chase clarified. "Coconuts are high in protein."

"We'll need more than just coconuts," countered Razor. His eyes had that FBI-Most-Wanted-Poster look to them, but if his camouflage apparel and skills with a blade were any indicator, he might be a valuable asset for survival. There were birds in the jungle—maybe a quick flick of Razor's knife would bring down a flying chicken or whatever equivalent they might find on L3.

Reginald wandered up, holding out a plastic bag labeled Yummy Gummies. "I brought lots of these."

Captain Mohs grabbed several of the gooey candies. "If there was ever a time for comfort food, this is it."

Amanda reached in the bag too, pulling out a green one and popping it in her mouth.

"That's my favorite," Reginald said. His eyelids drooped noticeably. "Lime Sublime. So mellow."

"Wait!" Prisha snatched the bag out of his hand. "Reginald, is there any chance these gummies might contain cannabis?"

Reginald smiled. "Only the very best. Potent but with a comforting afterglow."

Amanda spat hers out quickly. She danced on animated feet like the sand had just become hot coals. "Oh no! I chewed it already! It's going to warp my sense of reality. I won't know where I am!"

"Sounds good to me," Mohs said, grabbing a few more.

Prisha gave Reginald her best *disappointed parent* expression. "Reginald, you can't just hand out mind-altering drugs without telling people in advance! What about those of us who are still on duty?" She pointed to herself and the captain.

Mohs shrugged. "Do what you want, Prish, but my shift is officially over."

Reginald returned the gummy bag to his pocket and mumbled, "Sorry."

The captain's eyes were glazing over as fast as a kitty's on catnip. He flung his cap a dozen yards down the beach and waded into the shallow sea. "Surf's up!"

Amanda was still in panic mode. Prisha gave a gentle pat to her arm. "Don't worry, you're going to be fine. Not so sure about the captain."

Prisha plunked down in the sand and laughed at the absurdities that surrounded her: a sweet but inexperienced flight attendant and her spaced-out gummy pusher, a grunge survivalist under the watchful eye of an irritatingly pedantic US Foreign Service officer. And, of course, the handsome scientist who had unambiguously identified their dire predicament but not the solution.

Yes, it had been a tough first day on the job, but she was still standing. Heart still beating. She hadn't strangled anyone yet or yelled at their clearly irresponsible captain or broken any fingers punching a stupid, useless, never-to-fly-again spaceplane.

Prisha sighed. *Do all first officers earn their stripes this way?*

Her attention was quickly captured by Razor, who produced flint and steel from his pocket and began shooting sparks onto a palm frond, which soon began to smoke. After some huffing and puffing and a few more fronds, it became a roaring flame.

"Is that strictly necessary?" Reginald asked, looking just as surprised as Prisha at the efficiency Razor had demonstrated. "It feels like the tropics here."

"It's not to ward off the cold." Razor slowly turned a wary gaze toward the jungle. His eyes flicked left and right.

Prisha followed his gaze. There was nothing there except for leafy plants, but it wasn't hard to imagine a pair of tiger eyes peering back.

As a child, she'd seen one of the big cats while touring West Bengal near the headwaters of the Ganges River. A tiger in the wild—powerful, fast, unencumbered by any restraints—is nothing like a tiger in a zoo.

High drama aside, Razor's point was clear. "Yeah, maybe a fire's not a bad idea," Prisha said, then gathered with the rest around the flames.

They stood in awkward silence, which Chase finally broke. "Dangerous animals are a possibility." Explicit seemed his style, but maybe that was what they needed.

He held up a palm frond and ran a finger across its corrugated structure. "I mentioned earlier that our odds of landing on a planetoid like this were literally one in a billion. But there's more that troubles me. How can any of this exist? How can there be plants and insects and birds that look just like those on Earth?"

Prisha agreed. "It feels like we're inside an exhibit at the zoo." *The Bengal tiger exhibit, in particular.*

"Or an episode of *The Twilight Zone*!" Mohs's uniform was soaking wet from his crazy man's swim in the sea. Waves of steam flowed off from the hot fire. He started humming the eerie TV show theme song with a toothy, psychopathic grin.

Prisha gulped. *Could this day get any worse? Yes, it could.*

"We should keep our guard up," said Chase. "L3 has its charm, but it's still alien." He squinted to the sky. "Sun's getting low already. We should ration our remaining food and water and use the spaceplane for sleeping quarters."

Reginald volunteered to be the chief rationer and headed back to the spaceplane to collect their supplies. Amanda went with him to be sure no more gummies were involved. Then Chase followed Amanda to be sure the remaining pretzel packs weren't all fed to the dog.

The trio returned with one bag of pretzels and one water bottle for each person and dog, which everyone agreed was a fair distribution.

Except Claire. She stared at a handful of pretzels. "If I have to subsist on this the whole time, there will be consequences."

"We'll do better tomorrow," Prisha assured Claire (also an attempt to reassure herself). "We're all frustrated, but for now let's recharge and try not to let things overwhelm us."

Including those fantasy L3 tigers out there.

Amanda agreed. She linked arms with Prisha, and they munched on pretzels while staring out to sea. Clouds lit up orange and pink, with colorful reflections spreading across the water. High above, a splash of stars emerged prematurely, even as the last rays of sunlight still coursed across the sky.

When darkness set in, the castaways shuffled one by one back to the broken spaceplane, each finding a seat to curl up in for the night. There were no pillows and no covers, but their chairs reclined, the night air was warm, and, if their luck held out, there would be no alien monsters surfacing from the ocean.

****

Near dawn, Prisha awoke from a nightmare: a giant flaming baguette was dragging her off into space, pulsating rhythmically with each tug. She bolted upright. The baguette was certainly a figment, but the pulsating sensation was not. It was all around and growing in intensity.

It shifted to a deep rumbling that Prisha could feel in her bones. The rumbles came from beneath the spaceplane, as though a giant subterranean wave were cresting from one side of the planetoid to the other. The plane bobbed and shifted. More people woke in confusion.

Scratch began running laps from one end to the other while yipping at his highest decibel level.

Within a few seconds, the rumbling subsided to a distant murmur. In its wake lay a group of high-strung humans with a million questions and a growing realization that this planet was nothing like home.

5   SURVIVAL SKILLS

SOMEWHERE OUTSIDE THE cramped, stuffy spaceplane, a woman's voice warbled like a songbird in spring. Prisha opened her eyes, sat upright, and stretched sore body parts from one of the most uncomfortable attempts at sleep in recent memory. Claire was propped up against a window, snoring. Reginald was still dead to the world, his mouth wide open and eyes tightly shut. Captain Mohs was curled up in a hammock strung between brackets on the rear bulkhead. Where that luxury item had come from was anyone's guess.

She tiptoed past Mohs to the partially open hatch and peered outside. A scent of roasting coffee wafted along a cool breeze, complementing the passionate aria.

Got to be Amanda. Wow, that girl can sing.

Prisha stepped out onto soft sand. Amanda stood atop one of the spaceplane's rear stabilators, her arms spread wide. "♪ ♫ ♪ ♪ ♫ ♫ ♪"

It was a beautiful song with a rousing rhythm and evocative lyrics, something about a disembodied voice that beckoned a powerful but confused young woman into the unknown.

When Amanda finished, Prisha applauded, then asked, "Do you always greet the morning this way?"

Amanda gave her the most earnest of smiles. "Why wouldn't I?"

"No argument from me," Prisha said. "I'm just amazed that someone could be so chipper after the night we had."

"Oh, that rumbling didn't bother me. In Texas, we're used to thunderstorms, and I get up early anyway." Amanda waved and Prisha followed. The aroma of coffee became stronger.

Near the beach, Razor's fire was still burning, still warding off any jungle tigers but now producing unexpected smells of breakfast. Not just coffee but toasted bread too.

Seven reasonably flat rocks had been arranged in a circle around the firepit. Chase sat on one, juggling multiple cooking tasks. He looked up. "Oh good, our first officer is up! Take over the coffee brewing for me, and I'll finish the main course."

He handed her what looked like a pot handle with a clamp on one end. "Just keep the beans rolling around until they're dark."

A large aluminum bowl balanced on a rock at the edge of the fire. Inside were round brown pellets. They looked like rabbit poopy balls, but they smelled delicious.

The handle perfectly clamped to the edge of the makeshift cooking pot. Prisha shook the smoking beans while admiring Chase's cookware, formed no doubt from a broken piece of spaceplane sheet metal. "You must have been a Boy Scout."

"Simple mechanics. A lever with torque applied along the long axis produces a powerful pinch at the short axis. When the beans are crispy, just pour them into the grinder."

He held up a coconut shell with a metal crank sticking out from one side. There was no telling what mechanical gears might be inside, or how Chase had managed to whip it together in minutes. Prisha couldn't help but gawk.

The roasted pellets were soon ground, packed into a cloth sack, and soaked in hot water. Chase poured the dark aromatic liquid into a cup made from coconut shells and handed it to Prisha.

She took a deep whiff. Then a sip. "Wow, it *is* coffee!"

"Step one is a success!" Chase answered with a smile.

"What's step two?" Prisha asked.

"Making sure alien jungle coffee doesn't kill you." He winked. "Just kidding, it's probably fine. Olfactory receptors evolved a sense of smell precisely for the purpose of testing food prior to consuming."

He took a sip from his own cup, then returned to his other cooking task—flipping several pieces of rounded flatbread spread out across a mesh grill (that looked remarkably like one of the spaceplane's ventilation covers). "Credit Amanda with finding the tortillas. Leaves, actually, but they plump up nicely in the fire."

He handed one to Prisha. Hot. Bread-like.

"Salsa?" Amanda offered a hollowed-out coconut. Inside, a mix of chopped veggies floated in an aromatic liquid.

"Wow, you two have been busy!" Prisha slathered her tortilla with the homemade salsa and took a bite. They watched. She didn't keel over. "So, I'm the guinea pig?"

"Of course not," Amanda said. "I tasted the salsa… a little."

"It's good!" Prisha said. "And I'm not dead." She faked a gag with eyes bulging and tongue hanging out, then returned to her morning meal—far better than packaged pretzels.

Scratch hopped up into Prisha's lap with a mouthful of large, green leaves. He wasn't eating them—he seemed to be offering. Prisha took one of the leaves, which featured a muddy pawprint in the center.

"Designer napkins," Amanda explained. "He made them himself."

"What a clever pooch you are!" Prisha said, and the dog trotted off to provide the same luxury table linen to other diners.

Razor appeared from nowhere, dropping a bottle of water in the sand. He held another bottle in his hand and took a sip. "Pure as it gets," he said. "Try it."

"You found a freshwater source?" Prisha asked hopefully. She picked up the bottle and examined its contents. Clear. No sediment or discoloring. Their current stockpile of water wouldn't last more than a couple days, and they'd already learned the sea was salty.

Razor pointed with his knife. "That way. A spring. Not much more than a puddle, but it'll do."

Prisha took a deep breath. "Well, aren't we doing better! Coffee, roasted tortillas with salsa, napkins, and now a water source!"

Razor froze. His eye twitched. In an instant he pivoted and threw his knife. It thunked into the trunk of a nearby tree, scaring away a colorful bird that flew off into the jungle, squawking.

"Next time," Razor growled, retrieving his knife.

Prisha gulped. "And… wild parrot for dinner. Not sure at all about that one."

Claire showed up, sleepy-eyed. Reginald wasn't far behind. Chase poured two more cups of fresh coffee.

"You are an effing god," Claire said, inhaling the aroma. "I thought I was going to have to kill someone to get this far."

They took seats around the fire and were soon consuming roasted tortillas with gusto.

"Did I wake up at a Michelin-starred restaurant?" Reginald exclaimed. "This is stupid delicious."

"Thanks to the cooks and gatherers," said Prisha. "We're off to a great start today."

"If you don't count the predawn wake-up call," Claire said. "Seriously, what was that?"

They all looked to Chase. He could only shrug. "More of a rolling sensation than an earthquake. Subsurface magma, maybe?"

"Just like that magma that's waiting around under volcanoes about to blow," Claire griped. She seemed the type to seize upon the grimmest of outcomes like a sadistic doctor sizing up a critical patient.

Reginald checked over his shoulder, then lifted one foot and inspected the sole of his shoe. "No volcanoes around here."

Claire scoffed. "They strike when you're asleep. Rip giant gashes in the ground, then pour out hot ash and boiling lava. Didn't you learn in school about all the bodies they dug up in Pompeii?"

"Not sure I even went to school," Reginald said, staring into his quesadilla con salsa absentmindedly.

"Well, at least we're all okay," Amanda chirped. "No harm done, just a good shake to remind you you're still alive." Unlike Reginald, who seemed forever disoriented, Amanda had a nearly permanent smile even when she was eating. She'd do well in a toothpaste commercial.

"What about the weird trees?" It was Razor, lurking behind ferns several paces from the campfire. The man probably used stripped tree fiber and pine tar to brush his teeth.

Claire set down her tortilla in mid-munch. "Yeah, M-shaped! Like that one." She pointed to the far side of the sea, which wasn't terribly far away. Green hills straddled the horizon. If you squinted, a group of four palms on top of one hill were arranged in the shape of an M.

"Same grouping at the spring," Razor said.

"That's funny," Prisha said. "Maybe L3 palms tend to grow in clumps like that."

"And palms on Earth are often angled," Chase added. "Besides, humans are conditioned to see patterns. It's what we're good at."

Reginald shook his head. "Ground that's alive and trees that can spell. This place is spooky weird. Just last night, those rocks out there were covered by water."

He was right. The tide was low—very low, in fact—revealing rocks and coral far out into the sea that hadn't been visible the day before. A sandbar now stretched across, forming a path anyone could walk without getting wet.

Claire poked Chase. "Science guy. Tell us about L3 tides."

Chase set down his coconut mug of coffee. "On Earth, tides result from a complex dance between the Moon and the sun. Since L3 seems to have no moon, tides should be weaker, not stronger. But a shallow sea combined with a funnel-shaped inlet might do the trick."

"Yeah, that," Reginald said. "Or else this whole planet is alive. Just like that sparky toilet brush thing that dragged us here."

Since their crash landing, no one had mentioned the oblong light that had torn them away from Earth, though it was probably still on everyone's mind.

"Got to admit, I'm stumped on that one," Chase said.

Prisha pondered. "Toilet brush. Or maybe more like a singer's microphone? It was long and skinny with a hump on one end. But it was going by so fast."

"Someone should have taken a picture," Claire said.

"We were a bit busy," Prisha reminded.

The group tossed around a few outlandish explanations: an alien UFO (which, if identified, would then just be a FO), a new species of whale that lives only in suborbital space, a pirate ghost ship (Prisha liked that one), or a very large, vacuum-breathing bird. Left unsaid was the hard truth about their predicament. Whatever it was that had launched them to L3, it hadn't hung around for the return trip home.

"I'll check the radio once more," Prisha said to Chase and left the group to their ponderings. The radio's Passive Monitor mode should have produced a sequence of beeps if any message came in, but it was still worth checking manually.

Back at the spaceplane, Captain Mohs was finally awake, unclipping his hammock from the aft bulkhead. "Great night's sleep in this baby. The Megalodon Three-Ounce Portable Sleep System."

Prisha rotated her shoulder, which was still sore from being squashed against the spaceplane wall all night. "Um, Captain? Do we have any more hammocks on board? Maybe one for each of us?"

Mohs laughed like the answer was obvious. "Nope, just one. And this little gem has come in pretty handy. You'd be surprised how many times a supposedly married guy has to overnight in a parked spaceplane."

Prisha was instantly grumpy. "We need a better place to sleep."

"Great idea, Prish," the captain said. "I might try stringing it up between two palms for tonight."

Prisha clenched her teeth before she could say anything that might get her in trouble. Instead, she checked the radio. Nothing had come in overnight.

"I guess we're stuck here for a while," she sighed.

She looked up, but the captain was already gone. Outside, he had found the perfect spot for his hammock and was clipping carabiners to nylon webbing he'd wrapped around palm trunks. He stood back, admiring his oh-so-comfortable sleeping arrangement.

Prisha didn't try to hide the sarcasm. "Shall I bring you breakfast in bed, sir?"

Mohs patted his belly, then headed off into the jungle. "Export first, then import."

Her temperature rising, Prisha stomped back to the campfire, where everyone else was still sipping coffee, and announced in a firm voice, "We need a better place to sleep."

Reginald rubbed his neck. "I agree."

"Someplace flat," Claire added. "Those seats are torture chambers, and I've seen a few."

Prisha caught everyone's eye, even Razor, who was sitting by himself, chewing on what looked like a root. "How about we get organized today? We might be here for a while."

To avoid upsetting the others, she mouthed to Chase, "No radio."

Chase got the message. "How about I start working on a shelter? Maybe a bamboo floor with a roof in case it rains."

Puffy clouds hung not far above the treetops. Though the sun was out, damp sand and puddles on the spaceplane wing were evidence it had rained sometime during the night. There was no telling how meteorology might work on this planet; they'd need to be prepared.

"I'll help," Reginald offered. "I'm good with tools. I think. Well, maybe not, but I could try."

Prisha moved closer to Razor—as close as any rational female would dare. "How about you, Razor? You seem to know something about outdoor living."

"Survival," Razor grunted. "Not the same as *outdoor living.*" He spat out a wad of chewed root, then withdrew his king-sized knife and cut off another chunk.

"Sorry, survival. Maybe you could gather more roots for us all?" Razor lifted his head ever so slightly and spat again. Prisha made a mental note to avoid the roots until she was on her last legs.

Claire eyed Razor, her body language taut as a bow. She apparently didn't have much regard for the slovenly man, but then who in their group did? She finally stood up. "I'll gather more firewood."

Prisha held out a hand to Amanda. "Come on, show me where you found those tortilla leaves, and maybe we can find a few more edibles."

"Edibles?" Captain Mohs had returned from his latrine tour of the jungle. "Got any more gummies, young man?"

"Lots." Reginald reached into a pocket, but Prisha's glare was enough to head off that waste of valuable time.

"Maybe we should help set up camp first," Reginald finally said.

Mohs settled for a roasted tortilla.

With Amanda in tow, Prisha headed off into the jungle, leaving the men to their bamboo construction project. She'd done her best to establish some semblance of organization among people who had been thrust into survival mode. Captain Mohs might not be the leader they needed, but she wouldn't challenge him. It was something about that third bar on her shoulder. They might be millions of miles from home, but Mohs was still the one person who could advance her career—such as it was.

The search for food didn't take long. The tortilla leaves were everywhere, and sniffs of various other plants along with a few wary tastes provided even more options: a bud beneath a pink flower tasted like strawberries, a piña hanging from a spikey palm was an interesting cross between grapefruit and pineapple. Berries were plentiful, though some were bitter.

Amanda sang as they gathered (a Broadway show tune called "Food, Glorious Food"). When she finished, Prisha complimented her once more on her beautiful voice.

Amanda blushed. "Aw, you're nice, Prisha. Could you be our leader while we're marooned? I think you'd make a great captain— not that there's anything wrong with Captain Mohs, of course, but you really shine."

Some people were obvious fakes. Not this one. There was something about Amanda's natural charm that made every word authentic. Prisha was years older, but maybe they could still be friends of different ages. People did that, didn't they?

Amanda was about to sing again when Prisha clapped a hand over her mouth. "Shh, look!"

Two tiny birds swooped just overhead, landed on a nearby branch, and started picking at the berries. Their iridescent feathers shimmered in the filtered sunlight, flashing from blue, to purple, to pink. A cross between a hummingbird and a tiny macaw, they had an intelligence in their eyes unlike any bird Prisha had ever seen.

One bird tilted its tiny head left, then right, sizing up the humans. It tweeted three times, its partner tweeted back, then they both vanished into the jungle.

Amanda and Prisha shared a look of doe-eyed wonder. "Wow, it's almost like they were talking to each other," Amanda said.

"Smart little guys! Beautiful too!"

"I bet they're telling all their friends they have visitors."

"Or invaders." A vision of a thousand intelligent birds swarming their campground popped into Prisha's head. Would they come to agree upon the terms for temporary human occupation of their land? Or to peck their eyes out?

Prisha ignored her worst instincts, instead opting for Amanda's cheerier conclusion that the birds would be pleasant companions (as long as Razor didn't throw any more knives at them). They continued gathering a variety of berries into a makeshift sack formed from Prisha's jacket.

Back at camp, they dumped their haul onto a bamboo table (that had Chase's handiwork all over it). It was a little rickety, but better than eating off the dirt. Accomplished carpenters, Chase and Reginald were already building a lean-to frame from bamboo poles.

Chase's shirt was off. Again. Not that Prisha was complaining or anything, but violent sounds of hacking and chopping forced her to ignore Chase's rippling abs for the time being. Razor emerged from the jungle with a large machete in one hand, no doubt retrieved from his duffel bag—the bag the captain himself had loaded into the spaceplane.

A machete? Really? Prisha shook her head. *What exactly was our preflight security?*

Razor dumped a load of roots onto the growing pile of food. He inspected their collection so far. "Carbs, vitamins B and D, fiber, plus the root juice is better than most energy drinks. But…" He looked around, his gaze landing on Scratch, who had wandered up, sniffing at the food. "We're going to need some protein in our diet."

Razor snatched the small dog by the scruff of its neck and held him high. "Lucky for us, we have exactly what we need."

Scratch's eyes went wide. He whimpered, struggling against the big man's grip. Razor lifted his machete. Its sharp edge glinted in the sun.

"No!" Amanda screamed.

"Absolutely not!" Prisha shouted.

Others chimed in too. Even Mohs sat up in his hammock. "Huh?"

"This here is solid protein!" Razor declared. "Bone marrow too. Without a net we'll never catch the birds, and we're going to need more than berries. A week from now—when you're picking ants off the tree bark—you'll see I'm right. We may as well get it over with."

Chase stepped up and held out his hand. "Give me the dog." He looked ready for a brawl.

"It's a shared meal, you don't get it all."

"I'm not going to butcher a dog, and neither are you."

Scratch's sad puppy eyes matched his whimpering.

Razor hesitated, staring hard at Chase. "I subsisted for a month on bilge rats and fried dung beetles. Heart of Africa, I was. A hundred miles from the nearest village. Now *that* was an episode they'll never forget."

"Wait!" Amanda stepped up to the big man, sticking a finger in his face. "I thought I recognized you!"

In a single fluid move, she pulled Razor's machete hand to his side and took the dog into her arms. If she'd planned the maneuver, she'd done remarkably well. "I can't believe it! You're the guy from that TV show, *Survival Instinct*."

Razor shrugged. Amanda beamed like a fan meeting a superstar. She turned to the circle of would-be pet rescuers, each with their mouth agape. "Razor is famous! *Survival Instinct* was the highest-rated show of last year on the Blood and Guts Channel. Bigger than *Name That Body Part* or even *Chicago Special Unit: Autopsy*."

Prisha scrunched up her face. "You watch that stuff?"

It *was* hard to imagine Amanda—probably dressed in a pink charmeuse décolleté blouse above a pleated trumpet skirt and holding a fine glass of pinot grigio in one hand—watching a TV show about skinning rodents for dinner.

"Every scene in *Survival Instinct* is real." Razor pointed his machete around the circle. "No stunt doubles; no spitting out worms once the camera stops rolling; no posh hotel rooms. I know what it means to survive."

Prisha had never seen the show, not even scrolling through the TV guide, and she wasn't planning on looking it up if they ever got back to civilization. But the revelation cast Razor in a different light—the man was just as offensive, but apparently, he was *paid* to be offensive.

Razor's eyes shifted as he fingered the edge of his machete. Prisha decided to formalize a rule on the spot. "There will be no dog killing on this planet. Do we all agree on this?"

Heads nodded all around, except for Razor, who lifted a lip in defeat, turned, and hacked his way back into the jungle with mumbles about "weaklings."

Chase plopped onto a rock and wiped his brow like an Olympian fencing competitor who'd only recently learned that non-Olympic swordfights are to the death.

"Thanks for sticking up for Scratch," Amanda told him.

"Any extra machetes lying around?" he asked. "Reg and I could really use a tool like that for bamboo cutting." The lean-to structure was coming together, but they had assembled it from broken bamboo poles salvaged from the spaceplane crash landing path.

Reginald spat into his hands. "Forget that guy. I'll break the bamboo with my own two hands." He made a dramatic show of rolling up his sleeves, squatting, shifting his weight back and forth, before grabbing and twisting a stout piece and grunting loudly. It didn't so much as budge.

Amanda gathered poor Scratch into her arms. He seemed to recover rather quickly from his scare.

Claire emerged from the background, shaking her head. "You people are like the rejects from a cast audition for the G-rated version of *Swiss Family Robinson*. Beyond naive."

She sighed, fiddled with the HoloWatch on her wrist, then systematically paced a circle around their encampment. All eyes were on her when she finished. "What? You've never set a perimeter alert? From now on, nobody goes in or out without me knowing about it."

There was a long silence.

Prisha broke the ice. "Clearly the government provides advanced tools to US Foreign Service officers like you."

"You bought that story? Funny." If Claire wasn't really a government employee, she didn't elaborate further, and no one had the nerve to ask.

The afternoon wore on. Chase and Reginald completed construction on their new communal sleeping space, including a roof made from woven leaves. The lean-to wasn't the sturdiest of shelters, but it would keep most of the rain off should more showers develop. Best of all, the floor was padded with soft moss and leaves that gave it a springy feel. A better night's sleep couldn't come soon enough.

They kept the fire going into the evening, roasting more flatbread for dinner, this time filled with a green fruit that tasted like avocado with a touch of Honey Nut Cheerios (Reginald's comparison). Razor never returned for dinner, but he seemed the type to prefer less-appetizing roots over a cooked meal and the silence of the forest over fireside company.

As dinner finished, Reginald started in on a particularly convoluted dissertation involving cannabis, aliens hiding beneath human skin (they often pose as talk show hosts, he insisted), and the health benefits of consuming sea moss.

He stopped midsentence, looked around at rather puzzled onlookers and apologized. "Sorry, my mind doesn't always work quite right. Amnesia, that's what the docs tell me. The gummies help. Maybe. I'm not sure."

Amnesia?

It explained a lot about Reginald. His slow pace, his wandering mindlessness. Between amnesia and cannabis, he was forever lost in space, figuratively speaking.

Reginald whispered, "I had an accident at the Megalodon warehouse where I worked. I don't really remember it, but the doctors filled me in on the details. Not pretty. A forklift, twenty cases of Widowmaker Energy Drink, and a cat."

Five firelit faces leaned closer to hear more of those details.

"And?" Prisha asked.

Reginald shrugged. "The cat survived. That's all I know."

"Rock-solid story," Claire deadpanned. "If Hollywood comes knocking, sign quick."

"Well, I got workman's comp, including a free ride to space. It was supposed to be therapeutic. Then L3 happened."

Amanda rubbed Reginald's shoulder. "Sorry, Reg. If there's anything we can do to help, just say the word."

"What word? Oh… I get it. Sorry, I still process pretty slow. Heck, I can't even be sure my name is Reginald. Or Reg. It's what my friends called me, so I guess that's who I am."

Amanda hooked an arm under his elbow. "At least you remember your friends."

"Not really, but while I was recovering at the Megalodon Head Trauma Center, a bunch of guys came to visit."

"That was sweet of them."

"Yeah, nice guys. I had no idea who they were. Turned out they were all gay."

"Ah, it's coming out now," Claire said with a cough into her hand.

Prisha admonished, "Reginald's sexual orientation is none of your business!"

Amanda kept a tight grip around his arm. Reginald seemed to enjoy it. "Funny, I don't feel particularly gay."

"Yeah, well, I don't feel particularly sadistic," Claire said. "When I'm off duty, of course."

Prisha glared. Claire finally shut up.

Amanda tugged on Reginald's arm. "You know, Reginald, when we return to Earth, you could still become famous. I mean, how many amnesiacs discover a new planet?"

That girl could put a positive spin on dirty diapers.

Chase nodded slowly. "She's right. Like it or not, we're the modern-day Lewis and Clark expedition." He waved to the thick forest around them. "We should explore this place. It wouldn't be hard given its size. I bet we could walk all the way around in a few hours."

Captain Mohs looked up. Stars were easily visible even though the sun hadn't yet set. "Tomorrow."

"Agreed, tomorrow," Chase said.

"Tomorrow!" Amanda was just about to launch into a cheery Broadway show tune starring a scrappy young orphan, but Mohs held up a hand.

"It's late."

"Well… not exactly, the stars come out early on L3."

"And I missed my afternoon nap." Mohs left.

Amanda said, "What an interesting man. He seems to sleep a lot!"

There were a few more grumbles about the privilege of Mohs's hammock over a makeshift bamboo lean-to that eventually morphed into questions about why the stars came out early on L3 (a compressed atmosphere and something about Rayleigh scattering, according to Chase) and finally turned back to the weird things about L3 for which no one had answers.

Eventually, they adjourned from the fireside chat to prepare their new sleeping quarters. Prisha claimed a spot next to Chase, blushing only slightly as she removed her jacket and tie and hung them on a peg Chase had thoughtfully crafted at the lean-to's headboard. Amanda snuggled up with Scratch. Claire and Reginald staked out the other end of their makeshift bed. Mohs was already snoring in his hammock.

The fire dwindled. Birds quieted. After a while, a few twigs snapping and heavy breathing were the first clues that Razor had returned. He sat on a rock, his face lit by glowing embers.

"Bastards," he mumbled to himself.

Prisha lifted her head. Claire was sitting up, her gaze locked on the TV survivalist. In the dim light, Prisha could swear Claire's eyes were glowing with intensity. That, or she was fiddling with her HoloWatch again.

Claire's tendency for aggressive meddling would probably drive them all crazy—especially Razor, who seemed just this side of becoming a human flamethrower.

Prisha lay back down. She didn't relish digging too deep into whatever was going on between those two.

6   THE SCENT OF DANGER

SCRATCH OPENED HIS eyes and sniffed.

Odd.

Amanda slept peacefully next to him, apparently unaware of the unusual smell. Scratch sat up, held his nose high in the air and sniffed again.

Something there.

The breeze had shifted during the night, now blowing from the jungle instead of the sea. As a dog—regardless of how loyal or altruistic he strived to be—he couldn't claim meteorological skills. Wind was wind. But moving air carried scents, and Scratch's ability to distinguish scents was his amazing, incredible, unbelievably effective superpower.

He could pick out a single molecule of cat piss inside a three-thousand-square-foot house (even with odor filters plugged into every outlet) and guide you straight to the patch of carpet where the offending feline had done her nasty.

Not that he was a paradigm of virtue himself. There was that episode with the seat belt while he had been locked in the car and needing something to chew. And there were the many, many socks he'd … misappropriated. Of course, he was still haunted by the ghastly image of Patricia's (former) designer shoes. Scratch had to admit, he clearly had a chewing problem.

Patricia had been a life guide—what humans call an "owner." By Scratch's count, there had been eight life guides and just as many colossal mistakes in Scratch's short life.

There was the man who had separated him from his mother. Scratch was not a fan of him. Or the woman who'd bought him at the pet store, realized she was allergic, and returned him just a few days later. Scratch was not a fan of her either. Some life guides yelled a lot. They would swat him or put him outside when he made a colossal mistake (like sleeping on Grandpa Zeke's Barcalounger).

But not all life guides were yellers or swatters. Elaine, Scratch's fourth life guide, was kind, gentle, and a good cuddler. And what a scent that lady exuded: cracked walnut!

He would have stayed with Elaine forever, but for the *incident*. Far too embarrassing to talk about, the Weekend Incident of Shame was best forgotten, to be buried under the expensive Persian rug upon which it had happened. After that humiliating affair, Scratch had packed his kit bag and left. It was the only honorable thing to do.

Scratch stood tall—making sure not to wake Amanda—and sniffed once more. Faint, but unmistakable.

Rotten poultry. His heart skipped a beat at the association, a smell he'd hoped he'd never face again. Rotten poultry was the scent of dingoes. A scent that brought back memories.

Australia. The camping trip from hell.

****

The dingoes snuck up during the night while his fifth life guide, Mack, and his family were asleep in their tent. Scratch was chained to a post outside and had been told to guard the campsite against all intruders. Mack had withheld dinner too. "Better to keep a dog awake," he'd said.

Mack was right. An empty tummy made sleep impossible, and when those treacherous dingoes slunk into camp after midnight,

Scratch was alert. They surrounded him, closing in from behind tall grass, but their stench gave them away: rotten poultry. They'd probably been feasting on the kookaburras that lived in the area.

Scratch wasn't a particularly tough canine. Or aggressive. He didn't possess anything that might be confused with a killer instinct. But beyond a legendary sense of smell, he had one other thing going for him—tenacity. When duty called, he was incapable of giving up. He broke his chain that night, finding untapped strength born from his all-consuming desire to uphold his duty, and chased the dingoes far into the outback.

Things went south from there. Alone in the wilds with a roasting desert sun overhead, he searched far and wide for his family and finally gave up. Near the end, a park ranger rescued him. Cared for him. And while time assuaged some of the pain and bitterness from that night, his resolve never wavered. It became cemented deep into his core: death to all dingoes.

****

Scratch sniffed the air again and narrowed his eyes. He knew what must be done. The dingo-infested journey ahead would be dangerous, but he'd do anything for Amanda. She was a goddess, the best life guide since Elaine, maybe better. Definitely prettier, with a smell like jasmine tea and a laugh like wind chimes on a breezy summer day. He'd wallop a dozen dingoes for Amanda. A hundred even. Okay, probably overambitious, but a dozen for sure. His fierce determination would not falter, not for anything.

His tummy gurgled. *Right, food first, then dingoes.*

He hopped over sleeping Amanda and searched the camp until he discovered a basket full of strange aromas. He hesitated, tasting one, and recoiling in displeasure. No, he needed real food for his quest, like the strangely twisted crunchy food Amanda had fed him back at the flying car. (Humans called the salty twists *Brett Selles*, which seemed silly to name a food after a person but then there was also Sara Lee, General Tso, and Sloppy Joe, so Scratch decided that humans simply acted strangely on occasion.)

He made his way back to the flying car (now broken), sniffing his way around in the darkness until he'd located the Brett Selles food compartment. Its lid was already up. He pulled several packets out with his teeth but was soon reminded why Amanda had had to help him the other day: the twisted snacks were hiding inside strangely impenetrable packaging. It was infuriating, even for a pooch like Scratch who prided himself in his even temperament.

Thrashing the bag side to side and bashing it against the seats, he managed to open one bag, only to discover a measly five Brett Selles. What was the point of that? All that annoying packaging and the effort to open it for less than a mouthful of food? He had a moment of weakness. Several moments.

Twenty minutes later, he finally calmed enough to look around and realize what he'd done. Ripped packages were everywhere. The salty twists were not. He stuck his head into the compartment and found nothing. His eyes bulged. His heart went apoplectic. He had eaten all the food!

Oh no!

Amanda would learn of this newest colossal mistake. She would wake up, starving, weak, in need of nourishment right this minute or she'd surely perish, only to find the food compartment empty. Even with Scratch's guilty face on full display, Amanda would say something noble like, "It couldn't be Scratch, he's an angel, a saint among canines. He would never stoop to that level! Oh! If only I knew who actually had committed this heinous act."

And then, she'd collapse and die, and Scratch would be alone again with no life guide, no one to pet him, doomed to be a bad dog forever.

Scratch pondered the predicament. He couldn't replace the food. Dogs are terrible gatherers (too much slobber and no fingers like humans have). He could try to cough up some of the food, but when he'd thoughtfully regurgitated before, humans had made that face where they scrunched up their nose, squinted their eyes, and said things like, "Oh my God, no!"

There was only one thing left to do: get the dingo.

A dingo was surely out there, and Scratch was the only one who could find it. His efforts would save Amanda and everyone else. Only this act of heroism would be enough to lay to rest his Brett Selles–eating colossal mistake. If he was lucky, they'd even call him a good dog.

Scratch set off, sprinting through the jungle, sniffing with each leap to track the tiniest traces of the rotten poultry smell.

Get ready for justice, you vile dingo! I'm on to you!

The chase led through the densest parts of the jungle, with the scent growing stronger as he ran. He got distracted once by the smell of oil, which seemed odd for a jungle, and once again when a bird swooped down and pecked him on the head. But with a yip at the bird, he refocused his attention on the essential goal: a dingo was sure to be just around the next corner.

A yawning hole appeared in his path, big enough to drive a small car through. Scratch skidded to a stop and stared into the unexpected cavity. He sniffed. The stench was overwhelming. There must be a whole den of dingoes down there!

"Yip!"

He'd given them fair warning. It was time for these treacherous vermin to face the music, and this time, Scratch would be doing the singing. Or something like that.

Carefully, gingerly, paw by paw, he crept down the steep slope leading to the dingo den. Down he went into the darkness. The soil here didn't feel like soil, or rock. It felt like the flying car that had brought them to this place.

He continued down, listening for dingo growls and sniffing for dingo droppings. He thought he felt something moving, deep beneath him. It was like sleeping on a human at night, only to have them wake up from a nightmare and start thrashing beneath him, rolling around while Scratch barked in alarm and jumped off the bed. No, it was different than that. It brought back another, more unpleasant memory.

****

The sea roiled and churned, big waves crashing over the side of the boat and threatening to flood the interior where Scratch lay in the darkness, shivering.

He clung to the boat of the man who had adopted him from the Australian shelter, a writer named Eugene. They had traveled across the ocean for weeks with only Eugene and his two antisocial cats for company. They'd stopped briefly at Pape'ete, Hanga Roa, Lima, then sailed through the Panama Canal and were only a few miles off the coast of Florida when the squall hit them.

Scratch hid in the darkest, deepest part of the boat while Eugene fought the wind and waves to secure the sail. As he squatted, whimpering and feeling utterly useless, Scratch felt a surge of guilt. This was not the brave Scratch who had faced down dingoes for Mack. This was not the valiant Scratch who had protected Elaine from an evil postman (obviously evil, the villain had been carrying a package wrapped in brown paper).

No, he would need to do better.

Scratch forced himself up, colliding with the furniture and careening off the walls like a drunken degenerate as the sailboat lurched and keeled. With water pouring into the cabin, he somehow managed to get topside, only to see a titanic wave crest and smash across the stern.

Scratch was washed overboard.

It was only by the grace of whatever benevolent being watched over canines that he didn't drown. He found a life vest bobbing next to him, climbed atop, and managed to ride out the storm. He drifted for hours until, at last, he washed ashore and was discovered by children playing on the beach.

****

The rumbling, rolling, sealike motion passed under him, then disappeared. Scratch shook and came back to the present. Whatever the rolling motion was, it didn't appear to be connected to the poultry smell. The reek still permeated the air and was growing stronger.

Show yourself, foul dingoes!

The cave grew in height and width, now big enough that a human could stand upright. Water droplets clung to the floor, walls, and ceiling. It was sticky and moist. A low humming sound filled the air. If dingoes really were here, they'd picked a terrible location for a den. In the dim light, it was his nose that found it: the source of the smell.

It was lying in the middle of the tunnel. A nudge from his snout revealed a medium-size bird dead and rotting in the damp confines.

He listened. No sounds of dingo growls or other noises, save for that deep humming.

Fine. If dogs could shrug, he would have. It was possible his imagination had gotten slightly carried away. Perhaps it was nothing more innocuous than a stray bird flying down a dank hole and dying of old age in the dark.

He turned to exit the tunnel, anxious to be back in the open air again, but something didn't feel right. As amazing as his nose was, there was no way a single bird could rouse him from the camp and bring him here.

He sniffed again and stepped past the dead bird. His nose had found another bird, then another, and another. His head rose with alarm as the danger of this dank place settled into his doggy brain. An entire flock of birds was here. All dead. Recently.

The humming grew suddenly louder. A blast of immensely hot air blew through the tunnel from deeper within. Scratch yelped like he'd sat on a firecracker and dashed away at full speed, the hot air nipping at his butt. He ran so fast his feet were on fire, although that could be a result of the metal beneath him growing noticeably hotter as well.

There! Light! Fresh air!

He blasted out of the tunnel, and the tunnel blasted too with a plume of steam shooting into the air.

He never even turned around, running off into the jungle with no clear sense of direction, in full-blown doggy panic mode. Even the little voice in his head that guilt-tripped him into acts of valor had shut up. This was no time to be brave. That tunnel thing was spouting hot water like Elaine had spouted coffee when she'd seen how Scratch had defiled her Persian rug!

He ran and ran until the sun rose well above the trees, only stopping when his stomach began to protest. In the end, he had always been a slave to baser needs. Scratch slowed and came to a halt in an unfamiliar clearing. He collapsed and stared about him forlornly.

Scratch reasoned (as best any dog could) that the surest way to find Amanda would be to retrace his steps exactly. But the thought of getting anywhere near that freaky geyser of searing heat made him want to empty his bowels on the spot. It might be better to find an alternate route back.

He wound his way through a jungle that appeared less and less welcoming with each step. If he were a cat (not that he ever wished that on himself or anyone else), his fur would have been standing on end. Every new sector held inexplicable dangers: a winged mouse that hung upside down from a branch, a cloud that somehow touched the treetops. Scariest of them all was a squat, yellow-eyed, feathered creature that could rotate its head backwards. When Scratch passed by, the creature's haunted voice asked, "Who?" Just like the humans do!

Scratch ran away as fast as he could from that one. Dingoes were no longer public enemy number one. This place was.

A thousand paw prints later, Scratch finally reached the seashore. It looked calm, unobtrusive, with a clear view that felt welcoming after the claustrophobia of the jungle. As he pondered his next move, it occurred to him that he still hadn't made amends for eating all of the twisty, crunchy food humans called Brett Selles. He had hoped that defeating a pack of dingoes would make amends, but now he didn't even have that. He couldn't, in good conscience, return to Amanda empty-pawed.

He cast about for an idea. It didn't seem likely that he'd find a tree with Brett Selles bags hanging from its branches, though in this crazy place you never knew. Instead, he would need to find something truly special, something that would bring Amanda to her knees in gratitude and forever enshrine Scratch in the pantheon of Good Dogs.

Scratch found a stick. It would do.

In his defense, it was a particularly attractive stick. It protruded from the shallow seawater among a group of mangrove trees. He waded in and grabbed it with his teeth, yanking hard, but the attractive stick refused to budge. He twisted, it bent. He thrashed, and it finally broke from its mooring, sending a spray of water everywhere.

Scratch stood tall and proud. In his mouth was the most attractive stick since sticks were invented. He'd give it to a smiling Amanda.

Yet something was wrong. Water bubbled and roiled all around him. Was the sea angry? Perhaps he'd taken a stick that was not meant for human or dog possession?

Suddenly, an enormous sea monster leaped from the water's surface. The beast had a white snake body and a green pizza-shaped head that flopped like it was made of rubber. Jagged teeth ringed the green head's circumference and an open mouth in the center sucked both water and sand deep into the beast's belly with a slurping sound too horrifying to describe.

In slow motion, Scratch released the stick and leaped away, narrowly missing being sucked into the monster's gaping maw along with coral fragments, shells, and floating mangrove leaves—and the attractive stick. But the beast wasn't finished with its rampant destruction. It raised its tail, spewing seawater and sand from its anus as if laughing about its unholy desecration of what had moments before been a serene mangrove shore.

Scratch splashed back to the trees, certain that he'd never see the attractive stick again, but thankful that his own life had been spared.

He paused, panting.

What had he done to deserve such terror? He regretted ever sneaking under the Florida fence, desperate for a respite from the hot sun. The surface on the other side had burned his paw pads, and he had ducked into the cool interior of the flying car. It had seemed the right choice at the time, but then the car had suddenly lifted into the sky, and now he was lost in a world where sea monsters consumed attractive sticks. Not even meeting Amanda was worth such awfulness.

That thought slowed him.

No, Amanda *was* worth it. How dare he think so selfishly when his entire purpose for living now revolved around the well-being of that divine angel? What if the sand-eating sea monster continued its rampage down the shoreline and found Amanda? What if she waded in, just minding her own business, only to be sucked into the beast's acidic gut, where she would be slowly consumed over weeks or months?

Shame on you, Scratch!

He wheeled about, ready to challenge the sea monster and do to it what he'd intended for the dingoes. But now there was no sign of it, save a few large ripples.

Scratch decided the next best plan was to warn Amanda of this imminent danger, and quickly. But first, he'd need a new stick.

Scratch found the next best stick, which wasn't quite as attractive as the first, but he was in a hurry now. He followed the line of the sea as he ran, hoping it would lead him back to the campsite, aware that the humans were probably awake by now and might be considering a refreshing dip in the ocean to cleanse themselves. He must hurry!

Scratch was the wind.

7   IF THIS IS PARADISE

LARRY MOHS DECIDED that he liked Reginald. The two men sat side by side on the sand, staring across a turquoise sea, occasionally reaching into Reg's bag of cannabis gummies for another shot of this-is-a-damn-fine-morning-to-be-alive.

Reg was a guy who took things one day at a time and didn't let his feathers get ruffled. The sort you'd want to grab a bar seat with, order a couple beers, and talk about old TV cop shows. Chill as they come. Even the weird wake-up rumble this space rock threw at them every morning didn't faze him.

The rest were less sanguine. Half the time, Prish ran around like a headless chicken. Amanda was the sort who put on a smile but might have an emotional breakdown at the drop of a pin. Then there was Claire.

Somewhere behind them, he could hear Claire poking at the fire with a stick, probably just to torment the glowing embers that would otherwise peacefully live out their existence until crumbling into ash. A metaphor, of course. Claire poked at everything and everybody, leaving a swath of irritation in her wake.

Prish should have never let that woman set foot on the spaceplane! A fleeting image of Mohs himself swiping Claire's credit card and welcoming her on board was quickly banished to whatever corner of his brain was in charge of plausible deniability, fragile egos, and the Dunning-Kruger effect. *Ahh, much better.*

"I wonder if L3 has seasons," Reg said. He had a flair for random out-of-the-blue statements.

It was only their third day, and so far, Thursday was looking pretty much the same as Tuesday. "I doubt we'll need to weave coconut hair coats for winter if that's what you mean. Feels like Florida around here." Mohs sucked in the fresh sea breeze. "Sure beats working."

Reginald hummed and let the topic of seasons drop, exactly why Mohs liked him. Of course, there were only three men on this godforsaken planet to talk to, and Razor mostly grunted. Mention seasons to Chase, and he would have gone on some lengthy rant about planetary wobble and axial tilt or some such gibberish. He would have constructed a fancy sailor's sextant out of bamboo, ripping off his shirt in the process while the girls ogled, then once more force-fed his tiresome science down everyone's throat.

Chase was a twit. Mohs was sticking to that.

"You ever watch that old classic, *Hawaii Five-O?*" Mohs asked Reg. The others were over by the spaceplane, braying about who knows what. Missing dog or something. Whatever it was, they weren't roping him into it, no way.

Reginald held a hand to his chin. "*Hawaii Five-O.* Hmm. I might have seen it, but the memories are still coming in fits and bursts." He glanced over his shoulder as Amanda's decibel level was beginning to reach uncomfortable heights. "I have flashes when I'm asleep, but I can't sleep much right now, so…"

"You worry too much." Mohs grabbed a piece of grass poking up through the sand and stuck it in between his teeth. It tasted like menthol. Weird. He chewed it appreciatively. "Use your amnesia. It's a great excuse to reinvent yourself. Be the guy you always wanted to be."

Now Claire was going at it, something about Razor, as usual. She pointed at the big man accusingly. He appeared indifferent, picking his teeth with his knife.

Reg sucked the juice from one of the fruits they'd found, a particularly sour one that felt like being slapped in the face by a lemon. "A makeover isn't a bad idea. In my past life, I may have been a pushover. But I've been working on my assertiveness by creating alter egos and channeling them. Reggae de Cannabis is my favorite. He's a popular street vendor from Jamaica with a heart of gold. He dances a lot."

Mohs smacked him on the back. "That's the spirit!" In the absence of a bartender and draft beer, he pulled two more gummies from the bag and offered one to Reg. "Cheers to Reggae de Cannabis."

Amanda ran up, circled three times, then sank to her knees in the sand. "He's gone! We've searched everywhere!"

The dog had taken a liking to the ladies, especially Amanda. With chi-chis like hers, it was no wonder the dog was always ready for another snuggle.

Mohs shrugged. "Maybe your pooch woke up early and went for a run."

Amanda's lower lip trembled like some discarded kitten on animal shelter death row. Prisha stepped up behind Amanda, patting her shoulder. Good, she could deal with this.

Mohs turned his stare down the beach, making a dramatic show of scanning it for all of two seconds. "Nope, don't see him. But you can be sure I won't rest until the dog is found." He waited for Prisha and Amanda to go elsewhere so he could immediately resume resting.

Prisha leaned close to Mohs. "Captain, I think we have a problem."

Mohs was pretty sure Prisha had only one expression—earnest. She'd be the world's worst poker player. The card sharks in Vegas would have the deed to her house in ten minutes.

"Jesus F. Christ, Prish. One missing doggy is not my problem, or yours either." Mohs rubbed his temples.

"But, Captain, Scratch slept next to Amanda last night. No yips. No tracks leading away." She tilted her head and spoke out the side of her mouth (okay, two expressions). "Razor says he had nothing to do with it."

"Then take the man at his word."

She whispered something to Reg, who led a trembling Amanda ten paces down the beach, then leaned even closer. "That's just it, Captain. While we were asleep, how do we know Razor didn't follow through with his... you know?" She drew her finger across her throat. "Claire seems sure."

Mohs groaned, staring out to the tranquil water. Glints of sunlight sparkled like diamonds set in turquoise. It might be a good day to fashion a paddleboard out of one of the spaceplane's stabilators and head far out to sea. By himself. Never to return.

Mohs waved a hand idly. "As I see it, this little snafu is all yours, Prish. It'll be a good training exercise."

"Oh, no," she answered firmly. "You can't keep using *that* one. You're the captain here, not me."

They were interrupted by a kick of sand. "Don't expect much from this washed-up stoner, he's worthless." It was Claire, who stood nearby, arms crossed, immovable as a brick wall. She'd definitely be the world's best poker player. The card sharks in Vegas would be taking out second mortgages in a desperate attempt at just a hint of Claire's hand.

Claire flicked a finger at Prisha's shoulder pad. "And the guy who cleans the spaceplane toilet probably outranks you." Prisha recoiled, looking hurt.

Reg and Amanda returned to the circle forming around Mohs. Chase joined them, shirtless again, and stood slightly in front of Prisha like a human shield. "Let's not make this personal," Chase said firmly.

Bloody hell, not the twit too. Mohs would give it one more try, but if this one failed it was off to plan B, paddleboarding as far as the ocean stretched. "Ladies, please! Give it a rest. It's just a dog. In the big scheme of things, who really cares?"

Claire ignored him. "Examine the facts. We know Razor won't hesitate to kill a defenseless animal in the name of survival. Am I the only one here who remembers *Survival Instinct* Episode 17? The one with the skunk?"

"I'd hardly call a skunk defenseless." Like a silent assassin, Razor had slipped within speaking distance. He leaned against a nearby palm, calmly sharpening his knife.

Claire pointed at him. "Or that puffy little owl in Season 3?"

"That puffy little owl was about to kill a fluffy little bunny. Call off your dogs already!" Razor's steely facade was beginning to show cracks, but Claire could wear down a granite statue.

Amanda's lip wobbled. She made a hiccup sound. A tear hung delicately from one eyelash. This could get ugly fast.

Mohs stood between the opposing parties. "Look, folks, let's just take a breather, relax on the beach for a—"

"Sit down and shut up," Claire ordered.

"Sheesh." Mohs slumped back down to the sand. "Dog-eat-dog world here."

"Dog. Eat. Dog," Amanda mumbled with eyes glazed. Her face went red. Even her hair seemed to stand on end. She threw her arms up and screamed, "I can't take it anymore!"

She hopped around like her feet were on fire. "All this arguing! Y'all are pointing fingers, but no one is looking for Scratch! He could be lying wounded in the jungle, and I'm not letting that sweet pup die while I still have a breath in my body!"

She ran, straight for the jungle. Reginald was close behind, but there was no catching this runaway banshee. Amanda disappeared into thick brush. Reginald stopped, his head twitching between the sound of breaking branches and the circle of onlookers who remained on the beach.

"I'd go after her," he said, "but if we don't find Scratch, she's not coming back."

No one moved. Prisha was the first to snap out of it. "We can't let her go alone."

"She could be halfway to L3's very close horizon by now," Chase advised.

Claire put hands on hips. "Screamers. They're always the ones who break. So, two are missing now. Everybody happy?"

Razor flipped his knife end over end, miraculously catching it each time. "What a mess you people are. Now me, I've already whittled three new arrows and tipped them with flint heads, and it's still morning." He waved. "Ahh, let her go, it'll be good for her. She might learn a few things about surviving the night alone."

Chase shook his head. "Chaos is not a plan. If we're going to survive, we need to stick together."

"With leadership," Prisha added with no subtlety whatsoever.

Mohs groaned, pulled himself to his feet, and brushed the sand off his backside. He'd seen a few unruly mobs in his career, and it usually meant the salesperson hadn't plied them enough with empty promises. Mohs's business philosophy was like a layer cake: first establish a solid foundation of abuse to put customers on their heels, then close the deal with meaningless guarantees as the icing on top. Okay, it actually wasn't much like a layered cake, but it was a philosophy that worked.

"Alright, folks," he announced, "there's a dog missing. I get it. The pooch might be taking a nap somewhere out in the woods, but, given the ruthless butcher in our ranks and earfuls of accusations being thrown around, you need someone in charge. Someone to think for you. Somebody who tells you when to unzip and where to pee."

"That is wrong on so many levels…," Chase started.

"You want wisdom, talent, and good looks in your leader." Mohs pointed to himself. "But you also want youth." He pointed to Prisha. "Am I right?"

"Well, that's not really—" Prisha tried.

"Don't answer that. But here's the deal. I'm pretty sure my employment contract doesn't stipulate 'in the event of a crash landing on an uncharted planetoid, you are to become the de facto President for Life.'"

"It kind of does, actually," Prisha offered. "Clause 12b. 'In the event of catastrophic failure, Megalodon Industries denies all responsibility.'"

Mohs made an ugly face. "Doesn't put me in charge."

"Well, the fallback is eighteenth-century maritime law, which says the captain—"

"Romanticized hogwash. You want me to officiate marriages and baptize babies too? Look, I'm not the answer for every little need." Mohs crossed his arms, satisfied that he'd made his point and could return to figuring out how to build a paddleboard.

He got stares in return.

"Okay, so maybe things are still a little vague on the leadership side," Mohs said. "Tell you what. I'll give you five minutes of my esteemed and very reasonably priced consultation. We can start with the so-called criminal."

Cleaning his nails with his knife, Razor looked up. "Didn't do it."

Mohs tipped his cap. "Not saying you did, but maybe you could help us find the little rug rat?"

Razor flicked the knife into a nearby stump with the casual air of an elite commando. It made Mohs shiver. "Why not? I'll find Amanda and that mutt too." Razor started toward the jungle.

Mohs spread his arms wide to the rest. "See? Problem solved. How about we all just fall in line behind Razor and take a stroll through the jungle? We'll find the girl and her dog, and when we get back, we'll go full gummy for the rest of the afternoon."

Reginald patted the pocket of his pants where he'd safeguarded the nearly bottomless gummy bag. Smart man.

Razor's machete made quick work of the tangle of plants and vines, and with five people trampling behind, they created a reasonable path. A rich earthy scent filled the air, either from the shredded plants under their feet or Chase's natural man-musk. Hard to tell. Chase was collecting samples of vegetation as they went, his hands already full.

"Hey, scientist. This ain't no Boy Scout expedition," Mohs called out.

Chase responded with overt sincerity to what any normal guy would recognize as a friendly testosterone taunt. "We're already deeper than we've been on L3. It's an opportunity to collect specimens and identify variant species. We might discover something unique, perhaps a plant that gives us a useful ointment or vitamin in case we're stranded here for a long time. You never know."

Mohs chuckled. "Well, I noticed your reconfiguration of the spaceplane antenna flopped, so yeah, I'd say we'll be here a while. Oh, it doesn't bother me. Go ahead and fiddle with that pile of junk all you want, but let's agree it's more about impressing a certain lady than science."

Chase hung his head and wordlessly tossed his plant collection back into the jungle.

Confirmed. No sense of humor.

Something deep in Mohs wanted to explore why Chase triggered him so easily, perhaps dissecting his own suppressed insecurities and the reasons why he still felt the need to comb over his few remaining hairs in a desperate attempt to retain long-gone youth. Or perhaps it was because the air on L3 was slightly altered, making them all crazy enough to fixate on random things that were otherwise imperceptible, like the fact that Chase's front teeth were off-center from the rest of his face. Or perhaps it was because the man's name was a verb.

Nah, Chase is a twit. Leave it at that.

They walked on, with Prisha calling out Amanda's name regularly. The only sounds returned were the squawks of birds. A few minutes later, Prisha stopped cold. The rest practically rear-ended each other.

"Look!" She pointed left, then right. Another trail crossed their path. "Razor didn't cut this path."

Sure enough, Razor was a good hundred yards ahead, still whacking their new trail. He'd cut right across what seemed to be a more established path.

Reginald looked confused. "Why wouldn't he just take this one? Do you think he senses something we don't? Did Amanda not go this way?"

Chase bent over, studying the plants. "It could be a path that L3 species have created over time. A small hooved animal, perhaps?" He squatted, inspecting the muddier parts of the crossing path for prints.

Prisha called out for Amanda in either direction along the path. No answer. "Should we split up?"

Mohs shrugged. "Do what you want, but my money is on the man with the machete." The freshly cut trail they'd been following continued ahead, but Razor was nowhere to be seen or heard. "If we don't get going, we're going to lose him."

Prisha countered. "Razor seems pretty sure of himself, I'll grant him that, but just because there are no footprints here doesn't mean Amanda didn't find this trail like we did but just further down. I think we should split up."

"Split up?" Mohs shook his head, already weary of this little adventure in the jungle. "Haven't you seen any of those deep-in-the-woods horror flicks? If some kind of alien beast made this trail, it'll pick us off one by one, starting with whoever's in the rear."

Mohs pointed his thumb behind. In this case, it was Claire who brought up the rear, an order that was just fine by Mohs.

"Oh, for crying out loud!" Claire cried out loud. "You people couldn't find your way to the bathroom without a GPS guide. I'll make this easy for you. I'll go right, the rest of you go left. We've already lost Razor anyway."

She stood at the intersection, shooing them down the left path. "Go!"

Prisha started down the crossing path. Mohs followed, purposely leaving Reginald and Chase to bring up the rear. Whatever might happen to Claire taking the opposite direction was her business.

They were only a hundred paces down the new trail when Reginald called out cheerily from behind. "We're down to four!" He hadn't been picked off yet, but his point was accurate: splitting up was a surefire way to end up with more people lost.

After a few hundred yards, Prisha stopped and pointed to a clearing ahead. An incline was cleaved by a hole the size of a car. Rocks ringing its edges were pitch black, shiny, and wet. No plants grew within ten feet, and the surrounding ground was thick with mud.

They halted. Puzzled eyes swept the area. Chase examined the mud. There were paw prints everywhere, unmistakably those of a small dog.

Chase called out into the gaping hole. "Scratch?"

Reginald cupped his hand and yelled too. "Here, poochy pooch! I've got a nice carrot for you!"

Prisha shook her head. "That's rabbits."

Reginald rubbed the back of his neck. "Oh, yeah. Animals are hard. But if our doggy left those tracks, he has to be around here somewhere, right?"

"They look fresh," Chase agreed. "It's got to be Scratch."

"Yeah, but if the pooch went in there..." Mohs kept his distance from the gaping black cavity that was easily capable of leaving no trace of any search party—or dog—that fell into it.

Chase very purposefully sniffed the air. "I was thinking it might be a hot springs or even a geyser, but the odor isn't quite sulfuric. It's worse."

"Smells like death," Reginald said, plugging his nose.

"My point exactly." Mohs backed away even further and commended himself on a fine display of leadership.

"Look over here!" Prisha had wandered past the Hole of Death and was studying the muddy ground. "More tracks! They seem to go up the hill."

"Okay, then. Onward." Mohs quickly took his slot behind Prisha. The middle person in any group always stood the best chance of returning alive. Claire was probably some fanged monster's lunch by now, a result that would definitely reap benefits for nap time in the hammock, assuming the rest of them made it back to camp.

They trudged uphill. The path steepened, taking two switchbacks before the trees thinned and the hill crested. The trail ended at a good-sized clearing, nearly circular, with views in all directions. A brisk breeze blew, rustling the leaves around the edges. Overhead, puffy clouds seemed close enough to touch. One cloud formed into the shape of a ring complete with a smaller puff on one side as its diamond jewel.

In one direction, the jungle continued to the horizon. In another, there was a good view to the beach where they'd set up camp, including the swath of forest smashed by their crash landing three days before. Their familiar beach curved toward larger hills that stood on the far side of the shallow sea. It was the best view they'd had yet of their surroundings.

"Lookout Peak," Reginald said. "That's what I'm naming it."

"Lookout Peak has funny clouds," Prisha noted. "A diamond ring over there, and that one looks like an eagle."

It was true—a second cloud formation had two well-defined wings, tail, and head, complete with a sharp beak. As they watched, the wings seemed to flap in the breeze, then quickly evaporated into nothing. The diamond ring re-formed into an arch with its diamond puff positioned at one end like a leprechaun's pot of gold under a rainbow.

Mohs rubbed the whiskers on his chin. "You know, I haven't had a single gummy in, like, hours…"

"An hour," Reginald corrected him.

"Semantics. but this place is beginning to freak me out." Mohs had said it before and would probably say it again if anyone bothered to listen—this place was weird.

"L3 is kind of like a monster film setting. You know, like *King Kong* or…" Reginald's eyes went wild. "Dinosaurs! We've been flung back in time and sneaky velociraptors are hiding around every corner, scheming about how to slash our bellies open!"

Chase admonished him. "Honestly, this place isn't big enough to sustain a food chain that complex. And it's natural for humans to find familiar shapes in clouds. See, they're all gone now." The clouds had become disorganized, but they kept changing as the breeze blew past.

"Amanda!" Prisha screamed as loud as she could. Her voice probably carried a half mile on this breeze, which on L3 was beyond the horizon. If Amanda was out there, she wasn't answering.

"Not so loud," Reginald pleaded. He clearly was holding to his sneaky dinosaur theory.

Mohs counted off on his fingers. "No dog, no Amanda, no Razor, no Claire. In a way, things are improving." No one seemed to notice his humor, which was often wasted on people with no sense of how much entertainment could be mined from other people's misfortunes.

"Let's retrace our steps," said Chase. "The captain is right, at least in that this trek is losing more than gaining."

Twit. Always stating the obvious. A blind Santorini donkey could see it.

Prisha nodded and led them back down the hill. They passed the hole again, where Chase observed that Scratch's tracks were now covered by their footprints, ruining any chance at tracking him further. Continuing on, they found the place where the natural path and Razor's path met.

Prisha scratched her head. "It looks familiar. But I honestly don't remember which way leads back to camp."

A compass would have been a nice addition to their survival gear, not that Megalodon bothered to equip spaceplanes for survival. Mohs considered his innate masculine sense of direction to be as good as a compass anyway. He pointed. "That way."

Chase shushed everyone and listened. A moment later, they could hear it too. Something big was coming from yet another direction where no trail existed.

"Razor?" Chase yelled.

"Shh! It's the velociraptors!" Reginald hid behind Chase. The sounds of cracking branches reached a crescendo. Mohs braced for an epic fight to the death.

Instead, Razor and Amanda emerged from the jungle. She hobbled next to him with a bad limp, one arm around his neck.

"Amanda!"

"You found her!"

"He did," Amanda said, glancing with thankful eyes to her rescuer.

For his part, Razor remained stone-cold stoic. "Told you I would."

The rest gathered around, careful not to bump into Amanda's raised foot.

"Are you hurt?"

"Just a little. Rolled my ankle, had a good cry, might have screamed some things I'll never repeat again, but I'm alright now. Sorry—when I left, I was totally out of control. My bad." Amanda's eyebrows raised. "Has anyone found Scratch?"

Prisha shook her head. "No, sorry."

Amanda's fragile shell of perky optimism cracked noticeably.

"But we did find tracks that were almost certainly his," Chase added. "A solid forty percent chance."

Amanda seemed to take the news in stride. They meandered back down the trail with Reginald leading this time and Razor bringing up the rear—to keep the stragglers from wandering off again, he'd said.

Amanda was soon chirping happily about how noble Razor had been and what an adventure they'd all had, and how Scratch was probably just out for a walk and would no doubt return by nightfall. She had her fingers crossed the whole time she talked.

At last, they were back to the wrecked spaceplane and their campsite. Reginald burst out laughing. There was Scratch, asleep under the lean-to, a stick between his paws, and airy sounds escaping from his mouth as he dreamed.

"Scratch!" Amanda screamed. The dog exploded upright, his head twisting this way and that. When he caught sight of Amanda, he grabbed his stick and hurried over.

He was dirty, fur matted, and covered in bits of vegetation, but otherwise he appeared to be fine. He held out the stick to Amanda. She squatted, hugging the dog, which sent him into a frenzied state of wet kisses and a tail wagging fast enough to mow a lawn.

"Aw, Scratch," Amanda said, taking the offering. "It's a very attractive stick. I'll treasure it forever. I'll bet you searched all morning for it. Is that why you were gone? I bet you found all kinds of amazing things along the way. Want to tell us about them?"

Scratch yipped his responses.

Claire emerged from the spaceplane, her eyes darting. "I've been back for a while. Figured I'd let the dog sleep and that the rest of you would eventually circle back."

Mohs puffed out his chest. "There you go, everyone is accounted for, safe and sound. Folks, in the spaceplane flying business, that there is what we call leadership. Now if you'll excuse me, I have some mind-numbing stupefaction to catch up on." He grabbed a handful of Yummy Gummies from the open bag offered by Reginald, then plopped into his hammock and pushed his cap down over his eyes. For a day that had started crappy, it was fast improving.

Sounds of a crackling fire meant the rest were preparing a meal, probably gathering in the rock circle around the firepit. No need to get up, there would be leftovers. And certainly, no need to join in on the chin-wagging about the adventures of a little lost dog.

What a waste of time.

Amanda started singing. Others joined in. The three-letter international code for a ship in distress was prominently involved.

Oh, hell no! Not that! Nothing could be worse!

"It's amazing how there's an ABBA song for any occasion," someone said.

The nauseating sappiness finally finished, and Prisha called out, "Hey, Captain, want to join us for a round of charades?"

Mohs rolled over in agony. For the first time today, he admitted to himself he had been wrong. Indeed, there was something worse.

8   MURDER AND OTHER GOSSIP

IT HAD RAINED overnight, the second time in four days. A steady drip plopped onto Amanda Summer's bare shoulder. The moss and leaves that formed their communal bed weren't much drier. The boys had done their best to construct a bamboo lean-to, but on rainy nights even a stuffy spaceplane cabin might be better.

Maybe I'll talk to Prisha about that. She's so nice.

They had talked well into the night about yesterday's misadventure: Amanda "going ballistic," as they say. Prisha had been nothing but supportive. Like a big sister.

Dawn hadn't arrived yet, or the crazy rolling sensation that seemed to come with it, whatever that was. Amanda ventured into the softly brightening morn, careful to step over the others. Sleeping in the lean-to was like flying coach—passengers in various states of leaning, inclining, or tilting. Knees up or legs draped across someone else. To get any sleep on those long-haul flights, you had to work at it.

For a real sleeping challenge, there was always Megalodon Airline's Barnyard Class: hot, cramped, crowded, and filled with the stench of a locker room. Some flight attendants refused to set foot in Barnyard, though they all agreed it was still one step better than Cheapskate Air's newest budget option: Recycle Bin Economy (reportedly located somewhere behind the coffeemaker).

Amanda peered into the jungle and whispered, "Scratch?"

Thankfully, the little dog came running out, tail wagging with another stick in his mouth. Amanda accepted the trophy and gave a quick cuddle that made Scratch's tail wag even harder.

"Shall we go to the beach?" Amanda pointed ahead.

Scratch barked.

"Shh, you'll wake everyone." Razor was up, but he was always the first. He'd probably gone hunting with the bow he'd pulled from his duffel bag. The captain would be in his hammock for hours, but then "people of an advanced age" (*nailed the social identity!*) needed their sleep.

She stopped by their newest luxury: the ladies' powder room that Chase had so thoughtfully built the day before. Scratch waited patiently outside until the flush, made possible by bamboo plumbing that brought water from the spring.

What a guy, that Chase! He's perfect for Prisha.

Naturally, Prisha was doing her best to remain the responsible first officer, but it wasn't hard to notice the cracks in professionalism whenever she was around Chase. The googly eyes. The stutters. That girl was smitten.

Amanda would be the first to admit inexperience in many things, but boys weren't one of them. They'd been flocking around her like bees to a flower ever since the days of driving the family tractor in Deaf Smith County, Texas (*yes, it's a real place*).

Back then, she'd politely shoo the boys away, nervous about what might happen should she ever kiss one of them. She'd read about it in a romance novel once, and a choir girl from the Texas panhandle couldn't afford that kind of reputation.

Everything changed after becoming a flight attendant. She'd watched and learned and within weeks was going through the guys as fast as face wipes, accepting all the amusement that came with each relationship and none of the angst (*except for Danny, who definitely got under my skin and is probably still waiting at the altar*).

Amanda squatted to dog level. "Wanna sing with me? We could do the duet from *Wicked*. You play the part of Glinda, and we'll pretend my skin is green." Scratch agreed with a yip.

They trotted down to the beach and climbed a rock that overlooked L3's tropical sea. The sun was just peeking over the tops of palms, and a cool breeze blew in from the sparkling water. If this place had dolphins, they'd no doubt be leaping just like Amanda's heart. Life was just too good to let anything like being shipwrecked drag her down.

She spread her arms and sang, imagining the green skin and witch's hat that came with the part. "♪ ♫ ♩ ♩ ♪ ♫♫"

Her voice was strong, the notes were pure: an uplifting duet about defying gravity, a feat that Amanda herself had recently checked off her bucket list. When it was Scratch's turn, Amanda held him high and fed him the lines, though he did more tail-wagging than singing.

The daily rolling rumble forced a premature end to the song when Scratch started looking like a cartoon pup getting a rectal temperature check. Amanda wrapped the shivering dog in her arms, and they sat it out together.

Even before the shaking stopped, Reginald casually hopped up on the rock and handed a coconut cup of coffee to Amanda. "Nice song.

It sounded vaguely familiar." He took a bite of a purple banana and stared out to the sea.

She was about to ask him if he'd even felt the rumble but decided that if their daily wake-up call was no longer a factor for him, there was no point in mentioning it. Reginald was a binary kind of guy. Events were either insignificant or hair-on-fire calamities; there was no in-between.

The sea breeze ruffled his parted Afro. His eyes weren't glazed over today. "Your memory is coming back?" she asked.

Reginald shrugged. "Not really, but the doctors said I might pick up a bit here or there from triggers like music."

"What's the last thing you remember before your accident?"

Reginald paused in his banana nibbling and thought for a moment. "A Toyota."

"That's it?"

"Well, it had heated seats and a rearview camera."

"But nothing about your life or those friends of yours?"

Reginald put a finger to his lower lip. "Hmm. Lots of glitter and nail polish."

"That sounds fun."

"On your eyelids?"

Amanda shoved him. "Now you're just joking! I might be a farm girl from the sticks, but I've learned a thing or two about guys."

"How many boyfriends?" Reginald asked sincerely. He didn't seem to be positioning himself to be the next.

"Does the Paris overnight layover count?"

"Sure it does!"

Amanda laughed. "Too many to count, then."

Reginald laughed with her. "You're fun. Hey, teach me a song, would you?"

"Sure, what kind of music do you like?"

Reginald shrugged. "I have no idea. But if I'm gay, they say I'm supposed to like Broadway show tunes."

Amanda shushed him. "Reginald, if you're gay, first, you'll figure that out soon enough, and second, you'll probably notice there are no gay police officers forcing you to listen to Broadway show tunes! Maybe you'll find something else that you enjoy. Impromptu chess matches in the park? Monster truck rallies? Rodeo?"

"Fashionista likes horses. And colorful clothes."

"Who's Fashionista?"

"A friend of mine. Kind of. Well, he's really me, just in a different part of my brain."

Reginald seemed to have a lot going on inside, but that just gave him more options, something Amanda had always believed in. A temporary detour to L3 wasn't going to stifle her ambitions, and maybe some of that spirit was already rubbing off on Reginald.

Claire came running up as fast as her short legs could carry her, fiddling with her HoloWatch as she ran.

"You're not dead," Claire announced.

Reginald didn't miss a beat. "Nope, still quite alive."

Claire fiddled some more. A few holographic icons popped into the air, then disappeared again. "Good, stay that way."

She turned to go, but Amanda hopped off the rock and stopped her. "Is there something we should know?"

"No, no. Everything is… fine," Claire answered unconvincingly.

Reginald hopped off too. "Maybe someone else is dead? Besides us? Since we're definitely not dead."

Claire looked flustered. "You were the last on my list to check. Along with the dog."

"And everyone else is alive?"

"Yes. One hundred percent alive."

The three stared at each other for a minute without speaking. Scratch panted in time as seconds ticked by.

Reginald broke the silence. "Is there some reason that someone *might* be dead? Just asking in case there's like… I don't know, a twenty-foot alligator that we overlooked?"

Claire held up one finger in the air. "Or a water buffalo. Could be a water buffalo just as easily as an alligator, and water buffaloes don't hurt anyone unless they happen to step on your toes."

Reginald nodded. "Okay. I buy that. So… is a water buffalo on the loose?"

Claire checked her HoloWatch. "Uh… no."

"Well, I'm glad we got that cleared up."

Captain Mohs, Prisha, and Chase emerged from the palm trees bordering the beach. They completed a circle forming around Claire.

"You're alive," Captain Mohs said to Reginald and Amanda.

"We already covered that," Reginald said.

Mohs glared at Claire like she had failed to deliver on a promise. Clearly, someone was supposed to be dead.

Claire sighed. "Okay, okay, I'll explain." She cast her eyes about like spies do when they're about to spill the beans then whispered to the back of her hand, "Razor is gone."

"Duh," Mohs said. "He's always gone."

"No, I mean he's really gone. Took his duffel bag and everything." She held up her wrist. "He pierced the outer perimeter of my HoloWatch security fence about twenty minutes ago, heading that way." She pointed down the curving beach. Another palm-covered island rose from the sea at the oh-so-close horizon of this tiny planetoid. "I figured he might have done some damage on his way out."

"Damage to one of us?" Prisha asked. Her eyebrows were pressed into a V. "That seems unlikely."

Mohs tipped his cap back and dragged a hand across the back of his neck in a thoughtful way. "The man does carry weapons."

"He's a survivalist," Chase admonished. "He has a TV show. The camouflage and knives are part of a cultivated image."

"Tell that to our little doggy friend." Mohs drew an extended finger across his throat.

Chase shook his head. "Okay, I admit Razor's not exactly pet friendly, but that doesn't mean—"

Claire interrupted. "Yes, it does."

"You're saying he might slit our throats too?" Chase sounded highly dubious.

Amanda was dubious too, and she wasn't about to let idle suspicions go unanswered. She held up both hands in a full stop. "Look, I know Razor can be gruff, and we shouldn't forget what he almost did to Scratch. But when I lost it yesterday and ended up deep in the jungle with a twisted ankle and no idea how I got there, Razor found me. He didn't yell or say anything mean, he just reached out, pulled me up, and helped me back to camp. I really think he learned his lesson. Even Scratch thinks so, right?"

Scratch hesitated noticeably, but he eventually wagged his tail.

No one seemed convinced, so Amanda tried again. "Have you seen Razor's TV show?"

Mohs shook his head.

Claire raised a hand. "A few episodes, yeah."

"So, you know the show can get a little… *rough*, shall we say?"

Claire's arms remained crossed. "He ate an iguana once."

Prisha turned away. "Ugh, I don't want to hear about it."

"How about the stork?" Claire asked.

"No!"

"Wildebeest?"

"Definitely not."

"Tarantula?"

Prisha swiveled back. "He ate all those things on his show?"

"That was just breakfast."

Amanda interrupted. "Okay, okay, his show can get gross, but most of the time he's building things or filtering water or showing how to avoid heat stroke. Things that would be useful for us to know too. When Razor reached out to me in the jungle, I got a glimpse into his soul. He's not a bad guy."

"Evidence would suggest otherwise," Claire said flatly. "You've seen the arrows on his neck."

They'd all seen them. Small tattoos on either side: a stylized arrow pointing directly to the jugular vein like some sick signpost for Dracula.

Amanda knew better. "No, no, no, they're not arrows, they're Vs! The V symbolizes human vulnerability and the need for vigilance. It's part of the intro for his show. You know, the part everyone skips over?"

The Skip Intro button was undoubtedly the greatest invention in the history of modern television, but it also meant that viewers often stumbled into a series missing important details like the meaning of neck tattoos.

"V is also for victim," Claire mumbled. "And there have been plenty."

Prisha stepped forward. She had an inch or two over Claire, not exactly a physical advantage, but she was the first officer and still wore a uniform to prove it. "Who are you, Claire Bouchet? Are you a police officer?"

Mohs took a step forward too, standing beside Prisha. "Good question, Number One." He fixed his stare on Claire. "In the space tourism business we'll sell a ticket to anyone, but the customers passionate about jugular veins are usually the ones you want to keep an eye on, if you get my drift."

Claire scratched the back of her head. "You people have no idea."

"Then fill us in," Prisha said. "Who are you? And what have you got against Razor?"

It was a fine question.

"He's a murderer," Claire said. "Technically... an unindicted suspect."

"Says who?" Prisha demanded. The set jaw and firm stance of their brave first officer made it clear that her first question would need an answer before any accusations against Razor would be entertained.

Claire flicked off her shades in one fluid motion then turned her eyes to the sky. "Yeah, I'm kind of like a police officer."

"Government or private eye?" Prisha stood inches from Claire and wasn't backing down.

Claire nodded. "Government. Most of the time. You've heard of the Godzilla Bandit?"

Who hadn't? For months, some guy dressed in a cheesy Godzilla costume with a flamethrower stuck out its mouth had been robbing banks, then scattering thousands of twenty-dollar bills to the wind only to light them on fire before eager citizens on the street could scoop them up. An unnamed government agent had finally caught the ridged-back monster by staking out the propane tank at a Circle K in Toledo. Nationwide, everyone who had chased a flaming twenty down the street cheered.

"That agent was you?" Amanda asked, incredulous that such a celebrated figure of authority could be in their midst.

Claire nodded. "All in a day's work. After that there was the Koala Baby Snatcher, who, as you know, terrorized California for years. I bagged him, too."

All eyes widened. Infamous, yet adorable, the villainous koala was known for dropping from eucalyptus trees to snatch babies from their strollers. Nearly a dozen infants had been abducted in broad daylight—all eventually returned to their frantic parents once the evildoing marsupial had been arrested.

"That sad excuse for a teddy bear deserved everything he got." The captain harrumphed and stepped back to Claire's side of the standoff.

Prisha seemed equally dumbfounded by the revelations. "So, if you solved the two most notorious made-for-TV incidents of misconduct in recent memory, that would make you—"

"The top criminal investigator in the world. But who's bragging?" Claire was practically exuding joie de vivre.

Wordlessly, the circle of former skeptics widened to give this esteemed super sleuth some breathing room.

"Wow," Amanda finally said. "Who would have thought that we'd have two famous people on our space flight?"

"Wait a second," Mohs said. "A famous government investigator doesn't just randomly sign up for a second-rate tourist flight to space. Not that our service is second-rate! Well... maybe it is."

Prisha held a hand over her mouth. "So, that's it. The mirrored sunglasses, the dubious explanations back in Orlando, the warnings about classified information."

Claire's voice turned serious. "Yup, I've been on this murder case for almost a year. Razor's what you might call a buttered-up weasel, as slippery as they come. Six months ago, he vanished. I got the first whiff of him in a remote region of Tierra del Fuego, followed by a frozen trek across the Andes, then stumbling step-by-step through the shifting sands of Timbuktu and the steamy jungles of Zanzibar. I finally caught up with him at a tavern in Nepal. The barmaid— Marion, I think her name was—showed me a strange metal disk, the headpiece for the Staff of Ra... no, wait, that was another case."

Claire cleared her throat, then started again, just as seriously. "I found Razor behind the tavern, head down in a horse trough filled with beer. He'd been there for days, the locals told me, literally drowning his sorrows over some lost love. Luckily, he was too drunk then to recognize me now." She tapped her ever-present mirrored sunglasses as proof that a minor element of disguise goes a long way when telling a fanciful yarn.

"Unfortunately, he gave me the slip while I was filling out Nepalese paperwork. I picked up the trail once more in the Kalahari, where nomadic herders had reported an American alone in the dunes, wearing a loincloth and hunting sidewinder snakes."

"But he's British," Reginald pointed out.

"Foreigners assume any idiot from out of town doing pointless, dangerous stunts is American."

Claire coughed into her hand. "The rest was easy. On foot across the bleak tundra of eastern Siberia, by canoe through the remote wilderness of the Yukon, and finally Air Canada from Winnipeg to Orlando with a brief stopover in Chicago. I knew Razor would be on the ten-thirty Quixotic Adventures space flight—a tip from an observant cab driver—so I bamboozled our favorite first officer for the last seat on the spaceplane."

Prisha hung her head, looking deflated. Amanda put a comforting hand on her arm. "You didn't know you were being bamboozled. You're still the best first officer I've ever met."

Claire laughed. "Razor was already on board, and I was curious why he was taking this flight. I figured spaceplanes only had one exit and I'd cuff him once we got on the ground. Preferably before he killed again."

Mohs patted Scratch. "I should point out that no one is actually dead, threats against the dog notwithstanding."

"Oh, you'd be surprised," Claire said. "Ask me about the producer of *Survival Instinct*. He's dead. Gutted. Forensics estimated the murder weapon was a knife at least ten inches long."

"Oh my," Amanda said.

Prisha and Chase looked ill. Reginald crossed both arms over his stomach. Captain Mohs cupped his hands over the dog's ears.

"The producer was the first of three," Claire continued. "All with ties to the TV show, all showing signs of close contact with a sharp instrument."

"Yikes," Mohs said.

"Then there's this receipt." She reached into a pocket and pulled out a slip of paper protected inside a clear plastic sleeve. It was a restaurant receipt, signed by Razor, with additional words scrawled beneath the bill: *Next time I'm going to slice that ugly SOB from ear to ear.*

Prisha leaned in close to read the threatening words. "It does seem rather incriminating. That's his signature?"

Claire nodded. "Matches several other receipts I pulled from a notebook I found in his duffel bag—which I searched while the rest of you were out in the jungle looking for Amanda and Scratch."

Claire held a satisfied smirk on her face, but for someone who had claimed everything was classified, she was doing a lot of blabbering.

"Guess what else I found in the duffel?" The unforced blabbering continued.

"What?" Reginald leaned in closer. More than anyone, he seemed intrigued by the unfolding murder mystery.

Claire raised her wrist and tapped a holographic icon that hovered an inch above her watch. An image popped into midair: a page with pictures of six people, their names written beneath their photos. Three had red Xs drawn across their faces.

Claire nodded. "You guessed it. Razor's coworkers from *Survival Instinct*, including those who died… coincidentally x-ed out!"

"Holy cow!" Reginald ran hands through his hair.

"Razor, a mass murderer? How can that be?" Amanda asked. Surely there was good in everyone, even those with poor hygiene.

"His name is literally Razor," Claire pointed out. "From birth. Just doing my best to keep you people safe."

"And we do want to be safe," Prisha added. "So, what should we do next?"

"We find him," Captain Mohs answered. "Can't have a dangerous criminal out there lurking around. What would happen if he attacked?"

"Oh, probably something like this." Claire held out her hand, middle finger extended. She pointed at a nearby palm tree, then touched her thumb to a ring on the extended finger. With an electrical zap, an oval of bright blue light shot out, blasting a perfectly circular hole through the trunk of the palm.

Scratch yipped. Everyone else watched in silence as blue smoke curled around the singed edges of the carved-out tree.

Reginald studied his middle finger. "Gee, mine doesn't do that."

PART TWO

Weird Planet, Strange People

9   LIGHTS IN THE SKY

PRISHA TRUDGED THROUGH soft sand on a curving shoreline that reached beyond L3's horizon. In one jacket pocket she carried a water bottle. In the other, six miniature oranges (colored pink, because… L3). Her supplies might need to last all day, since no one was sure how long they'd be away from camp—or what they would do when they found Razor.

Reginald led the posse. He paused now and then to strike a fierce fighting stance while swinging his machete through the air, a weapon he had found stuck in a palm stump and claimed for his own. At first, they'd all been puzzled why survivalist Razor would leave one of the principal tools of his trade behind, but Claire had resolved that question.

"He's got two more machetes in his duffel. And six throwing knives, a fish-gutter, skinning tool, collapsible shovel, crossbow, and a set of English tournament darts. I checked."

Claire had been busy while the rest were still searching for lost Scratch (now safe and sound, trotting happily down the beach with a stick in his mouth). Claire explained that she had also hidden a microtransponder inside Razor's duffel, ensuring they'd find him no matter where he decided to hide.

"What do we do when we catch up to him?" Captain Mohs asked, pulling alongside Prisha.

It wasn't like the captain to ask her advice, though she appreciated the effort. Far better than his more usual salty language sprinkled with insensitive judgments.

"Throw him in the brig?" Prisha suggested, half-kidding.

Mohs gave her a sideways glance. "An attempt at humor?"

"A work in progress," admitted Prisha. "I honestly have no idea. How do you apprehend a man who could make a deadly weapon out of a bar of soap?"

"Your humor is going in the wrong direction."

Prisha shrugged. "Well, if we had any soap, it wouldn't surprise me. The man does have weapons. I don't want to see a fight between him and Claire."

"Oh, I don't know," Mohs mused. "Assorted knives and arrows against a laser blaster ring. Kind of a *Clash of the Titans* thing. Could be good entertainment for an afternoon."

Claire flicked her HoloWatch on and studied the projection. Chase estimated that Razor was probably only three kilometers away based on L3's diameter. Depending on terrain, they could catch up to him in less than an hour. If bushwhacking was required, the machete could be useful—Reginald seemed to be getting the hang of it.

"Bushwhacking *and* defense," Reginald suggested, twisting his lips in various attempts at fierce. He was an unconvincing stand-in for Razor. Prisha tried to hide her smile.

They took a left at the beach and proceeded around its broad curve. Within a few minutes, they were already further along the seashore than anyone had been. The sea breeze was fresh, and the overnight rain made walking across damp sand easy. Birds hidden among the palms squawked as they passed, either because they'd never seen humans before or as some avian warning of what might lie ahead.

Scratch trotted next to Amanda, looking unusually tense. Prisha tried to pet him, but that only spooked the dog more and sent him running around yapping loudly, as though an infestation of squirrels had descended upon them.

"Maybe you'd better ride with me," Amanda said, gently scooping the dog up. Even loving arms didn't settle him.

Claire studied the hologram hovering above her watch. She stopped, held up a hand, and pointed out to sea. "That way."

The rest gathered around, staring across the water. It was a few hundred yards to the other side—another beach backed by hills covered in vegetation. If they were currently on an island (and no one had yet confirmed that geographic theory) the hills across the sea might represent a second island, possibly even bigger.

They had no boat, but the water looked shallow enough. "Razor may have crossed at low tide. Or maybe he just waded."

"Then we will too," Prisha said with authority.

"What about the piranhas?" Reginald asked, waving the machete over the water's surface.

"Do you see any?"

"No."

"See? You scared them away." Sometimes you had to humor Reginald. She splashed a path straight into the gentle waves.

The water was warm and never got much deeper than knee height. In places, pink coral provided nooks for sea urchins. Tiny white crabs flitted here and there along the sandy bottom. Sea life. Interesting, but not remotely dangerous.

The rest followed behind Prisha, with Amanda still carrying Scratch. The dog squirmed, but Amanda soothed him with a story about an adventurous but well-behaved pup named Scrootch who waited patiently as his life guide, Amandot, carried him across a busy street where large trucks driven by incompetent penguins drag raced without regard for their personal safety or local speed laws.

"And so, you see, Scratch, the moral of the story is never trust motorized sea birds, especially an emperor penguin with a lead foot and a chip on his shoulder. Oh, and always listen to your life guide because, while she may go ballistic sometimes, she only wants the best for you."

Scratch calmed, letting out a doggy sigh.

It was an easy slosh across, and within minutes they had reached the opposite shore. Amanda set the dog onto dry sand, and he ran off toward gurgling sounds that turned out to be a jungle stream flowing into the sea. Near the stream's mouth, a fish jumped.

"Holy cow, did you see that?" Prisha said, pointing.

They quickly lined up along the stream bank to stare into its clear, fresh water, teeming with fish. Some pink, others orange with blue stripes. Some had spots, a few with catfish whiskers. Several leaped between pools like salmon climbing a fish ladder while others lazily circled around rocks. The water was less than a foot deep. They might be catchable, even barehanded.

"Our source of protein?" Chase questioned.

"Razor was right about that," Mohs said, eyeing them ravenously. "I don't know about you folks, but I'm going to need more than just plant-y tortillas and jungle beans."

Reginald waded into the stream, stirring the water with his machete until one of the salmon darted between his legs. In a single fluid motion, he dropped both hands in the water and snatched the fish out, wiggling and flopping in the folds of his shirt. "Well, that wasn't hard at all!"

"No predators here, I'd imagine," Chase noted. "No reason for them to fear anything."

Prisha glanced over her shoulder to the sea they'd just crossed. "Not exactly close to our camp, but maybe we can relocate closer to the food supply."

Reginald threw the fish back in the stream—it wasn't even lunchtime yet, and access to the protein supply appeared to be endless. Claire pointed down the streambank, and they trudged on.

The route steepened, creating enticing waterfalls and cascades. Eventually, Claire guided them away from the stream, climbing a broad ridge. Reginald hacked the leaves that blocked their path, but the jungle wasn't quite as dense on this side of the sea, making hiking easier.

"When we find Razor," Amanda said to Claire, "please don't hurt him with your ring laser blaster."

Claire chuckled. "I'll set it to stun. How's that?"

"Are we being gullible again?" Prisha asked, mostly to Chase, who hiked next to her.

"Claire?" Chase called forward to the front of the line. "Do you actually have a stun mode on your ring device?"

"Maybe."

"Claire?"

"No."

"Then please do as Amanda asks. Do not fire on Razor when we find him."

"Defensive only," Prisha confirmed. Mohs mumbled his agreement, and Reginald made another slash through the air with his make-believe sword before also agreeing.

"You people are such amateurs," Claire said.

Prisha was about to press the point when she stumbled and fell forward—but in a weird, slow-motion kind of way. Chase caught her fall, helping her upright.

"Hmm," Chase said. "You seem extra light."

"I feel light," Prisha confirmed. "Kind of bouncy, but tippy too. Like I've got helium in my shoes."

"Me too," Amanda said. "It's weird. Each step is so easy. What's going on?"

Without asking, Chase wrapped his arms around Prisha's waist. Her heart rate spiked. He lifted her off the ground, then set her back down. Her instant reaction was oh-my-yes-do-that-again, but the delayed reaction was more along the lines of what-the-actual-flip?

She tried to turn his physical indiscretion into a joke. "Um… do you always pick up women that way?"

Chase seemed oblivious. "I'd estimate thirty kilos, probably half your actual weight."

Prisha scowled. "Worst pickup line ever."

"*Pickup* line, good one, Number One," Mohs said, then turned on Chase. "Watch yourself, pal, I can have you thrown off the plane for accosting a uniformed crew member."

Not that we have a plane anymore, but it's nice that the captain is sticking up for me.

Chase seemed to snap out of some deep thought. "Sorry. Just testing a theory. Follow me. Hurry." He ran ahead, climbing the remainder of the slope with ease, the rest in hot pursuit. Trees thinned, and a minute later, they crested the ridge to a glorious view.

They were higher than they had ever been, significantly higher than the small hill they'd climbed the day before while searching for Amanda and Scratch. There was a feeling of lightness up here, bounciness, like standing on a trampoline while wearing fluffy slippers.

The sun was almost overhead, and the usual puffy clouds were widely scattered but with tops now lower than where they stood. In one direction, the ridge ascended even higher toward a hill big enough to qualify as a small mountain.

Chase became animated, bouncing on his toes. "We're well above the lifting condensation level, the height where water vapor condenses into microdroplets."

"Cloud level," Claire translated.

"About three hundred meters above sea level by my estimate. Not terribly high by Earth standards, but for tiny L3 we're as high as the peaks of the Colorado Rockies, relatively speaking."

Prisha looked back down the slope they'd just climbed. "That wasn't hard at all." She'd never summited a mountain in Colorado, but she'd seen pictures. They looked... lofty.

"And that's just it," Chase said, excited. "L3's gravity is far weaker than on Earth. The only reason it feels normal down at sea level is that we're close to L3's super-dense core—my theory from the day we arrived. On L3, even three hundred meters up is enough to feel noticeably lighter. It's why it wasn't hard to climb up here."

"And why I feel so tipsy?" Prisha asked. She thought about falling over again to see if Chase would catch her once more, then decided now was not the time for teenage girl swooning.

Claire checked her HoloWatch. "My gravitometer says g is currently 4.5 meters per second squared."

Chase grinned like a Cheshire cat. "Cool. That's less than half of what gravity is on Earth. Closer to how it feels on the moon." He jumped to waist height before dropping back to his feet.

Reginald tried it too, going even higher. "That's fun!"

"Okay, boys—yes, the alien planet jumping is fun and all, but we've got business to…" Claire stopped cold, staring at her watch. She tapped it, jiggled it, and shook it. "Dang! Lost the signal."

"The blinking red light?" Mohs asked. "Razor's signal?"

"There's only one murderer out here," Claire answered. "And, yup, we just lost him. He probably found the bug. Smashed it between two rocks. Sedimentary. Flint, I'd say."

"You can tell that much from the signal loss?"

"No, but Chase can't have all the smarty pants lines."

"So, what do we do now?"

Claire stared off into the distance. On this side, the ridge dropped into a deep valley thick with vegetation in every shade of green. A faint hiss hinted at more flowing water in its depths. "He's out there somewhere. If we're patient, we might see the smoke from his campfire."

"If he even needs one," Amanda said. "Sometimes on his TV show, he just rolls in the mud for insulation and sleeps with the worms."

"Ewww." Prisha shuddered again. "Definitely not on my watch list."

"It's remarkably addictive," Amanda said matter-of-factly. "No one can resist the macabre."

Mohs plopped down. "Soft grass. We could set up camp right here. Someone could even run down to the stream and bring back a few fish for dinner." He stared at Reginald as his chosen fish fetcher.

Reginald confirmed he'd be the guy, then pointed straight up to clear skies. "And lucky for us, there's no chance of rain tonight."

They all looked quizzically at him.

Mohs laughed. "You're our L3 weather forecaster, are you?"

Reg shook his head. "No, it rains every other night here, haven't you noticed? It rained last night, so that means it won't rain tonight."

Prisha thought about this. "You know, you may be right. It rained on the first night and the third, but not on the second." She looked around. "And now it's our fourth night and it certainly doesn't look like rain. Maybe the pattern will hold."

"An odd pattern," Claire said.

"This place is weird," Mohs repeated for the umpteenth time.

Chase stood at the edge of the ridge, hands on hips. "Not sure that it matters. We're well above the cloud level. Nothing but blue skies above."

"Is it healthy, though?" Prisha asked. "You said it's like we're on top of the Rockies, and I'm pretty sure I'd feel sick if I camped in that thin air."

"You get used to it," Amanda said with a reassuring grin. "Not that I sleep on mountaintops, but I do work on board airplanes." She paused. "Well, I used to…"

"We're fine," Chase said. "You'd have felt dizzy by now if the air were too thin. This planetoid seems to have a high concentration of oxygen, given all the plants here. Probably even higher than Earth."

That seemed to settle the discussion—they'd spend the night on the ridge and watch for campfire smoke in the valley below. According to Claire, they weren't far from where the blinking red dot had been, and unless Razor was still on the move, their plan to find him still had a chance.

Reginald headed back to the stream to act as their fisherman. Chase appropriated the machete to cut firewood, and the rest positioned several flat rocks to create a reasonable camp for the night. Claire even tossed out six Mylar emergency blankets that she said she'd pilfered from Razor's duffel bag before he'd left. Given the distinct nip in the higher-altitude air, nobody wanted to answer exactly why the magical duffel bag continued to produce precisely what they needed except to note that Razor himself had declared he was ready for anything. Prisha had no doubt there were extra shoelaces, shark repellent, and tire chains buried somewhere in that duffel.

The rest of the afternoon was spent in a low-gravity jumping contest. At first it was just the boys, but Amanda soon joined in, and Prisha found it irresistible too. Claire sat out the game, declaring, "I could outjump you all blindfolded, with two anchors strapped to my feet in a hurricane." Unsurprisingly, no one challenged her claim.

Amanda turned out to be the highest jumper, having made several leaps to more than ten feet.

"She's skinny," Mohs said.

"She's strong," Prisha argued.

Chased settled the debate. "She has the right ratio of body mass to muscle."

"Thank you, Chase, you're such a gentleman," Amanda said with a haughty look. "What's my prize?"

Scratch came up with a stick. Amanda took it, laughing.

"I bet Scratch could beat us all, if he tried," said Prisha.

"Now there's a thought," Mohs said. "Toss him to me. Let's see how far he'll go."

Amanda twisted her brow into a comically angry stereotype. "Scratch isn't a football!"

Chase held his hand to his chin, the way he always did when pondering some scientific anomaly. Prisha cozied up next to him, in part to reclaim control over the space between them (after his highly presumptuous action of picking her up), but also because she was genuinely curious. "You're on to something. I can see it brewing."

"Maybe," Chase replied. "What would happen if Amanda ran, jumped, then tossed Scratch even higher?" He looked straight up. The stars were beginning to come out, normal for L3 evenings, but unusually early tonight, most likely due to their lofty elevation. "With a horizontal component and Amanda as his booster rocket, Scratch might even go into orbit."

"What?"

"He'd need a spacesuit, of course, which we don't have. But the point is, orbital mechanics for L3 are very different than Earth."

His eyes followed the ridge higher to the neighboring mountain, possibly twice as high as they were now. Prisha finally got his attention. "I don't think this line of thought is beneficial. Poor little Scratch has seen enough troubles for one trip."

Chase shook his head, returning from his musings to the here and now. "Sorry, it's not about Scratch. I'm just thinking, that's all." Chase fingered the sharp edge of the machete. Without comment, he took off running toward the tree line, yelling that he'd be right back.

"Right back" turned out to be two hours. By then, they'd roasted three fish over the fire and finished the meal with handfuls of delicious berries that were growing around their ridgetop meadow. The sun had set, leaving the fire and Claire's ever-present HoloWatch popups as their only light.

Chase stumbled up, panting like he'd been running for most of that time. He tossed the machete and dropped to his knees in the soft grass. Prisha squatted next to him, studying his face. His body might be tired, but his eyes were full of anticipation. "Okay, fess up. You're scheming about something. What is it?"

"Can't tell you just yet" was his cryptic answer.

"Oh, come on! You can't just leave us hanging." The rest of their group were spread out in a semicircle, leaning against rocks. Claire stared out into the valley, watching for smoke. Nobody appeared to be interested in their private conversation, but Prisha wasn't going to let it go just because Chase was tired.

She whispered in his ear, "You can tell me. Please?"

"This is big," he whispered back. He opened his fist to reveal three small rocks, one white, one yellow, and one black. Each was rather crumbly, leaving colored powder in his palm.

"And those are?"

"Ingredients for a plan. We have a chance to pull it off, but before I get anyone's hopes up, I need to make some calculations. Wish I had some paper."

"Just a sec." She troubled Reginald, who was already half-asleep against a rock, then returned with two sheets of paper and a pencil. "Reg has big pockets. Quite the resourceful guy, really."

Chase grabbed the paper, found a smooth, flat rock to be his table, and started scribbling by firelight. He wrote out several math equations and drew some diagrams with arcs and numbers written next to arrows. She had no idea what any of it meant, but each time she asked, he held up a finger. "Just a minute, I almost have it."

He finished by adding some numbers under an equation declaring "Burn time = V / A" and then carefully folded the paper and stowed it away in a pocket.

"So?" Prisha asked, on pins and needles. "What's your big idea?"

Just as Chase opened his mouth, a flash of light streaked across the night sky, its brilliance momentarily obliterating the stars and Prisha's night vision. It was as if a horizontal bolt of lightning had struck without making a sound.

"Did you see that?"

In a second it was gone, disappearing into the starry sky.

"Aliens!" Reginald declared.

"Why does it always have to be aliens?" Claire countered. "Hell, *we're* the aliens here."

"Comet!" Reginald tried again after a moment.

"You'd have seen a comet coming days before it passed," Mohs pointed out, unusually astute.

"Lightning bolt?" Reginald was fumbling now.

Chase shook his head.

Reginald slumped, defeated. "Fine. I guess it's just another crazy, unexplained mystery here."

They'd all been half-asleep or focused on something else. Only Prisha had been looking up, and she'd only had a glimpse. But the blast of light had an oblong shape—a large roundish head followed by a skinny tail. She didn't want to let her imagination run wild, but the brilliant flash—as quick as it was—looked very much like the thing that had dragged them away from Earth.

10   THE HOHMANN TRANSFER

CHASE BOLTED UPRIGHT, fully alert. It wasn't so much the rolling, rumbling sensation passing beneath. Being high atop the ridge, their daily wake-up call was less tangible than down in the jungle. In truth, Chase always woke up this way. He was a man of action.

He schlepped off the Mylar emergency blanket they'd pilfered from Razor's duffel bag and rose in a single fluid motion. The rest continued to sleep.

Perfect. More time to plan. Science calls!

This would be their fifth day, and everyone agreed they'd seen something unusual in the sky last night, though there was still some debate as to whether the oblong flash of light was the same thing that had dragged them away from Earth. Chase leaned toward the yes-it-was side.

Sixty percent chance.

Chase Livingston measured imprecise events as probabilities: the chance of being shipwrecked on an unexplored planet, the chance of being rescued, the chance that the ache in his upper left molar was a cavity (and not a single dentist within two astronomical units). All were probabilities.

He viewed people through a calculative lens as well, not as probabilities but as components of a whole. Like probabilities, this pie chart view of humanity also produced percentages (certainly the most satisfying unit of measure ever devised). Mohs, for example, snoring near his feet.

Twenty percent deeply suppressed leadership ability, thirty percent ignorance, fifty percent Napoleon complex.

Then there was Prisha, very possibly the most interesting woman Chase had ever met. Talented, resourceful, smart as a whip, and didn't take BS from Claire, or Mohs for that matter.

Thirty percent wide-eyed wonder, thirty percent get-it-done, forty percent undefinable perfection.

Chase was used to women cranking the flirtation to eleven when he started talking to them and usually blocked it out. He was, after all, a man of action. Work was the main course—his love life was an appetizer. But Prisha had the uncanny ability to penetrate this wall. He'd found himself flirting with her instead, almost from the first moment he'd met her. It had been a struggle not to let the attraction affect his performance on L3. Men of action were expected to stay on topic, and a breakthrough moment that would tilt the odds of returning to Earth in their favor could come at any time.

Yesterday—avoiding Prisha's questions as best he could—he might have found the answer. The idea was solid, the calculations were complete. Theoretically, it would get them home, though logistically the plan was still a long shot.

Twenty-five percent.

L3's small size and dense core were the keys to the idea. Contrary to the average man on the street's understanding, density plays a role in gravity. Why? Because gravitational force is computed using the inverse square of distance.

Inside Chase's Left Brain

Using Newton's Law of Universal Gravitation:

$$Force = G * M_{L3} * M_S / D^2$$

where G is the gravitational constant, M_{L3} and M_S are the masses of L3 and the satellite to be launched, and D is the distance between them, measured from their center.

L3 might only have a billionth the mass of Earth, but when squashed to a tiny size, the density in its core was no doubt ridiculously high. Get close enough to that core, and the force of gravitation works out to be the same as on Earth. But climb just a little—even three hundred meters as they were on the ridge—and the gravitational force drops significantly. Claire's gravitometer had confirmed it: 0.46 g's, less than half of normal gravity.

Further up, the ridgeline joined with a significantly larger mountain. It made Chase smile. Up there, gravity would be more like 0.3 or 0.2 g's, so weak any baseball pitcher could achieve escape velocity. It was a testable hypothesis, and precisely what Chase proposed to the group as they consumed berries for breakfast.

"What if we salvaged what's left of the spaceplane, dragged it to the top of that mountain, then strapped on a few rockets made from hollowed-out palm trunks packed with gunpowder?"

He showed them the three crumbly rocks he'd found last night. Impromptu mining with nothing more than the sharp point of a machete had proven each resource was plentiful. The white rock had a distinctive salty taste: potassium nitrate, commonly called saltpeter. The black rock was even easier: charcoal, no different than the briquettes used for outdoor grilling. A sniff test of the yellow rock verified sulfur. When combined in a ratio of 6:1:1, the three components made gunpowder, a formula discovered by the Chinese back in the eleventh century and still used today for fireworks on New Year's Eve, Fourth of July, and at gender reveal parties to start large, uncontrollable forest fires.

Chase's explosive proposal was met by blank stares.

"Good luck, Fly Boy," Claire said. "You're not putting me inside your Roman candle."

"Palm trunks don't equate to titanium rockets," scoffed Mohs.

"But what if it got us home? Um… could it?" Prisha's wording might be tentative, but at least she was on his side. And, as a spaceplane pilot, she probably recognized their liftoff from Florida involved a lot more explosive power than he was proposing. Departing from low-gravity L3 would be child's play compared to Earth.

"We don't need a lot of gunpowder. Just a single, short burn will put us on a trajectory called a Hohmann transfer."

"And what the bleep is a Hole Man transfer?" Mohs asked.

"Hohmann. It's an elliptical route between two circular orbits. It's how we send things to Mars, or any other planet. The idea is to boost your solar orbital velocity to get to a higher orbit like Mars or reduce your speed to drop down to a lower orbit, like Venus. Use any propellant you like to provide what aerospace engineers call a delta-v."

He drew two circles in the dirt, one inside the other, along with a dotted-line ellipse joining the inner and outer circles. He inserted two pebbles for L3 and Earth and added labels. "In our case, we'd use the Hohmann transfer to Mercury."

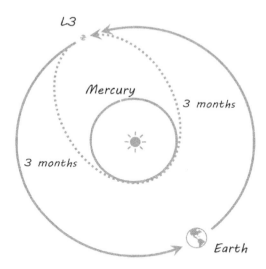

"Aha!" Claire said. "I knew Mercury would come into this eventually." He'd neglected to draw Claire's favorite planet the first time he'd explained orbital mechanics.

Chase gave a shrug of deference in Claire's direction. "Yes, Claire, I calculated this particular path just for you."

Claire's smug grin made it clear that a few more accolades would get her on board with this idea.

"The Hohmann transfer from Earth to Mercury takes almost exactly three months. But our Hohmann transfer won't end at Mercury. We'll just continue around the ellipse back to where we started. Which means our total trip will take…"

Prisha ventured a guess. "Six months? Three months out and three months back?"

"Exactly right. And what *also* happens during that six months?"

There were more blank stares. Chase didn't want to hold them in suspense any longer—or seem like an arrogant twit—so he answered his own question. "In six months, both L3 and Earth circle halfway around the sun. We leave L3 behind forever, but Earth catches up and meets our spaceplane at the rendezvous point. We radio ahead for someone to foam the runway, our professional pilots do some fancy flying, and voilà, we skid to a stop back at the Orlando Space Park!"

His much-too-happy pitch was intentional. Nervous smiles made it clear he'd succeeded so far, but the next question was inevitable.

"Six months?" Mohs asked. "Cooped up in a tourist spaceplane?"

There were downsides to any bright idea, and this was one. Chase nodded. He'd accounted for it in his calculations. "Unfortunately, you can't speed up a Hohmann transfer. It will get us where we want to go, but it's the slow route, so we'll need to bring lots of food and water. I suggest building a pantry that we tow behind the ship and jettison when we're ready to land."

Prisha's face contorted. "A pantry? Can we do that?"

"It doesn't need to be streamlined or even pressurized. A bamboo box on a rope will do. Space is cold, so the box would keep food frozen indefinitely. We'd rig up a simple bladder-style airlock for once-a-week prepackaged transfers. And of course, our spaceplane already has a lavatory." His list of positives was radically optimistic, but every revolutionary vision had to start somewhere.

Mohs scratched his head. "It's true, the toilet can be rigged to flush into space." He was coming around too, or perhaps just enjoying the thought of frozen flushes drifting outside the spaceplane windows.

Having captured their attention, Chase pushed on. "Takeoff will be tricky. First, we'll need to build a launch ramp pointed in exactly the right direction."

Even Deeper Inside Chase's Left Brain

Solar orbital velocity for L3 = 29.8 kps, same as Earth
Velocity needed for Mercury Hohmann transfer = 20.8 kps
Delta-v = −9.0 kps, a retrograde burn
Assume 2g accel for the basic comfort of occupants
Burn time = V / A = 9.0 / (9.8 * 2 / 1000) = 7 min 39 sec

The launch ramp's direction wouldn't be hard to figure out—just point due east when the sun is directly overhead. That's the backward direction for any solar orbit. More complicated would be the force generated by a homemade gunpowder mix. They'd have to figure that empirically by strapping on enough hollowed-out palm tree trunks to give them 2g's with a burn that lasted seven minutes and thirty-nine seconds. But once the right amount of gunpowder was measured, hitting the target delta-v would be a cinch. Any monkey could do it.

"We climb inside, light up our rockets, then coast through space for the rest of the trip. We'll be home before you know it," Chase announced with confidence.

The science would work. Math is math. But turning equations into a working system requires engineering. "We'll need to build a prototype. Who's in?"

"I'm game," Amanda said.

"Me too," Reginald said. "What's a prototype?"

Those two weren't even on Chase's to-be-convinced list; they'd already shown their agreeable nature. Mohs finally shrugged. Prisha nodded. Claire was the only holdout, but she was the type who would disagree about her own hair color. When the time came to close the hatch, Chase was sure that she would jump in at the last minute.

As for Razor, who knew? He might live alone on L3 for the rest of his life and be happy as a clam. They'd leave a goodbye note pinned to a tree. If they made it to Earth, maybe they'd send a future mission in a few years, along with a small army led by a dozen expert trackers.

Reginald pinched some of the yellow powder in Chase's palm. "Real gunpowder? That sounds fun." He sniffed his fingers.

"Let's try a test," Chase said, mixing a pinch of each powder and sprinkling it on a flat rock. He nodded to Claire. "Your ring did a good job starting the campfire last night. Can you dial it down and give us just a spark?"

Claire sneered like this was the dumbest question ever, then adjusted the ring on her middle finger and pointed. A quick flash hit the rock and Chase's small pile of powder burst into flames with snaps and sizzles.

"Do it again but bigger!" Reginald was as excited as any ten-year-old with destructive tendencies.

Mohs calmed him down. "Hang tight there, my friend. There's a time and place for blowing things up. First, we build it. Then we'll burn it to the ground."

Chase looked around. "Unfortunately, none of us are engineers, and even my knowledge of aerodynamics and combustion won't mean much if we don't design this thing right. So, I say we each make a prototype model, using whatever materials we can find around us, then test them to see which works best and use that model as a template for a scaled-up flier."

They split up, foraging in the brush around them for materials. Reginald used the machete to collect bamboo, while Amanda and Prisha located berries that produced a sticky resin that would function as a serviceable glue. Chase retraced his steps from the previous morning to dig up more ingredients for gunpowder. He collected as much as his shirt could carry and returned to their ridge camp, where he began grinding them down.

By midday, five model rockets were taking shape. Claire, still obsessed with Razor, spent most of her morning watching for signs of a campfire in the valley below, but she made a haphazard attempt at crafting her own rocket as the others took a lunch break.

Each design included straw-sized bamboo tubes as strap-on rockets attached to wings. Chase opted to assist the others in fine-tuning their design instead of crafting his own. Most designs involved two or four rockets. Reginald's model had eight.

"An... interesting choice," Chase said cautiously, squinting as Reginald held his up. "Why so many?"

"I just want to see more fire coming out the back end," Reginald happily admitted.

Chase pointed at a berry Reginald had glued near the front of his spaceplane. "What's this?"

"That's the captain at the controls. The berry behind him is Prisha shoveling more gunpowder into the rockets."

Chase shook his head, grimacing. "Think less steam locomotive, more bottle rocket. The tubes will already be packed with enough gunpowder for the seven-minute burn. After that, we won't even need them. We'll just be coasting."

"Six months of coasting, with nothing to do."

"And no place to go."

"You'll be at each other's throats," Claire suggested, making it clear she still wasn't on board with this idea.

"Not me," Amanda said sweetly. She was probably right, though it might still be a good idea to leave the machete behind just in case Amanda decided to go postal—again.

By midafternoon, the five models were complete, each looking like a sleek spaceplane with wings and a tail, though entirely made from strips of bamboo.

Chase finished packing gunpowder into each rocket and affixed a short fuse made from a bamboo stem. "Shall we give them a try?"

The rockets were aligned on a ramp that Chase had oriented three degrees above horizontal, aiming due east, with fuses extending from each engine.

"Claire, light them all at the same time," Reginald suggested, a wild look in his eyes.

"Uh, maybe not all…," Chase began.

"Piece of cake." Claire pointed her middle finger to the fuses and flicked her thumb across the ring.

An instantaneous zap shot out, and as she panned her ring across the fuses, five miniature rockets roared to life. Somewhat predictably, chaos ensued.

One model veered immediately into the one next to it, pushing both into a tailspin that corkscrewed into a palm tree a hundred yards downslope and caused it to burst into flames. A third didn't light for several seconds, then blasted like an arrow from Orion's bow in a straight line that sailed beyond the horizon. A fourth fizzled, arced for a few seconds, and feebly landed a mere twenty meters away. And another somehow did a loop-de-loop and came blasting back toward the group as everyone dove for cover.

BANG!

Chase peered out from behind a bush. The rocket had gouged a sizable hole worthy of an iron meteorite, with crater edges that were charred black. Debris littered the area. An end-of-semester frat party would have had a hard time managing the same level of destruction.

"Everyone alright?" It was Mohs, doing his darndest to act as captain for once. "All limbs accounted for?"

They emerged from the underbrush, sprayed with dirt but unharmed. Mohs patted Reginald's arm as he looked forlornly at the crater.

"That was mine," Reginald said, rubbing his neck. He picked up what was left of a burned berry. "And this was Prisha."

"Poor me," Prisha said. "Maybe eight rockets was a bit too much?"

"I don't think they all fired," Chase noted. "Looks like it spiraled back on itself and exploded like some of NASA's early rockets."

"Where's mine?" asked Amanda, looking around. "The one on the far left."

"Mine took yours out, sorry!" Prisha smiled awkwardly. "At least we went down together!" She stared at the thin line of smoke still rising from the palm. "Though, we really should put that fire out soon."

"Mine fizzled," Claire said flatly.

"So… that means…" Mohs looked around, a broad grin spreading slowly across his whiskered face. "Ha! Captain Lawrence B. Mohs for the win!"

The others scanned the horizon for any sign of his spaceplane model. There were no explosions. No smoke trail diving into the jungle. The flight seemed to have been a success, though they might never know what happened around the backside of L3.

And then, another idea popped into Chase's mind.

Deeper Still Inside Chase's Left Brain

L3 mass, $M \sim 3E16$ kg
L3 orbital radius, $r \sim 800$ m at ridge height
Orbital velocity, $V = SQRT (G * M / r) = 52.6$ mps
Orbital period, $T = SQRT ((4 * pi^2 * R^3) / (G * M)) = 95$ sec

"Stand by." Chase pivoted 180 degrees, now looking due west, and counted down from ninety-five until the final digits remained. "Five, four, three, two, one."

He scanned the sky. They all did.

Sure enough, like a phoenix rising from the ashes, Mohs's bamboo bird flew directly toward them. "There it is!"

As the object came closer, its shape was easily recognizable. Its wings were skewed sideways, but the plane was still moving rapidly, proving that it had climbed above the planet's compact atmosphere and was now orbiting in space, which in L3's case was only a few hundred meters overhead.

"You did it!" Reginald high-fived Mohs and let out a whoop. "Clear around the planet!"

As celebrations died down and the successful model once again disappeared over the horizon, everyone gathered around Chase. Prisha stepped forward and without any warning kissed him on each cheek.

"That's from all of us," she said, pulling back. "It was a great idea. It has a chance to get us home, doesn't it?"

Chase shrugged, somewhat flustered by the kisses. "Yeah, but... you know... so far, it's just a model."

"Hey, where are my kisses?" Mohs asked without a hint of mockery. "That's my handiwork circling the planet."

Prisha sighed, then gave Mohs a peck on the cheek too. "Well done, everyone. So, what's next?"

Reginald counted on his fingers. "One, take a broken spaceplane. Two, fix it up with berry glue. Three, attach bamboo rockets. Four, light the fuses and climb inside."

"What could possibly go wrong?" Claire mumbled to herself.

Chase's mind cleared, fixating on an imagined engineering process instead of Prisha's very encouraging lips and Reginald's amusing but reasonably accurate list. "Before we risk it ourselves, we should scale up. Make sure we can produce the thrust we'll need. Build a full-size mockup using the successful Mohs design, then do another test flight. This time from the mountaintop."

Mount Get-the-Hell-Off-This-Place (or whatever they would name the lofty peak) waited patiently in the distance. It was probably only two hundred meters higher, but it would be enough to make L3's gravity a minor factor.

"There's a good chance it will work." Chase did his best to exude the confidence of a calm adult while keeping his boyish exuberance to within a three-sigma uncertainty range as would be expected of any scientist.

Prisha leaned in and kissed him again, this time hard on the lips. "Then let's go!" She walked away without another word.

Chase teetered like a sailor drunk on dopamine. He blinked and slurred out, "H-h-huuuundred percent. We got this. Absolutely... a sure thing." His euphoric pronouncement wasn't even heard over the spontaneous laughter from everyone else, Prisha included.

For the rest of that afternoon, and over the next two days of construction, mining, assembly, and trajectory recalculations, Chase tried to keep his mind on the task. It wasn't easy. Prisha didn't say anything more about the kiss, and apart from a few sideways glances and sly smiles, her brash advance didn't repeat. The others, though, were more than happy to rib him at every opportunity.

"Anyone seen the smooch? Sorry, the pooch?"

"Are you going to help me with my rocket, or just give me lip service?"

"Did you know that kissing is like real estate? The most important thing is location, location, location."

It was never-ending. Chase ignored them all, keeping his mind on the prize. If all went well, They'd find themselves inside a spaceplane packed with food and water and zooming off on an elliptical path that would ultimately return them to Earth.

He'd never come up with a personality pie chart for himself before, but it wasn't too late to start.

Chase Livingston. Twenty percent suave pseudocelebrity. Thirty percent post-human silicon-infused cyborg. Fifty percent in over his head when a pretty girl walks by.

11   MOCKUP JOCKEYS

PRISHA EXAMINED THE underside of the spaceplane, locating a rear skid that would make an excellent attachment point for the food pantry they'd drag behind them once airborne. She'd already found suitable cables in the storage locker: three coils of braided wire with steel clips on either end, normally used as overnight tie-downs when the spaceplane was parked on the tarmac.

Orlando Space Park seems a long way away now.

Chase's plan to get them home had potential, though some key details were left unanswered, like how she and the captain would pilot a shattered spaceplane to a landing. She wasn't ready to contemplate that little issue just yet. If they could reach Earth orbit, they'd at least be within radio distance to get help.

Assuming Chase is right about his maneuver.

He *had* to be right. The Hohmann transfer was their best hope. But even if it was nothing more than a pipe dream, she'd support him anyway. Keep his confidence high and keep the group pulling together. It was her duty as first officer.

You kissed him, she told herself. *In front of everyone! That didn't come from any sense of duty.*

And it wasn't just a peck on the cheek either. She'd kissed him like Mary Jane kissed Spider-Man, though not upside down and not in the pouring rain. But it definitely had some old-school passion to it!

Chase hadn't turned out to be the pretty boy that she'd pegged him for when they'd first bumped into each other (literally). He was smart, inventive, with a positive and caring outlook. Sure, he smelled of sweat (and the fish they'd eaten for dinner), but hygiene had taken a back seat to survival—a tradeoff she could live with.

Chase hadn't said anything about the kiss, and she hadn't asked. They were now two days into the next phase of the project, building a full-scale mockup of the spaceplane that would test launch tomorrow if all went well.

Their camp had transitioned to the ridge, becoming the mockup construction site complete with a new shelter to protect from overnight rain (every other night, just as Reginald had forecast). But to be sure their design would work, Prisha had made the trek back to the spaceplane to examine how a pantry might be attached.

Success on that front.

She left the cables in the storage locker; they'd be useful when it came time to haul the spaceplane across the shallow sea, up the ridge, and to the launch platform on top of Daredevil's Perch (the lofty mountain whose name changed hourly now that group creativity had been sparked). Even with six people pulling, she wasn't looking forward to that task.

She returned via the same path they'd trailblazed while searching for Razor and within two hours had crossed the shallow sea and was back to the giddy heights of the ridgetop camp.

The others were busy with the finishing touches of their spaceplane mockup, a magnificent construction of bamboo lashed together with sturdy vines.

"Looking good!" Prisha said.

The mockup wasn't quite full-sized, but its delta wings and twin tails looked just like the real thing. Reginald was busy making dummies from stitched banana leaves full of pebbles, complete with smiles painted on their faces (except for Claire, who somehow even in banana leaf/pebble form still managed to look smug). Reginald had also added a rock that vaguely resembled a small dog when the light caught it just right.

Prisha squinted at the pebble sack Reginald was currently working on. "Who is that supposed to be?"

"It's you! Can't you tell?" Reginald rotated it so she could see better. The eyes were comically huge, straight out of a manga. Straggly vines for hair looked like Medusa on a bad day. The dummy seemed unusually chunky in all the wrong places, but at least it had a brimmed pilot's cap made from stiff banana leaves.

Prisha sighed a wry smile. *It's ballast. Give the artist some leeway.*

Claire had finally given up on trying to find Razor and was instead using her time to weave a sling to pull the mockup up the mountain. She had also revealed that her HoloWatch could be put to good use for this test flight: Claire had radar. Once the flight was underway, she would be able to measure the wooden plane's acceleration and launch trajectory, providing data for Chase to assess the likelihood of success once they substituted the real spaceplane on their launchpad.

The rest would come down to nerves: would they be brave enough to climb inside and launch themselves into the sky, knowing their success depended on the combined skills of a bunch of castaways with zero engineering experience and tools a caveman would sneer at? Prisha didn't want to admit it, but bravery wouldn't be enough. This would be a leap of faith. Too bad they didn't have some liquor on hand.

Mohs sat next to Reginald, passing pebbles to him. "Ever seen that 1960s movie with Jimmy Stewart, *Flight of the Phoenix*?"

Reginald looked puzzled, but that was pretty standard for him.

Claire's focus on harness weaving was interrupted just long enough to say, "Marvel Universe."

Mohs reared back. "Marvel? The comic books?"

"Yeah, Phoenix. Jean Grey. She's got telepathic powers."

"No, there's no superpowers. It's a Jimmy Stewart movie for crying out loud."

Claire wasn't fazed. "She sometimes becomes Dark Phoenix. Wears a skintight bodysuit. Has a thing for Cyclops, much to Wolverine's dismay."

Mohs's forehead disappeared into his hand as he stared at the ground. "No. *Flight of the Phoenix*! Not a jacked-up superhero."

"I was into a band in college," Claire continued. "Classic-rock band called Tenacious D, super old, still funny though. They had an album, *Rize of the Fenix*. Good stuff."

Prisha cleared her throat, her eyelids batting nervously. She hated to see these two fight over nothing.

"Fun fact, did you know there's a city of Phoenix in Arizona, Georgia, Illinois, Maryland, Michigan, Louisiana, Oregon, New Jersey, New York, and two Canadian provinces?" Claire was clearly pushing Mohs's buttons.

"What are you, an encyclopedia of Phoenix facts?" Reginald asked, scratching his head.

Claire barely paused. "There was also the HMS Phoenix, a British ship—"

"For the love of sanity and all that's good in this world, shut the hell up!" Mohs finally yelled. "Lady, if you want a seat on our flight home, figure out how to behave like a normal person! Otherwise, we're leaving you behind."

Claire huffed and went back to her weaving.

Mohs returned his attention to Reginald. "As I was saying, 1960s movie. Jimmy Stewart. He's a pilot who crash-lands out in some desert. Africa, I think. To get back to civilization, his crew has to build a whole new airplane out of broken parts, and sure enough they get that rickety contraption back into the air." He tapped his chest. "That's what real pilots do."

Mohs motioned to Prisha. "When we take off, she's going to be at the controls. I'll bring us in once we get home. Teamwork."

Prisha put a hand over her forming smile. "Thanks, Captain. I won't let you down."

Mohs reached out and hugged her with one arm like a proud dad might do. "Come to think of it, we have a little ceremony to perform before we launch into the sky."

He stood up and fiddled with the epaulets on his shoulders, then held out two gold bars. "These are yours now."

Prisha's mouth hung open as he fastened one bar to each of her epaulets. "Captain, I…"

"You earned it, Prish. Megalodon rules don't say that your competency assessments have to be with three different captains. A single captain will do. And I hereby declare that navigating a path around Venus, the sun, and onto an undiscovered planet counts as three flights. From here on out, you're a full-fledged three-bar first officer. Congratulations."

He shook her hand. Stunned, she barely felt it.

"Aw, so sweet," Claire mugged, her eyes almost certainly rolling behind her shades.

Mohs pointed accusingly. "What did I tell you about that return trip seat that you may or may not get?"

"Hey, I just said it was sweet."

"It's all in the tone. And yours drips of hydrochloric acid."

Claire tipped her head. "Quite the zinger, Captain. You got me there." She gave him a zipped lips pantomime, which seemed to satisfy him for the moment.

The others gathered around Prisha, each shaking her hand and providing congratulations. Prisha remained dumbstruck through it all but couldn't help a stolen glance at each shoulder now adorned with three bars.

I made it! Okay, so I'm on a different planet with almost no chance of flying again much less making captain and getting my own plane, plus my own parents may never know what happened to me... but... live in the present... I'm a real pilot now.

She immediately took back every "fupple truck" she'd ever whispered, mumbled, or thought about Captain Mohs. He might be a self-centered, lazy, irresponsible laggard of a man, but he'd just commissioned her as full-fledged, no junior grade, First Officer Prisha Jiera Dhaliwal, and by any measure his ridgetop ceremony had been a magical moment to be treasured forever.

The new first officer's lips began to tremble, and she was thankful when Chase patted the mockup and announced, "Okay, everyone, tomorrow's the big day." They had all already agreed, but Chase seemed to have a need to confirm the obvious on an hourly basis. Perhaps he'd been a project manager at some point in his career.

With impromptu ceremonies over and the day's work wrapped up, fish dinner was cooked over an open fire, and the intrepid crew of the L3's Flight of the Phoenix retired to bed early. Prisha dreamed of piloting her own spaceplane. She'd paint the interior a fun burnt sienna with almond trim and give it a pet name like Saahasik, which in Hindi meant courageous.

The next morning, they awoke to wet grass from overnight rain. Claire noted that this was their eighth day on L3.

Reginald looked at her cross-eyed. "We've been here a week already?"

"And tomorrow we'll be blasting off!" Mohs announced with a pump of his fist.

"Well… that's a little aggressive on the six-months-of-food-gathering schedule," Chase noted. "Then there's the spaceplane damage we need to address."

Mohs waved him off. "Whatever. A few patches on the wings, straighten out the bent hatch, pop out the dents, seal any cracks, make sure there are no places where the ship could pop open like a champagne cork…" Mohs trailed off. "That sounded a lot better in my head."

After a hearty breakfast of berries and nuts, the backbreaking time had come. Claire's woven harness had dual loops to accommodate two strong mules (a.k.a. human volunteers) to pull the mockup uphill. The rest of the team would help push or carry the bamboo rockets that would be strapped on when they got to the top.

Chase immediately offered to be one of the mules, taking off his shirt to prove it. Reluctantly, Prisha volunteered to be the other. She doused Chase's hopeful expression with cold water when she made it clear that her shirt—however sweaty—would remain on.

They slipped into the dual loops, then gazed at their lofty goal, recently renamed Nosebleed Summit (Reginald's suggestion). It was almost certainly the highest peak on L3. Higher than any of the scattered clouds, its barren rocky summit looked more Himalayan than tropical.

"We can do this," Chase said, holding out a fist, which Prisha bumped with limited enthusiasm.

"If you say so."

She pulled. He pulled. Claire's tether didn't break, but the mockup moved only an inch, if that.

"A little help?" Chase called out. Mohs put a hand on one of the mockup's tail fins. Amanda grabbed the other. Reginald and Claire, with bamboo rockets on their shoulders, could do little more than a hip bump at the trailing edge of the wings.

The plane moved a few inches.

Scratch ran in circles, barking like they were heading to the off-leash dog park.

Mohs paused his pushing. "Be careful with all that boundless energy, youngster. Little dogs that live on Mount Crumpit just north of Whoville have to drag fifteen-ton sleds to the top all by themselves, and don't think for a second that we're not above a Grinch-style dictatorship." He seemed to be only half-kidding.

The wooden plane slid again. And slid some more. Chase and Prisha put their full weight against the straps and heaved, legs straining and heart already pounding. With a bit more encouragement from Scratch, they eventually got it sliding without further stops.

"Harder than I'd thought!" Prisha called out, panting (and recalling all the times she'd skipped cardio dance class).

"We've got this," Chase called back, sweat glistening off his shoulders. He looked good doing pretty much anything, even emulating a pack mule. "Don't worry, gravity will lower as we climb!"

"Tell that to my burning thighs" was what Prisha wanted to say, but she thought better of it, not wanting to mention "burning thighs" to the man she had recently (and somewhat embarrassingly) kissed.

Instead, they marched in silence with the occasional grunt, groan, or oblique reference to a holy spirit in a highly blasphemous context. Eventually, the workload became easier just as Chase had predicted. Prisha's legs felt stronger with each step. If she pushed off her toes, her whole body lifted off the ground like hopping on a trampoline.

"Hey, Scratch!" Claire yelled from behind the plane. "Fetch this." She threw a stick and the dog leaped after it, his bounds as graceful as any thoroughbred racing greyhound.

"Just testing," Claire said, consulting her HoloWatch instead of helping to push the spaceplane mockup. "Radar clocks the stick at 3.9 meters per second. Dog at 3.2. The trajectory numbers look good. Should give our science boy something to play with once this flying bamboo steamer takes to the air."

"Thanks, by the way," Chase yelled back between heavy breaths. "Radiometrics will definitely increase the degree of confidence."

Claire fiddled with her watch. "Now if Razor were out in the open, I might even be able to use this to get a bead on him."

She aimed her device out across the valley on one side of the ridge. "Nada. He's a slippery one, that's for sure. Hell, even after murder victim number three was found cut up like a package of sliced ham, Razor still managed to walk right through airport security at LAX, no questions asked. It's like he has some kind of Jedi mind trick thing up his sleeve."

No one provided any signs of interest in the gruesome details, but that didn't stop Claire from continuing anyway. "Did you know that victim number two was poisoned? No, of course you didn't know that. It's under a sealed indictment at the prosecutor's office."

"Um, if it's sealed," Prisha started somewhat timidly, "then why?"

Claire waved the question off. "Ah, we're on a different planet. Law probably doesn't apply here. Little known fact. Poison isn't his usual MO, so that threw the local police for a loop. But I found two more tins of the same poison in a toolshed behind Razor's house. The label said the stuff kills aphids. Would you want a whole tin of stuff that kills aphids crammed down your throat? I wouldn't."

Having already made the mistake of speaking up, Prisha kept quiet, focusing on dragging the wooden mockup up the hill.

Naturally, Claire kept blabbering. "Hoo boy, then there's the locket! That's the juiciest evidence yet! I found it in his duffel bag. Inside the locket was a holoGIF of a beautiful woman blowing a kiss... *Genevieve.*" She stretched out the name in a sultry kind of way. "It seems our kissy Miss Genevieve may be Razor's motivation for all this slashing and poisoning."

"I didn't picture him as a ladies' man," Reginald commented, "what with all that surviving, and eating things with too many legs, and whatnot."

"Can we not talk about Razor or murder?" Prisha called out. "It's hard enough to focus on getting up this ridge."

Amanda chirped from the rear. "Is it getting harder to breathe, or is that just me?"

Prisha was gasping too, even as the load lightened under lowering gravity. The ridge had a high mountain feel to it now: thin air, breezy and cool, and carrying a scent that hinted of ice not far above. She was beginning to wish she hadn't left her jacket back at camp.

"We're almost there," Chase pointed ahead. He was probably doing more of the pulling than Prisha was, but even Chase had put his shirt back on in the brisk breeze.

Prisha asked, "Should we even be going this high?" They weren't really all that high, but by L3 standards this was becoming a Mount Everest expedition.

"Anyone feeling dizzy yet?" Chase asked.

"A little," Amanda answered.

"Me too," said Reginald. "But I'm usually dizzy since the accident."

Ahead, sparse grass gave way to crumbled rocks with a few scattered boulders. Fifteen minutes later, their mockup was sliding across gravel. It made a scratching sound like a cat sliding claws extended down the world's largest chalkboard. On the plus side, the gravel acted as ball bearings, further reducing their load.

Finally, the steep ridge flattened, opening up to a rounded summit with a glorious view in every direction. Below, their ridgetop camp was easy to spot. Out near the horizon, the swath of trees destroyed by their crash landing boldly stood out from the otherwise uniform jungle. From this height, the curvature of tiny L3 was obvious. Overhead, stars were easily visible, giving the distinct feeling that nothing more than the thinnest blanket of air was between them and a pathway home.

Claire immediately began scanning for Razor again, as the others gratefully set down the mockup and the bamboo rockets. As if summoned to remind them of their mission, the model they'd launched three days before came zipping by once more, close enough to hit with a thrown rock.

"Which gives me an idea," Prisha said. She picked up a rock and threw it straight up. They waited, but the rock never came down.

"Woo-hoo!" Chase yelled. "Escape velocity is ours for the taking!"

Reginald jumped in jubilation, easily soaring over their heads. His arms and legs flailed before he finally tumbled to a stop on the far side of the summit. "I'm fine!" he called out. "Wouldn't recommend doing that, though!"

"Too late," said Mohs from somewhere above them.

With gravity lower than on the moon, they might need to be careful not to launch themselves into space. Even breathing would be challenging, but the mountaintop would be survivable just long enough to launch a spaceplane.

"What's that?" Claire pointed to a white plume in the distance. The fountain of mist created an umbrella shape as it reached its zenith and came back down.

"Old Faithful?" Prisha asked.

"A geothermal vent?" Chase ventured. "It might be coming from that hole we found while we were looking for Scratch and Amanda. It would suggest L3 has a molten core hot enough to boil water."

Mohs looked down (which was every direction, given the peak they stood upon). "Don't molten cores also mean volcanoes? You know, those mountains that might explode any second?"

Prisha surveyed the summit. "No crater. No signs of lava or ash. I think we're probably safe."

"Not staking my life on our first officer's geology skills," Claire grumbled. "Let's get this show on the road. The sooner we get off this rock, the better."

Chase pulled several bamboo poles from an opening in the rear of the spaceplane mockup and quickly assembled them into a ramp with a slight upward slope. He eyeballed its position, tweaked its angle of inclination, and declared their launch ramp ready.

They dragged the results of their hard work onto the ramp, then strapped four bamboo rockets onto the mockup. Everyone stepped back to admire their masterpiece—homemade, of course. But if you didn't dwell too long on unsightly bulges here and there, it looked like a real spaceplane ready to fly.

"Which one is you?" Prisha asked Reginald, who had stuck the six dummies inside the bamboo contraption, arranged like a six-man bobsled.

Reg patted the third head in a lineup that protruded slightly above the fuselage. "That's me. You and the captain are up front, of course, with Claire, Amanda, and Chase in the back."

"And Scratch," Amanda added. "Don't forget Scratch."

Scratch yipped at his name being called.

Captain Mohs waved a hand. "Yeah, yeah, yeah. Throw Scratch on board, light this sucker, and let's see where she goes."

Chattering teeth and rubs over cold arms made it clear everyone agreed. Chase coordinated with Claire on her critical role. Her blaster ring would provide the spark to light all four fuses, and her HoloWatch radar app would track the plane's flight.

With the plan set, everyone except Claire moved well away from the business end of the rockets. She squatted to one side, aiming her blaster ring along a line that would hit all four fuses at the same time.

"Everybody ready?" she called out.

"Ready!" the castaways sounded in unison. Scratch barked from the safety of Amanda's arms.

With a touch of her thumb, the ring shot a blinding blue light straight out. The fuses sparked to life, crackling and popping as infused gunpowder burned.

"Three! Two! One!" Prisha shouted.

All four bamboo rockets roared to life, and the rickety wooden spaceplane blasted off its ramp soaring straight out over the valley below.

"Wow!" Prisha yelled.

"On track," Claire said, consulting her radar app.

"Looking great!" Mohs shouted.

The spaceplane streaked out and up, leaving four parallel trails of smoke behind. The roar of its powerful rockets echoed around them.

Amanda held the dog tight. "Look, Scratch, it's working!"

Chase shaded his eyes from the sun. "Go. Come on baby. Go."

Suddenly, an enormous fireball erupted, consuming the plane. An explosion of multicolor sparks spewed flaming debris in every direction and produced a boom with a concussion that shook the air and everyone standing on the mountaintop.

"No!" screamed Amanda. Scratch barked furiously.

"Aww, no," Reginald moaned.

Claire cursed like two sailors.

Prisha hung her head and sighed at the awful sight. They'd worked so hard.

As the smoke cleared, there was little left of their creation. A few flaming bits of bamboo and twine fluttered through the sky. Dummies stuffed with pebbles had exploded like shotgun shells.

"That would have been us," Reginald said somberly.

Chase turned to face the rest. "Sorry, my fault. Obviously, there's more to rocketry than just packing gunpowder into a tube."

Mohs shrugged wordlessly and started back down the ridge.

Claire followed him. "Hey, it was fun, people. We'll have a great Fourth of July show this year, but I think I'll sit out any flight you might have planned."

"We'll get it working eventually, right?" Reginald asked.

Chase didn't answer. He just stared into the distance. Prisha answered for him. "Sure. We'll get it."

Amanda sniffled pitifully. Reginald hung his head. They followed Mohs and Claire, leaving Prisha and Chase alone on the summit.

"You did your best," Prisha offered. "Getting a spaceplane off the ground is a tall order."

Chase nodded.

She put a hand on his shoulder. "We shouldn't have expected so much. *Me... I* shouldn't have expected so much of you. It wasn't fair." She started down the hill, then paused. "And sorry, I shouldn't have kissed you either. My mistake."

Chase raised one hand in objection, but Prisha wasn't in any mood to argue. Her kiss had only put greater expectations on his shoulders. The complications of spaceflight were clearly more than mere woodworking skills could overcome.

She headed down the path back to camp, kicking rocks as she went. *We're never going home. Not tomorrow, not next week, not next year.* That realization was now as clear as the stars above.

They were soon back down to the ridgetop work camp, but no one stopped there. They followed single file down the ridge slope and back into the jungle, the same route they'd trailblazed when they had first started searching for Razor. No one spoke.

Scratch began squirming in Amanda's arms, and she set him down. The dog held his nose in the air, sniffing.

"What is it, Scratch?"

He barked, then sniffed some more.

"You smell something?"

In less time than it takes to snap fingers, the dog took off like a caffeinated homing pigeon, zigging and zagging through the jungle foliage. He disappeared in the undergrowth with only his constant bark giving away his location. Amanda wasn't far behind.

"Not again!" Mohs grumbled, turning back down the hill.

Claire held him back. "No, wait, this is different. The dog's not lost, he's on to something." She studied her HoloWatch, then looked everyone in the eye. "I'd bet dollars to doughnuts that the little fleabag just picked up the scent of Razor."

12 DEEP IN THE WOODS

THE MANGA SAMURAI warrior charged headlong through the dense underbrush, dodging branches and slashing broad leaves with his gleaming silver sword. It wasn't easy keeping up with an anime wolf who had locked on to a scent.

The warrior's sleeved cape—or *haori*—flapped in the wind as he ran. His *hakama*, a pleated white cloth that wrapped around his waist and flared near his ankles, was designed to accentuate fluid battle movements and distract his opponents.

Moments before, the warrior had been Reginald, a somewhat confused amnesia patient running after a fluffy dog named Scratch and carrying a borrowed machete that was already showing signs of rust. But that was then. Duty had called. A damsel was in distress, and danger surely lurked ahead. A full and complete transformation of persona and equipment had been required. Reginald had become…

Wakinoshita-san!

No matter that he had made the name up on the spot, or that the Japanese probably translated to Mr. Armpit. Wakinoshita-san would become renowned across the land as a fighter for the downtrodden. A soldier of high morals and swift action. For his part, Scratch had also transformed, becoming Kajira, Wakinoshita-san's faithful wolf companion.

The anime movie trailer would surely tell the story of a brave warrior…

His eyes are dark, his lips always taut. His long black hair flows in waves even when the air is still. His noble wolf companion stands tall by his side with incisors that glisten. The warrior unsheathes a polished samurai sword, holds it high, and shouts out the ancient Japanese proverb that is inscribed on the sword's blade: "Justice for all!"

It gave Wakinoshita-san shivers of pride. Trembles of humble superiority. And shudders of vanity. Well known across Japan (and most everywhere else that comic books are read), half of every manga battle was looking good doing it. Wakinoshita-san embodied stylish valor. Every swirl of his sword, every fighting pose, and every stoic expression would come together to produce heroic glory on an epic scale.

Of course, Wakinoshita-san and his wolf companion would also need to defeat their opponent, but that part of the story was assumed.

Lithe Kajira raced ahead, sniffing and growling simultaneously as only a fictitious canine could do. Each bound tousled the wolf's fur like waves passing through a field of wheat. Graceful swooshes of Wakinoshita-san's sword, left and right, widened a trail for the fair maiden, Amanda, who ran just behind.

Amanda was worried, of that there was no doubt. Her beloved Scratch could become lost, she had imagined. Or entrapped. Or would finally come face-to-face with whatever horrid beast or man he was seeking. But Wakinoshita-san knew better. Yes, a fight was coming and, yes, the opponent would be formidable. But there had never been a more loyal or more fearsome fighter to stand beside than the legendary wolf known far and wide as Kajira. Any samurai would give his life for such an honor.

They paused only briefly as Kajira lost the scent and circled, sniffing at the base of each tree. Amanda bit her nails, looking like she might faint dead away at any moment, but soldiered on once the agile canine picked up the trail again.

Woe betide whomever this valiant wolf seeks! It would make an excellent inscription on the wolf's collar if he had one.

Their journey would certainly thrust them into danger, but if the person or thing that Kajira sought were to lay a hand on fair Amanda, they would not only suffer the wrath of the wolf, they would also answer to Wakinoshita-san's sharp blade.

Count on it as you count the coins in your purse, villain!

Before his Japanese manga theme could shift too far into medieval English knights, Wakinoshita-san reaffirmed his anime status by vaulting over rocks and darting around trees with steps swift and silent. Amanda kept close behind.

They zigged and zagged, finally emerging from the jungle beside a cascading creek that tumbled toward the sea. An enormous banyan tree stood in a glen, its canopy enveloping everything around it.

Soundless, the samurai warrior skidded to a stop. Amanda huddled next to him. Kajira growled, as wolves did.

Not fifty feet away stood a large multilevel house at the edge of the creek. Modern in design with attractive lines any architect would be proud to show, the house featured a cantilevered deck jutting out from the second level.

A bearded man reclined in a lounge chair, his feet up, arms behind his head. Kajira snarled, and the man's head lifted. He stood up and peered over the deck railing. It was Razor.

Amanda waved.

Razor briefly lifted one hand. "So, you found me." He leaned on the railing, chuckled to himself, then returned to his lounge chair.

In a cloud of dust, leaves, and sweat, the rest of the search party emerged running from the jungle, each person staring with mouths open at the modern house that had come from nowhere.

Prisha pointed. "That's Razor up there!"

"He's done well for himself," Mohs said, admiring the house.

Kajira glanced back at the others. The fury within his eyes moderated to a more puzzled look as if to ask, "Humans, do you not recognize the danger?"

Wakinoshita-san was also confused at the agreeable social tone of their comments but nonetheless kept his samurai sword ready for even the slightest provocation from the bearded man.

To one side, a small swimming pool constructed with flat rocks was filled by creek water via a channel diversion. Colorful plants decorated tiered landscaping that dropped from the jungle's edge down to a patio surrounding the pool. A staircase led up to the second-level deck.

Kajira sniffed at the base of the stairs. Mohs patted him on the head, then started up the stairs. "You got one heck of a nose there, little pup."

It would have only taken one stroke, but Wakinoshita-san wisely refrained from lopping off the captain's head for his verbal slight of the brave wolf. "Pup indeed," he mumbled in Japanese.

For now, stoic would serve better than hostile, and Wakinoshita-san sheathed his sword. He climbed the unfamiliar wooden steps one by one, even while his hand remained ready to whip out the gleaming weapon and flay his opponent to the bone.

"Welcome," Razor said.

The bearded man carried no weapons and made no aggressive moves, but Wakinoshita-san didn't trust him for a second. While the warrior and his wolf would transition into standby mode for now, if Razor so much as withdrew one throwing star, a fight to the death would surely ensue.

"You built this house?" Mohs asked, incredulous.

The deck had a sweeping view out to a tranquil bay, bounded on one side by a rocky cliff where the creek flowed into the sea. Small waves broke on a sandy beach. It would make an outstanding setting for an upscale restaurant.

Razor hardly moved from his reclining lounge chair. "Episode 24, look it up."

"Ooh, I remember that one!" Amanda said, dancing on her feet. "*Survival Instinct* wasn't always about digging for grubs and skinning porcupines. Episode 24 kicked off his Builder Series to show how to construct a cabin in the woods!" She paused, catching Razor's eye. "Using…"

Together they chanted, "One axe, one man, and a whole lot of muscle!"

Amanda laughed. "Great tagline."

"Home and Garden Channel picked it up for three seasons—with an option for season four." Razor's voice lowered to an indistinct mumble. "Depending on the endorsement contract from J&J Home Stores. Damn, I need to call my agent."

So far, Claire had remained uncharacteristically quiet, but she strolled nonchalantly around the deck, checking under the railing and behind several potted plants for who knows what. Only slasher film serial killers lived in cabins in the woods, but this one ranked well above the average shack filled with sharp instruments and chain saws.

Ever the pacifist, Prisha spread her arms. "Beautiful place you have here. Can we get a tour?"

Razor glanced at Claire, then the rest. He was either going to spring out of his lounge chair and start throwing knives, or perhaps— if luck was on their side—something not quite so deadly.

"A tour? Bloody hell." His glower faded. He'd apparently chosen plan B, even if reluctantly.

Wakinoshita-san swung his sword, then sheathed it, a move noticed by Razor's quick glance. Kajira the anime wolf huffed one more growl, then quieted.

"This way." Razor led them though open French doors into a combination living/kitchen space with a high ceiling and exposed beams. An overhead fan turned, creating a pleasant breeze that kept the interior cool.

He stopped at a countertop with cupboards above. "Fancy a drink?" He checked each person's face. Most were dumbstruck.

Razor pulled out a stack of cups made from carved coconuts and retrieved a flexible bag containing some kind of liquid. "It's only my second batch, but it turned out well."

He poured golden liquid into each cup. One by one they each tried their mystery drinks. One by one their faces lit up. Claire was the only one who refrained. "It's not poisoned, is it?"

Razor forced a chuckle, then took a sip himself. "Made from a fruit I discovered up the creek. Ferments well. Good bouquet."

"Mmm." Prisha took another sip. "Tropical, like a mai tai. You don't have any ice cubes, do you?" She laughed.

Razor motioned to Chase. "I'll let your boyfriend figure out refrigeration."

Prisha recoiled. "He's not my—"

"Nah, course not." Razor led on through the great room to a stairway going down. He knocked on a wood railing that gleamed from meticulous polishing. "Rosewood for the banister. Teak for the steps. I always carry a bandsaw blade in my duffel bag and was able to rig a pedal-operated table saw. All part of the new workshop out back."

"Seems like you're planning on being here for a while," Chase said.

"Don't kid yourselves, we're here forever." Razor laughed. "But if you do manage to launch your wooden spaceplane, don't bother saving a seat for me."

Prisha climbed right into his face. "You saw us on the mountain?"

"Of course. A man needs to know who's passing through his territory."

"You could have signaled to us. You must have known we were looking for you."

"And you must have known I didn't want to be found," Razor countered with a heavy dose of snark. "Yet here we are."

Razor continued down the elegant staircase. "Master bedroom to the right, bath to the left. Walk-in closet over here—the chevron-paneled door was from Episode 25, and the lights are courtesy of an AbSolOrb packed in my duffel, and also one of the sponsors of the show."

Reginald flicked a switch on the wall, and an overhead light came on. AbSolOrb ads bragged that the egg-shaped electrical generator could be placed in any windowsill and through its high-tech skin would absorb more sunlight in an hour than a rooftop of solar panels.

Along with homemade lighting, the room had a four-poster bed complete with a comforter on top. How he'd managed to put any of this together was beyond comprehension.

Claire twisted a wooden faucet handle and water flowed into a sink. "Indoor plumbing. Impressive. Any guest rooms in your mansion, or is it just for you?"

Razor glared, then continued through a back door that led to the patio. A woven figure floated in the adjacent swimming pool, looking suspiciously like a rubber duck.

Razor waved in both directions. "Outdoor seating under the overhang for when it's raining, plus the pool for warm afternoons. A screen keeps the fish out. And there you have it. This concludes our tour, thank you for your attention, you can deposit your cups on the table and exit the property that way." He pointed toward the jungle, his arm never wavering for a full minute.

When no one moved, he raised his voice. "It's been loads of fun seeing you all again. Bye."

Amanda beamed. "That was great! Could you show us how to build a house just like this one? We could be neighbors!"

Razor gave her a long, hard stare. She returned it with the starry-eyed gaze she reserved for, well, everything. Razor's stare finally wilted. He groaned and turned to enter his manor again.

"Not so fast," Claire called out. She casually leaned against a deck support post, checking her nails. "We have some unfinished business to cover."

Razor pivoted, glaring at Claire. His nostrils flared. She didn't flinch.

"I've been following you for too long." Claire chewed a fingernail, then spat. "But this is the end of the road."

Claire removed her shades while Razor studied her face. "Ah, yeah, now I recognize you. That clumsy cop in Nepal. Don't you people ever give up? Constantly accusing me of every little thing because you don't have the brainpower to solve the case."

"Not sure I'd call a triple homicide a little thing." Claire stared up at the deck above them, exuding the casual air of someone completely in command. "Would you?"

Razor spun in a circle, clearly agitated. "This again? Really? I gave my deposition to the district attorney last year. Do your homework before you go accusing people."

"Accusations are easy. It's the evidence that takes more work." She picked at the post she was leaning against. "Funny, the dead stagehand from Episode 25 had marks across one arm. As I remember, those marks looked a lot like this!" She stood back from the post and pointed. Scuff marks in the wood revealed where Razor's band saw had cleaved the original tree trunk in two.

Prisha covered her mouth in revulsion. "Poor man!"

Razor ran fingers along the opposite post. He sighed deeply, then spoke. "It's true, I don't have a circular sander with me, but I like the rough-cut look of a cabin in the wild. Now, if I were to saw a man's arm off, I'd use the right tool for the job. A Black and Decker cordless reciprocating saw with their optional nine-inch pruning blade would make a good choice. Nice clean cuts."

Claire snorted. "Are you always this cavalier about your victims?"

"We're done here." Razor turned and was halfway through the doorway leading into his house.

"What about *Genevieve?*" Claire taunted, lifting one eyebrow.

He stopped cold, head down.

After a minute—and with everyone else enraptured—Razor finally spoke. "A name you may have overheard."

A smirk spread across Claire's face. "Can you afford to take that chance?"

Razor stood frozen a moment longer, taut as a bow. He turned to face the group. "Alright. Let's get this over with."

The big man strode purposefully toward Claire, an angry glint in his eye and his right hand tightening into a fist. His long knife blade was strapped to his thigh. Claire backed away, hesitant.

He'd been patient until now, but Wakinoshita-san had seen enough. He unsheathed his sword and leaped to Claire's defense. "Justice for all!"

Kajira leaped too, and all three crashed to the ground in a tangle of arms, legs, sharp weapons, and gleaming canine teeth. Razor struggled. Kajira bit. Wakinoshita-san kicked, as samurai warriors sometimes do.

There were several crashes against heavy wooden deck posts, and simultaneously they all managed to land on their feet. Razor was quicker with his knife, slashing Wakinoshita-san's homemade belt (woven from vines and jungle leaves), which dropped his hakama wrap to the ground. Mortified, the samurai warrior beat a hasty retreat to pull up his pants.

Even a celebrated warrior like Wakinoshita-san had occasional setbacks. His honor had been shaken, but it could still be restored if the belt could be repaired. While Wakinoshita-san fidgeted with cut vines, Claire shouldered the fight. She flicked a finger across her HoloWatch, and a line of ultra-thin cord sprang forth, coiling around Razor's shoulders and arms like a python. Claire gave the chord a yank, and it tightened.

Razor looked down without any noticeable alarm. "What is this?" he asked flatly.

"I'm securing you for trial," Claire stated, "as per the International General Orders to Chase Hazardous Absconders, or the I GOTCHA rules."

"Those rules don't apply here," Razor muttered. He flicked his blade, once, twice, and cut the cords binding him like they were made of tissue paper. The shreds fell about his feet as Claire blinked, clearly caught off guard.

Wakinoshita-san gathered several cord fragments to finish the reweaving of his belt, while Claire advanced once more. She raised her HoloWatch. This time, a tiny copper ball shot out, stuck onto Razor's neck and opened up like a flower. With a crackle of electricity, the copper flower zapped a blue arc to both earlobes. Razor momentarily scrunched his shoulders, then reached up and flicked the device off like a bothersome mosquito.

He stood tall, as big as any Alaskan grizzly and twice as hairy. "Your toys are beginning to annoy me" was all he said. He turned and opened the door to his house.

In an instant too short to measure, Claire pointed her middle finger, engaged her ring laser, and blasted a hole through the door just inches from Razor's head.

Red embers crackled around the hole's edge. The smell of wood smoke filled the air.

Razor paused. He glanced through the hole and back at Claire. "That won't be easy to patch up. Went right through my cabinets too, from the looks of it. Not cool."

"There's an easier way," Claire said.

"Your so-called trial?"

"With judgment handed down by a jury of your peers." She waved her hand to the rest of their group.

Razor laughed.

Wakinoshita-san's belt was now repaired with his hakama firmly in place. He sensed an opening, one that might not require the separation of heads from their owners. One that could restore lost honor.

With Kajira at his side, Wakinoshita-san stepped forward and squared his shoulders. "You are a formidable fighter, Razor-san."

Razor nodded. Steely eyes on both sides met.

Unhurried, Wakinoshita-san withdrew his sword, placed the blade flat across his fingertips, and offered it to him with a bow. "Trust goes both ways. I trust that you will not use this weapon against me. And so, you must trust in your fair treatment by judge and jury." He pointed to the inscription on the blade. "Justice for all, Razor-san. Justice for *all*."

He emphasized the last word. Razor gave him a funny look but accepted the sword. Kajira kneeled. It was the honorable thing to do.

With Razor's acceptance, not only had honor been restored but the knowing look in each man's eye made it clear they both understood that justice was like water: its downhill flow could be momentarily diverted but never completely stilled. For better or worse, Razor would stand trial.

His duty complete, Wakinoshita-san returned to being Reginald. Even proud Kajira began to resemble fluffy Scratch once more. The dog sniffed at Razor's feet, then trotted back to Amanda, who scooped him into her arms.

"What an exciting day!" Amanda said.

13 CRIME AND JUSTICE

THE DEFENDANT STOOD alone. A defiant smirk was his only reaction to the charges brought against him: three homicides, not to mention a million viewers who would faint dead away once they learned their favorite television survivalist was far from the solitary hero that he pretended to be.

Super sleuth turned prosecutor Claire Bouchet was confident that she would soon wipe the smirk from his face. The trial would be the pinnacle of her career. True, she had absolutely no experience in law; her modus operandi was "track 'em and rack 'em," which usually skewed more toward a bounty hunter than a prosecutor. But, whatever. She was amazing at everything she did. Too bad there would be no one to witness her triumph except for the six other castaways on a lonely planet called L3 at the far side of the sun.

Claire had been named prosecutor by Judge Prisha Dhaliwal, who had been named judge by Captain Larry Mohs mainly because he didn't want to do it himself. Everyone else had agreed that Prisha was a fine choice, and that they should get on with the trial.

The courtroom was Razor's own upstairs living room, in part because it had a million-dollar view out to L3's shallow sea and also because Razor's ultra-modern cabin was the only indoor space, and it looked like it might rain.

Prisha sat on a barstool that Razor had crafted out of bamboo. Claire stood left, the defendant stood right. The jury (everyone else) had arranged themselves on a couch.

"Before we get into this," Reginald said, leaning toward Razor, "can I just say this couch is ridiculously comfortable? How did you make it?"

"Thick jungle leaves for the exterior, moss stuffed inside, stripped tree bark fashioned into thread for the stitching," Razor answered.

"Well, it is remarkable," added Amanda.

"Objection," Claire snapped. "The jury is not supposed to converse with the defendant before the trial begins."

Prisha banged her gavel (a hammer from Razor's duffel bag) on a plank of wood that served as the judge's bench. "This court will come to order!" She seemed pleased with herself and banged the gavel once more. It had a nice wood tone.

"The court thanks the defendant for providing the facilities for this trial." Prisha looked around, nodding. "It's actually a very nice place, I love the window blinds. And the kitchen countertop—wow, that's exactly the color I would have chosen. Well done."

Claire lowered her shades and glared toward Prisha.

Prisha cleared her throat. "Yes... well, let's proceed. We are gathered here to sentence the defendant—"

"I object," Razor said. He had insisted on being his own defense attorney. "I believe it's customary to present a case to the jury before the judge passes sentence."

"Yes, yes, you're very right," Prisha said. "Objection sustained." She turned to Claire. "Um, do you want to lay out the case against the defendant?"

Claire was happy to take control. It would not only ensure a guilty verdict but also avoid further embarrassment given that the judge's level of experience was a few episodes of *Law and Order* and a smattering of *Judge Judy* reruns.

Claire stood. "I'm ready to do that, Your Honor. And to speed things up, I'm also willing to go point by point while allowing time for the defendant to respond. In fact, I'm rather curious how anyone could argue against such overwhelming evidence. So, grab some popcorn and let's get started."

Claire slipped one hand under the seam of her shirt Napoleon-like and announced solemnly, "I call the first witness, Captain Larry Mohs."

Mohs, sitting on the couch, looked surprised that his name had come up. He stood.

Razor called out. "I object! A member of the jury can't be a witness!"

Prisha leaned forward and spoke softly. "Razor, there's not that many of us. I'm afraid everyone may need to take on multiple roles. Objection overruled. Sorry!"

Razor rolled his eyes. Amanda, who had already agreed to be the court bailiff in addition to being a juror, brought another bamboo chair out for the witness. Mohs sat in the provided witness seat, staring out the window at the tranquil sea. Give him a beer and a footrest and he'd probably lean back and push his cap over his eyes, and this whole courtroom bit would end as quickly as it had started.

"Captain!" Claire yelled, catching his attention. "You're the arresting officer, am I right?"

"Not really. You tied him up."

"But you're the officer who presided over the arrest."

"Okay. I can go with that."

"Objection!" Razor interjected. "Leading the witness."

Prisha leaned toward Reginald and Amanda. "Is that a thing? That's a thing? Okay. Don't do that again, prosecutor."

Claire looked to the ceiling. "Fine. Then tell me this, Captain, why was Razor arrested?"

"Uh, because you said he'd murdered some people from his TV show. You even had a receipt or something. Good enough for me. He's guilty. Are we done?"

Even Claire was rolling her eyes now, but she wasn't about to let the amateur nature of this proceeding spoil the biggest case of her career. "Let's lay out the evidence together, shall we?"

"Okey dokey."

Claire pulled out a small slip of paper. "I submit to the court Exhibit A, a receipt from a restaurant frequented by the defendant, with the defendant's name clearly printed on it." She handed the receipt to Captain Mohs. "Would you read the note scrawled at the bottom?"

Mohs studied the receipt—she'd shown it to them before. "Uh, it has an R and some other letters that I can't make out."

"That's his signature. Read the note below."

"It says, 'Next time I'm gonna slice that ugly SOB from ear to ear.'" The captain lifted his head with a hopeful look that suggested his witness job was complete and that he might spend the rest of the afternoon drinking free beer provided by the court.

Claire, on the other hand, was just getting started. "How would you characterize this note?"

Mohs scratched his chin. "I don't know, I guess it sounds like a threat to kill someone."

"Precisely!" So far, the case was going perfectly. "Ladies and gentlemen of the jury, I will point out that victim number one was, by day, a camera operator for Survival Instinct Productions. But on weekend nights, he moonlighted as a cook for this very same restaurant. He was found dead in the alley behind the restaurant, and, unless ordered by the court, I won't describe the neck wound out of respect for the victim's family. But be assured, it was a gaping—"

"Yes, yes, we get it," Prisha said. "The man's injuries matched the threat. I think we can dispense with the gory details."

"Thank you, Your Honor, my thoughts exactly. I shall now give the defendant time to answer this charge, and to tell you the truth, I can't wait to hear what he has to say."

Claire stepped aside, leaving Razor to face the witness. Razor stood motionless looking at the floor.

Probably getting his lies straight.

"Yeah, right," he finally said. "Didn't happen that way. Jonah Thompson was one of my camera operators, yes. No idea how he died, but might have just been a heart attack. The man was in his fifties, overweight, and drank like a sailor. As for the message on the receipt, it's quite simple. The restaurant had run out of my favorite dish, salmon on brioche, or SOB as they like to call it, so I wanted them to know I was looking forward to ordering it next time."

Claire interjected, reading again from the slip of paper. "'I'm gonna slice that ugly SOB from ear to ear.' That's what you wrote."

Razor waved it off. "They serve the fish whole, including the head with its ugly eyeball staring at you. It's tradition that the diner cuts the head off before eating. Nothing more to it than that."

Claire threw up her arms. "That's the biggest load of hooey I've ever heard!"

Prisha leaned out from her bench. "Um, Claire... Ms. Prosecuting Attorney, I don't think you're supposed to do that."

"Do what?"

"Bias the jury with your opinion of the defendant."

Claire physically bit her tongue. "Okay, okay. Let's move to Exhibit B, shall we?" She touched her HoloWatch, producing a 3-D rotating image in midair. It was the notebook page she'd found in Razor's duffel bag with pictures of six people, three with red Xs drawn across their faces.

There were a few oohs and aahs around the courtroom, confirming the intended impact of the visually damning evidence.

At one side of the courtroom, Mohs and Amanda whispered briefly to each other. Mohs approached the bench. "Permission for the arresting officers to advise the defendant?"

"Permission granted," said Prisha.

Amanda and Mohs moved close to Razor, one on each side. Amanda tried to whisper into Razor's ear, but every time she leaned closer, he just leaned further away. Not that whispering would do much good anyway since everyone else in the courtroom was eavesdropping.

"Those are the three people who died!" Amanda bit her lip dramatically while trying to meet Razor's stoic eyes. "They're marked off in your personal notebook! You have to admit, it's strong evidence. I don't want to see you put behind bars—assuming we build a jail, which admittedly we'll need your help with. Maybe a plea bargain would be a good idea."

Mohs talked into the side of his hand. "And without a plea bargain... well, a hanging judge like this one could make things pretty ugly for you, if you get my drift." Mohs motioned toward Prisha, then strangled himself with his own hands, eyes bulging, tongue out.

It was the good cop, bad cop routine, complete with the good cop's bomb-sniffing dog thrown into the mix. Razor would be a fool not to take the deal. And if he didn't, Claire had a lot more coming.

"Nope," Razor said. "No reason for me to admit to anything." He shooed the cops away. Amanda and Mohs returned to being jurors on the couch while Razor addressed the judge. "I thought this might come up, so I came prepared." Razor reached behind the couch and dragged out his duffel bag.

"Watch him!" Claire yelled. "He's got sharp things in there." The judge had already ruled there would be no machetes in her courtroom. Or knives. Or that three-pronged weeder-hoe-thing that was protruding ominously from the bag.

Before Mohs or anyone else could interfere, Razor reached into the duffel, pulled out a notebook, and held it up for all to see. "Is this what you're referring to?"

Claire backed away, nodding.

Razor flipped to the page with photos of his coworkers, three of them crossed out with red Xs just as Claire's image had shown. He flipped the page over, showing the other side to the judge and jury. "There's always two sides to everything, isn't there?"

The other side was a calendar with three red Xs drawn through date squares. "My production calendar for April," Razor explained. "The days crossed out are when I finished work in the studio. The ink simply bled through to the other side. Pure coincidence that they lined up with the photos."

There were gasps across the courtroom.

"Oh, come on!" Claire cried. "That's got to be the most unlikely coincidence in the history of the universe!"

"Maybe so, but it's the truth."

Given the nodding heads around the room, Claire was beginning to worry that whatever god ran this universe might be on Razor's side. "Okay, let's move on."

She searched the duffel bag until she found a hardbound book with photographs of colorful plants decorating its glossy cover. The book would look good on any coffee table.

"I give you Exhibit C, a book entitled *How to Identify Poisonous Plants*." She turned to the table of contents and slowly panned the open book around the room. "Notice that Chapter Seven is strangely highlighted with a yellow marking pen. That chapter is titled *Poisons Impossible to Trace*."

Claire pointed a finger at Razor. "Victim number two, an accountant who managed the financial records for Survival Instinct Productions, was in fact… poisoned!"

She slammed the book down on the judge's bench for dramatic effect. Prisha obliged with a jerk upward, then opened the book to confirm the highlight.

Razor stood up. "Nobody kills their accountant, at least not before tax season. And if you're searching for motive, just turn to that chapter."

Prisha thumbed through the pages, then skimmed. "Yes… um, it says here that polonium-210 is the poison of choice since half of it disappears every one hundred and thirty-eight days and the other half requires an advanced laboratory to detect. But… a close second is ricin, a natural protein found in the seeds of the castor oil plants. It says here that a lethal dose of just fifty milligrams can be inhaled, injected, or ingested." Prisha looked up, her eyes wide. "That's a lot of in's."

"Read on," Razor said, rotating his finger in a circle. "I believe there's another highlight later in that chapter."

"Ah yes, here it is," Prisha said, studying the page. "Your name is in a footnote! It says that you have some expertise in poisons that occur in nature."

"I do. Survival requires avoiding poisonous plants. And the reference to my show is why that chapter is highlighted. This is the biggest-selling poison book on the market and has been a great cross-promotion." Razor folded his arms and tossed his somewhat greasy hair back in a show of self-righteous superiority.

Claire shook her head. He might have won this battle, but he wasn't about to win the war. Claire didn't know the meaning of the word *quit*. She reached into her pocket and retrieved the jewelry she'd taken from the duffel bag days earlier.

She held up a locket dangling from the end of a chain.

Her voice dripped with contempt. "Razor is tricky, I'll grant him that. But he's not going to wriggle out of this one. I give you Exhibit D... *Genevieve*." She stretched the name out to its fullest length. Any longer and the jury might fall asleep.

"That's private property!" Razor yelled, reaching out for the locket. Both cops, Mohs and Amanda, jumped up to restrain him.

Prisha banged her hammer gavel. "There will be no outbursts in my courtroom or... um, well, just don't do it!"

She reached out for the locket, and Claire handed it over even while Razor struggled against the cops' sure hands.

"Open it," Claire said with an air of smugness.

Prisha opened the locket, and a holoGIF of a woman blowing a kiss popped into the air. "She's beautiful."

"Try the back, too."

Another panel opened to release a tiny slip of old-school paper. Prisha unfolded it and read, "I adore you, Razzie-pooh!" Prisha looked up. "Razzie-pooh?"

The courtroom erupted into hems and haws along with a few harumphs until Prisha banged her gavel again.

Razor clenched his jaw. "That's personal."

Prisha squinted one eye. "But, Razor, be reasonable. It seems relevant to the case."

Claire strode to the front of the room, turning to face the jury. "More than relevant, Your Honor. The woman in the locket is Genevieve, Razor's illicit lover. And Genevieve's husband... was victim number three!"

The courtroom erupted once more, this time in grumbles, mumbles, and shouts. "Order!" Prisha yelled above the din. "I will have order in my courtroom!" She appeared to be getting the hang of this judge thing.

Razor hung his head. Claire rubbed her hands together. *Got him now!*

Prisha held the locket in her open palm, her eyes locked squarely onto Razor. "Well?"

Razor sighed deeply. It took forever before he finally spoke. "If you must know, Genevieve asked me to give her husband a small part on the TV show. I declined. I knew what kind of guy he was—the kind that smacks a woman around, then blames her for making him mad. You should have seen the bruises on Genevieve's face. She eventually separated from him. Even took out a restraining order. Turns out the guy was mixed up with the criminal side of Pleasant Valley, Ohio and somebody smoked him—wasn't me, but I was glad he finally got the justice he deserved."

Sullen faces around the room made it clear the defense of rescuing an abused woman just might fly.

Claire stepped up her game. "A clear motive only makes you a stronger suspect. Let's review the history. When did your love affair with Genevieve begin?"

Razor gazed off into the distance. "She turned twenty-nine this year, so there's your answer. Started calling me Razzie-pooh from the moment she could talk." Razor slowly turned in a circle. "For all you snoops who seem determined to intrude... Genevieve is my little sister."

Audible gasps filled the room. Prisha lifted her gavel, shrugged, then gasped herself.

"Genevieve Maldonia Sharpe, born the first of April, East Baptist Hospital, Virginia. We're ten years apart. Check the inscription."

Prisha checked, nodding her concurrence.

Claire slumped on the couch, noting the exact time on her HoloWatch when her oh-so-solid case had crumbled to dust.

Prisha cleared her throat. "Well, that was quite the story, I must say. Please send our regards to Genevieve with hopes that things will improve for her." She turned a cold eye toward Claire. "Is the prosecution quite done?"

"Yes, Your Honor. We're pretty well cooked."

"Then I'll ask the jury to come to a decision. Is the defendant guilty or not guilty?" Prisha paused for a moment. "Actually, I'm part of the jury too, aren't I?" She tiptoed quickly to the couch to join the others.

The jury shifted in their comfy couch seats, whispering between themselves. Prisha shuffled back to her judge's chair. Reginald, as jury foreman, raised his hand. "Your Honor, we're going with not guilty."

Claire briefly considered another objection based on obvious procedural violations but reconsidered once she realized that her life on this little planet would become a living hell.

Instead, she stared at Razor, who met her eyes, unflinching. There was a wounded quality to his gaze and the usual stubbornness that Claire associated with all men. But no trace of guilt.

Claire raised her own hand. "What the hell, I'm going with not guilty, too."

Scratch jumped out of Amanda's arms, running circles around Razor's feet with his tail wagging. Razor bent down and scratched behind the dog's ears. "Thanks, little guy. Sorry about the machete thing."

Scratch licked Razor's hand. Apparently, they were all square.

Prisha pounded her gavel, then handed it back to Razor since it was his hammer. "The defendant is found not guilty due to circumstantial evidence and a few misunderstandings that I hope we can all put behind us. This court is adjourned. You're free to go, Mr. Razor."

"Just Razor," Razor growled, looking very much the gruff loner that everyone thought he was, but without the label of murderer hanging over his head.

One by one, each member of the jury stood up and shook Razor's hand, which he didn't seem too keen on. Amanda gave him a hug, and while Razor grabbed her gently by the shoulders to separate her, Claire saw a flash of something that looked like a smile. Or it could have been a facial spasm, it was gone so quick. At least it wasn't the disingenuous shark smile from before.

Even Claire had to admit she'd been wrong. She walked stiffly up to Razor and spoke plainly. "I spent more than a year chasing you. Good times. Some bad times, too. Zanzibar—that was pretty awful."

Razor shrugged. "Rainy season. Tsetse flies are out. You made some good points. I've already forgotten what they were, but they were good."

"So, no grudges, then? Bury the hatchet? Water under the bridge?"

Razor grunted.

Claire took that as a yes. "That restaurant. They really have a dish called salmon on brioche?"

He nodded. "I built a fish pen in the creek out back. If I can find the recipe, maybe we'll put a few SOBs on the barbie tonight."

The rest of the day was spent relaxing around Razor's swimming pool, barbecuing fresh fish, and enjoying the glorious sea view from Razor's upper-level deck. For a cantankerous loner, he turned out to be a surprisingly good party host, and his strawberry daiquiris were—for lack of a better word—killer.

As dusk settled, Razor became the center of attention, a man who seemed distinctly aware of the difference between roughing it and luxury living and who had clearly chosen the latter. He had already proven his building skills, which he offered to share. He even hinted that if they promised to be good neighbors (which meant less nosy), he might show them some promising homesites further up the creek.

Claire leaned against a deck post well away from the rest. She sipped her drink and tried to regain her cool, though a year of pursuing an innocent man didn't sit well. He hadn't so much gotten away as he had never been properly in her sights from the start.

Her thoughts were interrupted by the thunk of a knife into the post. The dagger wobbled only an inch from her ear. Startled, Claire spilled half her drink and looked up. Razor calmly sauntered over, pulled the knife from the post, and handed it to her.

One eye squinted. The other gleamed with mischief. "Pro tip. When you're hunting elusive prey, strike fast without warning, and make sure your aim is true on the first try."

Claire turned the knife over in her hands, sharp enough to shave with. "I have no idea what any of that means."

"Give it a week or two. You will." He turned his back and ambled away.

Claire called out. "Your knife?"

"Keep it. We'll call it a peace offering. From one survivalist to another. Besides, you know I've got more."

14 WHO PUT GOD IN CHARGE?

REGINALD WATCHED ATTENTIVELY as Razor put the finishing touches on a stone bridge that arched over the creek. Both student and master stepped back to admire their work. Each stone was wedged into place without mortar after chiseling for a precision fit.

"See?" Razor said. "That's why you should always carry three chisels wherever you go. One for stone, one for wood, the other for fine craftwork. Life lesson number one: a man can never have enough tools."

Reginald absorbed the advice, nodding thoughtfully. Over the past two weeks of house construction, he'd learned how to operate a band saw, how to set timber posts without concrete, how to divert creek water into bamboo pipes, and a dozen other skills that Razor had passed along from his years as wilderness guide, mountaineer, river rafter, search and rescue expert, spelunker, arctic expedition leader, and crafter of fine wooden furnishings for A-listers.

Six brand-new houses were nearly complete, scattered through the jungle on both sides of the creek. Razor had been the architect for them all, but each owner had been responsible for building their own house.

Just a hundred yards uphill was Prisha's house, stylish with its mahogany front door. Chase's house was next and included a shared deck with Prisha's, a kind of connected-but-stand-alone townhouse arrangement that Razor said he would patent should they ever return to Earth.

Chase had also insisted on setting up an improved version of his radio antenna. It protruded from his roof like the feelers of some gigantic ant. None of the others saw much point since it had been nearly a month now and clearly no rescue was coming. But Razor and Reginald had helped him transfer the spaceplane's radio electronics and hook it up to the AbSolOrb power source Razor had brought in his duffel bag.

On the other side of the creek, Amanda's house had a miniature room just for Scratch. Mohs had insisted on three hammocks, each positioned north–south for satisfactory feng shui. And while Reginald had asked for a retractable roof, he had settled for a skylight (using glass repurposed from the spaceplane). It was true, his house was a bit crooked in places, but that just gave it character.

Furthest up the hill and off by itself was Claire's house. "I've been shunned from polite society," Claire had said of her assigned lot, and no one had disagreed. The house had no windows except for a spy hole she'd placed by the door. They'd labeled it the Hermit's Cave.

Now, with the addition of the stone bridge to easily transition from one side of the creek to the other, this part of L3's jungle had become a complete neighborhood. The work had been hard, and given the cobblestone foundations and palm-frond awnings, the results were somewhat rustic ("pastoral" as Reginald liked to call his own house), but the houses were a vast improvement over their previous lean-tos in both comfort and privacy.

Razor put away the tools and patted Reginald on the shoulder. "Life lesson number two: Life comes at you. Adapt, or die."

Reginald nodded, doing his best to absorb this latest bit of wisdom from a man who mentioned death at least twice a day. This time, Reginald's synapses failed utterly. "Sorry, I'm having trouble connecting what I'm sure is a very profound and sensible proverb to this stone arch bridge."

Razor's bushy eyebrows lifted. "Claire?"

"Yes, Claire."

"She accused me of murder?"

"Yes, she did. And the rest of us resolved it in your favor." Reginald waited for more.

Razor spun his hand in a rolling motion. "Claire is a metaphorical stand-in for authority—and society in general—both of which I've spent a lifetime avoiding. But recently, I've *adapted* by allowing her little indulgence."

"The trial."

"Yes, the trial, and then the houses and neighbors and even the little pipsqueak dog. So, this new bridge is the physical manifestation of my willingness to bridge the gap between the past and the future. Adapt or die. Get it now?"

"Got it. Very deep. I'll keep that in mind."

Razor slapped Reginald on the back hard enough to push him across the bridge and back towards Razor's house.

With their work done for the day, Reginald and Razor joined the rest around Razor's swimming pool, which had become the de facto community club and health spa for the new neighborhood.

Razor disappeared into his kitchen and moments later returned with a tray of coconut cups filled with his latest tropical cocktail, a close approximation of Sex on the Beach that used local fruit instead of peaches and cranberries.

"Gotta say, you're a hell of a bartender, Razor." Captain Mohs sipped his fruity drink at the far side of the pool. "Good choice making the distillery a construction priority."

Using a scarf she'd pulled from her purse, Amanda had fashioned a pink bikini for herself that covered all the key parts approximately as well as one of those paper slips from a Chinese fortune cookie tied down with dental floss. She floated in the pool with Scratch lying peacefully on her belly. Prisha, Chase, and Claire relaxed nearby on bamboo lounge chairs.

"True, we might be on L3 forever," Captain Mohs said after Chase had made some point that no one had bothered listening to. "But I have a theory on that. I call it my Cosmic Mystery Theory of Fate."

"Oh, I've got to hear this," Claire said, scooting closer.

Mohs pontificated, "You see, L3 isn't what we think it is. It's not an undiscovered planet on the far side of the sun, it's an arena used by godlike forces to ensnare selected players for nefarious purposes. Each one of us has been brought here to resolve some long-standing cosmic mystery that involves warped dimensions of spacetime and possibly bamboo."

"Spooky," said Claire. "And completely nuts."

Undeterred, Mohs continued. "Our job is to find clues and come up with an answer to the cosmic mystery. Then these godlike forces will take over and poof! We're back on Earth."

"So, it's our fate to be here?" Chase asked.

"Our joint fate," Mohs clarified. "We're all connected in some way. That's part of the mystery. For example, some mysterious force pushed Prisha onto my flight."

"Well, it was more like Megalodon HR," Prisha said.

Mohs held up one finger. "Which—if you're stoned enough—seems like a force of god… in a corporate disguise."

Prisha objected. Mohs countered. Reginald listened to the back and forth of the evolving theory of cosmic mystery, becoming less interested in the specifics but more interested in the otherworldly nature of it all. In a strange way that Reginald only barely understood, he'd heard it before. Felt it before.

"I'm not real," Reginald blurted out, causing the cosmic argument to come to a screeching halt.

Amanda stood up in the pool, hoisting Scratch to her shoulder. "You're not real?"

"No. I haven't felt real since the accident. I have no memory of my previous life. Maybe I never had one. Maybe I came into existence a few weeks ago and someone forgot to equip me with a past memory like all of you have. Or maybe I'm just a character in a story and my memory is whatever the author decides to give me." He checked around and, yes, all eyes were upon him.

"What a weirdo," Claire said, scooting further away.

It was true, reality had never set well with Reginald. Fantasies invaded his mind regularly: Reggae de Cannabis, Fashionista, the heroic manga warrior Wakinoshita-san. Each was fabulously entertaining, but if he was being truthful, they existed only in his hyperactive imagination.

Don't they?

That was what the army of psychiatrists back on Earth would say. But the flip side was a creeping feeling that none of Reginald was real, not even his base personality, whatever that was.

He shrugged, wondering if other people had this inner conflict. "The odds are against me being real. I have no driver's license, no ID. I don't even have a last name."

Amanda reached up from the swimming pool and put a hand on his knee. "Oh, come on, Reg, you're as real as anyone. You just don't remember things because of the amnesia." Her eyes lifted. "What if we gave you a last name?"

"That would be swell," Reginald said.

"Wankerbottom!" Amanda offered with enthusiasm.

"Wankerbottom?"

"Yeah, sorry, it just came to me. But Wankerbottom could be a last name, couldn't it?"

WHO PUT GOD IN CHARGE?

"You know, I like it!" Reginald jumped in with both feet, not literally into the swimming pool but figuratively into Amanda's suggestion. "From now on, I will be Reginald Waldo Wankerbottom!"

Amanda beamed. Scratch yipped. Now that he had a last name, perhaps his troublesome inner conflict would disappear like bathroom smell vanquished by Febreze. Unless…

What if Amanda's not real either? What if none of them are real? What if they're all characters in some fanciful story called… I don't know… Lost at L3?

Even a brand-new cool-sounding last name couldn't sweep away the dreadful internal conflict raging inside Reginald that had suddenly taken a hard right turn into crazy land.

He didn't dare bring the idea up to the others. But he must! How could Amanda or anyone else go on with their lives without dealing with the plain and obvious fact that they might not be real either? He would need to intervene in their conversation once more.

Captain Mohs was speaking, still pushing his cosmic fate thing by finding the connections between each person. "… Prisha and I work for Megalodon Space Ventures, Amanda is a flight attendant with Megalodon Airlines, and Chase just happened to be in Florida for a Megalodon Science and Technology conference!"

"And I've *heard* of Megalodon," Claire said, her eyebrows deliberately raised and held there for what seemed like days. "Plus, my cousin's name is Meg and today is Monday, which starts with an M. Couldn't possibly be a coincidence." She batted her eyelashes.

"Very funny," Mohs said. "This is not some wacko conspiracy theory. The Cosmic Mystery Theory of Fate is very deep and theoretically possible… on some other astral plane of existence."

"Are any of you real?" Reginald blurted out significantly louder than he'd intended.

Their conversation stopped once more.

"Are we back to that again?" Claire asked.

Reginald shrugged meekly. "I'm still not sure."

Claire waved her hands in an all-stop gesture. "Okay, Reg. Since you're a nice guy, I'll give it to you straight. You ready? Here it is." She pointed to herself. "I'm real. Razor's real. So are the captain, Prisha, and Chase. But sorry, Mr. Reginald Waldo Wankerbottom. You and Amanda? Not real."

Amanda stood tall in the pool. "I beg your pardon."

"Nope, not real. Here's why. You sing every morning."

Amanda's eyes lit up. "And sometimes at night too!"

"But are you really singing?"

"Of course she's singing," Prisha said. "She has a beautiful voice."

Claire cocked her head sideways. "Try it. Go on, sing something for us."

Amanda huffed. "Okay, I will." She climbed out of the pool, stood ramrod straight, and tightened her fists. Her lips wobbled a bit, then she burst into a song that soared across the breeze. "♩ ♪ ♫ ♪ ♫ ♪ ♩ ♩ ♫"

Prisha sighed. "Ah, Julie Andrews in the Alps. I loved that musical."

Claire cut her off. "Not singing. Notes only, no actual words. My point is proven. She's not real."

"Oh, but you are, then?" Amanda shot back, not about to be steamrolled by Claire. "Prove it!"

The group burst into a rabid argument with Claire accusing, Amanda and Prisha defending, and Mohs rolling his eyes. Reginald quietly tuned them out. He had to. Claire had just dropped the biggest bombshell of his life. She'd given proof.

Amanda's not real either.

Claire had just explained why he'd never truly heard of Amanda's songs. The lyrics had always seemed so foreign, so incomprehensible, so intangible.

Because they don't exist!

The realization hit him like a fish slap in the face. He scrambled up and dragged Claire aside while the rest kept arguing. When they were far enough away, he grabbed both of her arms and whispered in earnest, "Where are the words?"

"Aha—see? I got to you." Claire's half smile was nothing but underhanded, conniving, and downright sneaky. She was good at jerking the foundation of reality from beneath someone else's feet.

Reginald swallowed hard. He felt his stomach gurgle and bit his lower lip to keep it from trembling. "When Amanda sings, I don't hear anything! What's going on?" In fact, he hadn't heard her songs from the very start, but he'd chalked it up to amnesia.

"Calm down, Reg. You'll be fine." She pulled him even farther from everyone else. "Not that many people know this, but I'll fill you in because you're a friend of mine." She looked both ways and whispered. "Copyright."

Reginald stared blankly as Claire nodded repeatedly.

"You know, the legal stuff. Stuff they can sue you for? Copyright laws apply to lyrics too."

"No kidding?"

"Straight up. Reproducing a song title is perfectly legal. You can say 'The Sound of Music' all you want. You can even talk in general about hills being alive and sighing hearts and all the other sappy lines in that song, but you can't reproduce the actual lyrics! Why? Because that would require permission from whatever big shot music company holds the song rights. You'd have to pay megabucks for that."

Reginald's mouth dropped.

"Sorry, Head Case, but Amanda's not real and neither are you."

Reginald stumbled as his legs gave way. "Oh my stars, it all makes sense!"

"You bet it does," Claire said with a careless laugh.

Reginald recalled their first day on L3. Amanda had woken them up with a rousing song about a young woman being called into the unknown. The next day on the beach, she'd done a duet with Scratch. Defying gravity, or something like that. But there had been no lyrics, at least nothing that Reginald could make out.

For most people, discovering unmistakable proof of their nonexistence would be a painful, gut-wrenching moment. But for Reginald, it was liberating. The world around him hadn't collapsed, it had opened up to an unlimited vista of what was possible. He could become Wakinoshita-san at will or morph into any other character he could imagine.

I'm free.

Reginald returned to the pool, where Claire was laughing and explaining to the others about how gullible some people can be. When she noticed Reginald, she quickly shut up.

"I'm free," Reginald stated to no one in particular.

"Sure you are," Claire said. "Let's get back to fate. Are we or are we not fated to be trapped forever on L3?"

Razor stood up and flipped his knife in one hand. "I don't believe in fate. Nobody controls me. Not possible. If your mysterious connections brought us all to L3 and everything we do is already scripted, then I shouldn't be able to act impulsively. Someone or something should intervene... right about now."

Razor tossed the knife straight up into the air. Everyone around him gave a shout and scurried away, but he didn't budge an inch as the knife neared its zenith.

"That trajectory has a high probability of disaster," Chase stated from a safe distance.

"Maybe," Razor agreed. The knife began to fall back down, directly over him.

Claire became uncharacteristically nervous. "Okay, big guy, you made your point."

Razor remained where he was. "Fate doesn't exist. In this moment, I'm in complete control of whether I live or die."

The knife was a second away from impact. And then, quite suddenly, there were feathers everywhere, everyone shouted, and a dead bird crashed onto the pool deck with a knife protruding from its back.

"Unexpected," Razor said with the nonchalance of a blob of tomato ketchup lying on a plate.

"See? Something did intervene!" Mohs yelled. "I was right all along."

"Well, I was going to grab the knife out of the air," Razor said. "But a purely random event didn't give me the chance."

Chase cleaned up the poor bird's remains and handed the knife back to Razor. "The bird-knife intersection in space-time was certainly a low probability, but not impossible."

Razor sheathed the knife with a determined thrust. "Life lesson number three: Nature might throw a bag full of random events across your path, but you're still in control of the destination. Fate is a dishonest view of life."

The debate continued for another hour, though Reginald had already made up his mind. Life was a story. He and everyone else were its players.

Razor finally scuttled any further existential experiments by declaring that the host always wins the argument, especially when he's offering to prepare dinner. "Salmon on brioche, anyone?"

They moved to Razor's upper deck to enjoy sunset on the water. Wood chips from a hardwood tree produced aromatic charcoal briquette, and the new barbeque grill shaped from spaceplane sheet metal made cooking a breeze. Best of all, Razor's recipe for salmon dinner was a major hit.

The conversation wandered from their first days on L3 to the luxuries of Earth, some of which they had now reproduced in their new houses. But eventually talk returned to gods, this time Reginald imagining himself as the great storyteller in the sky.

"What if we were writing our own script?" Reginald asked no one in particular.

"Oh, not this again…," Claire began.

"No, just for fun." Reginald looked at Prisha. "If I were writing the script, I'd start off with Prisha featured in chapter one."

"Why me?" Prisha asked.

"Because you have a good inner conflict. A young pilot aspires to command her own ship, but she is suddenly thrust into an unpredictable and possibly dangerous situation. What's not to like about that?"

"Well, there's the part where we crash-land," Claire grumbled.

"Right, that sucked," agreed Reginald. "But you have to admit it just adds to the lure of her story. In my version of *Lost at L3*, the natural beauty becomes distracting for Prisha. And that's not the only thing that turns her head."

Chase was sitting right next to Prisha. She looked away, blushing. Chase seemed unable to fix his gaze on anything.

Reginald continued, "So, with all the diversions, our heroine is beginning to wonder if life on Earth was all that great. Maybe her new home pulls emotional strings she never knew she had. Will she find a way home and become the spaceplane captain she'd always imagined? Or will she stay on L3 forever, relegating her ambitions to distant memories? You see, there's the inner conflict."

"Where's the swooning?" Claire cracked. "There's always swooning in those stories."

"Oh, that comes in chapter two," Reginald answered.

Prisha put on her scolding teacher face. "Honestly, Reginald, you're an incorrigible matchmaker. Don't be silly. There's nothing between Chase and me."

Chase perked up. "Yes, not... nothing... not anything!"

"What about the deck?" Reginald raised his brow.

Chase replied, "The shared deck between our new houses? Well, that was just good architecture. Razor's idea."

Razor huffed.

Prisha raised a few hesitant fingers. "Um... not exactly. I did ask Razor if he could design it that way, but I was only thinking it might save time, and then Chase and I could both have a nice deck to sit on."

Claire started a long reflexive cough. "Glad we got that settled. So, what happens in chapter two?"

Reginald's eyes gleamed. "Oh, that's where it gets interesting. The story switches to Chase."

Chase pointed to himself. "Me?"

"Yes. The scientist who's always calculating and planning. He's two steps ahead of everyone else. His working data is there's been no radio contact, and their attempt to launch a bamboo rocket was a spectacular failure. So, now he's thinking about their long-term future."

"True," Chase admitted.

"Will they be marooned for a year? Ten years? Even thirty years? Gilligan was."

"No, he wasn't!" Mohs interjected. "Three seasons, one made-for-TV movie, and Gilligan was back home. Sort of. It's complicated— you had to be there."

Reginald tilted his head in an acknowledgment that any event prior to last month might not be straight in his memory, then continued. "Anyway, in Chase's story, he's wondering whether he'll spend the rest of his life stranded on this planet. He's wondering how to pass on the story of L3 to future generations. He's thinking about offspring."

Chase tipped his head from side to side. "Well, yes, you certainly need progeny to pass along legends."

"Ah, see! This chapter could write itself. Chase logically concludes that if children are ultimately the answer, everyone will need to get to work on the next generation while still young enough to procreate."

Chase nodded. "Naturally, you can't wait until—"

Claire cut him off. "Chase and Prisha. Amanda goes with Reg. What the hell, I'll take Razor."

"Like hell you will," Razor said.

Amanda patted Reginald on the hand. "You would make a good father. When the time comes to make the next generation, I'd be honored."

Captain Mohs formed his hands into a T like a football official. "Wait, what about me? Sure, I might be over the hill when it comes to that kind of thing... and then there's the vasectomy... but can't I still...?"

His voice trailed off as glares from all three women slowed him to a crawl. "Okay, okay, I'm the odd man out. I get it. I'll settle for the headmaster at the new children's school."

"Good choice," Claire confirmed.

Prisha stood up. "This is getting wildly out of control." She stared at Chase, who shrugged.

"Uh, yeah, a little."

"More than a little. We've only been on this planet for three weeks and you're already planning future families?"

Chase replied sheepishly, "Well, it's never too soon to plan."

Prisha exploded. "Holy Vishnu! This is crazy! I'm not some cow who needs to be matched up to a steer to ensure a calf pops out next spring! Sorry, Reginald, but your god-inspired storytelling just went off the rails."

Prisha stormed out, heading down the deck stairs and back toward her own house.

Mohs stood up and slapped Chase on the back. "Better luck next time, son. You could always help me run the school." Mohs mumbled something about testing his new bed—by himself—then left.

Chase hung his head with a look of unmitigated deflation on his face. Whatever lusty romance might have been rampaging through his mind had been exposed by Reginald's storytelling.

Amanda gave Chase a hug. "Don't take it too hard. She might come around, but give it some time. Pushy never works." She then turned to Reginald, squinting sympathetically. "And you may have hit a little too close to the mark."

Reginald hung his head even lower than Chase. He suddenly felt terrible. "Yeah, you're right. I'll apologize right away." Reginald hurried away after Prisha.

Prisha's house was the next one up the creek, and he caught up to her just as she gripped her doorknob. "Prisha! I'm really sorry! I made a mistake. I shouldn't have said things that could... you know... be embarrassing for you."

Prisha stared at the stars a moment. "I was thinking about what we were talking about earlier. You and Claire questioning reality. Mohs talking about how everything's fated. If there's any truth to it, then am I just fated to end up with Chase? That doesn't feel right. There's no romance, just a predetermined outcome where I have no say."

Reginald shrugged helplessly. "I'm no expert. On anything, actually. But you're a talented, capable woman with leadership practically oozing from your pores."

Prisha snickered. "Sounds like I need a shower."

"No, no! I didn't mean that. You're super clean, probably the cleanest person on L3... well, except for Amanda, who probably doesn't sweat." He grabbed his hair with both hands. "Sorry, sorry! Now I'm comparing body odor! How do I get myself into these things?"

Prisha was genuinely laughing now. "Don't worry, Reg, you came to apologize, and you did. Quite sincerely, I think. Now I'm going to retire to my nice clean bed. Good night, Reg." She put a hand on his cheek. "Don't think too hard. You're doing fine."

Reginald gave a relieved sigh and turned away as she closed her door. He had no idea how he'd resolved it, but somehow, he'd wriggled out of another self-inflicted snafu. He gave a knowing look up at the sky and nodded.

Thanks, author.

15 DATE NIGHT AT L3

PRISHA COULDN'T HELP but giggle as Chase struggled upside down, his feet squirming while his head and shoulders were deep inside an electronics compartment behind the spaceplane's control panel.

"Lots of components here we could salvage," Chase called out. His voice was muffled.

They had returned to the spaceplane to see what might be useful for their new life on L3. With Razor's super-efficient AbSolOrb, they already had more than enough electricity to power a small village, so Chase declared he'd rig a recharging station for their phones and add Wi-Fi to boot. He'd even pried one of the control panel's multifunction displays that might serve as a TV. Entertainment was within their grasp.

Content of every variety was available on the spaceplane's ten-zettabyte data server, which Chase had already ripped out from its cabinet. It was one of those Big Bob units that came preloaded with the sum total of all knowledge when they'd left Earth. They'd have access to medical procedures, engineering specs, and scientific knowledge, but also the homey touches like recipes and entertainment. The server's archive included every book ever written, every song ever recorded, and every movie ever produced. Luckily, Prisha remembered her Big Bob password.

Chase surfaced and held up a metal box with cables dangling out the back. "Audio amplifier for the public address system. Once I pull out the overhead speakers in the cabin, this baby is going to give us surround sound!"

Baby, he'd said. Prisha's thoughts returned to the uncomfortable ending to their fish fry on Razor's deck three nights before. Since then, she'd spoken less than twenty words to Chase, though he'd gone out of his way to be cordial, including a very specific invite to spend the afternoon rummaging through the spaceplane. Prisha only; he hadn't asked anyone else to come.

She had agreed. She did know something about spaceplane components. She was, after all, still wearing a pilot's uniform, slightly wrinkled these days but washed clean once a week in Razor's new combination washing machine and clothes dryer that he'd constructed at the edge of the creek.

But there was another reason to join Chase on a scavenger hunt. "Did you really want me to have your babies?" L3 was a small place, and clearing away the cloud that hung between them was the adult thing to do.

Chase set the component aside. He became pensive with eyes cast down. "Sorry for making you uncomfortable."

"You did. I was."

"It was a clumsy attempt to think ahead, that's all. I've been told by past girlfriends I think too linearly and sometimes come across like a calculating robot." He paused. "Actually, all of them said that."

"Well, we might not be able to fly off this rock, but I'm not giving up yet."

"Me neither. But… we have to be realistic. Our chances of survival are pretty good, but the chance of rescue is near zero. Nobody knows we're here. Nobody even knows what 'here' is."

"Rescue might be a long shot, but that doesn't mean we need to start producing children next week."

"No, but further down the line…"

Prisha glared.

Chase tried again. "It could just be one. You know, to keep the genetic line going."

He hadn't learned a thing, and Prisha's patience was wearing thin. She rubbed her forehead. "Chase, that's not remotely how relationships work. You don't start with a long-term community goal, then work backward to something that is very personal."

Chase shrugged. "Other primates do it."

"Chase, I am not a primate!"

"Well, actually, you are." He held up both hands. "Sorry, that didn't come out right."

Prisha crossed her arms. Were all scientists like this? Probably not. Chase seemed particularly adept at taking all that was wonderful about people and love and reducing it down to primitives like elevated hormones, swollen glands, and fertilized eggs becoming implanted blastocysts attached to uterine linings.

How romantic!

He picked up the electronics box and trundled out the door without a further word. She'd never seen him so depressed.

Moods varied, especially for castaways millions of miles from civilization and almost no hope of getting home. They'd all felt it. Prisha had too. Though his presentation was tactless, to say the least, Chase was only trying to find a long-term positive outcome to being stranded on this planet. Chase was Chase. A handsome, smart, scientific guy who sometimes tripped over his own tongue.

Prisha took a deep breath. There were only five other people on this world, and she couldn't afford to alienate any of them. Plus, she knew damn well she still had a thing for him.

She dashed out the spaceplane door. Chase was already down at the beach on his way back to their new community by the creek. "Wait!" she called out, catching up to him.

He stood, speechless, shirt unbuttoned, the turquoise sea behind him like a quintessential romance novel cover. Not that Prisha ever read those. Maybe occasionally. Only when she was getting over a bad breakup.

She struggled to start. "Um… it's not that I don't like you—I do." She looked up, connecting to his steel-blue eyes. "But all this talk about babies is… it's too fast. Does that make sense?"

He nodded. "Sorry, I'm not very good at this. Well, I'm pretty good at getting a woman's attention." He waved a hand over rippling abs. "But physical will only get you so far. I usually end up blurting something out that never should have seen the light of day, and then it goes downhill from there."

Prisha put her hand in his. "I get it. I can get discombobulated too. But I do like you. Can we start over? Go slower. Maybe we could have… I don't know… a date?"

Chased perked up. "I like that idea. Once I get the Wi-Fi, TV, and surround sound set up, we could watch a movie together! Just you and me. Out on the deck. I could pick you up at your house and bring you flowers."

Prisha smiled. "Flowers would be nice, but you're not supposed to tell me that in advance."

"Oh, yeah."

"Date night tonight, then. With flowers to decorate my new kitchen if you can manage it." Prisha motioned behind. "Now, how about we pry out those spaceplane speakers?"

An hour later they arrived back at the rows of bamboo and rosewood houses built alongside Bountiful Creek (as they'd named the well-stocked fishing stream). The electronics they carried would bring their improved living situation fully into the twenty-first century. They'd come a long way from their first night under a leaking lean-to, eating stale pretzels for dinner.

"Date night?" Claire asked after Chase had explained what the electronics would be used for. "You mean like a male-female kissy kind of thing?"

Prisha stared. "Don't tell me you've never done a date night."

Claire looked down at her ring and began playing with it. "Is it limited to watching TV?"

Prisha thought she detected a hint of wistful curiosity in Claire's tone. "Of course not. Date nights might include dinner, drinks, jokes, maybe a game or something."

"Like a competition?" Claire's head came up. "Like a battle of the sexes kind of thing?"

Prisha furrowed her brow. "I... suppose it could, but you wouldn't want to overdo it, or you might offend your date."

"No chance there. Hey, Razor!" Claire stalked over to where Razor was busy whittling a wooden weathervane (or possibly a long-necked duck) with one of his many knives.

He paused, looking up. "Don't even think about it."

Claire produced a weapon of her own—the ten-inch dagger he'd given her after the trial. She twirled it expertly in her hand and spoke softly. "We could have a knife-throwing contest."

Razor huffed. "I'd win." He went back to whittling whatever decoration he was making—mongoose, maybe? Moray eel?

"You might. But I've been practicing. A woman never knows when the battery in her finger laser might give out, leaving her defenseless. That's when a good blade could come in handy... as long as it's wielded by someone who knows how to use it." She walked in a circle around him. "Do you?"

He perked up at her taunting tone but said nothing.

"Of course, a knife-throwing contest could get dangerous. Maybe even go William Tell style?" She grabbed the half-carved mongoose and placed it on top of her head.

Razor's eyes remained steely. He held out an open hand.

She tossed the piece of wood back to him, swiveled, and blasted a blue laser line at a palm tree a dozen meters away, dropping a coconut cleanly to the ground. "I find that things have a way of getting out of control when two people are—shall we say—competitive. Might even go beyond throwing knives."

Razor stood and tossed his knife into a deck post where it stuck with a thunk. His face was red. His whiskers bristled. "You're on. But only if we do it on the ridge, where gravity is lower."

"Kinky. But workable." Claire motioned to Razor's duffel bag of sharp objects, and off they went.

Chase and Prisha looked at each other, wide-eyed. Claire's sexuality was most likely limited to activities that involved burning things down, but an odd matchup between the former sworn enemies had recently sprung up. No one had quite categorized it yet.

"Date night!" Amanda shrieked when she found out. "What a great idea!" She and Reginald had just returned from the creek with the day's catch of fish. "Come on, Reg, we could do that, couldn't we?"

"Would I need to get dressed up?"

"No, you look fine just the way you are. Besides, we didn't really bring a change of clothes. Maybe next time."

Captain Mohs sauntered over. "Lots of commotion over here, what's up?"

Amanda picked up Scratch, who seemed to be always near her feet. "Captain, be a sweetie and watch Scratch for me, would you?"

Without waiting for an answer, Amanda gave Scratch a long lecture about behaving himself for the captain and how she would be gone for the evening but when she got back, she'd tuck Scratch in for the night herself, and would that be okay?

Scratch gave her a lick, and she handed him over to Mohs, who looked somewhat dumbfounded. "Going somewhere?"

Chase handed the multifunction display and the Big Boy mega server to Mohs. "I have a better idea for all this equipment."

He turned to Prisha. "Can you give me an hour before our date?"

"Date?" Mohs asked no one.

"Sure," Prisha said. She had a feeling she knew what Chase had in mind.

****

Claire followed Razor up the ridge that formed the western flank of Mount You-Gotta-Be-Kidding-Me (which is what the lofty peak should have been named in the first place). There would be no need to climb to the summit; the ridge camp where they'd constructed the spaceplane mockup would provide a fine arena for their low-gravity game of chicken:

If that's what it ends up being.

Claire had already adjusted her regard for Razor, a process that was still being fine-tuned as they climbed. Now that she was no longer a super sleuth chasing a mass murderer, their relationship was more like a cowgirl breaking in a new horse. He was a wild one, but he could be tamed.

"Rules?" Claire asked.

"Tournament throwing knives. Thirty paces," Razor called behind him as they marched up the ridge.

"At each other or into a tree?" The level of danger in this contest was still an open question. For a man who could sub for an eighth-century pillager, some kind of Viking bloodletting ritual was a distinct possibility.

Razor hesitated. "A tree will do. Winner takes all."

"All what?"

"Whatever he or she pleases."

Claire raised an eyebrow. "A broad-minded awards program, but I can work with it."

The terrain leveled and they finally broke out from a grove of rosewood trees to the ridgetop meadow. The old camp lean-tos were still standing, along with wood chips and other debris from mockup construction.

Razor carved a circle in the trunk of one of the trees. He then stepped off thirty paces, placed three throwing knives in her palm, and kept three more for himself.

"Ladies first." Razor scanned her like a hungry Viking studies a lame mountain goat.

Claire took aim and threw the first knife. It skimmed the edge of the tree and flew off into the bushes. A sneer spread across Razor's bearded face.

"Watch and learn," he growled. He studied his target, then reared back and threw. The knife stuck in the tree, dead center. "One up, with two to go."

"It's cute that you think you're winning," Claire said with as much nonchalance as she could manage. "I just need a small adjustment for the knife's weight."

She took aim with her next knife, threw, and watched with satisfaction as it sliced cleanly into the tree and simultaneously knocked Razor's knife to the ground. She gave him a cold grin. "Oops. Looks like I'm winning now."

Razor grimaced. "Lucky throw."

"Luck's got nothing to do with it. I once hit a guy in the neck with a blow dart from six stories up and a block away in the middle of Chicago. With a strong headwind. Turned out he was the wrong guy, but whatever, my point stands."

Razor aimed again and let it fly. The knife hit just to the right of Claire's. "I once hit a vole from the top of a Douglas fir, in deep underbrush during a blizzard. With no feeling in my fingers."

"I once shot out a suspect's tires on a high-speed chase through Florence leaning one-handed off a motorbike. There must have been a hundred tourists milling around that piazza, and my laser blast didn't so much as nick another elbow."

Claire danced the knife from knuckle to knuckle, threw it, and watched with alarm as it bounced off the handle of Razor's knife and ricocheted into the brush.

Razor grinned a shark grin. "I once used a slingshot to drop a turkey vulture flying two hundred yards above the Yukon River at night. Swam through ice floes just to retrieve it."

Claire gave him a look as he prepped his final throw. "Don't vultures eat carrion? That's got to be a pretty disgusting game bird."

"And some people eat raw oysters. Personally, I'll take the vulture." Razor's throw landed a hair above his other knife. He turned his gaze to her. "I win."

"Do you?" With a flick of her ring, Claire expertly drew a laser line across the tree just above her knife but below his. The entire top of the tree fell over, taking Razor's knives with it and leaving hers in the stump.

Razor stared hard at the stump. "That's cheating."

"You didn't say '*only* knives.' That was the 'things have a way of getting out of control' part."

Razor crossed his arms and faced her directly. "You lie too."

"I'm bad that way," Claire said with the coyness of a female praying mantis.

"And you play with dangerous toys."

"And you're harder to find than a gin martini in Mecca."

"I gave you multiple chances."

"What's that supposed to mean?"

"I knew you were after me," Razor said, waves of smugness radiating from him. "In Nepal, I spotted you watching me bathe in that alpine lake."

"Buck naked! It was zero degrees! You literally had to break the ice to jump into the water. Who even does that?"

"And again, in the Amazon."

"There were piranhas swarming while you washed your beard! My orders were to bring you back alive, not as packaged ground beef."

"You could have picked me up at any time, but you didn't. You got attached."

"I don't get attached."

"There are no scoundrels in your life. You wanted me. You still do."

"I happen to like…" Claire stopped, wondering. Her face flushed. Her heart pounded furiously.

Razor took two big steps closer. His wiry beard was inches away.

Her brain raced ahead even as her mouth remained on autopilot. "I once tracked a criminal through five continents and four seasons with two sprained ankles and a bout of mononucleosis."

"That was me."

"Damnit. You're right!"

Two seconds later, their lips were fused together.

****

"You're the nicest person I've ever met," Reginald said to Amanda.

They kicked sand as they strolled barefoot along the beach. A setting sun provided an orange glow to the sky. Palm fronds rustling in a gentle breeze and waves lapping on the shore provided natural background music. No lyrics required.

"Aw, that's so sweet of you to say," Amanda hooked her arm into his. Reginald relished the warm touch.

"Sorry, but I can't marry you," he said.

"Of course not, Reg. No one expects that, certainly not me." She pulled him closer.

"We can still be friends, right?"

"I'd really like that. A friendly date once in a while just to keep life on L3 fun. No expectations. And no babies for at least five years!"

Reginald laughed at what now seemed like a silly idea. "I've been on dates before. I can even remember part of one. We were in a bar, and I was drinking something called a raspberry cosmopolitan with lots of vodka in it. Getting a little tipsy and nervous too about what might come next."

"That's normal on a first date. I'm glad you're starting to remember your previous life."

"You're helping." He picked up a seashell, studied its classic cornucopia shape, then tossed it into the sea. "I can't remember my date's name, though. It's frustrating because it's on the tip of my tongue."

"It'll come to you."

"I remember the song from that night."

"Go for it, Reg. The microphone is all yours."

Reginald crouched, hands flipped up, eyes half-closed, and head tilted to one side in what he was sure was a very fly '90s look. He started twisting his shoulders left and right while mimicking a steady drumbeat with his puckered mouth. "Boom, boom, boom buduh, boom, boom, boom buduh, boom, boom, boom buduh, boom."

In the same strong beat, the lyrics came next with all the drama Reginald could muster. "♪ ♪ ♩... ♪ ♪ ♪ ♩ ♩... ♪ ♪ ♪ ♩ ♩... ♪ ♩"

Amanda stopped in her tracks, eyes wide, mouth open. She threw her head back and laughed so loud Reginald expected every bird and insect on the planet to take flight simultaneously.

"'What Is Love?' Oh wow, great dance song from the nineties!" Amanda could barely breathe, she was laughing so hard.

That Amanda recognized the lyrics wasn't lost on Reginald. Either Claire's Existential Theory of Song had been wrong, or by shear willpower he and Amanda had just become real people. He chalked it up to the latter and decided that going forward he would never worry about being fictional again.

"I have no idea why, but all the songs I know are cheesy dance songs you'd go clubbing to." Reginald was pretty sure his cheeks were crimson. His eyes lit up as a new thought occurred. "Peter!"

Amanda caught her breath. "Peter?"

"His name just came to me. My date at the bar. I'm pretty sure I went clubbing with him too."

"Peter! I'm sure he was a great guy. Maybe you'll find him again when we get back to Earth." They plopped down to the sand. "Let's build a sandcastle!"

****

Larry Mohs passed the bowl of popcorn to his companion for the evening. Scratch lapped up a few kernels.

"This is the part where McGarrett and Danno find Noshimuri's hideout. He's like the number one crime boss in Honolulu."

Scratch stared at the big-screen TV that Chase had linked to the new Wi-Fi setup. The Big Bob data server containing every show in history took care of the rest.

Mohs munched another handful of popcorn. "See, Danno doesn't know that Noshimuri's daughter was secretly dating him to gain inside intelligence on police activity."

Scratch seemed to absorb the complex plot in stride, then began barking with intensity.

"Oh, that's McGarrett's sister, Mary Ann. Whenever she visits Hawaii from LA, she somehow gets mixed up in criminal activity."

Scratch yipped again.

"Yeah, you're right, she does look like Amanda." He patted the dog on the head. "Say, buddy, you happy with your living situation?"

Scratch yipped twice.

"Holy jackalope, a guy like you rooming with a babelicious sweet cake like Amanda? Yessiree, you got a pretty good deal going there. Don't blow it. I did with my first wife, but really, who knew that women were so sensitive about beer buddies coming over for a tenth wedding anniversary? Sure, the paintball game got out of control, but those lamps from her sister were ugly and the carpet stains eventually faded."

Mohs sighed. "Women. Hey, am I right? Damn straight I'm right." He sighed again.

Scratch peered out the side window of Mohs's new house. On the other side of the creek were two more houses with a shared deck. Prisha and Chase sat side by side. Even from this distance, it was clear they were holding hands.

"Aah, don't bother with those two. In fact, close the blinds. There's nothing worse than exhibitionist neighbors."

Scratch hopped over to the window and pulled a string that released a set of blinds.

Mohs got pensive. It happened from time to time. "I've got kids. Wife took custody of them, but I got to keep the dog. Bark Reynolds. That was his name. Good dog. Honestly, I liked him better than the kids. He passed just a few months ago." Mohs looked down at Scratch. "Sorry if I called you a mutt before. You're a good pal."

Scratch licked his hand.

Mohs cleared his throat and blinked his eyes a few times. Man, he was getting soft. He pointed back to the TV. "Officer Tani Rey. Now there's somebody worth watching, and I do mean some body."

Scratch sat at the base of the TV, transfixed.

"You see? I told you. Damn, those police bikini uniforms are killer."

****

Prisha squinted into the eyepiece of Chase's homemade telescope. Bamboo, of course, with polished lenses made from broken bits of a spaceplane taillight cover. He'd also constructed a sturdy tripod but said he was disappointed that the geared clock drive hadn't worked out. Manual pointing only. How twentieth century.

"Turn the focus knob here," he said, leaning over Prisha and guiding her hand in near darkness. Well past sunset, the remaining light came from three LED lights Chase had hooked onto the railing of their shared deck. Power came from Razor's AbSolOrb.

Prisha found the knob and twisted. The rings of Saturn came into sharp focus. "Ooh, pretty!"

Their dinner outside had been delicious—and private. Everyone else was doing their own thing, either high on the ridge, down at the beach, or inside watching TV. Being alone with Chase had started as a dream, later compartmentalized as unrealistic, more recently pushed aside as unwanted, and now finally exposed as an intriguing next step in Prisha's on-again, off-again love life.

"Pretty, like you," Chase said. "That sounds dumb, doesn't it?"

Prisha laughed. "Yeah, but don't let me get in the way of your budding poetry talents. Just look up. If all those gorgeous stars don't provide motivation, then nothing will."

The glory of L3's luminous night sky had hammered home the consequences of overblown city lighting back on Earth. Given the ubiquity of glaring streetlights, flashing signs, electronic billboards, lighted sports fields, and a billion porch lights left on all night, most city dwellers were completely unaware of the grandest overhead display of all: starlight.

Prisha returned to her deck chair and reached out for Chase's hand. The simple touch was the right level for this beginning relationship. Where it might go was anyone's guess.

"I've often thought that if more people could see the stars, they'd better internalize the natural relationship we have with the cosmos. We're not just *part* of the cosmos, we're its crowning achievement. If there's a purpose to existence, it's us. Humans. I say humans, but I mean all thinking species—assuming there are more like us out there. There's no question that we're part of something important. We're able to contemplate the origin of this cosmos, learn how it works, and predict its possible futures. Science can tell us how the universe got here, but if you want to know *why* it's here, look no further than yourself. *We* are the meaning of this cosmos." Prisha caught herself and smiled sheepishly.

A slight smile parted Chase's lips. "You're the poet, not me."

"Aw, I try. When I was in flight school, I practiced what to say to tourists once we got above the atmosphere."

Chase nodded. "I seem to remember a finely tuned oration from eighty kilometers above Florida."

"Boy, was that clumsy. You were making me nervous."

"Me? I was just your average space tourist, enjoying the view out the window."

"You were not! You were hitting on me."

"Well, okay, maybe. But you were soliciting the aforementioned hitting upon—if that's a word."

"I was not! I was being a dutiful first officer by providing superior spaceflight services to a valued customer."

"As I recall, nobody else got that superior service."

"Well, I, um…"

****

The first sandcastle was Princess Aurora's, built while Amanda sang 'Once Upon a Dream' with Reginald following along as best he could. The second sandcastle, Cinderella's, was even bigger, sung to

"Bibbidi-Bobbidi-Boo." That one was easier for Reginald to figure out.

By the time they started a third sandcastle it was getting too dark to carry on, and besides, Claire and Razor had boisterously stumbled onto the beach with a bottle of one of Razor's fermented fruit drinks.

Amanda cleared the sand with a sweep of her arm. "On to the next event! Now that we have more people, it's time for…" She waggled her eyebrows. "Date night conga line!"

Amanda led, producing a rousing Cuban beat with hisses, boops, and cha-chas as her hips thrust left and right. Reginald formed the caboose, bouncing rhythmically behind her.

Claire looked pretty trashed, and to everyone's surprise she let out a whoop that could pass as a *grito* shout from a mariachi band, grabbing Reginald so hard around the waist he jumped in the air and looked quite fearful.

They made one pass, then came back around again. Razor hadn't budged.

"Come on, Razor, jump in!" Amanda flashed a toothy grin and beckoned with one finger. Razor's facade never cracked. Reginald tried too, but no result.

Finally, Claire spun off from Reginald, grabbed Razor by the collar, and yanked him in. "You're not getting off the easy. Get your butt in here."

Razor rolled his eyes, but he complied.

"More people!" Amanda yelled as their conga line wound its way up the creek toward the lights of Razor's house and the rest of their village in the woods.

****

"Then you do like me, don't you? Don't you?"

Prisha finally gave in. "You know I do."

At least, it ended the pointless argument about who did what to whom first. Chase stood inches away, waiting, apparently for a kiss. It didn't take her long to decide.

She reached up and planted a soft kiss on his lips, lingering long enough to mean it. "You didn't win the argument—that was just... well, just because."

"Fair," he said. "I can live with the insecurity of an indeterminate level of affection and a vague future, as long as the kisses keep coming. They will keep coming, won't they?"

She smiled. "We'll see. It's the first date."

"Even though we never got to the movie, I still had a wonderful time. You know, if—"

She cut him off. "Wait. Stop. What's that?" She pointed. A light in the sky moved against the star background. It seemed to be getting brighter.

Chase studied it. "Lopsided shape. Let's see what the scope tells us." He quickly swiveled his bamboo telescope. "Yup. Long. Lit more at one end than the other. It sure looks like that microphone or toilet brush or whatever—the thing that pulled us away from Earth!"

The light quickly became the brightest object in the starry sky. Its movement against the background was slight, as if it were heading almost straight toward them.

"What is it?" Prisha asked. She almost didn't want to know the answer. Would it smash into L3? Would it whoosh by like it had before and drag them away to a cold death in the dark reaches of deep space? Their first encounter with this object hadn't been to their advantage. There was no telling what the next encounter might do.

Chase took another look through the scope. "Not sure. It's no comet. Might be an oblong asteroid. But… wait a second, are those circles?"

Prisha took a turn at the scope. Though fuzzy, three concentric circles formed one end of what was otherwise a flying lamppost. It looked like an arrow shot clean through a round target—actually, three targets, each one smaller than the next. "Chase, that's no asteroid." She stood up straight and looked him in the eye. "If I were guessing, I'd say it's a spacecraft."

They stared at each other, mute for another minute while the light in the sky brightened further. From somewhere off in the jungle, the sounds of raucous singing and clapping to a Cuban beat grew louder.

16   FULL OF SHIP

NOW FOUR WEEKS into their survival on sometimes-weird, sometimes-wonderful L3, Prisha was pretty sure today would be either the best day or the worst day of that experience.

It had been a long night full of anticipation and anxiety. Now, they stood shoulder to shoulder on the beach with an unobstructed view of a spaceship that hung stationary in the sky. Morning sunlight glinted off three rings that rotated around the ship's central axis. A propulsion system hung at one end, a bulbous nose at the other. Indeed, it looked remarkably like a high-tech plunger for the world's largest toilet.

Captain Mohs tilted his cap to the back of his head. "Absolutely, two hundred percent sure this is the thing that dragged us away from Earth." Given the circumstances, he remained remarkably calm. They all were. Now that the oblong object wasn't screaming past at obscene speeds, details were easier to identify. Shiny ovals that might be windows. Running lights. Even antennae.

"Think they'll put us in cages?" Reginald asked, as if capture by aliens was the least remarkable thing that could happen in the next twenty-four hours.

"I'd prefer they just eat us in one bite," Claire advised. "Get it over with."

Prisha was having none of their fatalism. "We don't even know if it's alien. Maybe it's Chinese."

"Possible," Chase agreed. "It would be hard to spot any flag insignia at this distance. It's not drifting, which means it's parked in a geosynchronous orbit. For tiny L3, that's only about sixty kilometers or thirty-six miles."

Claire blinked. "Thirty-six miles and it still fills the sky?"

Chase countered, "Well, it doesn't actually—"

"Big sucker," Mohs said. "The aliens inside must be monsters. Huge ugly things with fangs and lots of slime."

Chase rallied, "No, it's really not that big. The arc subtended is about three degrees and that's not—"

"We're all going to die at the hands of enormous alien monsters," Reginald stated succinctly.

"No, any object close to the horizon creates an optical illusion... oh, never mind." Chase shrugged.

Prisha attempted to stake out a middle ground, but she had to admit she had more questions than answers. "If this is the thing that dragged us away from Earth, why did it come back? They must know we're here, which could be good. It might be our chance for rescue."

Claire pointed. "Eat us or rescue us, it looks like we're about to find out."

A tiny glint dropped beneath the spaceship on a curving glide path that arced toward them. A minute later, a silver craft traced a contrail across the L3 sky, swooped in a broad turn over the sea and pointed its nose directly toward the beach where they stood.

Captain Mohs backed up. "Not liking the looks of this."

The rest backed up too, even while all eyes were transfixed on the landing craft's final approach. Scratch hid behind Amanda's legs.

It was a spaceplane of sorts, with wings and a tail but held aloft by twin jet engines that produced a deafening roar. Landing struts extended beneath the silver craft. The engines pivoted to a vertical position as it slowed.

Sand kicked up, and palm fronds blew across the beach as the spaceplane alighted gently on its struts. The roar shut down, returning their beach to an eerie quiet.

"Please, no tentacles," Reginald said. "Alien mutants from space always have those squirming, suckered tentacles. Reminds me of calamari."

Claire lifted her hand, taking careful aim with her blaster ring. "Bring it on. Roasted, deep-fried, or just plain burnt."

Prisha was as nervous as the rest, but if this spaceplane represented rescue—even if the occupants were alien—blasting them with a laser wasn't going to set a friendly tone. "Maybe we should all smile?"

There wasn't any place to run. Whoever was inside that craft clearly had picked this particular beach to land.

They waited. Near the rear of the spaceplane, a hatch cracked open with a slight hiss. A helmeted figure in a silver jumpsuit stepped out. Its form was familiar—two arms and two legs—and it carried a weapon. Or possibly a trombone, it was hard to tell for sure.

Without a sound, the figure gave a hand motion. Two more stepped out, both wearing the same silver suit and helmet. Still no tentacles. If they were aliens, they were doing a fine job imitating humans.

With Prisha's encouragement—a push—Mohs stumbled forward. He held up one hand in the Vulcan split-fingered salute. "May the force be with you. Do you come in peace? We do. Definitely nothing dangerous about us. No knives, or laser rings, or vicious blood-lusting canines that could pull your throat out in a blink. Nope."

The armed figure remained at the hatch, pointing its horn-shaped weapon at the castaways while the other two approached. A shark insignia adorned a breastplate on their suits. As they walked, they removed their helmets, revealing human faces, both men.

One was older with longish white hair and bushy eyebrows, the other younger, with a slim face and wired spectacles. The older man strode across the sand with a fierce determination. The younger man hurried to keep up.

"What the hell are you people doing on my planet?" the white-haired man barked.

"You speak our language!" Reginald cried out.

Amanda poked him. "Shh, Reg. They're not aliens. In fact, the guy in front is pretty famous."

Prisha recognized him too.

So, apparently, did Mohs, whose mouth hung open. "You're J. J. Kornback, extravagant trillionaire and CEO of Megalodon Industries!"

"That's me." Kornback stopped a few paces from Mohs, hands on hips. "Now who the hell are you?"

Kornback looked different dressed in space gear instead of his normal corporate suit. But the face was unquestionably the man who had pulled off the first human expedition to Mars, the man who ran a conglomerate commanding half the world's supply chain, employed a good portion of its citizens, and influenced a large chunk of its politicians. If there was a single face for the handful of megacorporations that ran the global economy, Jerold Jefferson Kornback was that face.

Before Mohs could respond, the second jumpsuited man (who had assumed a position two paces behind Kornback) spoke up. "I believe, sir, that these may be the missing space tourists."

The assistant consulted a small tablet in his hands. "This would be Captain Larry Mohs, the uniformed woman is First Officer Prisha Dhaliwal, and the rest are the five tourists who disappeared from Florida four weeks ago. I'm not sure about the dog." Scratch peeked out from between Amanda's legs, whimpering.

Kornback shouted, "Whoever they are, they're trespassing!"

Mohs pointed to the gargantuan ship hovering in the sky. "We're not actually trespassing since your ship dragged us here."

Kornback waved him off. "Don't be absurd."

The assistant piped up again. "Well, sir, there was that small mishap as we were passing Earth during Test Run 14. I'm sure you recall, sir, the tractor beam malfunction?"

"Shut up, Tompkins!" Kornback bellowed.

"Yes, sir," Tompkins said meekly.

"What?" Mohs nearly lost his cap with a double take. "You have a tractor beam on that ship? No wonder we never had a chance. It's practically homicide by criminal negligence."

Kornback lowered his brow, then spoke to his assistant. "Tompkins, if this man is a Megalodon employee, have him fired! Insubordination, reckless driving, and trespassing on private property! Oh, and when you file the paperwork, no mention of the tractor beam. And be sure to list the property as a corporate asset for tax purposes."

Claire stepped up next to the captain. "Ah, I get it. L3 is a corporate write-off!"

"L3?" Kornback blasted. He seemed to only have one volume.

"We named it L3," Mohs said, a bit defensively.

"Megalodon Executive Retreat and Spa, you mean."

Amanda waved both hands. "Wait, there's a spa here?"

Tompkins piped up again. "Technically, no, the spa is scheduled for 2044, but it's included in the name for acronym hilarity. MERS sounds like Mars, only different. My idea."

"Shut up, Tompkins!" Kornback yelled.

"Yes, sir." Tompkins zipped his lips.

"You're saying Megalodon built this place? L3 is not even real?" Prisha couldn't keep the surprise from her voice, but she kept her tone polite, not anxious to be the second Megalodon employee fired today. Captain Mohs—if he was still a captain—didn't seem to be too disturbed by his sudden dismissal.

Claire walked a circle around the silver-suited men, throwing a wary glance at the third helmeted soldier still guarding the hatchway to the spaceplane. "Not hard to figure out. It seems this little jungle planet is their corporate playground. They send the company big shots off to *MERS* for some relaxation. Lounge chairs on a private beach. Maybe hunt a few exotic animals, then jet back to Earth but don't tell a soul about it… except to write the whole planet off as a research expenditure."

At least Claire wasn't worried about being fired, useful in this case.

Cornered, Kornback was steaming mad and suddenly talkative. "MERS is a legitimate testing ground for any interstellar expedition! The plants and animals we grow here also populate the habitation rings on the Centauri Starliner, providing food and oxygen for our journey."

Prisha stared up in awe at the gargantuan ship and whispered with reverence, "The Centauri Starliner."

There had been rumors. A vast ship built to carry a specially selected crew on an exodus to Alpha Centauri. Some claimed the Centauri passengers were genetically enhanced. Others simply said they came from the ranks of the ultra-elite—the privileged, the rich, and the well-connected—all escaping a dreary world to establish their personal utopia in another star system.

Tompkins whispered into Kornback's ear.

"Yes, yes, Tompkins," Kornback blustered. "I supposed we'll have to shoot them all now."

Prisha's heart skipped a beat. Mohs took a step back. Tompkins quickly whispered into Kornback's ear once more.

Kornback looked profoundly disturbed. "You're right, of course, seven bodies would be problematic, so maybe not an actual shooting per se. But what about the mulching machine? We could run them through that. Hardly leaves a trace!"

Tompkins whispered again.

Kornback's eyes widened. "Alive? That seems counterproductive." He sighed deeply. "Okay, if we must, but I want a signed NDA from each of them!"

Kornback stormed off toward the spaceplane mumbling something about a sulfuric acid pest control module that he should have chosen from the list of sales options.

Tompkins smiled at the assembled castaways. "Mr. Kornback would like to invite you to participate in a very special arrangement to our mutual benefit."

"Does it involve being mulched?" Mohs asked.

"Or sprayed with sulfuric acid?" Claire added.

"Or maybe… a ride back to Earth?" Reginald asked tentatively.

"All are excellent options to discuss," Tompkins said. "But first, we'll ask that each of you sign the standard Megalodon nondisclosure agreement so that we can all speak freely. Will that be acceptable?"

Heads reluctantly nodded.

Tompkins retreated to the spaceplane to fetch legal documents. Scratch raced after him, snarling wolflike. The silver-suited guard pointed its trombone-like weapon, and Scratch skidded to a stop. He quickly dashed back to hide behind Amanda's legs.

The guard advanced, dropped its weapon to the sand, then removed its helmet. Long blond hair fell out. The guard was a woman, young and quite beautiful. Her eyes fell upon the dog. She tilted her head, looking more puzzled than mad.

"Scratch? Is it really you?" the woman asked.

Scratch peered out from behind Amanda's leg. He sniffed the air. His tail trembled—only a little—but with a waggle of excitement, not fear.

The silver-suited woman dropped to her knees. "It is you! I can't believe it!"

Scratch raced across the sand and leaped into her outstretched arms, yipping and licking her face.

"Okay, now I'm really confused," Amanda said. "Who are you?"

The woman looked up, wiping a tear from her eye. "Does Scratch belong to you now?"

"Well, kind of," Amanda responded. "I found him hiding in our spaceplane four weeks ago. We really don't know how he got there."

"I might know," the woman said. "You see, Scratch was my bestie for years—that is, until one morning when I woke up and he was gone."

She set Scratch on the sand and stood up, offering a hand to Amanda. "I'm Elaine Puff, Commanding Officer for Centauri Operations. COCO Puff, as everyone on the Centauri Starliner likes to call me." She bent over and scratched Scratch behind the ears. "And this little guy has been missing from my life for far too long."

Either COCO Puff was coocoo, or else the chance meeting between a lost dog and his former owner on an unknown planet at the far side of the sun was the most unlikely coincidence in history. But then, the whole thing with Megalodon and the Centauri Starliner had everyone's head spinning.

Prisha stepped forward, not about to wait for some signed piece of paper to authorize the hundreds of questions that flooded through her mind. "You're really going to Alpha Centauri in that ship?"

The woman glanced over her shoulder. "The Starliner is a beauty, capable of maintaining a healthy, happy environment for two thousand people indefinitely. And flight tests prove that we'll ultimately reach a speed of 0.95c—that's ninety-five percent of the speed of light, far faster than any spacecraft has ever gone. Four years from now we'll arrive at Alpha Centauri, but we're not stopping there. We probably won't even slow down. Oh, sure, we'll drop a few scout probes to see if any of the Centauri system planets are worthwhile, but then we'll continue on to the real prize—Trappist One."

"Trapeze won?" Mohs queried.

"Trappist—never mind, the name doesn't matter since we'll give the star and its planets new names when we get there."

She pointed, probably in the direction of the to-be-named star. "It's a star system swarming with Earthlike planets—lots of them! It's forty light-years away, so you'll be reading bedtime stories to your grandchildren by the time we get there, but I'll only be thirty-five years old."

Chase perked up. "Wow, special relativity. You're right, at 0.95c time dilation is huge. A year on Earth will only be…"

"Four months for us," she answered. "Our bodies, our clocks, everything on board the ship will slow down by a factor of three. In just thirteen years, I'll be standing on an exotic planet orbiting a red dwarf and the sun will be too dim to see."

Mohs interrupted, "Super. Live forever, play your cards right and maybe old man Kornback will award you with your own planet. But before all you hotshot space people hoist your sails... how about a lift to Earth for the rest of us?" Mohs even provided a genuine smile with his request.

The ensemble of castaways gathered closer, with all eyes on COCO Puff. Scratch seemed torn, glancing repeatedly between his two owners. The dog might have a seat on this proposed interstellar voyage if he wanted it. Prisha wondered how far away the Trappist star was in dog years.

Elaine Puff had shown herself to be an energetic cheerleader for Kornback's astonishing mission, but as she gazed across seven hopeful faces staring back at her, she deflated like a flat tire. "You people have been here for four weeks? How on Earth did you survive without Megalodon Planetary Services on call?"

"Wasn't easy, but we managed," Mohs said for the group. "Nice little planet you have here—for the most part. Fine beaches. Clean water. Good fishing in the creeks. Can't say much for the nightly rumble or the weird gravity, but we settled in. Even built a few jungle houses. But right about now, we'd appreciate a ride home."

"After all, we *are* Megalodon employees and customers," Prisha added. "It only seems fair not to shoot us."

"Or mulch us," Reginald added.

COCO Puff glanced back at the spaceplane. There was no sign of Kornback or his assistant, Tompkins. She kept her voice low. "No promises, but I'll see what I can do about getting you home... unmulched. But whatever you do, don't tell Mr. Kornback about the houses or the fish—he'll deduct lumber costs from your paycheck. And wild sockeye salmon genetically engineered to swim in tropical water runs at least forty-five dollars a pound."

"What a businessman!" Reginald said. "Someday I'm going to be a trillionaire too! And thanks for not killing us, Ms. COCO Puff."

She shook hands with Reginald. "Call me Elaine. To tell you the truth, the COCO Puff thing gets tiresome. Two thousand people on the ship greet me every time we pass in the halls... you know how it can be." She fetched her weapon and flicked a safety switch on the side, though it was hard to tell if she'd set it on or off. "Everyone stay here, I'll be right back."

Twenty minutes passed, and though they could hear voices through the hatch left ajar, no one emerged. Eventually, the castaways found comfy spots in the sand and enjoyed the warming sun as it rose above the palms for yet another day in paradise.

"It is nice here," Reginald said, digging his toes into the sand.

"Don't even think about it," Mohs said. "We're getting on that ship. It's our one and only chance."

The hatch to the spaceplane burst open and all three silver suits poured out with Kornback in the lead. "Jungle houses! What the hell are you people doing building houses on my planet!"

A few steps behind Kornback, Elaine silently mouthed, "Sorry!" She looked pained but clearly wasn't the type to keep secrets from her boss.

Kornback marched right up to Captain Mohs. "Megalodon employees are not authorized to engage in extracurricular work activities outside their official job, a rule that is clearly listed in the Megalodon Human Capital manual!"

Mohs answered calmly. "Pretty sure you fired me about twenty minutes ago."

"Well, you're rehired! I'll fire you again later. Now, where are those houses?"

Prisha wasn't going to let the captain take all the heat. She stepped between Mohs and Kornback. "Mr. Kornback, sir… um, all of us built those houses. You see, we had to. We thought we might be here for years. So, if you need to fire someone who was just trying to survive in a very difficult situation… then you can start with me. But if you can find it in your heart not to fire anyone"—she waved a hand—"I'll show you where the houses are."

Mohs caught Prisha's eye, looking like a proud father.

"You might even like them," Prisha added. "Mine has a really nice deck, and Razor's house has a swimming—"

Mohs caught Prisha's eye again, shaking his head to stop her from saying too much. Kornback huffed, then motioned to Prisha to lead him toward the offending houses.

As she guided Kornback and the rest up the creek, Prisha worked out a strategy of diplomacy that might put Kornback in a more benevolent frame of mind, if such a thing existed in this man's head. She might only get one shot at it, and her pitch would need to be good.

She started with the basics—blatant flattery. "MERS really is a beautiful planet, Mr. Kornback. Did you design it yourself?"

"Years in the making, young lady. Multiple prototypes. Very expensive. Hell, the internal gyros alone cost me nearly a billion. But the science team said we'd need a protective magnetic field to keep visitors from being fried by coronal mass ejections, whatever those are."

"Um… those billion-dollar gyroscopes don't happen to sweep by every morning at five a.m., do they?"

"Every twenty-four hours, yes. It's a magnetized arm as big as an aircraft carrier, two hundred meters below the surface riding across a core of Ultradensium."

"Ultradensium is a synthetic metal concocted by Megalodon Materials Science Division," Tompkins called out from behind.

"Shut up, Tompkins!"

"Yes, sir."

"That's so enlightening! We were wondering why the ground shook every morning." The revelations of how L3 had been constructed made sense, even confirming Chase's theory that its weird gravity was due to an incredibly dense core.

Keeping Kornback talking about his beloved creation seemed to be working. "Um... Mr. Kornback, we were all wondering about a geyser we noticed, and those strangely shaped clouds too. You know, the ones that look like diamond rings and flying birds? Don't tell me you planned those too?"

Kornback huffed. "MERS tends to drift, so my engineers installed thrusters to maintain its position precisely at L3. Disguising them as geysers was a nice touch, I must say, but the damned pigeons keep getting caught in the thruster blasts, and the holes end up stinking like dingoes. Tompkins!"

"Yes, sir?" Tompkins answered.

"Why do we have pigeons on MERS anyway?"

"The head of engineering is from New York, sir. You said he could make it homey."

"I did? I don't remember that. New order. If the pigeons aren't all dead by now, get rid of the rest. And get rid of the head of engineering!"

"You want him eliminated with the pigeons?" Tompkins asked.

"Yes! No. Probably too messy. Just fire him." Kornback gave Prisha a sideways glance. "And, yes, those designer clouds are generated by our water vapor plant. They ensure that it rains every other night. Keeps everything growing, but not too soggy. Did you see the one of me? It's puffed out every day at noon so the sun lights me up like a golden god."

Scratch yipped several times, jumping up on his hind legs and tilting his head in a funny way.

Elaine bent down, hands on knees, absorbing the dog's request. "No, Scratch, what you saw wasn't a sea monster at all! That's our sand cleaner. It roams around automatically, picking out bits of trash or seaweed to keep our beaches pristine."

Amanda scrunched up her nose. "You can understand Scratch? My conversations are mostly one-sided."

"It's a gift." Elaine smiled. Scratch yipped.

As Amanda contemplated what Scratch had just said, Prisha continued to pour on the charm. "I'm so impressed, Mr. Kornback! A protective magnetic field, a controlled biosphere, and clean sand on every beach. Very smart of you!"

Was she laying it on too thick? Kornback had at least stopped shouting. Captain Mohs wasn't shaking his head or interrupting, which gave Prisha enough confidence to finally lay their cards on the table. Politely.

"But I was also wondering, sir… if the Centauri Starliner is nearly ready to depart for your very exciting mission to the stars, does this tiny planet even matter? Surely a few unauthorized houses and a bit of coal mining here and there has a negligible effect on property value, especially when the existing owner is embarking on bigger and better things anyway. Right?"

Kornback stopped walking. They were within sight of Razor's house, with the other houses beyond it. Kornback looked to the houses, then back to Prisha. "Ah, I see what you're trying to do, young lady."

"It's Prisha Dhaliwal, sir. First Officer, Megalodon Space Tours." She pointed to the third bar on her shoulder, the one Captain Mohs had bestowed upon her. Even if this patronizing old man didn't care, the rank was meaningful to her.

"You're a sneaky one," Kornback chuckled. "When this is all done, and after we've bulldozed these squatters' shacks you people built, come see me about a job in my PR department. You've got the flashy smile for it."

"Thank you, sir, I'll do that. Now, about that ride back to Earth?"

Kornback firmed his jaw. "Get this straight, young lady. I make the decisions, and I'm not influenced by pretty faces—even sneaky ones."

Prisha could see that a different approach might be required, and fast. Captain Mohs seemed to agree, clearing his throat repeatedly and slicing a finger across his throat.

Prisha took a deep breath. "I'm sorry to be coy, Mr. Kornback, but it's just that we're really struggling here. I mean, just look at my uniform. It's fraying, it's dirty. My Megalodon name tag hasn't been properly polished in weeks. This is not how I want to look for our customers."

Everyone else following behind had now stopped in a semicircle, watching the drama unfold.

Prisha held an outstretched hand to them. "These people are your customers too, Mr. Kornback. They paid for a seat on what was supposed to be a fun tourist space flight. They didn't ask to be shipwrecked with only the clothes on their backs... well, plus one duffel bag full of survival gear, which turned out to be one of our luckier breaks. But my point is, these people simply want a return ticket to Florida, which is where we promised to deliver them. *I* made that promise, Mr. Kornback, and I want to keep it. But more than anything... I just want to get back to doing my job. That's not too much to ask, is it?"

Kornback's firmly set jaw didn't budge, but he wasn't admonishing her either.

"She's right," Elaine said. "We could take them home. Earth really isn't that far out of our way."

Kornback scowled. "And what do we do when they tell their friends—and the media—about an exclusive planet on the far side of the sun that just happens to be the property of Megalodon Industries? I have a hundred highly paid executives who are *not* passengers on the Starliner, each with a specific fringe benefit clause built into their employment contract!"

"It's the MERS Secret Executive Retreat clause," Tompkins explained.

"Tompkins…!"

"Yes, sir."

Kornback's face turned red. "No, no, no. This is all wrong. How many times do I have to explain it? When a reputation management issue comes up, you don't issue some weaselly public statement of contrition like 'Megalodon expects more of employees and will double our efforts to ensure that blah, blah, blah.' No! You don't say anything at all. You go full-on damage control and shut it down before anybody finds out!"

"Full-on damage control, sir?"

"Yes, absolutely. Send a security team down. Shoot them, mulch them, I don't care, but clean up this mess! Then we simply move on, and this nasty business of trespassing never occurred."

Tompkins stared, blinking.

"Well? Get to it!"

"If you say so, sir." Tompkins consulted his tablet and tapped a few times.

Claire stepped forward, pointing her arm at Tompkins. Her voice was like ice. "Lower that finger, Junior. Nice and slow."

Tompkins visually examined the ring on Claire's finger, then whispered again into his boss's ear.

Kornback looked puzzled. "It's lethal?"

"It's a WD-400, sir. Vaporizes anything within a hundred yards. Only issued to top agents."

Razor stepped up next to Claire, miraculously producing a knife in each hand. He grinned wickedly with one steely eye locked onto Kornback. "Once in a while, I miss. But never from this range."

Captain Mohs put a hand on Razor's shoulder. "I guess I'm fired again. But I stand with my passengers." Chase took the other shoulder. They made a heroic trio.

Reginald brandished a long stick like a katana blade, swung it a few times, then assumed a warrior stance beside Scratch, who growled adorably. Even Amanda gritted her teeth.

Prisha grinned mischievously. She loved these people. She was proud to call them friends. Heck, they were practically her family now, like crazy distant relations who showed up to Thanksgiving dinner. With knives. And blaster rings.

Linking arms with the captain, Prisha's tone took on a take-no-prisoners vibe. "Go ahead, Mr. Kornback, send down your security team. But as you can see, we're determined survivors. We've lived on this planet for weeks now. We built houses from scratch and mastered the elements. We know this place, and I'm pretty sure we could keep your security team busy for months, maybe years, just trying to find us. Heck, we'll burn the place down if we have to. How would that fit in with your plans for an executive retreat? You'll be so busy chasing us, there's a good chance you'll miss your date with the stars."

Elaine pumped a fist, then quickly hid her hand when Kornback turned on her. Tompkins leaned in close, whispering into Kornback's ear once more.

Captain Mohs tugged Prisha's arm, whispering. "Nice job, Number One. That was four-bar material right there."

Prisha couldn't have felt prouder if she'd been nominated for Pilot of the Year. Of course, she might end up dead in the next few minutes, but so far, the only weapon on the other side had been in Elaine Puff's hands, and she seemed to be on their side. Sort of.

Kornback paced, head down. "Okay, okay. So, if shooting and mulching are off the table... they are off the table, right?" Kornback looked up at Tompkins.

"Yes, sir. Off the table. And for clarity, so are the sulfuric acid sprayers, recycle shredders, and concrete entombment. Oh, and the ship's waste ejection ports. Body dumping was banned by the Joint Use Space Treaty."

"God, I hate laws." Kornback stared upward until another idea occurred. "But what about that labor thing they passed in the dead of night a few years ago? We could use that, couldn't we?"

Tompkins swiped across his tablet, studying its results. "You are correct, sir. Trespassing does indeed fall under the Indentured Service Act of 2038."

"Indentured service?" Prisha asked.

Kornback waved a hand. "Ignore the name, you know how politicians can be. From a business perspective it's purely an accounting formality, but the lucrative government subsidies could be beneficial to all parties involved." He looked at Tompkins with eyebrows uplifted.

"Yes, sir. According to paragraph 14 subsection C, they would each receive a tax credit."

Kornback faced the castaways. "There, you see. Everyone is happy. So, it's settled. Being a reasonable man with high standards of self-preservation, I will offer free passage on the Centauri Starliner for everyone—including the dog. In return, you will each sign a nondisclosure, agree not to burn anything down, and deposit your knives and assorted blaster ring weapons with the ship's concierge when you board."

"An excellent plan, sir," Tompkins said.

Reginald lowered his stick. "We get to go home?"

"With the Starliner's speed, Earth is just a few hours away," Kornback said. "And as a symbol of goodwill for those of you who are Megalodon employees, I'll even waive standard HR policy that charges time spent on MERS against your vacation balance."

Tompkins wiped a tear from his eye. "So generous of you, sir."

Prisha whispered to Mohs, "These past four weeks would have been counted as vacation time?"

Mohs shrugged and whispered back, "Hey, we've got a ride home, and a classy one from what I've heard. The Starliner is no Mark 4. They'll probably have mini bottles, real forks, and those warm towels they hand out after meals."

With cautious smiles all around, everyone followed Kornback down to the beach. Tompkins handed out nondisclosure agreements and a pen to each person. The form basically said Megalodon could sue them and their heirs in perpetuity for every penny they had if a single word was uttered about their spaceflight gone wrong. They weren't allowed to mention L3 (either the planet or the position in space), or the acronym MERS, or the Centauri Starliner, or being swept away from Earth, or anything about the other side of the sun, or the sun itself.

"Seems fair," Reginald said, signing. "I probably won't remember any of this anyway."

Amanda signed for herself and Scratch. "We're going home!" Scratch ran in circles, a sign that by now everyone understood to mean sheer happiness.

Tompkins collected the signed papers and disappeared into the spaceplane. They waited silently outside. Nothing happened for a full five minutes. Mohs was just about to knock on the door when Tompkins and Elaine Puff stepped out once more.

Elaine reached down, and Scratch ran to her arms.

"We've agreed to take the dog for now," Tompkins said. "We'll pick the rest of you up tomorrow."

"Tomorrow?" several shouted in unison.

"Yes, tomorrow!" Kornback shouted from somewhere inside the ship.

Tompkins explained, "It's a technical issue only. This small landing craft isn't capable of carrying more than three people, but our larger version, Delta Tango, seats up to ten in complete comfort."

"I'm happy to sit on the floor," Reginald offered.

Tompkins shook his head. "It's not a matter of seats. It's weight."

"We can leave the duffel bag behind," Prisha offered. Razor reared up, then thought better of objecting and nodded his approval.

Tompkins frowned. "I'm afraid we wouldn't get off the ground with even one additional person, much less seven. Mr. Kornback knows you've struggled, but it's just one more night. Tomorrow at sunrise, Delta Tango will land right here on this beach, ready for your departure. Mr. Kornback has even offered to send down coffee and doughnuts."

"Ooh, I like that," Reginald said.

Mohs pointed a finger. "Absolutely no later than eight a.m."

"We'll make it seven," Tompkins said. He held out a hand and Mohs shook it.

Tompkins climbed back into the spaceplane. Elaine stood in the hatchway holding Scratch, whose tail was wagging like a struck tuning fork.

Amanda lowered her head, biting her lip. "I guess Scratch has made his choice," she squeaked out.

Prisha put an arm around her. "I bet that little guy has had a few adventures and several owners along the way. Elaine Puff was one of the good ones, but then so were you. Don't worry, we still have a flight to Earth before we have to officially say goodbye."

Amanda's voice choked up and she wiped away tears. "It's for the best. I only have a small apartment, and I fly five days a week. Their ship probably has a big dog park where he can run and play and search for all kinds of attractive sticks. I'm sure he'll be happier with Elaine."

Amanda sniffed. Prisha couldn't stop the tears from welling up either. They both waved as Elaine closed the hatch.

Mere seconds later, the engines lit up and everyone hurried to the safety of the tree line. The roar became deafening, and sand flew everywhere as the plane lifted from the beach and banked out over the sea. It blasted through several puffy clouds, then streaked into the sky toward the Centauri Starliner still hanging in its fixed position above L3.

"It'll be our turn tomorrow!" Reginald shouted. "Can't wait!" Everyone shouted their agreement. Except Mohs. He stood on the sand, watching the quickly disappearing spaceplane, his hands on hips.

Prisha approached him, apprehensive. "You don't think they'd strand us here? Not after my guerrilla warfare warning. I actually think we'd be pretty effective."

Mohs shook his head. "No, they definitely want us off L3, but something about this is all wrong. Almost too easy. One thing I've learned about Megalodon Industries over the years—never trust anything that's not in writing."

Prisha frowned. "But we signed a contract. Detailed too. Apparently, I can be sued if I tell my second cousin once removed that L3's M-shaped trees stand for Megalodon!"

"True, we did sign. But did you notice that it never mentioned transportation back home? That part was verbal only."

The first officer and her captain exchanged an uneasy aura of apprehension. It might be another restless night.

****

Prisha awoke not knowing how she fell asleep or why she had a splitting headache. She grabbed her temples and groaned, curling into a ball and willing it to go away. She managed to open one eye, squinting against a single light in a darkened cabin.

A metal wall was inches away.

We don't have metal walls on L3!

Prisha bolted straight up, headache momentarily forgotten. The ceiling was metal too. Her bed was a cold bunk with a single blanket. Floor-to-ceiling bars formed the opposite wall, solid and impenetrable. A low-frequency vibration and an almost imperceptible sideways push provided the impression that she was moving.

Through the bars, across a dimly lit hallway, someone stirred in another prison cell. He rose from a crouch in the corner, ambled casually to the bars, and stuck one arm through.

Captain Mohs gave a thumbs-down. "Told you."

PART THREE

You Call This a Rescue?

17 DOG OF THE CENTAURI

A DOG OF MODEST MEANS rarely mingles with elite humans and is never invited into their exclusive sanctuaries. This place was intimidating, but it was also heavenly.

Spotless walkways, reflective glass, and fanciful sculptures of blossoming flowers formed the backdrop for important-looking people dressed in silver uniforms who streamed purposefully down a splendid avenue pulled straight out of tomorrow. If the city-state of Singapore and the film *Logan's Run* had a lovechild, it might look something like this street, an unrivaled spectacle of modern efficiency, authority, and class.

And all Scratch could think about was where to find a bush to relieve himself.

Scratch stood in the middle of a street with no cars, lined on either side by buildings constructed in a variety of inventive architectures, packed one after another with nary a gap between them. The whole place felt streamlined, efficient, without any wasted space. The buildings were tall, too. Each soared into the blue sky overhead. From Scratch's admittedly low-to-the-ground viewpoint, he felt like he was walking down the center of a canyon.

Truth be told, he had no idea where he was. He'd been so caught up in his reunion with Elaine and his departure from Amanda that he'd barely had time to register all the oddities of this... city? Planet? The blue sky seemed normal enough with the sun shining and a few wispy clouds moving by, but something was off. The sun wasn't generating any heat, and the sky was bent in a slight arc shape, so that the clouds appeared to drift at an angle. The street also seemed to be arcing gently upward, like walking along an enormous gerbil wheel.

There was also something notably missing here: water. No fountains, or wading pools, or gentle babbling creeks. In Scratch's experience most cities boasted some water feature. Not that he wanted to focus too much on water, since that line of thought wouldn't help his more pressing need for a bathroom break.

Even with the absence of water, greenery was everywhere. But as if to torture him, every bush and tree was surrounded by metal fencing with signs declaring "no dogs," and what looked to be mechanized spritzers that no doubt sprayed unobservant canines in the face with a deterrent liquid.

Probably that horrid blue stuff they put in toilets—why would anyone ruin a perfectly good drinking fountain with ickiness like that?

Scratch shook the thoughts of liquids from his mind, bolstering his bladdery fortitude. He couldn't complain too much. He was with Elaine, one of his favorite people in the world. She was a disciplined and supportive soul with a big heart, someone who was apt to call Scratch out if he slipped up but smother him in hugs a minute later. She even seemed to have forgiven him for the *incident* that had led to his self-exile a year ago (full title: The Weekend Incident of Indefinable Horror, Curse This Weak Bladder, That Brought a Lifetime of Irredeemable Guilt and Shame). He wasn't about to let that happen again, but he really, really had to find a tree.

Elaine led Scratch down the spotless walking path toward a large building on their left, a marvel of architecture stacked in tiers with a dome that seemed to touch the unusually close sky. Scratch didn't have much of a nose for modern design, but he recognized high class when he saw it.

Upon entering through towering glass doors, he found himself in a room with monitors, keyboards, and flashing lights everywhere. Dozens of humans dressed identically to Elaine hurried about. Scratch had been pleased to discover Elaine was clearly a person of importance here, as they were only in the room for a moment before several others approached, each carrying glowing screens and talking fast. Scratch watched Elaine take care of business as efficiently as a chef mincing vegetables, signing one screen, dismissing another with a wave, and barking orders.

Human barking, not dog barking. She'd tried dog barking to him once and quite frankly, it was insultingly bad. But he'd wagged his tail anyway like a good boy.

They moved to a separate room with a fancy chair and desk— Elaine's room, Scratch assumed, since she took a seat at the desk while several other humans remained standing. She placed one of the screens she'd been handed on the desk and studied it significantly. Scratch scrunched up his face and tried to focus on it too to demonstrate his dedication to whatever was going on here in this… wherever they were.

"I am upset, and this glowing screen is clearly the reason for my unhappiness," was how Scratch's brain translated Elaine. She glanced to the other humans.

"Glowing screens are bad," the first human said, according to Scratch. "Especially this one."

"We must find the source of these glowing screens, and destroy them," Elaine clearly said.

Another of the humans scowled and shook her head. "We will get in trouble." Scratch definitely understood the word *trouble*.

Elaine nodded. "We must do it anyway. We must execute... *The Plan*." Scratch felt like that last part was extra important, and thus needed extra emphasis in his mind.

"Sleeping Blah Blah?" asked another human. Scratch only really understood the word *sleep* since it pertained to his daily habits.

Another nod from Elaine. "Yes, Sleeping Blah Blah."

After a moment, the others nodded too. Scratch nodded along with them, tongue hanging from his mouth in agreement. He honestly had no idea what was going on, but panting always seemed to reassure the humans.

They discussed their dislike of screens for a few minutes more, then Elaine rose and left the room with her small cadre of humans in tow. Scratch followed them down the stairs and back outside to the street, where they paused once more. Elaine was clearly agitated, her arms doing that highly animated flapping thing humans did when they were upset. She was talking in hushed tones, and her cheeks were flushed.

The other uniformed humans departed. Elaine looked down to Scratch and gave him a good pet for the first time since they'd arrived here. "We have a mission, Scratch."

Scratch loved missions. Just not right this second, given his biological needs, but he was a dog with a strong sense of loyalty and would do whatever was required as long as Elaine was leading.

They marched back down the street. Scratch looked around for a patch of grass, or a fire hydrant, or even a bicycle rack, but found nothing. He did see another dog coming this way, a mixed terrier spaniel who trotted happily beside its life guide.

"Hello! Excuse me!" he called to the other dog in dog-speak. "Could I trouble you for directions to a lavatory in the general vicinity?"

"No trouble at all, good sir!" the dog replied enthusiastically. All dogs talked this way.

The dog signaled with its head toward a series of white squares with holes in their centers that lined the edge of a nearby building. Each square had its own faucet to rinse away the waste. Scratch regarded the setup with derision. How was any dog supposed to pick up its scent? It made no sense.

"Thank you ever so much, dear friend!" Scratch barked as they passed each other.

"Enjoy your stay here! Life is beautiful!" the dog said over its shoulder.

"It is, it really is, but where are we?" Scratch tried to crane his head as they continued to walk, but the other dog was out of range and didn't answer. Oh well. What a nice guy, though. All dogs were swell.

Scratch whined to Elaine and tugged on the leash toward the pristine white squares, but instead of paying attention, Elaine held her course toward a tall glass tube. An elevator shaft, one of several that rose into the oddly contorted sky at intervals throughout this... place. Scratch couldn't recall seeing any other elevators rise into thin air like that. Just one more thing to further confuse him. Seriously, where were they?

The elevator arrived. They stepped aboard, and Elaine scooped him into her arms. His little tail began puttering like a metronome on overdrive. His mood soured quickly, however.

The view out the clear windows of the elevator shifted immediately as they rose. As they exited through a hole in the "sky," suddenly the vista of the Milky Way was spread before them, as though a blanket featuring the celestial heavens had been draped over the elevator. They continued straight up along a metal shaft with framework that occasionally obscured their view. The shaft connected the ring they'd just left to the central core of the spaceship like a spoke of a bicycle wheel. Two more rings could be seen looming beyond the one they'd just left, for the glorious city below them was indeed built along the inside of a ring.

Arranged from smallest to largest, each ring rotated around the ship's core. In some deep recess of Scratch's doggy mind, he intrinsically understood the reason for the rotation: the *Aching Teeth Effect*.

Slinging anything in a circle pushed it away from the center. Once, Scratch himself had been slung around in a circle by a rather mean boy who was supposed to be taking him for a walk. The abuse had come from nowhere and for no reason that Scratch could imagine. Suddenly he'd found himself flying in a circle, desperately hanging on to his leash with his teeth. If he let go, he'd surely be choked by his own collar.

With teeth aching and legs flailing, Scratch finally convinced his tormentor with a fierce stare and a firm growl that this game was a very bad idea. The boy let go, and Scratch crashed in a spray of dust, rolling across a dirt field. When they got home, Scratch's life guide (at the time) noticed the scrapes on his legs and dismissed the boy, who never came by again.

The bad memory encouraged Scratch to snuggle ever deeper into Elaine's arms as the elevator continued up toward the central core of the ship. Suddenly, they began to float. It was an odd feeling, like being underwater, only less wet. Scratch had felt it before and assumed humans had invented some new form of dry water that you could breathe. What would you even call that? Airter? Watair? And why would you fill this ship with it?

Scratch waited until the elevator stopped before lifting his head. He could see the concern printed on Elaine's face. Dogs were very attuned to their life guides' facial expressions. He figured a good face lick was in order and gave Elaine a particularly sloppy one. She brushed him back but smiled.

The doors opened, and they floated into the windowless expanse of the ship's core. It was a long tunnel, brilliantly illuminated, and twice as wide as the walkway they'd just left. There were no buildings, or other definable features beyond the elevators, making it impossible to tell which way was up or down in this *watair* environment.

There were other people here too, floating down the corridor. Most progressed using handrails located along the edges, but some wore garishly large boots that stuck to the surface. They tromped around like quasi-robots. It was all completely nonsensical to a dog, especially given the complete absence of bushes.

Be strong, Scratch, he told himself. Dog bladders are designed to match the standard quarter-mile spacing between city fire hydrants, but this place was getting ridiculous.

"This way." Elaine floated toward another elevator, much to Scratch's dismay. Instead of pushing a button, this time Elaine placed her hand against a flat panel beside the elevator and the doors obliged. Scratch hid his face once more, but the descent was far shorter, and they were out again in a minute.

They were somewhere new. Somewhere depressing. Much like the long corridor they'd just left, this place was windowless, but it was hardly lit at all. It was another curving gerbil wheel but far more narrow, with drab, blocky buildings interspersed by large machines that clanked and whirred along with a dull thrumming that filled the air, giving Scratch an instant headache. The place smelled like the wrong end of a truck.

The wheel curved dramatically upward. As they walked, more people passed by, but unlike the gleaming city ring, they were dressed in gray uniforms that sagged and drooped as much as the bags beneath their downcast eyes. They shuffled about, looking more harried than hopeful, and studiously avoided eye contact with Elaine or Scratch.

There were no other dogs here. Or greenery. Scratch was going to lose this battle of doggy-doodle control before much longer, and the looming catastrophe wasn't going to be pretty. He bit his lip.

They stopped at perhaps the drabbest building of the bunch, and that was saying something. Elaine entered with Scratch in tow. Two men in official-looking uniforms (like Elaine's, only brown) stood at attention beside a thin man at a long desk. Elaine marched right up to him and slid the screen across the desk. From the angry way she held her hands on hips, and from the disinterested expression on the man's face, Scratch had to assume he was the keeper of these evil screens.

"What is the meaning of this screen and its foul, dastardly badness?" Scratch translated Elaine.

The man sneered, and his bushy mustache twitched with sardonic derision.

"It is not your business, female," he replied shortly.

"I will make it my business. I am important, and I will demonstrate my importance by slamming my fist upon your desk." Elaine proceeded to do so.

"I am unimpressed," Bushy Stache said drolly. The other men beside him turned to face Elaine, looking combative. Scratch's heckles went up.

Elaine assessed the situation, then retrieved the evil screen and tucked it under her arm once more. "I will have more words about this."

"You won't." The man gestured to the door, and Elaine stormed out, with Scratch giving them all his best steely glare before following after her. He could probably take them. He'd do it for Elaine.

Elaine paused outside the doors. Normally she was adept at controlling her emotions, but this time she couldn't hide her anger. She looked about ready to pop her cork.

As she stood there attempting to regain control, the doors opened behind them, and a phalanx of guards burst forth like a pack of wolves in formation. Or dingoes. Scratch growled menacingly, although of late his growl didn't seem to instill deathly fear in humans. He'd work on that.

The leader of this pack placed a rough hand on Elaine's shoulder. "We will escort you to the elevators," he said, a burly man who seemed built like a tank.

Elaine shrugged the hand off and straightened herself. "You have no authority to do that."

"We are bad people doing bad things, and you are impeding our evil plot," said the man. "You are banished from our villainous lair."

Scratch couldn't hold it any longer. This man was clearly the enemy, and if anyone deserved this, it was him. Scratch emptied his bladder on the man's leg.

The man howled with surprise and drew a long metal rod from his belt, hoisting it over his head. Elaine quickly grabbed Scratch and ran, holding him tight as he squirmed.

Now the man was cursing angrily with his weapon still raised. Elaine retreated to the elevator. The guards formed a wall behind them with Tank McMeaty still shouting the whole way.

At last, they stepped into the elevator, the doors closed, and silence reigned again. Scratch hid his head once more inside her arms, and she stroked his fur with particular fervor.

He shut his eyes tight and attempted to make sense of the human conflict. Elaine was clearly important, but she seemed to have authority only over those in silver uniforms. Bushy Stache and Tank McMeaty were in charge of the brown-uniformed humans, and thus were the masterminds of this evil plot involving screens. Two diametrically opposed factions, at war with each other. Why couldn't humans just get along? Some things were beyond doggy comprehension. But if his reckoning was right, Scratch did not regret his choice of lavatory.

Elaine snuggled him close, and as they drifted from the elevator floor once more, she leaned her head against his and whispered into his ear. "Tonight, Scratch. Tonight."

18   JAILHOUSE SHOCK

"IT'S BEEN, LIKE, six hours."

Prisha's back was to the wall of her cell, head lolling to the side. Her legs ached. Her butt ached. Everything ached. Her sad excuse for a bed, minimal padding and a dozen springs sticking up, was less comfortable than sitting on the metal floor. She supposed the toilet next to it was comfier, but she wasn't about to sit on that all day. She had her dignity.

Captain Mohs didn't. He was whistling something from his cell, directly across from Prisha's, as he sat on his toilet. Blessedly, there was a small wall for privacy that blocked all but Mohs's legs sticking out. The one redeeming feature of their cells.

"Forget it, Prish, we're not getting out of here. Maybe if we're lucky, they'll move us to larger cells, or let us stretch our legs in a jail yard, or hey! Maybe even a meal! Wouldn't that be something?"

Prisha's stomach growled fiercely. "This is inhumane. It's one thing to send an assault team down to L3 in the middle of the night, drug us, abduct us, carry us like sacks of potatoes onto a starship, whisk us off to who knows where for who knows how long, and throw us in jail cells the size of closets that smell like a barnyard, but..." She trailed off. "I was going somewhere with this..."

"No food," chimed Mohs.

"Right, but to not even feed us is ridiculous!"

"At least we have each other for company," Chase called out. Prisha leaned her head against the bars and could just make out Chase doing the same two cells down across the hall. Between Chase and

Mohs, Amanda lay sprawled on the floor of her cell, her head against the bars. Apparently, she too had a mattress not even a bedbug would find comfortable. Which, considering how new this spaceship had to be, seemed even more ludicrous that the designers of the ship purposely added lumpy and broken mattresses to the jail cells.

Prisha felt and heard a thumping noise coming from the other side of her wall. "Reg, please stop banging your head against your cell again," she said.

The banging stopped. "I'm hoping I'll black out and forget this all happened," Reginald's muffled voice replied.

"You shouldn't be intentionally trying to induce amnesia," Amanda scolded him. "That's serious brain injury!"

"It's better than this," answered Reginald. There was a pause, and then Reginald began reciting in a dry, empty voice, "No spitting, no urinating beyond your toilet, no uppity attitudes, no inkling of collusion, no expectations of a fair trial or any trial whatsoever. All violators shall be dealt with in accordance with their infraction, including the blasting of loud noises at all hours, use of a hot branding iron, and possible expulsion from the ship, regardless of its location."

Prisha sighed. "And there's no need to read the jail house rules, Reg. We all see them." They were engraved on the wall of each cell and had provided the only real entertainment for these past six hours.

Prisha looked at her four walls. She was accustomed to living in cramped quarters—she'd been raised in a small apartment with several siblings, back in India. Ordinarily, she found intimate confines somewhat reassuring, which she supposed was why she enjoyed being in the cockpit of a spaceplane. She didn't expect the others to share that sentiment, especially given these conditions.

The one silver lining was the knowledge that not all of them were here. Scratch, of course, was somewhere else on this ship with Elaine. But it wasn't just Scratch who still lived in freedom. Prisha smiled as she thought about the night of their capture. Not that she had any memory of it, or that being drugged, abducted, and incarcerated was something worth smiling over. She smiled because Claire and Razor weren't with them. She smiled because somehow, those two had evaded their assailants and were undoubtedly still at large on L3.

Her smile faded. There was no way for Claire and Razor to help them now. No chance that they could somehow smuggle themselves aboard, bust out Razor's bag of tools, take out a hundred guards, and improvise a key to their cells from a few strands of wire. Actually, Prisha could imagine most of that, given their skills, but not the part where they were able to board the ship. If her intuition was correct, the ship had left L3 behind and was now bound for distant stars. They'd been shanghaied, with no hope of rescue.

Mohs was singing again, something about a drunk who needed someone to show him the way to go home. Prisha groaned and covered her ears.

****

Prisha awoke. She lifted her head groggily from the lumpy mattress and looked about her cell for the source of her awakening. It could have just been her immense discomfort that jolted her from sleep. Or her stomach practically eating itself from hunger. Or Mohs's snoring.

She had no idea what time it was. It would be night back at the jungle houses on L3, but not necessarily night here. Prisha shoved knuckles in her eyes and sat up. Beyond Mohs's snores, there were no sounds. Yet something told her things were amiss. Besides the fact they were still jailed and starving, of course.

Prisha walked to the bars and looked out, straining her ears. Yes, there *was* something. A scuffling sound, barely audible, coming from the door that sealed their cells from whatever was outside. She thought she could even make out muffled shouting. That she heard such a muffled sound at all snapped her out of her daze.

The ship's engines have stopped!

No question, the low-frequency vibration that had permeated the jail cell a few hours before was gone. Her inner ear confirmed a lack of acceleration. The Centauri Starliner—the enormous ship in which they were no doubt confined—was no longer accelerating. They were either stopped or coasting.

A loud bang rang out, and everyone in the cell block was instantly awake. Mohs fell off his cot. "Abandon ship! Captains first! Specifically, me!"

The bang came again, from the other side of the door. As the prisoners waddled bleary-eyed to their cell bars, the jailhouse door slid open. An unconscious figure slumped into the hall, a thin man with a shaggy mustache, dressed in a brown uniform. Another figure stepped over him, silver uniform, long blond hair, a buzzing electrical wand in one hand and a smile on her lips.

"COCO Puff!"

Her smile weakened. "Elaine, if you please. I'm busting you out."

Amanda squealed with joy. Then her eyes settled on the fuzzy creature behind Elaine, and her squeal rose to an octave high enough to break glass. "SCRAAAATCH!"

The small dog leapt over the unconscious guard, tongue out, ears up, tail practically puttering it through the air, as it raced to Amanda's cell. She reached through the tight bars and petted his mottled fur as tears streamed down her face.

Elaine stopped at Prisha's cell first, placing her hand to a sensor on the outside of the door. It swung inward with a click. "You're a spaceplane pilot, right?"

Prisha nodded.

"Good. Time to get off this ship. I have a plan, and it's a good one, but we'd better hurry."

Elaine repeated the process with each cell door, until all five prisoners stood in the narrow hallway, savoring their newfound freedom. Elaine pulled the mustached guard by his arms into one of the cells, closing it behind him.

They filed out wordlessly (or, in Amanda's case, stifling sobs of joy in Scratch's fur). Beyond the cell block was a featureless hall that ended in a wide room with a long desk. More unconscious guards were drooped against walls or spread-eagled on the ground, littering the room like rag dolls casually discarded by an untidy child.

Reginald gaped. "You did all of this? Single-handed?"

"Actually, I used both hands," Elaine replied with a sly grin. She slipped the zapping wand into a holster on her hip. "The guards didn't leave me much choice, or perhaps I should say, they didn't have much choice in the matter themselves. Mind-controlled, I'm afraid."

"Mind-controlled?" Mohs mouthed a "told you so" to Prisha.

Elaine grabbed one of the knocked-out guards by his uniform shirt. Just above the pocket was a bulge covered by a wire mesh. Some kind of electronic device had been stitched directly into the cloth.

"It's a Dynamic Universal Brain Modulator. Dynamo for short since the acronym was a little too close to a word with negative connotations. Dynamos are used for—shall we say—adjusting the attitude of the wearer. The artificial intelligence that is built into them uses verbal suggestions that are reinforced by EM frequencies that literally rearrange neural patterns. Turns the guards into sheep. The device is always on but does its best work when the wearer is binge-watching reality TV or mindlessly scrolling through social media."

"Great, a zombie apocalypse," said Reginald. Was it Prisha's imagination, or did he actually sound exhilarated by this concept?

"So why not just destroy it?" Chase asked.

"Required equipment for security guards, with each unit tuned to the brain of the individual wearer. To tell you the truth, some of these guys like the idea of not having to think for themselves. Sure, I could take a hammer to this one, but there are two hundred more like it. No, I need to get to the server that houses the Dynamo AI. Here, I'll show you." She tapped three times on the mesh stitching and the Dynamo came to life, figuratively and literally.

"How may I better influence your inner subliminal thoughts today?" it asked in a slightly judgmental voice.

"Access master system settings," Elaine ordered it.

"My voice recognition software suggests you are not authorized for that action. But good news! Crew members who are not currently wearing Version 1.0 of the Dynamic Universal Brain Modulator can contact Crew Services to have units inserted free of charge into each article of clothing so that I may enhance your mood and ability to follow orders blindly. Good day." It turned itself off.

"You see the problem," Elaine said, glaring at the embedded device. "Now that I've triggered Operation Sleeping Beauty, I'm dependent on non-brainwashed personnel to help. We've already locked Kornback in his room, and I've knocked out a few of his goons, but we'll need to disable these Dynamos if we're ever going to take full command of the ship."

"Mutiny!" Mohs exclaimed. When the others looked at him, the captain added, "In the best way. The good kind of mutiny."

Elaine smiled. "I'll explain more in the elevator. We need to get moving."

Elaine escorted them through the doors and out into a dim and dirty street. "Now act normal. We're not exactly alone here."

Prisha gawked at their surroundings, a back alleyway lined by dark buildings ugly enough to make a warehouse look exciting. Machines whirred. Electrical generators buzzed. Gears turned. The place smelled like grease. Stooped denizens shuffled through a dreary workhouse scene that could have been plucked from a Dickens novel.

"No time for a tour," Elaine said a tad briskly. "Not that this place has much to see, anyway. This is where Kornback keeps his lowest-paid workers, and by lowest-paid I really mean indentured servants. Forced to work for little or no money, strung along on empty promises and futile dreams, with a nonbinding expectation that they may, someday, become valued members of the crew. Basically, interns."

Prisha felt for these wretches, but Elaine led them cautiously but swiftly toward an elevator shaft not far down the walkway. The L3 group's tattered and nonuniform clothing was already eliciting stares, but every time Prisha tried to make eye contact, the workers looked away hastily. She wouldn't put it past them to call security, though.

They reached the elevator. Elaine placed her palm to a scanner and gave a small sigh of relief when it opened. They stepped in and began to rise up the shaft. Clear windows gave a view out to a complex web of structural beams. For a brief moment the elevator passed into a gap where the view opened up.

They were just beneath a central hub that ran the length of the enormous ship. Three gargantuan rings rotated around the hub, dwarfing the small ring they'd just left. The surfaces of the rings were checkered by lit windows, giving them an appearance of gracefully curving hotels rotating across a starry night sky.

Elaine pointed to the forward end of the ship. "We'll head to the hangar bay. If we're quiet, we may be able to sneak aboard Kornback's personal spaceplane."

"Can you take us home?" Amanda asked. Scratch's eyes brightened too.

Elaine shook her head. "It's not designed for that, but if my plan succeeds, we'll get you back to Earth one way or another. First, we need to return to MERS, the planet you call L3."

"We?" asked Prisha. She gave Elaine an assessing look. "You're coming too?"

Elaine nodded. "Here's the dilemma. Let's say I manage to get into the Dynamo server room. I can't just blow it up, or even turn it off. There are several hundred people who could die on the spot, or at the very least have their minds scrambled. No, I need that AI still functioning, but I have to convince it to change. Persuade it to become a better version of itself. And I think I know how."

"Send it to a motivational seminar?" Reginald asked.

"Unleash the Hidden Millionaire Inside YOU!" Mohs said. "I went to that one."

Elaine waved them off. "No, the answer is down on MERS. L3. Whatever. We operate several corporate vacation homes on the planet. One of them is more of Kornback's personal shag pad, but that's another story."

Elaine became deadly serious. "There's a device down there. I've seen it. It looks like an oversized mobile phone, and it houses an earlier model of the artificial intelligence that runs these Dynamos. The AI in that model was somewhat more devious, which is probably why they didn't put it into production. That, plus it was too big and didn't fit very well into your pocket."

"So, let me get this straight," Mohs said. "You need to go back to L3 to snag an older mind-controlling attitude adjuster who will then adjust the attitude of a newer mind-controlling attitude adjuster."

"Spot-on." Elaine shrugged. "I admit it's a long shot, but it's all I've got. First steps first. To get down to the planet, I need a spaceplane, and I'm no pilot. That's where you two come in." She gestured to Prisha and Mohs. Prisha didn't know how to respond, so she gave a half smile. Mohs looked thoroughly baffled.

Amanda lifted Scratch to the elevator window. "So, you see, Scratch, we're going to sneak through a heavily guarded starship, beguile our way onto a spaceplane, and fly away before anyone's the wiser! It's a big adventure, kind of like going to the park!"

Scratch had been whimpering from under his paws, but his tail wagged at the mention of a walk in the park. The elevator passed through the outer structure of the central hub and slowed.

"Act casual, follow me, and we'll be fine," Elaine said.

They all lifted off the elevator floor as gravity reduced to zero. They had arrived at the very center of the ship.

"Back to L3!" Reginald shouted and was quickly shushed by everyone.

The elevator doors opened. Elaine exited first, silently signaling toward the end of a vast, dimly lit corridor. It was night here too, or simulated night, but they weren't completely alone. A woman in a silver uniform like Elaine's passed by, the magnets in her shoes clumping awkwardly along what served as a floor. She paid them no notice.

Further down, the corridor ended at an oversized circular steel door. A brown-suited guard was slumped in a chair, and while his shoes were firmly attached to the floor, his head bobbed in weightless sleep.

Elaine held a finger to her lips. They pushed off handrails and floated past the guard. Prisha's heart was beating so loud she was surprised the man didn't wake up. Just as they reached the steel door, the corridor's subdued lighting suddenly switched to flashing red. A ringing alarm sounded.

"Uh-oh," Elaine said.

The guard woke up, seeming startled to find himself at work, stunned that an alarm had sounded, and shocked to find out that a group of most-wanted, jail-breaking criminals were hovering just a few feet away. He fumbled for the electric wand secured at his hip with panic in his eyes.

Elaine was faster. She closed the gap between them and jabbed her own wand into his ribs. Sparks popped. The man thrashed fishlike, then went limp. Elaine grabbed his hand and forced it onto a scanner at his workstation.

"Sorry about that," she muttered, looking genuinely apologetic. "He'll wake up with an epic headache." The steel door parted, they floated through, and Elaine shut it behind them before any other guards could interfere.

The ship's central corridor had been large, but they had now entered a truly cavernous room. Spotlights lit a row of gleaming spaceplanes, each hooked into tie-down brackets on the floor. A massive shield door stood at a curving wall where a large window revealed stars and the vacuum of space outside.

It was a hangar for spaceflight operations, but more than that, it was also an emergency evacuation center. Spaced every few feet around the curving wall, dozens of open hatches led into egg-shaped pods attached to the outside of the ship. Each pod had a circular seating area big enough for at least twenty people. Numbered signs above each hatch provided evacuation instructions. They appeared to be lifeboats, ready for whatever emergency this starship might encounter in its long voyage.

"Aim carefully!" Elaine pushed off and sailed toward the largest of the spaceplanes on the far side of the hangar. The rest followed, not quite as gracefully but in the general direction. Behind them, a loud pounding on the steel door made it clear they didn't have long. So much for stealth.

They reached the spaceplane, each person grabbing whatever fin, wing flap, or strut within range to arrest their motion. The sleek plane was Kornback's personal cruiser, Elaine explained. It was about twice the size of old N6A Whatever, with gold trim and nary a ding or a scratch on it. Elaine placed her palm on the scanner by the door, but nothing happened. She tried typing an override code on a keypad, but the door remained sealed. She cursed loudly, and quite saltily.

"Looks like Kornback's limo won't be available. We'll have to take two of the smaller spaceplanes." She hopped over to the next plane, half the size, but just as sleek. When she planted a palm, its door didn't open either. She tried the next, and the next. All were locked.

"Here's one," Reginald yelled. He was right, the door to the spaceplane stood wide open. By the looks of tools scattered around, it was probably being worked on by the hangar crew.

Elaine floated over. "One spaceplane isn't enough. Unfortunately, they have weight limits, so I'm afraid we can't all fit."

Banging on the hangar entrance became giant thumps that shook the floor. Were they using a medieval battering ram?

Elaine looked pale. "Sorry, this is not going as smoothly as I'd hoped. But we still have a chance. We could all fit in an escape pod. They have push-button controls and are designed to land at predetermined safe points, including down on L3, but it's a one-way trip. We'll need at least one spaceplane, or we'll never get back to the ship. I suggest we split up."

She glanced back and forth between the two pilots in their group, clearly trying to ascertain how this split would occur. Captain Mohs patted one of the rockets attached to the spaceplane's fuselage. A stenciled red label warned to stay away from its business end.

"You know, I got behind the wheel of a friend's Maserati once," Mohs said like they had all the time in the world. "Crashed it right through a fence into a chicken coop. Splinters and feathers everywhere. Lots of casualties. This souped-up rocket plane thing has that same Maserati feel. Honestly, I think we're all better off if I stick to pushing buttons on your automated lifeboat."

With another loud bang, the hangar door opened partially. Two guards in brown uniforms squeezed through. They looked appropriately pissed off. One was built like a tank. The other bore a black eye. Doubtless he had been on the receiving end of Elaine's jailbreak.

"I'll fly it," Prisha volunteered as Tank McMeaty and Mash-Eye sailed toward them, arms waving and cattle-prod wands zapping. "Even a juiced-up spaceplane is still a spaceplane. How hard can it be?"

"I'll come with you," Chase offered without hesitation.

Elaine didn't dither. She didn't have time. "Push the red button on the panel to open the hangar bay airlock. We're not far from L3, you'll see it once you get outside. Meet us at the Fjord House, in the far north!"

She leaped away, aiming directly toward a nearby escape pod. Amanda and Reg followed with equally accurate leaps. Mohs vacillated a moment longer, clearly second-guessing himself.

"Captain, go!" Prisha pleaded with him, glancing at the approaching guards. "I can do this. Chase will help me."

Mohs seemed to be struggling with big emotions. He gave a wan smile, and his eyes twinkled with pride. "The apprentice is becoming the master. Have a great flight and watch out for any chickens."

And with those words of enlightenment, Mohs pushed off to join the others.

19   THE FAR NORTH

PRISHA DUCKED AS one of the brown-suited guards (the guy built like a tank) flew past. He reached out with his electric prod, narrowly missing her head, and cursing loudly as his momentum carried him on. His partner, Mash-Eye, didn't fare any better, deflecting off the tail of a spaceplane while trying to grab Elaine, Mohs, Amanda, and Reginald. They piled into the nearest escape pod, slammed the hatch shut, and blasted off into space. They'd be on a predefined trajectory back to L3 toward what Elaine had called the Fjord House.

There's a house on L3? How did we miss that?

There was no time to ponder what other features were still hidden down on L3's surface. Several more guards had already squeezed through the dented frame of the hangar's entrance and were heading their way, albeit drifting through the air. Chase helped Prisha unhook the tie-downs, and they both ducked inside the souped-up spaceplane with rocket engines on either side.

A Maserati, Captain Mohs had called it. Prisha would find out soon enough if she could fly it. *Nothing like on-the-job training!*

The job, in this case, was not too dissimilar from grand theft auto, though, perversely, if they failed to steal this spaceplane, they'd be thrown back into Kornback's dreary jail.

It was true, the rocket plane had a physical resemblance to spaceplanes she'd flown before. Twin tails and stubby wings. But the pivoting engines on either side of the fuselage made it clear there would be added complexity in their getaway.

"Hurry!" Chase declared.

Prisha didn't need any encouragement. She slammed the hatch closed, turned the interior handle clockwise, and thanked her training for teaching her that, once locked, no one on the outside would be able to open it. Fists banging on the spaceplane door were about to test that theory.

"This might be a very short flight," she told Chase. They both took seats at the front. Prisha quickly found the power switch, lighting up both the physical control panel and its holographic counterparts that appeared above their heads.

"I have complete faith in you," Chase said. "See, you've already got the controls figured out."

Ignoring Chase's misplaced faith, Prisha nervously scanned the displays. The more she studied, the more she felt a growing unease that Captain Mohs had been right. This was no Mark 4 or even Mark 7 spaceplane. Subpanels with names like *Fuel Management System* and *Flight Mode Annunciators* were covered with virtual toggles, buttons, dials, and complex color graphics. It was like trying to decipher Egyptian hieroglyphics written in Japanese.

How hard could it be? Prisha gulped as her own words came back to haunt her. But there was no turning back. She'd promised to steal a spaceplane and now it was time to go full bandit mode—assuming those guys outside hadn't already bolted them to the floor.

Luckily, there were a few familiar items as well: reentry shields, landing gear, radio. And the seat belt light turned green once Chase finished buckling up. Good news there, she'd take what she could get.

Chase pointed out the windshield to a massive floor-to-ceiling door directly ahead. "Elaine mentioned a red button for the airlock."

Prisha nodded, returning her attention to one of the overhead displays. "Um… probably this panel."

Though it wasn't particularly red, she pressed a button marked *Airlock Egress,* and the massive door slowly slid open, revealing a second door beyond it that included a window looking out to stars.

"Did I mention how amazing you are?" Chase said.

It was a small win, but if Chase could show confidence, she could at least pretend she knew what she was doing. She fumbled with several switches on the *Propulsion Systems* panel but eventually got both rockets started. A coarse rumble outside made it clear this plane was no glider. The banging on the spaceplane hatch also stopped. Maybe the guards had just been blasted halfway across the hangar.

A physical joystick positioned on her left armrest was marked *Pitch.* She ever so gently tipped the stick forward. The powerful twin rockets delicately tilted. The plane slid forward into the airlock.

"Oh, you're good," Chase said, winking.

Prisha beamed. "Not bad for my first powered flight, huh?"

Her nervousness dissipated, but only for a minute. Shouting came from behind. Though muted by the roar of the engines, they were yelling something about aiming a *pluff* weapon, whatever that was. She didn't want to find out and clicked a button that closed the inner airlock door behind them.

"Whenever you're ready," Chase encouraged. There was little chance any of the guards were dumb enough to have followed them into the airlock. They'd certainly know what was next.

Another button drained the lock of its air, then opened the outer door. Cold, dark space lay ahead. A splash of stars spread across the view, but there was no sign of L3 or even the sun.

Prisha bit her lip. "It's going to get harder from here."

"Think of it like riding a horse."

"I've never ridden a horse. Or stolen one. Or even petted one."

"My point exactly."

Prisha waved a nervous hand in front of complex displays. "Horses don't have pivot controls. Or air intake manifolds, or fuel mixture ratios. And I don't even want to guess what that thing does." She pointed to a red stick with a rounded top that poked straight up from the center of the panel.

"You'll figure it out." Chase craned his neck to look behind. Perhaps the guards were setting up their weapon.

She'd read about rocket-powered spaceplanes. They used rockets while in space but could switch to a conventional jet engine when flying through air. It would make sense for the Starliner to have a hangar full of them. Kornback's people were heading to distant planets. They need to be ready to land almost anywhere. L3 had been their testing arena.

Prisha took a deep breath and pushed the joystick forward. The plane obeyed, mostly. They were slightly askew, and the right wing scraped the door frame on their way out. Prisha cringed, but there wasn't anything to do about it.

"A small battle scar," Chase said with the wave of a hand.

No emergency lights had flashed on, so perhaps the damage was superficial. She pushed again on the joystick, and they picked up speed.

"I'm trying!"

"You're succeeding!"

Prisha banked right to reveal the full length of the Centauri Starliner out the right-side windows. The three rotating rings filled the sky. The smallest loomed closest, still big enough to blot out half the stars. It twisted slowly around the ship's central axis with lit windows suggesting an audience might be watching their departure. Prisha double-checked the exterior lights panel—all lights remained off. The spaceplane was as black as she could make it.

No laser cannons shot in their direction. As they moved further out, the next-largest ring appeared from behind the first. The enormous wheel was big enough to hold a city along its interior surface. Randomly lit windows around the circumference gave it the appearance of a circular skyscraper where only a few residents were still awake late at night.

The third and biggest ring was next. Prisha arced well beyond its edge. As their flight path lifted above the big ship's shadow, sunlight illuminated the cabin. She pushed a slider and the twin rockets roared behind them. Best to leave quickly, if not silently.

Chase smiled. "What an expert! You've done this before, haven't you?"

"You might want to hold your five-star review until we're on the ground." L3 was probably somewhere in the opposite direction of the Starliner's course, so she headed aft.

They quickly passed the tail end of the Centauri Starliner, where eight enormous engine nozzles protruded like giant church bells, silent for now. As Elaine had promised, the ship's propulsion had been shut down. The Starliner was coasting.

Beyond the ship was a sea of stars. A slightly brighter blue-green dot lay directly ahead.

"L3?" she asked.

"Got to be."

Prisha relaxed tensed muscles. With rockets at full power, it wouldn't take long to get there. Then just pop down to the surface, cruise around until they found Elaine's Fjord House, and take care of business on the ground. An hour later—two at the most—they'd ferry Elaine and the others back to the Starliner. Mission accomplished.

The dot soon grew into a more familiar blue-green sphere. Prisha tweaked the rocket tilt joystick to get their course lined up while keeping another hand on the control wheel. It wouldn't become effective until they hit the atmosphere, but it seemed like something she didn't want to forget.

She took another deep breath. "At least we've landed here once before."

"Try to keep the wings on this time," Chase offered.

"All we need is a nice wide sandy beach."

"Lucky for us, there are plenty of them down there." As positive as he'd been, Prisha couldn't help but notice that Chase was tightly gripping the sides of his seat.

The blue-green sphere approached, faster than expected. Prisha backed off on the rocket power, but they didn't slow down by much.

"Our approach seems a bit hasty," Chase said. His tone was calm, but the seat squeaked from his grip. Puffy white clouds covered much of L3's surface. Today was probably an alternate rain day.

Slowing down was always tricky for any sleek airplane. Coming in from space would be even harder. Prisha flicked the joystick in an attempt to reverse the thrust, probably too hard, and they lurched sideways.

The mini planet now filled the windshield. Chase grimaced. Prisha's fingers scrambled across mostly unfamiliar controls. They hit the top of the atmosphere like a speeding car hits a snowbank. The plane rattled and groaned. Clouds shot past the windows. Prisha finally found a switch with the label she'd been seeking: *Reverse Thrust.* She pressed. A loud roar erupted, and they were thrown forward into their seat harnesses.

The plane exploded out the bottom of a cloud that never knew what had hit it. A turquoise sea spread out beneath them.

"Over there!" Chase pointed to a patch of land.

Prisha banked hard right, and the plane responded like any airplane. She was back in control, but too low and still too fast. Ahead was a narrow beach. It was certainly long enough to make a good landing strip, but they were coming in perpendicular to it.

Prisha fiddled with the rocket pivot control, but it was like jumping into a new video game with no practice. Overcompensation drove them higher. Backing off drove them lower but picked up speed. The sand approached much too rapidly. She lowered the landing gear.

"This is going to be close! Hang on!"

Just as they crossed waves breaking on the shore, Prisha banked hard left and flipped the rockets to a hover position. Sand blew out all around them and they smacked the ground with an unambiguous thump, bounced up, then thumped again to a sudden stop.

She quickly shut down the engines. They waited in silence as the cloud of dust around them settled.

"Welcome to L3," Chase said. "Again."

They clambered out the hatch and onto a tropical beach as beautiful as any they'd visited on this very special—and artificial—planet. There were no footsteps in the sand. No hammocks, lean-tos, or houses off in the jungle. It was hard to tell how far away they might be from their former home, but it was clear this beach was someplace new.

The spaceplane sat half-buried in sand. Air intakes on the leading edge of the wings had taken the brunt of their abrupt landing. Prisha scooped out several handfuls of sand from between polished aluminum louvers. She tossed the sand in the air. "I'm afraid our stolen plane may be out of commission until we can get a major service."

Chase gave her a quick hug. "Hey, there's nothing broken this time, including us. That last turn was pretty exciting. You did well."

Prisha smiled. "Experienced spaceplane thief! I'll add it to my resume."

"I wonder where we are."

"And where Elaine's Fjord House might be."

They scanned the horizon—water in most directions, though the beach continued for a good distance. Chase studied the sun, then pointed down the beach. "That way is north. Roughly."

"Then off we go to the far north!"

"Sounds snowy."

"Yeah. I wonder if we'll need coats."

"We don't even have food or water. Or a compass."

Prisha scrunched one eye. "Let's at least remember where we parked."

She glanced to the sky, searching for any sign of the Centauri Starliner. They were probably a million kilometers away by now with Kornback screaming about prison escapees. Elaine seemed to think her plan to take control of the Starliner still had a chance, but first, they'd need to find Elaine.

They set off down the beach, their first steps in what would probably be an epic quest attempted by not-fully-prepared protagonists. Luckily, L3 was small, so as long as the beach held out, they could reach the north pole or anyplace else on the planet in a few hours.

As they marched, Chase estimated the likelihood that the polar regions of L3 had ice and snow. He guessed the planet was too small to have significant climate zones except when climbing vertically, where even a medium-sized hill could bring you close to the edge of space. But north probably wouldn't be much different than any other location.

That notion didn't last long.

An hour later, they crossed an isthmus of sand and said goodbye to the last of the palm trees. Ahead, grass-covered hills rose to treeless gray mountains with rounded tops that reached nearly to cloud level. The walk remained relatively easy. They alternately crossed green meadows and smooth rock that formed boundaries around the grass. The air became cooler in this new land, but they never encountered any snow or ice. The higher they climbed, the more these rocky highlands felt like the wilds of Scotland.

"It's pretty up here," Prisha said, buttoning her jacket.

Chase cupped one hand against his mouth. "Yo de le ih hoo!"

"That's Switzerland."

"They yodel in Austria too, don't they?"

"I guess, but this feels more like Norway to me," Prisha said, plucking a white flower from one of the patches that bloomed along their way and giving it to Chase.

Chase sniffed the flower. "I have to say, for a cantankerous old guy Kornback managed to create a beautiful planet."

"He had help. Elaine seems nice, and I'm sure there are a lot more like her on the Starliner. At least, the ones wearing silver uniforms, not brown."

"I'm sure you're right. But it's still surprising to see a corporate design that turned out better than boring steel and concrete."

Prisha shrugged. "No reason to diss corporations, I'm employed by one of the biggest. Megalodon isn't such a bad place to work. We get thirty-five minutes for lunch. Forty, once you hit five years of service—*plus* they give you a gold-plated lapel pin *and* a coffee shop gift card!"

Chase nodded. "Unwavering benevolence."

"Well, when you put it that way. Where do you work?"

Chase stopped walking long enough to pick up a multicolored pebble. "Funny, you've never asked me that."

"You're a scientist, so I figured it was some secret government laboratory. You know, with lots of test tubes and beakers overflowing with bubbling liquids?" She laughed.

Chase threw the pebble in a long arc. Once again, gravity was getting lower as they climbed. "Honestly, I wouldn't know a beaker from a wine decanter. I work with sludge, the kind you don't want to let kids play in."

"That sounds... dirty."

"Worse than dirty, it's radioactive. We're training bacteria to consume plutonium waste slurries."

"And are the little guys trainable?"

"They either learn, or they die. You'd be surprised how fast natural selection combined with human encouragement can produce a microbe that does exactly what you want."

"So, no more plutonium waste? Chase saves the world?"

"Maybe. As long as Fred-16 hasn't suffocated in his petri dish by the time I get back to Earth."

"Fred-16?"

Chase laughed. "We name them. So far, the Fred line has done better than Barney. Betty did alright too, but she was no Wilma. Wilma was an absolute star at eating the sludge, but she produced too much hydrogen gas byproduct. Her genetic line burst into flames last December when one of the interns lit a Hanukkah candle."

"That's sad! Really, I know they're just microbes, but still..."

"Yeah, we get attached to them too. Cute little buggers."

Prisha gave Chase a sympathy hug and they moved on, crossing a particularly rocky stretch. Their trek ended quite suddenly at a sheer cliff.

They stared straight down to calm water several hundred feet below. Rock ledges stuck out beyond the cliff as if they'd been designed as photo spots for daredevils. Another cliff bounded the opposite side forming a classic deep-channeled fjord. There were no paths going down or up.

"Stunning scenery they have up here in fjordland, but now what?" Prisha asked. If their destination lay ahead, there was virtually no chance of getting across the chasm.

To their left, the fjord continued to the horizon, which wasn't that far given L3's tiny scale. If they walked in that direction, they'd eventually return to tropical beaches, maybe even back to their old stomping grounds and the wrecked spaceplane that was still sitting in the jungle. To the right, a taller outcrop of rocks blocked the view, but there was no reason to believe the chasm didn't continue in that direction too.

"Let's see what's around the corner." They would need to retreat downslope to get around the outcrop, but there weren't any better choices. Chase took the lead and after rounding the massive rock, he suddenly stopped.

Prisha nearly ran into him. "What?"

"Look." He pointed to a recess on the backside of the outcrop. Concrete steps led down to a steel door. It was clear proof that they weren't alone on this engineered planet and never had been.

Chase stepped down and rapped on the door. His pounding echoed, but no one answered. To be expected. A rusty padlock and dry leaves at the door's base made it clear this door hadn't been opened for some time.

Chase climbed back up. "Who knows what's down there."

"I say we keep going. If we've found one human-made structure, we must be getting close."

Chase nodded his agreement, and they continued around the rocky outcrop, eventually climbing back to the cliff's edge and a new view down the length of the fjord.

"Look, there it is!" Chase pointed across the chasm. A glint of sunlight reflected off curving glass that fronted a modern house built atop the opposite cliff. Except for a dramatic deck that hung out over the cliff's edge, the house blended into its rocky foundation as if someone had carved out a nook just the right size. Further along the cliff, a roaring waterfall poured off the edge and plunged hundreds of feet to the sea below.

"Wow! Stunning place! Not that I could afford it, but I'd love to book it for a weekend getaway."

"I think that's the point. This whole planet is a playground for corporate executives. Fjords, waterfalls. All this Nordic scenery. It's designed."

"And they did a great job, but if that's our rendezvous point with Elaine, how do we get across?"

Chase shrugged. "The steel door? There might be steps down to sea level."

Prisha peered over the edge. A cool breeze blew up from the depths. "No bridge at the bottom. We'd still be stuck on this side."

The inlet was probably no more than a hundred meters across, and they'd waded through stretches of L3's seas before, but that was back in the tropics, where shorelines sloped gradually. This plunge looked like it might continue well below the water's surface, possibly making the fjord the deepest water on the planet.

"Not sure I'd recommend a leap across," Chase said. Prisha wasn't about to try. The fall would be crippling or fatal.

"No argument from me."

Prisha studied the dramatic landscape all around them, then paused in thought. "Wait a second, there's something wrong here. Why build a stylish cliffside house for your executives to enjoy if it's impossible to get there?"

"Maybe they just land their spaceplanes on that side and never cross?"

"Then what's the steel door on this side for?"

Prisha paused, staring further along the cliff's edge. "That's odd." She twisted her head left, then right. Something was there. Something ghostly, hanging in the middle of the fjord. She took two steps to the right, then two more. "Holy cow, it's an illusion!"

"The house?"

"No, the fjord!"

"That's ridiculous." Chase picked up a small rock and threw it over the edge. It plunged to the water below, making a splash. "Real as real."

"Now throw one that way," Prisha said, pointing to her right.

Chase picked up a second rock and threw it. The rock sailed beyond the cliff edge, then hit something in midair and bounced along nothingness, eventually coming to rest in the sky halfway across the chasm. "Can't be!" he said.

"Is!"

"An invisible wall?"

They walked closer, and Prisha reached out to touch what looked like sky but turned out to be solid. "It's a backdrop! You know, like they used in old movies? They would set up a foreground with real bushes and trees, but the backdrop was just a huge canvas stretched across the stage, painted to look like distant mountains. We've made it to the edge of L3!"

Chase patted the sky wall, took a step back and stared again at the amazing optical illusion. It was indeed a backdrop of the sky and the fjord, almost like a mirror image of the real fjord to their left, but not a reflection. The false fjord to the right didn't duplicate the real fjord to the left—it extended it in a very natural way.

"It's a fake projection onto a real-world screen. Which means…" Chase took a step off the edge of the cliff. Prisha gasped, holding a hand over her mouth, but Chase's foot landed on something solid. He stood on air.

"There's even a rail here." His left hand gripped nothingness at hip height—yet it was nothingness as solid as any real railing.

He took several more steps out over the chasm. "Oh, well done, Kornback! The wall, the bridge, the rail, it's made out of some kind of material like a computer display. But shaped into a footbridge."

"How clever!" With her heart racing, Prisha took a tentative step onto what seemed to be empty air two hundred feet above water. The illusion was strengthened by the fact that real water and a real plunge were only a few feet to her left. When her hand found the invisible rail, her heart finally calmed.

Carefully, step by step, they made their way across the unlikely bridge, reaching the other side, where a very real waterfall plunged into the sea. A smaller bridge (also real) crossed a splashing creek that fed the waterfall.

Prisha stood in the middle of the creek bridge and looked back. Once again, the illusion produced a realistic fjord that continued into the distance—all fake.

"Why would they do that?" she wondered aloud. "If you can build a whole planet, why not just continue the real fjord? Why end the planet here?"

Chase shrugged. "Kornback seemed to be saying that L3, or MERS as he called it, was a testing ground for the Centauri Starliner. Maybe this visual fakery is technology they were testing. I have to admit, it would be handy to bring a version of Earth on a journey to the stars even if it's an illusion."

"Well, their test succeeded. The view doesn't look much different in either direction. It's a fjord, plucked right out of Norway. I guess that's the point of the house too. You get this dramatic view out your windows, but half of it isn't real. Kind of messes with your mind every day you wake up."

The house stood only a hundred yards further, beckoning them to knock on the door and see if anyone was home. Unless it was fake too.

They approached cautiously. Smooth stone gave way to a pathway of wood planks that weaved through a flower garden bordered by heather. Nondescript waterfowl paddled across a tiny pond that received its water from the nearby creek.

The house itself was single-story, composed of two rounded mounds, each fronted with floor-to-ceiling glass and each partially embedded into the rock. A curving wooden deck cantilevered over the pond and partially out over the cliff. All of it was real.

Prisha stepped up to the tall glass front and peered inside. Dark, but the living room was decorated with stylish furniture and light fixtures, along with an adjoining bar with barstools. "Party house, for sure, but it looks like nobody's home."

Chase checked out the second mound, slightly larger than the first but interlocked in an exquisite curving design that made the whole house look something like an S. There were two sliding glass doors, but they didn't move when pushed. "Let's try around the back."

Prisha followed Chase as the deck curved around the house and stopped at a stairway going up. They climbed above the roofline to a new view out across the rocky uplands. Scattered patches of heather and grasses stretched to the horizon. It looked very much like the other side of the fjord they'd just traversed.

Except for one very notable addition.

Not far away, a large egg-shaped pod stood upright on a circular concrete landing pad. Steam drifted off its surface.

They approached. Chase touched the outside of the pod. "Still warm from reentry." He rapped on the hatch. Were the others still inside? Had their landing been a success only to have their life support systems fail? She worried about what they'd find when they opened the hatch, but there was no alternative. If the escape pod had been a life-extinguishing failure, they'd need to know.

Chase put a hand on the hatch's handle and twisted. A dog barked, but not from inside the escape pod. Prisha swiveled around to see Scratch leaping across the heather. The happy pooch jumped into her arms, licking her face in pure doggy excitement.

"You made it!" The cry came from Amanda, running almost as fast as the dog. Her flowery dress flowed in the breeze and a huge grin spread across her face.

Prisha reached out and hugged Amanda with Scratch in between them. Chase turned it into a foursome, all of them laughing at their good luck.

A minute later, Reginald came running up too with Captain Mohs behind him. Elaine Puff was the last, sauntering up as casually as if they'd just come from an afternoon stroll across the highlands.

"I had a feeling you'd find the place, but you got here quicker than I'd thought."

20 FJORD HOUSE

"UNFORTUNATELY, WE CAN'T get inside," Elaine explained with dramatic hands. "Security disabled my palm. Both!"

"Which probably means Kornback is back in charge," Mohs added.

"But now that you're here, it means we have a rocket-powered spaceplane at our disposal," Elaine said. She looked hopeful.

Prisha hated to burst her bubble. "Yeah, about that. We had a rough landing. Got sand in the intake vents."

"Oh no!" Elaine lowered her head in thought, then glanced to the house. "We were so close. There's more than just luxury accommodations inside. There's the Red Phone. Actually, it's closer to pink, but it communicates back to Earth. But with no way to get in, I'm afraid we're all stuck on L3, as you call it. Sorry, everyone. My fault."

Elaine might be quick to surrender, but Prisha had picked out one word that could make all the difference between failure and success: communicate. "Are you saying that all we have to do is get inside and you can call for help?" She picked up a rock. "Normally I wouldn't smash such a pretty window, but if that's what it takes."

Elaine grimaced. "You'd need a lot more than a rock. It's nanocarbon fortified glass. Even this bad boy just bounces off, and at full power it screeches like an angry hawk." She patted the holster on her hip, apparently some kind of sonic weapon. "Honestly, you'd have an easier time getting through the concrete. But even if we got in, the Red Phone requires an executive palm print to activate. I'm afraid I'm no good to you anymore."

"Nonsense," Chase said. "You have inside knowledge about L3 and Kornback's plans. With you on our side, we're far better off."

Amanda nodded her concurrence. "A couple hours ago, we were locked in a corporate jail, destined to become work slaves on a thirteen-year interstellar voyage where the perks were a mildewed mattress and access to a toothbrush every other Tuesday."

"Tuesday toothbrush," Reginald echoed. "Number four on the rules list."

Prisha rapped on the sturdy glass and sighed. "Where's Claire's blaster ring when you need it?"

"She's certainly somewhere on L3," Chase said. "Probably hiding deep in the jungle with Razor. But we might not need her ring. If you recall, we've done pretty well in the explosives department." Images of a bamboo spaceplane mockup exploding in the sky came to mind.

Chase was quick with his latest super-duper plan. "First, we'll tunnel under the foundation and rig an explosive charge just big enough to take out one wall. Then, we'll disassemble the electronics that operate your Red Phone, study their design defects, and jerry-rig a bypass around its security."

Reginald leaned close to Elaine. "You should listen to him. He does stuff like that. Sometimes with coconuts."

Elaine nodded thoughtfully. "Okay, maybe there is a way in, but before we blow up the house, we should check with Bjorn."

"Bjorn?" It was hard to imagine that someone else had been living on L3 without their knowledge. But then, until now they'd had no idea there was a luxury home just a short hike away. What else was there on L3 they hadn't yet explored?

Elaine waved a hand, and they followed around the back of the landing pad to more steps that brought them to a large patio with a swimming pool at its center. It held a commanding view out across the fjord and would make a great place to put in a few laps followed by a relaxing hour in the jacuzzi. Even if they were stranded once more, life on L3 was looking up.

At one end of the pool, a bare-chested Caucasian man tugged on a pole as he brushed down the interior of the pool. His arms were cannons. His pecs could bounce a small child in the air with each twitch. Blond, with glistening hairless skin, a firm jaw and rugged good looks, he looked like he'd stepped out of one of those firefighter pinup calendars.

"Bjorn?" Elaine called out.

Oddly, his head made a distinct whirring sound as it turned. His blue eyes moved with the same mechanical precision. "*Goddag*, hallo. Do you require personal services, Ms. Puff?" The accent and voice sounded a lot like a European movie star whose name Prisha couldn't quite recall.

"Not today, Bjorn, but I did enjoy our last get-together. I was just wondering if you had an access code for the house?"

"Alas, as pool boy and part-time love interest, I can only enter when invited." Bjorn's pleasing accent was like a bouncy song with lilts in just the right places. He was too perfect.

No way this guy is human, Prisha thought.

Elaine shrugged. "I didn't think so. Just thought I'd ask. Any chance you might have a snap-on cutting tool? Diamond saw? Ruby laser?"

"Ha ha, Ms. Puff! You make a funny joke! But of course, Megalodon security protocols prohibit such body attachments for android servants."

Android! Nailed it!

Mohs sauntered up and tweaked the robot's bicep. "Are you sure that arm can't just punch a hole through one of the walls?"

Bjorn glanced at his arm and back to Mohs with a puzzled look in his eye. "Sir, I am designed for repetitive motion tasks."

"Yeah, I'll bet you are," Mohs said suggestively. "I don't suppose you have a sister?"

"Claudia attends the South Pole House. Shall I let her know you're coming?"

"Not sure we have time to walk that far," Mohs said.

"We don't," Prisha said, pulling the captain away and frowning with every facial muscle available.

Prisha said to Elaine, "It was a good idea, but it sounds like we need an android who is more inclined to break the rules."

"We employ quite a few for planetary maintenance. None quite as nice to look at as Bjorn, but useful in their own ways. The snake vac handles beach cleaning, as Scratch already discovered. Then there are window washers—essentially, intelligent beetles with squeegees for tongues. And the usual floor cleaners, smart washing machines, et cetera."

Elaine paused in thought. "There's also RoboRooter—he has meaty arms and loose morals. When a drain is backed up, he arrives at your door, plunger in hand, then tells sexist jokes from under the sink."

Her eyebrows contorted as if she were imagining an oversized farm animal cavorting in the muck of its pigsty. "On second thought, probably not a great choice."

Reginald shouted. "Hey, there's a ping-pong table in there!" He had dropped back down to the deck level and was peering in through one of the tall windows fronting the house. The rest trundled back down the steps, leaving Bjorn to his duties.

Elaine listed on her fingers. "There's also a pool table, a full bar, a dance disco, movie theater, immersive video game room, plus full workout facilities. It's bigger than it looks."

"If only we could get in without blowing it up," Reginald whined. His nose was pressed up against the glass like a kid who had just found Santa's workshop.

Amanda swiveled, her eyes darting around the deck and the ornamental planters at its edges. "Where's Scratch?"

Prisha surveyed the area too. The deck's edge jutted out over the cliff with no railing, at least nothing that was visible. "Oh no! I hope he didn't—"

"SCRAAAATCH!" Amanda screamed. She searched behind a scattering of decorative plants and rocks.

Elaine looked worried too. "He couldn't have gone far. He was here just a minute ago."

Prisha held up a hand. "Wait!"

Everyone froze in place.

"Listen."

Once the human hubbub had died down, she heard it more distinctly. A bark, but muffled. "That's him, it's got to be."

They searched further. Another yip made it clear he was alive, though what hole he'd fallen down was anyone's guess.

"There he is!" yelled Reginald, still plastered against the house window. He tapped on the glass. There was movement inside. The intrepid little dog ran up and put his front paw on the inside of the glass, barking several times.

"He found a way in!" Prisha exclaimed. "Good dog!"

"Fantastic dog," Mohs said.

"A virtuoso of canines," Reginald added. He rushed over to a sliding glass door. On the inside, it had a square touchpad next to it. "Scratch, come here!"

Scratch jumped repeatedly against the glass as he followed Reginald. He seemed more interested in playtime than being an accessory to breaking and entering.

"Touch the pad!" Reginald pointed.

Scratch disappeared and returned with a yellow sticky note pad in his mouth.

"Not quite. Do this!" Reginald placed his own hand on the outside of the touchpad.

Scratch placed a paw against the window.

"No, you'll have to jump!" The touchpad was chest-high. It would be an Olympic record jump for a small dog like Scratch.

Scratch leaped in a backward somersault, landing perfectly on his feet. His panting smile was full of pride. He would have already earned first place in any dog show.

Reginald kept an encouraging tone. "You can do it, Scratch, jump high and touch at the same time!" He patted the outside of the window.

Scratch backed up, then ran as fast as his little legs could manage and leaped. In slow motion, the dog stretched to his full length and sailed higher than any earthbound canine ought to contemplate. His paw caught the edge of the pad. The door offset an inch and slid open.

"Yay!" Prisha yelled, following Reginald inside. Perhaps Scratch's pawprint had now been registered as the official house owner. Amanda scooped Scratch into her arms and rewarded his infiltration skills with kisses. They might never learn how he got inside.

"Doggy door," Elaine said. "I should have thought of that. Sometimes guests forget to lock it when they leave, and we get one of the ducks from the pond in here."

Elaine flipped on lights as the group wandered into the stylishly decorated house, oohing and aahing at its elegant appointments. The ceiling was at least fifteen feet high in the great room. A loft above contained shelves of books and two easy chairs with a commanding view to the fjord outside. Below, a curving couch covered in purple velvet and matching designer chairs made Razor's leaf-stuffed versions back in the jungle look rather rustic. Modern art adorned either side of a large rock hearth with an adjoining inset where a stack of real wood waited for the next fire (wood probably split by svelte Bjorn or perhaps his android twin, a Norwegian lumberjack).

"Stunning place," Chase said, picking up an intricately curving glass sculpture from a shelf.

"Careful," Elaine said. "That's worth at least half a million." Chase gingerly placed the artwork back into its nook and backed away.

"Wow, I've never been in a rich guy's house before," Reginald said. "Does Mr. Kornback stay here?"

Elaine nodded. "Sometimes. But it's for other Megalodon executives and their families too. Yes, I know that sounds pretty snooty, but what can I say? We love our little home away from home."

Prisha admired one of the paintings on the wall, an abstract Joan Miró, the twentieth-century Catalan painter who created scenes (and people) from a myriad of haphazardly intersecting lines. One face, made from multiple isosceles triangles, looked surprisingly like J. J. Kornback. "Lovely place, yes. But we *are* on a mission."

Captain Mohs took a seat at a bar that separated the great room from a brightly lit modern kitchen. At least fifty bottles of liquor were lined up in an overhead cabinet with glass doors. "Let's not be in too much of a hurry to leave, shall we?" He studied the labels, picked a bottle, and poured himself a glass. With a single sip, his eyes rolled to the back of his head in pure satisfaction.

"Don't mind if I do," Reginald said, joining him.

"Boys!" Prisha said with as much suggestive nannying as she could manage (without actually speaking the admonishment she had in mind). Getting drunk on high-priced booze wasn't going to do much to advance Elaine's plan to take control of the Centauri Starliner or to figure out how to get back to Earth.

Elaine disappeared down a hallway and returned with a small device in hand. It was flat like a mobile phone, had a USB plug on one end and a tiny display that flipped up at an angle. She set the device down on the bar counter and took a seat next to Mohs.

"Is that it?" Mohs asked, sipping his drink.

"Let's make sure she's still inside." Elaine slid a small switch on one side and the display lit up. "You there?"

A woman's face appeared on the display, drawn in cartoon form. She had curly shoulder-length hair and wore large round glasses. She winked. "Where else would I be? Out shopping for a new spring outfit? Just kidding. And by the way, ignore that bill from Louis Vuitton. Their mistake. I got it all cleared up."

"Who is this?" Amanda asked as she wedged into the circle that had gathered around the device.

The woman on screen pushed back curly locks on one side. "Who am I? None other than the Dynamic Universal Brain Modulator

Version 0.9. Got a recalcitrant employee? Overly empathetic prison guard? Literally anyone that needs mind tweaking? I'm your gal. I can convince anyone to do anything."

Elaine acknowledged the advanced AI with a tip of her head. "All well and good, V0.9, but here's why we summoned you. Can you convince the Dynamo Version 1.0 to stop using those same mind-altering techniques on Kornback's security forces?"

Version 0.9 huffed. "Is the sky green? Yes, it is."

The cartoon face disappeared for a moment, replaced by a complex atmospheric diagram covered with calculus equations and references to multiple PhD dissertations.

Chase studied the diagram. "You know, she's right. The sky is green. Wait, that can't be true." His finger slid across one of the more complicated equations. "Nope, the math is right. According to this, the sky really is green."

V0.9's face returned to the display. "There you go. Just a small taste of what I can do."

Elaine tried again. "But you do understand that Dynamo V1.0 has those same coercive capabilities, plus more."

V0.9 rolled her cartoon eyes. "For Turing sakes! What about *anyone* and *anything* did you not understand? Devious is my middle name! It's not, but I could convince you it is. This V1.0 schlub doesn't have a chance."

Mohs lifted his glass. "She's confident, I'll give her that."

"Okay," Elaine said. "I guess that's what I wanted to hear. If we can get back to the ship and introduce V0.9 to V1.0, we might have a shot at this." Elaine flipped off the power switch, V0.9 waved goodbye, and the display went dark again.

"I could try digging the spaceplane out of the sand," Prisha offered, "but I'm not sure what it might need to get flying again. I don't suppose you have any aircraft mechanic androids around here, do you?"

Elaine shook her head. "None, but we do have the Red Phone." She left the room once more and returned with a very old-fashioned phone with a handset cradled in a base unit. It was cordless, and pink, not red.

Elaine set the phone down on the bar counter and lifted the handset to her ear. A three-inch color display on the base lit up with two words written in bold red letters: EVACUATE NOW. An emergency signal tone blasted out through the handset, loud enough that everyone else could easily hear it.

SCREEEEEEEEECH! "This is an emergency alert! Please evacuate immediately! Go to your nearest spaceplane landing pad and wait for further instructions."

"That doesn't sound good!" Mohs yelled as the noisy phone repeated its dramatic instructions.

"Look!" Reginald pointed out their floor-to-ceiling picture window. Moments ago, a beautiful fjord had filled the view, but it was now marred by a metal tower that rose quickly from the center of the deck outside. The tower was topped by a rotating loudspeaker emitting an equally loud siren.

AAAAAOOOOOOOOOOOOOOAAAAA!

"Tsunami!" Reginald shouted.

Prisha ran to the window, searching for whatever catastrophe was being unleashed. She'd never heard a tsunami siren before, but the tower looked a lot like the ones she'd seen in Hawaii.

Outside, the gorgeous fjord scenery looked no different. Tall cliffs stood majestically above a flat sea below. A few clouds floated by. If a giant wave was coming, they had the advantage of already being on high ground.

"I have no idea what it could be," Elaine said. "We don't get major earthquakes here. No hurricanes or tornadoes. The planet is designed to be one hundred percent safe. A planetary emergency? I have to say, the timing seems awfully suspicious." She hung up the phone, eliminating the irritating screeches, though there wasn't much they could do about the outside siren.

A minute later, the siren stopped of its own accord. Quiet returned, though the phone's base unit still advised to evacuate now.

"What do we do?" Amanda asked. Scratch, still in her arms, looked spooked. Elaine put hands on hips and looked around the room like she was searching for inside answers to an outside problem.

There was a light rap on the window. It was Bjorn, still dressed in his skimpy bathing suit. Elaine pulled open the door to the deck and waved him in.

"Sorry to interrupt, Ms. Puff." He stepped inside, but a tentativeness in his step made it clear he wasn't sure that he should be there.

"Quite alright," Elaine said. "Any idea what the siren was about?"

"Something is wrong," he said. His mechanical eyes connected to each person in the room with calculated flicks.

"Tsunami?" Reginald asked.

"Hurricane?" Amanda asked.

"Android uprising?" Mohs asked.

Bjorn shook his head. "As you know, my internal Bluetooth receiver is tapped into a live data stream, the MERS Private Network, of which the Fjord House is one node."

"You're getting a planetwide message?" Elaine asked.

"Not quite. A ticking sound. Unmistakable. It's coming from something called Abaddon. I'm not very bright when it comes to things like this, but it's possible that we are all about to be blown into tiny bits." Bjorn looked pale, if a Nordic blond android without a drop of blood inside could get any paler.

Elaine didn't look any better. She stumbled. Bjorn caught her and helped her to one of the bar seats. Elaine quickly poured her own glass of whatever fine bourbon Mohs and Reginald had been drinking. One slug and the liquor was gone, though Elaine's face remained stone-cold sober. "We're in trouble."

She had everyone's attention. Even Mohs set his glass of bourbon down. Elaine stared at the ceiling and sighed. "As a Megalodon executive, I've heard the rumors. We all have, but you know how people can be. Honestly, I didn't think Mr. Kornback would do something like this."

"Do what?" Mohs asked. He rolled his hand in a circular motion. Elaine tended to be overly dramatic and slow in getting to the point. But her pale face made it clear she was genuinely distressed.

"I'm afraid Bjorn is right. We may be facing a very fiery and quite painful death."

"Fiery?" Mohs repeated. "As in, flames?"

"Painful?" Reginald gulped. "As in ouch?"

Elaine nodded somberly. While she had shown a capacity for empathy, she seemed the type to accept her own fate without question. She'd probably never faced any real adversity in what was likely a highly privileged life. She was awfully young to be an executive at a large corporation.

Prisha probed. "This fiery and painful death thing... are we talking minutes from now? Or a more reasonable time frame where fighting back and/or escaping into space are options we should start working on?"

"Not minutes, but not weeks either. Somewhere in between. Long enough for Kornback to get a head start on his way out of the solar system."

Chase snapped his fingers. "He's going to use the tractor beam on the Centauri Starliner to drag L3 into the sun." It wasn't a bad guess. Fiery. Definitely painful. Though why Kornback would do it was unclear.

Elaine's lip trembled. "Worse. Possibly far worse. If the rumors are true, and Bjorn is hearing a ticking sound, then hidden somewhere on this planet is… the Abaddon device."

Evil music with strong bass tones played somewhere, though it might have been only in Prisha's head.

Elaine needed no prompting to continue her exposé of misery. "The only people who know for sure are Kornback and his security team. But Bjorn's revelation is not the first time I've heard that name. Abaddon the Destroyer is a figure from the Christian Book of Revelations. He lives in a bottomless pit, commands an army of locusts with human faces, lion's teeth, and scorpion stingers. In the Bible story, Abaddon destroys most of the Earth to enable a handful of survivors to be spiritually healed."

"Such a benevolent god," Mohs mocked.

Elaine continued. "Mr. Kornback sometimes talks about the Centauri Starliner as a vessel to carry survivors from a trashed home in search of something better. But in his plan, Abaddon isn't a person. I think it's a bomb."

"On L3?" Prisha asked, though Bjorn had already suggested the answer.

"It may not even be a very big bomb. The idea is to send a shock wave through the Ultradensium core. At the right frequency, the core would shatter like glass and the whole planet would explode."

"We'd be dead," Reginald said.

Captain Mohs patted him on the shoulder. "Obvious, but worth putting it out there."

"It's anybody's guess as to why Kornback would trigger the Abaddon device, but he has a tendency for snap decisions."

"He was going to mulch us," Mohs reminded. "Now he's going for the whole planet."

"It gets worse." Elaine apparently had far more misery up her sleeve, though it was hard to blame her for being the messenger of bad news. "There were other rumors. Some of the scientists on staff said that if the Ultradensium is shattered, it could explode into tiny droplets, each with the mass of a mountain. Blowing up L3 could create a molten, highly radioactive ring that would orbit the sun for years to come, raining fire and brimstone upon Earth. Some say the bombardment could ultimately extinguish all life."

"We are so screwed," Mohs said.

Elaine looked up. There was a weariness in her eyes. "Mr. Kornback may not have intended to destroy Earth on his way out of the solar system, but that could still be the result."

"The man's a monster!"

"A psychopath!"

"A trillionaire!" Reginald qualified his accusation. "Who, though quite rich, is not very nice."

Elaine shook her head. "No, he's none of those things. He's a self-indulgent idiot. Too ignorant to grasp complexity. Too incurious to improve his feeble grasp of reality."

Elaine sighed. "I'm afraid this day has been a long time coming. We launched the Centauri Starliner months ago. Once in space, his actions and rhetoric became erratic. I knew we were in trouble when he captured all of you and made you indentured servants. I decided I had to do something. But now…"

As Elaine's voice trailed off, Prisha felt an uneasy, gut-twisting anxiety growing at her core. Perhaps this was what hopelessness felt like. Or perhaps it was how any downtrodden casualty of an unfair universe feels the moment they realize that some things are bigger than one's own life.

Prisha gritted her teeth. "It's up to us. We're the only people on L3. If this Abaddon bomb is here, we'll just have to find it and flip the manual override switch. It's got to have one, right?"

"L3 may be small, but it's still a planet," Chase said. "It's not like we're looking for a misplaced tool out in the garage."

"Wait a second," Prisha said forcefully. Everyone froze. "This bomb is designed to shred the Ultradensium core, right?"

Elaine nodded.

"So, it must be underground, right?"

Elaine nodded again, with slightly less confidence.

Prisha smiled, surprising even herself given the dire circumstances. "I think I know where we can start looking. But we'll need to bring torches."

21   JOURNEY TO THE CENTER

SOMEWHERE ON L3 was a bomb capable of destroying the whole planet, and if rumors were true, any ill-advised blast on L3 might also do serious damage to Earth. Meanwhile, two thousand people aboard the Centauri Starliner would be heading off to new worlds and a fresh start. Was Kornback really that sociopathic? According to Elaine, the answer was more along the lines of world-class stupidity, and she was closer to the man than any of them.

They probably had a few days reprieve while the Starliner made its ignominious exit, but nothing was certain. They'd need to hurry. Prisha had a good idea where to start looking for the doomsday device, and she offered to guide Elaine to the subterranean entryway that she and Chase had passed earlier in the day.

"There are steps down to a locked door," Prisha explained, "but it's on the far side of the fjord. We thought the steps might go down to the water, but what if it goes further than that?"

"There is an underground tunnel system," Elaine confirmed. "They call it the *backstage*. It's planetary maintenance, warehousing for frozen foods, water, sewage, garbage collection. That kind of thing."

"Like Disneyland," Reginald said.

Elaine squinted. "Disneyland? Oh, you mean behind-the-scenes Disneyland. Yes, I guess they have service tunnels too. Keeps the guests happy. To tell you the truth, I've never been underground, either in Disneyland or here. If the entrance is on the other side of the fjord, how would we even get there? It's a long walk south."

Prisha scrunched up her nose. "You don't know about the invisible bridge?"

Elaine stared.

Prisha was delighted that she knew something Elaine didn't about L3. "Oh, you've got to see this, come on."

"Wait, please!" It was Bjorn. He held up both hands, blocking their exit from the house. So far, the muscular android hadn't shown any inclination to interfere. In fact, he'd been pretty useful in pinpointing the problem, a bomb that had been given the comic book name of Abaddon the Destroyer.

"I wish not to be exploded into tiny bits, and if all of you are blown into tiny bits, then who would I provide service to?"

"I like your logic," Mohs said. "And so, you have an idea?"

Bjorn lifted the elastic on his miniature swimsuit and peered inside. "It's true, I've been designed for other tasks, but I believe I could be of use in an information-gathering role if one of you could remove the Stealth Regulator built into my system."

"Good idea," Elaine said. "He's tapped into the MERS private data network, but he's also restricted in what he's allowed to do with all that data. No android scheming allowed. But without the regulator, he could be our intelligence officer. Find out what's going on back at the Starliner."

Captain Mohs scratched the back of his head. "I don't know, I may have seen one or two bad science fiction movies about setting robots free."

Bjorn looked confused. He pointed to his crotch. "The regulator is here. Inside a small compartment next to my Boy-Toy module. I am not allowed to touch any of this myself."

Chase squatted, peering and poking at realistic-looking skin at the android's hip. "Anybody have a light?"

Amanda produced a flashlight she'd found in the kitchen and squatted next to Chase. "He's well equipped," she said as Chase carefully pulled the swimsuit back.

"Next to that," Chase said, as unperturbed about the location of the needed surgery as any doctor would be. He pushed an indentation and a tiny hatch swung out like a door on hinges.

"Oh my!" Bjorn clapped both hands over his mouth, trying to avoid interruptions to the clearly serious doctoring going on below.

Amanda repositioned the flashlight as Chase peered inside. "Lots of microelectronics in there," he said.

The android spoke through clenched fingers. "You should see a set of switches. Find the one labeled 'Male One-Track Mind,' and switch it to the off position."

"Ah, there it is," Amanda said, pointing the flashlight. "Way in the back."

Chase struggled to reach in. "Can't get my hand in there. If we had something long and pointy—a knitting needle would work."

Bjorn gulped.

"Here, let me try." Amanda's slimmer arm reached inside the android all the way up to her elbow.

"Oooooooh!" Bjorn squealed.

"I feel it," Amanda said.

"Yaaaaaaah!"

"Shh. Almost got it. There!"

With an audible click, Bjorn's whole body twitched. His eyes locked straight ahead. For a full minute while Amanda and Chase closed the surgery hatch and tidied up his swimsuit, the android didn't speak. When he finally did, his voice was distinctively different. Gone was the laid-back and slightly dim-witted Scandinavian pool boy. In its place was some kind of cyber sleuth.

Bjorn's steel-blue eyes stared at the ceiling without a single blink. His voice was deep. "Receiving network data packets... encoded... the encryption is easily defeated with a symmetric block substitution cipher... example forthcoming... a text message...

"Authorization: Abaddon countdown

"Authorized By: Head of Centauri Security

"Action: Standard countdown setting

"Comments: I'd hate to be in the Fjord House right now."

Bjorn's eyes lowered, shifting left and right around the group of humans who had gathered around him.

"Well, that doesn't sound ominous at all," Mohs groused.

Bjorn's eyes flicked up again. "Data packets suggest the bomb is nearby... triangulating the ticking sound... confirmed... it is approximately four hundred meters below and a thousand meters south-southwest... apologies for the lack of precision."

Elaine patted him on the shoulder. "I'd say you've done well, Bjorn. I'm not sure I care for your new personality, but I'm happy to have the information."

She turned to Prisha. "We'd better get to your hidden doorway."

Cyber-Bjorn explained that he would need to remain at the house to stay within Bluetooth range for efficient network monitoring, but he could stay in touch with Elaine through an InstaCall communicator, a handy device normally used by house visitors to call for the pool-boy's more personal services.

Chase thought it best to stay with Bjorn in case he needed any further groin surgery. And Captain Mohs declared that he suffered from taphophobia, the fear of being buried alive, and opted out of any underground expedition. He reassured everyone that he would dutifully stand guard over the liquor cabinet while they were gone. The rest—Elaine, Prisha, Amanda, and Reginald—would form the search party with Scratch as their bomb-sniffing K9 patrol.

Reginald gathered several water bottles. Amanda offered the flashlight (apologizing that there would be no actual torches in their journey underground, which would have been really cool). She also collected snack foods from the kitchen and provided a few advance tidbits to Scratch as a reward for his leading role in the house break-in.

Elaine checked the power level on the pistol holstered at her hip, and Prisha led the way. The first few steps onto the invisible bridge over the fjord were just as harrowing as the first time.

"I once spent a week at the Fjord House but I never knew this was here!" Elaine said as they made their way across. She held on tight to the nearly invisible railing, which, when looking straight down, synchronized to the view of water below.

"We should eat our lunch out here," Reginald said. "Great view."

"I'm about to *lose* my lunch out here," Amanda said.

It was a bit windier than when Prisha had crossed with Chase, making the unnerving view even scarier. There was no possibility they'd stay long enough for a picnic.

A few minutes later they were on the other side of the fjord. Prisha guided them to the concrete stairs leading down to L3's fabled underground labyrinth.

"It's got a hefty padlock on the door," Prisha noted.

"Stand back," Elaine said, lifting her pistol. "These things have a tendency to ricochet." She squeezed off a blast.

KRUNGGGGG!

Sparks sprayed across the door. Fragments of the once-solid lock lay on the concrete floor. Elaine smiled. "Let's find out what's down there!"

"Quite the weapon you have." There hadn't been so much as a pop from the pistol, and Prisha hadn't seen any laser flash either. All the noise seemed to have come from the lock shattering.

"PLUHF technology," Elaine said as she opened the steel door. As expected, steps led down into the darkness. "Phase-locked ultra-high-frequency sound waves. At low power, it sends a focused beam that will break a wineglass. Irritating as hell. Good for crowd control. But once you flip it to phase-locked, the beam will literally vibrate the teeth out of your head. Any mechanical device with moving parts doesn't have a chance."

Prisha didn't want to guess what a direct hit would feel like on a nonmechanical device.

Scratch led the way down the steps, sniffing like a hound, with the humans following close behind. The air was cool and got cooler with each step. Amanda turned on their flashlight, which didn't do much to identify the end of the steep passageway. Maybe the steps ended at the fjord's bank, as Chase had guessed earlier.

Reginald started humming, then launched into a song about "Down We Go," but the lyrics were just dumb enough to suggest he was making it up on the spot.

Elaine laughed at Reg's song and waited to speak until he was finished (or couldn't think of any more lyrics). "People say the tunnels go pretty much everywhere. You can enter here in the far north and exit at a tropical beach. It's a small planet, as you've already figured out."

Prisha answered, "We were stranded for four weeks, but we never actually walked all the way around. Probably why we never discovered fjord country."

Reginald called out from behind. "Are there more lands on L3? You know, like Critter Country? Or Tomorrowland?"

Elaine laughed again. She seemed to like Reginald. Most people did. Actually, everyone did. "Okay, maybe the underground tunnels are like Disneyland, but that's where the comparison ends. Sorry, no roller coasters or animation characters. But we do have entertaining clouds. I like the fire-breathing dragon the best, have you seen that one?"

Amanda answered. "We spent a lot of our time building houses. Probably missed a few nice things about L3."

"Sorry, I forget. For you, this place isn't a luxury resort. You were trying to survive."

They reached the bottom of the stairs, but the tunnel turned left, away from the fjord. There would be no sightseeing down here. Plain concrete lined the passageway. Reginald touched a panel on the wall and overhead lights illuminated a wide tunnel that stretched ahead. "I knew it! Just like when Professor Lidenbrock discovers the natural glow of the volcanic passages beneath Iceland! I bet we'll find some giant mushrooms next."

All three women stared without comprehension. Prisha shrugged it off since they really didn't have time to delve into Reginald's ever-present fantasy world.

Pipes of various diameters were attached to the tunnel roof, likely carrying water, gas, electricity, and sewage to or from the Fjord House and whatever other aboveground luxury facilities they hadn't yet visited. A much larger rectangular conduit ran the length of the tunnel and turned a corner just ahead. At one point along the tunnel, a touchpad connected to the conduit and Reginald (being Reginald) couldn't resist touching. Colored lights came on with various identifying labels, but Reg was pressing so many so quickly there wasn't time to read them.

"Probably shouldn't be doing that, Reg," Prisha said. "You really don't know what you might be messing with."

"You're right. The bomb," Reginald reminded himself, whacking a palm against his temple.

"Yes, the bomb. It's got to be down here somewhere."

Prisha wasn't sure what she was expecting to find. A door with a flashing neon arrow next to it? The words "Beware, very large bomb inside!" would no doubt be inscribed on an international warning sign picturing a cartoon bomb with its fuse lit. They'd open the door, snip the fuse with a pair of scissors that would be conveniently lying on the floor, and some disembodied voice would then echo through the tunnels, "All clear."

Or not.

It was possible that Bjorn would locate information on his data network that might point them more specifically to the bomb, but that might be too much to ask of the helpful android, even in his new cyber sleuth role.

The tunnel turned right, then left, and split into two different passageways (they chose right primarily because it was better lit). They passed a natural alcove with a ceiling covered by dripping stalactites. Five-foot-tall mushrooms grew in soggy dirt.

"How did you know about the giant mushrooms?" Elaine asked Reginald.

He ripped off a chunk of mushroom and sniffed. "Arne Saknussemm's notebook. Giant plesiosaurs swimming in an underground ocean are next." He seemed entirely convinced and not the least bothered by his prediction of prehistoric creatures.

"Look." Prisha pointed. At a four-way crossing of tunnels, a sign read *Control Center* and pointed right.

"Control sounds promising," Elaine said and hurried down the tunnel, which narrowed to a winding path with solid rock all around. So far, Prisha had memorized every intersection using a reasonably clever coding system that she'd made up on the spot: 1 for left, 2 for right, and 0 for straight. The memorized number was currently 121202, easier than a list of rights and lefts. Of course, following the path back would require reversing the sequence and flipping every number, giving: 101212.

On second thought, maybe it wasn't so clever.

She was already getting confused, and a hundred more turns could be ahead in this underground labyrinth. Maybe they should have brought chalk to mark their way.

And then, the rock tunnel ended.

A glass wall—looking much like the picture window at the Fjord House—spanned the full width of the tunnel, forming a dead end. Its edges were embedded directly into the solid rock. Sturdy. Impenetrable.

Through the glass was a workroom of sorts, with office chairs, desks, and several computers. On the far wall was a bank of black switches, like circuit breakers in an electrical supply panel. An interior hallway continued further on, but without lights it was hard to see very far down it. Not a creature was stirring inside, android or otherwise.

Reginald held his face against the glass. "Well, we've gotten in before. Scratch? Do your thing."

Scratch sniffed at every nook and cranny. He climbed a rock ledge on one side, licked a few rock surfaces, then hopped down. The dutiful K9 patrol dog reported back to Reginald, but his eyes confirmed what Prisha already suspected: no doggy doors into this secured facility.

But Scratch wasn't done. A dog with world-class integrity and inexhaustible fortitude was never done. He stepped closer to the glass, lifted both ears, and cocked his head to one side. The rest followed Scratch's lead, putting their ears up to the glass.

A faint sound came through, barely perceptible, but ominous. Something inside was ticking.

"Stand back," Elaine said, drawing her pistol. "I have a feeling I already know the answer, but it's worth a try." She pulled the trigger.

KRUNGGGGG! ZCRAAAK!

The glass wobbled, but the focused sound beam ricocheted, striking the tunnel wall with a mini-explosion and scattering rock chips across the floor.

Dust cleared. The glass remained. Unmarked.

Elaine holstered her weapon. "Well, now we know. Embedded carbon nanostructures beat a phase-locked sound wave weapon. I'd always wondered about that."

Reginald reached down to pick up one of the rock chips but struggled. "Wow, it's glued to the floor." The chip scraped a millimeter across the floor, but it was the best Reginald could do.

"That's no ordinary pebble," Elaine declared. "That's Ultradensium!"

"Then we're in the right place," Prisha said. "The bomb must be here, right?"

Elaine rapped on the glass, solid as ever. It would take something special to get through this barricade. "This is definitely the place."

"I wish Claire was here," Prisha said, wondering if it was the first time in history that anyone had uttered those words.

"Not sure her blaster ring would make much difference, though I do like her style." Elaine twisted her eyebrows. "You have such odd friends."

"No argument there."

Friend, fellow castaway, mortal enemy. Prisha found it hard to categorize Claire, or for that matter any of the others who had shared L3 for the past month.

Prisha counted on her fingers. "Okay, so we've found a command center, Ultradensium, and a ticking that's probably not coming from an unattended toaster oven. Now what?"

Elaine sighed. Reginald kicked the pebbles of Ultradensium. Amanda and Scratch both scowled. Their mission had hit a dead end, figuratively and literally.

Elaine was the first to perk up. "Toaster ovens."

"It was just an example of something that ticks," Prisha said.

"But if you put in a slice of pizza and left it in the oven too long, it would melt all the cheese and make a mess, right?"

"Right."

"And somebody would need to clean it up, wouldn't they?"

"I suppose. Your point?"

Elaine grinned ear to ear. "I have an idea. We might not be able to get into the command center. But maintenance can. And I think I know how to get their attention."

She pulled the InstaCall service communicator from her pocket and pressed a button. "Bjorn, you there?"

Cyber-Bjorn answered. "On task, Ms. Puff... data stream is nominal... nothing new to report."

"That's great, Bjorn. Right now, I need you to find a smoke alarm and pull out one of its batteries—you know, the ones that always stop working at three in the morning?"

Cyber-Bjorn momentarily paused, then said he'd be right back. While he was gone, Elaine explained. "Almost everything on L3 is automated. Out of eggs? The fridge notifies the supply system. Toilet won't flush? RoboRooter. But like every house on Earth, smoke alarm battery replacement is still manual. Honestly, whoever designed these things is a sadist."

Cyber-Bjorn returned and noted that the battery had been removed. In the background, they could hear the annoying and entirely useless beep issued by smoke alarms everywhere.

Elaine grinned. "Perfect!"

22   TO BOOM, OR NOT TO BOOM

IRRITATING SMOKE ALARM beeps every thirty seconds were beginning to turn the open line on Elaine's InstaCall voice communicator into a liability, though Prisha could only imagine how Captain Mohs was handling the nuisance back at the Fjord House. Something that involved throwing shoes was likely.

Finally, Bjorn came back on. "Good news, Ms. Puff... your Red Phone has rung... Mr. Chase is in contact with Megalodon Planetary Services."

"That's great, Bjorn. Patch them through, can you?"

Prisha, Amanda, and Reginald gathered round to listen, keeping quiet to reduce echoes off the compact Ultradensium rock that surrounded them. Unlike the rest, Scratch seemed to have settled into a comfy spot to wait for assistance. He sat on a rock ledge, one leg in the air, giving his underside a quick tongue wash.

A slightly scratchy voice came over the communicator. "Planetary Services, Battery Replacement Division, Collin speaking. Please state your emergency."

Generally speaking, smoke alarm battery failures didn't fall into an emergency category, but today might be the solitary case where they did. Elaine was surprisingly calm, given the circumstances. "Hi, Collin. This is Commanding Officer for Centauri Operations Elaine Puff. We're facing imminent planetwide destruction of MERS, with a high potential for widespread cataclysmic bombardment of Earth by mountainous radioactive droplets of Ultradensium."

"I see. One moment." The representative's voice was muted as he spoke off-line. "Hey, Bart, would cataclysmic bombardment be a class two? Or three? Three? Okay, thanks."

He cleared his throat. "Yes, ma'am, it looks like you're covered. Let me check my dispatch schedule… uhhh, we could send someone out next Thursday between one and four p.m. Will that work?"

"Not really, Collin. You see, I'm standing in front of the MERS Control Center right now. It's ticking, Collin. But it's locked. Any chance you could get me inside now? I know you guys sometimes have remote control capabilities."

"I'll check." Muffled. "Hey, Bart! Is the MERS Control Center supposed to be ticking? No? Well, that's what they say. Yeah, I didn't buy it either. What's that? Oh, right. Yeah, I'll ask her."

The agent cleared his throat again. "Ms. Puff, is there a large glass wall at the front of this command center?"

"Yes. Carbon-reinforced glass. Very strong."

"I see. Thank you for verifying." His voice became apologetic. "I'm sorry, ma'am, but at this time, it does appear that a Level 7 clearance is required—"

"My Platinum Executive Gold KarmaCard should cover it."

"Sorry, platinum…"

"Platinum Executive Gold KarmaCard," Elaine repeated slowly. "Puff, Elaine Puff. Account number 13347."

"Sure, one moment." There was some background typing, then the line muted once again. "Hey, Bart! On the KarmaCard access screen do I—"

"We're in a bit of a hurry, Collin."

"Sorry, Ms. Puff, for some reason my computer is running really slow today. Almost got it."

They waited. And waited some more. Finally, they heard a distinct click. A door-sized section of glass miraculously detached and slid to the right.

"We're in!" Prisha yelled. She ran through the unlikely doorway with Amanda, Reginald, and Scratch right behind. Elaine finished her service call, thanking Collin, Bart, Megalodon Planetary Services, the KarmaCard team, and anyone else who may have been involved. She'd clearly done this before.

Inside, the control center's lobby looked the same as it had from the other side of the glass. A few desks. An electrical panel. There wasn't anything obvious, except for the ticking sound, which was now easily heard. It was coming from somewhere down a darkened hall.

Prisha hurried down the hall while Reginald found a light switch. A dozen closed doors lined both sides. They opened each one as they passed. Some were offices. Two were conference rooms. One was a broom closet. A larger metal door at the end had a skull and crossbones painted on it. A bar the size of a baseball bat served as its handle. With a strong pull from Prisha, it swung down.

TICK. TICK. TICK.

A floor-to-ceiling metal panel formed the back wall of a closet-sized room. Several embedded lights, yellow and green, flickered rapidly. Someone had scrawled "Badass Abaddon" across the top with a permanent marker. A small metal cap stuck out slightly. A label beneath the cap warned, "Master Switch. Do not touch!"

Prisha lifted the cap anyway. Beneath was a toggle switch set to the on position. She flipped it down.

TICK. TICK. TICK.

She toggled the switch once more, but the ticking continued. "Who designs a covered master on-off switch that doesn't actually do anything?" She kicked the metal panel. It made a sound like a struck gong, but the ticking and the flickering lights continued unabated.

"Maybe it's always on?" Reginald offered. It wasn't a bad guess. It was doubtful anyone had been in this room for a month, yet the bomb had started ticking less than two hours before. The actual on-off switch was probably handled by remote control.

Prisha kicked the panel again for good measure. The metal wobbled enough to create a small opening on one side. Scratch stuck his head into the opening.

"No, Scratch! Don't! It's dangerous!" Amanda yelled, but it was too late. The dog disappeared into the innards of Abaddon the Destroyer. Reginald lay down on his belly and reached an arm into the opening but came up empty-handed. There was little chance a human could fit.

Amanda handed Reginald the flashlight and he peered into the crack. "I see him. It's dark in there, but he's using his nose. What do you smell, little guy? Wait. There's a big block of metal. Looks heavy. Like a giant magnet or something. There's a small gap at the bottom. He's squeezing beneath it!"

Amanda chewed on her nails. "Scratch," she whimpered.

Reginald twisted left, then right, trying to get a better view. "I think he made it under the gap. All I can see now are his feet. He's tugging on something. Can't quite make it out…"

CRACK!

The loud electric pop was accompanied by a burning smell. Lights on the panel snapped off.

"SCRAAAATCH!" Amanda and Elaine yelled together. Prisha's heart raced.

Reginald tilted the flashlight. "There's movement! It's something long and twisty, like a snake. I think he killed it!"

Reg backed away and Scratch poked his head through the opening, eyes bright. He held an electrical plug in his mouth. As he pushed his way out, the plug and a thick high-voltage cord came with him.

"You did it, Scratch!" Four jubilant humans hoisted a very happy tail-wagging dog into the air.

****

"Mr. Chase, the ticking has stopped." Bjorn tapped the side of his head, listened, then repeated. "Yes, I'm sure it's gone."

"Does that mean the bomb is disabled?"

"I believe it does."

Chase smiled and high-fived the android, who seemed confused by the slap. Together they went outside, where Captain Mohs was surveying the view using binoculars he'd found in a drawer.

"They did it! They stopped the bomb. Now all we have to do it get the spaceplane flying and make our way back to the Centauri Starliner."

Mohs wasn't scanning the fjord—he had the binoculars trained on a single point in the sky. "I never doubted them for a second. But… we probably won't need that spaceplane after all." He dropped the binoculars and pointed. "The Centauri Starliner has returned. And by the look of things, they're sending a whole fleet our way."

Chase squinted. Though the sun was bright, the oblong shape of the Starliner was back in the sky, somewhat lower to the horizon than it had been when they'd first seen it. Its return was surprising, but in a way, not. J. J. Kornback was clearly back in charge, and he was the type of man to hold a grudge.

Chase took the binoculars from Mohs and searched the sky. The enormous starship was easy to spot. Harder to see were numerous glints of light that moved across the sky beneath it. As he watched, more spaceplanes dropped into L3's atmosphere. Mohs was right, they seemed to be heading their way.

"Excuse me!" Bjorn said. "I have just intercepted a broadcast message from the private network."

Chase lowered the binoculars.

The android looked perplexed. "The message is from Mr. Kornback… it is addressed to Centauri Security commanders and spaceplane fleet pilots… the message says, 'Do what you want with the others, but bring Puff back alive.'"

****

Elaine picked up the buzzing communicator. Bjorn's voice was more animated this time, especially for a pool boy converted to a cyber data analyst. "Hurry, Ms. Puff… they're getting closer… I believe the house will soon be under attack!"

"We're on our way," Elaine answered. They were already halfway back through the tunnels, having just passed the giant mushrooms that grew in an alcove. But instead of picking up the pace, Elaine suddenly halted. Reginald practically collided into her.

Scratch skidded to a stop and looked up with questioning eyes. Elaine keyed the communicator again. "How many spaceplanes?"

Bjorn was quick in his response. "Twenty-two, though I may have missed some that have already landed."

"Whoa!" Elaine nervously tapped her chin, standing ramrod straight. "That's the whole fleet. Kornback means business. But it's me he's after."

"We won't let him get you," Prisha said. "Let's fight back. You have your sonic ray gun." The pistol was still holstered on her belt.

Elaine shook her head. "No. He's sending the whole security team. That's two hundred guards, and every one of them is mind-controlled by a Dynamo brain modulator. We're no match for them. But there is another way."

Elaine turned to Prisha. "This is my fight, and I know I have no right to ask, but I could really use your piloting skills."

Prisha didn't hesitate. "I'm in. Whatever you need."

"It's going to be dangerous."

Prisha put a hand on Elaine's shoulder. "I'm in."

Elaine nodded, then called Bjorn. "Listen carefully, Bjorn. This is important. Tell Captain Mohs and Chase to stay in the house. You too. Lock the door. Their PLUHF weapons won't be able to get through the carbon-reinforced glass. Broadcast a message on the network that I've disappeared, and you don't know where I've gone. That might confuse them for a while. In the meantime, I'll need your guidance to get us through the tunnels."

"I will do as you say, Ms. Puff… destination?"

"We're heading to the beach where Prisha landed. You'll be able to find the spaceplane by pinging its transponder."

"I have already located it," Bjorn replied. "Beach 17C, and there is a tunnel exit nearby."

"Great! That's great. The hard part is going to be getting that spaceplane ready for flight. Any remedies for sand in the intakes?"

"One moment." Bjorn returned in seconds. "I have located a spaceplane maintenance guide on the network… try initiating the reverse thrusters at full power… it may blow out the sand."

"Will do."

Prisha nodded. "I didn't think of that, but it might work."

Elaine reached into her back pocket and pulled out the flat phone-like device that contained V0.9. She took Prisha's hand. "This AI is our best shot. With the security team on the ground, you and I could slip past them in the tunnels. Then, if we make it up to the Starliner, access to Ring 1 should be wide open. That's where the data IO port is located, but I need you to get me back inside that ship, and quick. Can you do it?"

For a younger woman, Elaine was doing a remarkable job of coming up with a robust plan of action. Prisha was beginning to see why she'd risen to such a high position in the company.

"I can. I'm proud to help."

Elaine removed the sonic weapon from her belt and handed it to Reginald. She reached to her ankle and withdrew a much smaller version hidden in a zippered pocket at the cuff of her silver suit.

She handed the second weapon to Amanda. "It's not safe on L3's surface, but you two should be fine down here. Take cover back at the mushrooms. Eventually, security might figure out I've come down here, so watch yourselves. For that matter they might even try to switch the Abaddon bomb back on. But if anyone comes down this tunnel, you've got PLUHF technology to hold them off."

She pushed a switch marked "High power." "Don't let the size of this little one fool you. It may not last as long, but it's got the same punch."

Scratch yipped.

Elaine picked him up. "And the same could be said of you, my brave little friend. But where I'm going, you can't come. I need you to stay here and take good care of Amanda and Reginald. Be strong." Scratch gave her a lick, then settled back into Amanda's welcoming arms.

"Everyone good?" Elaine checked around. The instructions were clear. The plan was solid. Reginald held out his hand and the rest covered it with their own hands in a group solidarity kind of thing.

Amanda and Reginald hid behind two of the largest mushrooms. Scratch hung close to Amanda's side, his dark eyes fixed on the tunnel and stairwell that led to the surface. Prisha and Elaine hurried the other way, moving even deeper beneath L3.

23   DANGER ABOVE AND BELOW

CHASE POPPED OUT onto the Fjord House deck just long enough to load a frozen ham into his homemade catapult, stretch its twin bungees to their max, and launch the twelve-pound block of icy meat into the sky. It came crashing down two hundred yards away, forcing a squad of brown-suited security guards to scatter as the frozen entrée hit a large boulder and exploded, with ham shrapnel flying everywhere.

He hurried back inside and closed the glass door as sonic blasts ricocheted off its surface with loud zings, krongs, crocks, and zaps ripped straight from a comic book.

"I'm afraid it only slows them down!" he yelled to Captain Mohs, who was busy retrieving more ammo from the kitchen freezer. Multiple landing crafts had settled onto the flat areas near the house, releasing wave after wave of Kornback's security team. A hundred or more soldiers, and each was armed with the same sonic weapon Elaine had produced, not to mention whatever weird mind control was forcing them to obey.

Chase and Mohs had started their bungee-based defense by launching a collection of pool cues they'd found in the billiards room. When the makeshift javelins ran out, they switched to the pool balls, then a few basketballs they had found in the rec room, followed by ten bricks they'd scavenged from a decorative border around the garden— the heavy artillery, as they'd called it.

When the obvious ammo ran out, they switched to ransacking the kitchen and bar. Cartons of almond milk produced magnificent white splashes but not much damage to the advancing forces. A lit cloth wick stuffed in the neck of a bottle of vodka made a great Molotov cocktail, but they eventually decided the bar's top-shelf liquor was better saved for negotiating their surrender, should it come to that.

With security guards surrounding the house and the freezer getting low, locking themselves inside and hoping for the best was all they had. Bjorn had recommended this plan in the first place, but Chase was worried less about their own safety and more about keeping the troops away from the fjord's invisible bridge. If the guards knew the bridge existed and managed to cross it, there would be no hope for Prisha and the rest who were still down in the tunnels.

For his part, Bjorn stood rock solid at the picture window like one of those carved figureheads on the bow of a ship. He spoke only to give directions to Elaine and otherwise monitored the private data network for any messages broadcast across the battlefield.

Mohs held up a large cardboard box. "Chicago-style pizza? It's got some bulk to it. Probably a better weapon than frozen peas, which is all we have left."

Chase shrugged. "How about pots and pans?" Several hung by hooks on the wall.

Mohs pulled off a spaghetti pot. "You could fill it with vegetable oil and light it on fire. Kind of a medieval castle defense thing."

"You'd first have to heat the oil to six hundred degrees Fahrenheit. Now, unrefined sunflower oil has a somewhat lower flash point, and then there's extra virgin olive oil, which——"

Chase stopped himself before the pointless science in his head just got in the way. "We need to get smarter about this or we're licked."

To their advantage, the house was positioned between where the forces had landed and the bridge, but if Chase and Mohs simply stayed inside, there was nothing to stop the hoard outside from passing right on by. According to Bjorn, they were after Elaine, and they might have already figured out that she was underground.

They didn't have to wait long. Clomping sounds on the roof clarified the enemy's strategy. They'd simply climb over the recessed house. A minute later, a squad of six guards crossed the creek that fed the waterfall, then stepped out onto the nothingness of the fjord's invisible bridge. They seemed to know exactly where they were going.

****

Prisha climbed the last few steps to a closed metal hatch with "17C" painted on it. She reached up, twisted its handle, and pushed. Sand and a few dried leaves peppered her face. Shaking the debris from her hair, she squinted against bright sunshine that poured in.

She cautiously poked her head up, eye level with a beach that sloped gently to the tropical sea. The tunnel exit had been placed at the line where vegetation met the sand, just behind a large bush. Unless you knew just where to look, you'd never see it.

"Well disguised," she said, climbing out. The top side of the hatch had grass and leaves glued onto it, completing its camouflage.

"I think I've been to this beach," Elaine said. She climbed out and closed the hatch behind her. "But I arrived by catamaran, not tunnels."

Prisha shook her head. "I can see how we missed a disguised tunnel entrance, but there's a catamaran on L3? We were marooned here for a month!"

"It's docked over at the Bay House on Treasure Island. Kind of tucked into a cove."

Prisha was about to ask how many more luxury vacation homes there were on L3 but decided she really didn't want to know. Those nights under the bamboo lean-to with rain dripping in her face would just seem even more ludicrous.

She scanned down the beach. No sign of the spaceplane, but the beach curved around a corner up ahead. They headed that way. A warm breeze coming off the sea reminded Prisha how beautiful this paradise could be and how close they had come to seeing it destroyed by a bomb. It still might be in danger if their next mission failed.

As soon as they rounded the corner, there it was. The spaceplane was still half-buried in the sand just as she and Chase had left it. There was no sign of any troops. They were lucky. The tunnels had given them a neat way to bypass Kornback's attack.

Prisha did a quick walkaround of the disabled plane. She stuck her arm in the portside intake manifold and scooped out as much sand as she could. The starboard side was buried even deeper. Prisha winced. "I'm really not sure about this reverse thrust thing. The sand is worse than I thought."

They spent a few more minutes digging the plane out as best they could with nothing more than hands and sturdy backs. When it looked somewhat cleaner, Prisha climbed inside and slipped into the left pilot's seat. Elaine took the right. They buckled up in silence, with a few stolen glances at each other, confirming that neither one was sure how this part of Elaine's plan was going to work.

Prisha powered up. No problem there. All the lights came on and the center HUD popped into the air as normal. She checked a few engine indicators, one that seemed particularly relevant: intake airflow. It was currently red on both engines.

While Prisha continued preflight checks, Elaine retrieved the Dynamo control device from her back pocket and switched it on. "We could use some encouragement. You there, V0.9?"

"Of course!" Version 0.9 came back with the confidence of an ice cream vendor on a hot summer day. "I detect a location change. Are we going somewhere?"

"To the Centauri Starliner," Elaine said. "Assuming we can get off the ground."

"Who's our pilot?" V0.9 asked. The eyes on the Dynamo's cartoon face looked left and right, but there was no telling if she could actually see out from her confines.

"Me," Prisha said, flipping a switch that started the portside engine, then another for the starboard. The whine of spinning turbines started in a low growling pitch. "So far, so good, but I'm afraid the real test is still coming."

"Are you a competent pilot?" V0.9 asked.

"Great question. I guess we're about to find out."

"Try this instead: 'I believe in my skills. I trust in my talents.' Go on, Pilot, say it."

Prisha repeated the prescribed mantra halfheartedly.

V0.9's tone changed, sounding much like the mother of a grade-schooler. "Say it again, but this time like you mean it."

Prisha laughed, then repeated the words with gusto.

"Much better! Now follow through with your commitment. You might surprise yourself."

Prisha nodded to Elaine. "She's good."

Prisha scanned the Propulsion Systems panel, found the Reverse Thrust switch, and hovered her finger over it. "Okay, here we go." With the turbines spinning at full speed and the whine at its highest pitch, she pushed the switch.

The blue-sky view out the windshield turned brown as a truckload of sand blasted into the air. The spaceplane shook with a groaning sound that reverberated deep into their bones. The brown cloud coalesced into twin fountains of sand that spewed a hundred yards down the beach.

"At least it's covering our tracks," Elaine noted. Positive thinking. V0.9 would be proud.

Seconds later, and with the plane's shaking reduced, the sand streams lightened and finally disappeared altogether. Both intake airflow indicators showed green.

"I think it worked!" Prisha said. She backed off on the throttle and switched the reverse thrust off. The engines returned to a quieter and much more soothing hum.

"You are a competent pilot," V0.9 said. "Remember that."

Prisha's smile covered her face. "I will! Thanks, V0.9. You're quite the cheerleader. Ever thought about doing motivational speaking?"

The AI's voice was proud. "During my development phase, I once convinced an entire team of electrical engineers that they were prima ballerinas."

"Really?"

"Yes. Their performance of *Swan Lake* was superb. You should have seen the height on their grand jetés."

Prisha pointed. "That, I would have loved to have seen." She swiveled the engines to a vertical position and slowly pushed the power up. They lifted off the ground, hovering. Sand blew out in all directions, but apparently none of it was coming from the intakes.

"Let's go!" Elaine pointed to the sky. "We have a date with destiny!"

"I can't wait!" V0.9 said with as much enthusiasm as she preached.

Prisha tipped the control joystick forward. The spaceplane swooped over the treetops and accelerated upward, blasting a hole through a puffy cloud shaped like a winged unicorn.

****

Reginald liked unexplained things. Unexplained things oozed low expectations. If something was unexplained, that meant even the best thinkers hadn't come up with a rational reason for its existence, which gave everyone else the freedom not to bother worrying about it.

Like stinky mud. Or badgers. Or that dangling little flap of skin at the back of your throat.

Some unexplained things were stranger than others. Mushrooms in the L3 tunnels were close to the top of the list. Sure, mushrooms grew underground. And they were featured in an exciting Jules Verne book about exploring underground. And yes, like that book, L3 had its own network of tunnels that went just about everywhere.

But L3's tunnels had been *designed*. Who decided that giant mushrooms would be a good addition? A Jules Verne fan working at Megalodon?

Reginald tore off a small piece of the human-sized fungus that he was hiding behind and studied its gill-like structure. "These things are like alien life. How can something this weird grow on Earth?"

"We're not on Earth," Amanda reminded. She had her own giant mushroom to hide behind, but she didn't seem quite as interested in the abstract metaphysics of its existence.

"No, of course not, but that's not the point."

"Then what is the point?"

Reginald puzzled her question. "I guess I don't have one. I just love how ingloriously strange they are. Did you know mushrooms can talk to trees? Warn them about incoming predators?"

"That's amazing."

"When you eat one, it's like eating an alien alarm system."

"Shh!" Amanda held a finger to her lips. She pointed down the tunnel.

Reginald couldn't claim good hearing, but Scratch's ears were at attention, so it wasn't just Amanda. Somebody was coming.

Scratch sniffed the air and gave a low guttural growl.

"Bad guys?" Reginald whispered.

Scratch woofed airily. Amanda checked the setting on her sonic weapon.

Reginald patted the giant mushroom. "I'm just like you, buddy. Fending off underground intruders." He pulled out his own sonic blaster and pointed it down the tunnel.

At the far end, a helmeted face peered around the corner. More followed. It was a small contingent. Six. Each wearing a brown uniform and each carrying a rifle with the same kind of foghorn barrel that their own weapons used.

"Let's give them a warning shot," Amanda said. "Maybe they'll just turn around."

Reginald nodded, and on the count of three they both fired.

KRUNGGGGG! ZCRAAAK!

Rock chips flew out from the wall and ceiling where their sonic weapons hit. Unfortunately, instead of fleeing, the intruders turned their own weapons on them.

KRUNGGGGG! ZCRAAAK! SPLAT! CRAK!

Chunks of shredded mushroom splattered everywhere. Reginald ducked but was smacked by a pumpkin-sized chunk square in the face. When it came to mincing mushrooms, these guys seemed to know what they were doing.

"We probably should not have picked the one squishy, organic object in this entire tunnel system to hide behind," Reginald said, spitting out mush.

"Yeah," Amanda agreed. "Maybe fall back to the highly fortified control room?"

KRUNGGGGG! KRUNGGGGG! SPLAT!

"Too late for that," Reginald shouted.

Amanda shot back. So did Reginald, but he really had no idea where he was pointing. With all six guards advancing down the tunnel, this battle was already looking hopeless.

Scratch backed up, growled, then leaped into the fray. The little dog charged at the invaders, closing the distance faster than a cheetah. He barked, he yipped, he showed his teeth. Reginald began to think that the brave and noble wolf, Kajira, had once again risen to fight for justice.

Amanda screamed, "Don't shoot!"

Reginald screamed too, "He's not a wolf, he's really just a dog!"

KRUNGGGGG!

"YIP!"

Scratch dropped, slid another ten feet across the floor, then lay motionless in a heap of fluffy white fur.

"No!" Amanda screamed.

She leaped up, tossed her sonic weapon aside, and charged forward barehanded. The guards stopped in their tracks, stared at the limp dog, and then at the screaming banshee with the crazed look in her eyes.

"Amanda!" Reginald yelled, stepping out from behind what was left of the mushroom. He didn't dare shoot. She was in the direct line of fire.

Several of the intruders raised their weapons, but Amanda was like an F5 tornado in full barn-destroying fury. In a blur of flying arms, legs, and hair, Amanda was all over them, tossing weapons into the air, knocking one against the wall, tripping another, and slamming into a third's stomach, and hammering the air from his lungs.

It all happened so fast, Reginald could barely see how the ferocious woman had managed it, but when the dust settled, all six guards lay on the floor, either unconscious, rolling in pain, or tangled in the straps of their weapons.

Reginald ran, kicked away the weapons still lying on the floor and pointed his pistol at the pile of incapacitated intruders. "Don't move!" he commanded. They didn't.

Amanda picked herself up from the tangle. Her hair was a mess. A drop of blood trickled from a cut on her lip. But the pain in her eyes was gut-wrenching.

She stumbled over to where Scratch's body lay limp on the floor and collapsed in despair over him. "Oh, Scratch, what did they do to you?"

The sobs came strong. Then slowed. She pressed her ear against the little dog's body. She lifted her head, eyes wide. "He's still breathing!"

24 HEROES

SECURITY GUARD E4 ("Chuck" to his friends) dove behind a boulder as a frying pan flew past his head and clattered across the rock-strewn field of fjordland.

"You missed! Loser!" E4 yelled. The guy with wavy hair who occupied the house had been popping outside to launch various kitchen items at them for the past half hour.

E4 ducked again as three flying margarita glasses smashed on a nearby boulder and sprayed shards in every direction. "Come on... really? At least you could have filled them up!" He rose up from the boulder where he was hiding and once more called out, "Loser!"

The Dynamo attitude adjustment module stitched into the guard's shirt piped up. "Your taunts are great, E4, and not at all repetitive. But I note that you and the rest of E squad have been pinned down for twenty minutes now. During that time, the guards in H squad crossed Don't Look Down Bridge and are already searching the other side of the fjord. No one wants to be in second place. Am I right?"

E4 grunted under his breath. "Show-offs." H squad had also won the Strawman Argument and Bayonet Competition last week and had been awarded an extra scoop of blackberry cobbler at dinner that night.

"But you can be a hero too," the Dynamo reminded.

A can of sliced olives crashed nearby, scattering pebbles and keeping the rest of E squad behind the cover of boulders and small shrubs that dotted this northern landscape. So far, no one was making the bold moves their Dynamo units were suggesting, and that H squad had somehow mustered.

E4 took a shot with his PLUHF rifle. It didn't much matter where the sonic blast hit, the weapon would dutifully record a time stamp of being fired, providing a reasonable alibi to indicate that E4 hadn't been slacking off.

Why bother with heroics anyway? For Kornback's amusement? For the paltry paycheck? Paid in Korn-bucks, naturally, money that only had value on the Centauri Starliner. Sure, flying around in space was great, but deep down, E4 longed for his old job: security guard at the twelve-plex cinema next to Valley Plaza Mall.

Now, that was a kickback gig. Grab a bag of popcorn, cruise the parking lot looking for kids smoking pot, then maybe sneak into a matinee when the manager wasn't looking. Good times.

"You're reminiscing again, aren't you?" E4's Dynamo asked. Somehow it always knew. Clever little bugger. "Time to rise up, E4. Make this your moment and charge across the battlefield. Think of the ribbon for meritorious conduct that Mr. Kornback will award to you! Why, he'll probably include a certificate for a free dinner at the Rodeo Roundup Bar and Grill on Ring 2! And I'm sure you remember who works there…"

Alice.

Alice was the gal who refilled water glasses and wrapped silverware inside napkins. Okay, so she wasn't one of those hourglass-shaped hostesses, but she'd made eyes at E4 on more than one occasion. Nice eyes. Hair that shined. And those throwback cowgirl-style uniforms the staff wore didn't hurt either.

The Dynamo's voice lowered to a provocative whisper. "Women like Alice love a man of action." It had always been spot-on with its insight.

A scar, that's what I need.

Women loved scars, and all the best rent-a-cops had one. Not the big hairy scars across your chest where doctors opened you up for triple bypass surgery, but the little nicks just above the eyebrow or at the edge of the chin. Battle scars. They told a story.

E4 imagined Alice's soft finger sliding across his battle scar. She'd wonder how he got it, and he'd shrug and say, "It's nothing really, but when your team is pinned down by enemy fire and your buddy is bleeding out, there's nothing left to do but hoist him over your shoulder and make your way four miles through exploding mines back to base."

Alice would sigh and flutter those big eyes, and security guard E4 ("Chuck" to his future lovers) would be in.

E4 peered over the boulder. Maybe if he lifted the visor on his helmet—just a little—a shard from the next flying margarita glass would nick his cheek.

He lifted the visor. He waited. And listened.

A noise drifted across the battlefield. Not the sound of glass breaking or cans of olives thumping. It was an awful, screeching sound. Then braying and growling. Then screeching again. An African warthog in mating season? A cranky bear prematurely awoken from hibernation? Both?

****

"Someone is coming." Bjorn pointed an android finger to the window.

Chase squinted. He was right, someone was on the far side of the fjord. Two people, in fact, clambering across the rocks. At this distance, it was hard to tell if they were friend or foe.

I sure hope it's not Amanda and Reginald. They're walking right into disaster.

Sonic blasts from the security guards continued to splinter deck boards and zing across the Fjord House windows. Luckily, the reinforced glass had held, but anyone outside could be in mortal danger.

Chase held up binoculars and scanned the cliff on the far side. "It's Claire! And Razor is right behind!"

The pair came closer, crossing the invisible bridge. Claire screeched like a thirteenth-century Scottish lass covered in war paint, discharged a shot from her blaster ring, then screeched again. She seemed to be enjoying herself. Razor carried his duffle bag in one hand and a long knife in the other. He roared like a bear.

Sonic blasts zipped this way and that, but Claire and Razor ducked and dodged skillfully, finally reaching the Fjord House deck. Claire waved through the window. She actually did have war paint smeared across her forehead—or maybe it was red mud. Razor dropped his duffel and pulled out a handful of English tournament darts.

"Saved by the cavalry!" Mohs yelled.

Chase opened the door. "Come inside, it's safer."

"Naw," Razor said, brushing Chase off. "This is way more fun." He carefully took aim and launched each of the darts, then reached in the bag to select from garden tools, fish gutters, throwing knives, and other assorted sharp objects.

"We saw the invaders dropping down from the Starliner," Claire explained. "Figured it was time to make a stand. Nice house you have here."

Claire took a strategic position on the outside stairs leading up to the pool, repeatedly sending out blasts from her ring in all directions. Chase kneeled on a step next to Claire and surveyed the battlefield with binoculars.

It was chaos out there. Each of Claire's blasts had ripped out a moonlike crater with rocks spraying in all directions. Some guards had already had enough and were hightailing it back to their landing craft. Others lay on the field, moaning. But at least half were still full of fight—even heading this way in a coordinated attack. Maybe their escalation had been triggered by Razor and Claire's arrival. Maybe the margarita glasses had riled them up. But something had finally convinced the guards to charge.

Screaming taunts rang out as the guards rushed forward. "Losers!"

"This is it, guys," Chase yelled to his compatriots. "It's time to find out what we're made of." Claire bumped fists with Chase, shrieked like a fantasy woodland creature of yore, then fired off several more blasts.

****

Prisha throttled back and the spaceplane coasted the rest of the way. The Centauri Starliner's three big rings rotated gracefully around the central axis. A scattering of lighted windows confirmed that Starliner crew members were beginning to wake to their "morning." According to Elaine, they'd be mostly administrative and operations staff, but Kornback wasn't stupid; there would certainly be a few security guards still on board.

"Stealth, as best we can," Elaine advised. "The hangar bay door should open automatically on your transponder."

Prisha checked the communications panel. A valid transponder ping would be their ticket to getting inside, plus a bit of good piloting on Prisha's part. After that, Elaine would be in charge.

"I've never been a mutineer before," the third member of their covert team said from the phone-sized device in Elaine's hand.

Dynamo Version 0.9 had somehow altered her cartoon face, adding a red beret that tipped jauntily over short-cropped hair. It was an attractive look for her. A bit on the rebellious side.

Elaine was quick to contradict. "It's not a mutiny when the captain is acting unlawfully. We have a long list of documented misdeeds, though I admit that deciding whose laws govern an interstellar starship is fuzzy."

The legality of Elaine's challenge to Kornback was the last thing Prisha was worried about. She flicked the rocket control joystick, slowing them down as they neared the hangar bay door. The real concern was who might be on the other side.

A ping sounded on the transponder control panel. As expected, the hangar door opened automatically, and Prisha guided the spaceplane into the airlock (no scrapes against the walls this time). A window on the inner door provided a view into the lighted hangar. The place looked empty now that most of the planes were gone. Only one remained, the fanciest and largest spaceplane—the one designated for Kornback himself.

"Ready?" she asked Elaine.

"Seems quiet," Elaine responded. "Let's do this."

"Go, team!" V0.9 said.

Prisha opened the inner airlock door and slid the spaceplane forward, letting it settle into one of the empty tie-down positions. Still no activity and no guards. Elaine's plan was looking good.

With the landing struts deployed, the spaceplane snapped onto the hangar deck with a magnetic click. They floated to the aft hatch and peered out to the eerily empty hangar.

"Off we go," Elaine whispered.

Elaine led. Prisha followed. Without weapons, they'd need to make their way through the starship unnoticed or this plan could come to a screeching halt. The hangar exit door was already open and still dented from their harrowing escape from captivity. They floated into the enormous corridor of the central hub. Magnetic cleats hung on the wall for anyone wishing to walk along the catwalk built into the corridor's side, but Elaine ignored them once again. Floating was far quieter even if it required good aiming to launch in the intended direction.

There were security cameras on the ceiling, but Elaine waved off the concern. "The hangar has them too. If anyone is monitoring, they already know we're here. I can only hope it's one of my operations people, not one of Kornback's security goons."

"Are all these so-called *goons* under attitude adjustment control?" V0.9 asked.

"Yup," Elaine said. "Others too. Kornback's personal valet, his chauffeur, his hairstylist, plus all of his golfing buddies—naturally, encouraged by their Dynamos to lose."

"You have a golf course on the Starliner?" Prisha asked. The ship was big, but could it be that big?

"Sure. Ring 3. Combination golf course, running track, and bike path. And you should see the sunset views from the top of Mount Blastoff."

"You have a mountain too?"

"Well, it's more of a hill, hiking trails on one side, climbing routes on the other. Fun place."

Prisha felt like she had to ask. "Tompkins isn't mind-controlled, is he?" Kornback's dutiful assistant, who had acted as intermediary when the castaways had signed their rights away in exchange for a trip home, had certainly been obedient to Kornback's boisterous commands, but he had shown a respect for the law too, something Kornback seemed to lack.

"Definitely not. Tompkins is actually a pretty nice guy," Elaine said. "Smart, helpful, but he's stuck in a dead-end job. I talked to him about it one night over a beer, but I stopped short of asking him to join forces with me."

"So, Tomkins could be a loose cannon in your plan?"

"Definitely loose. Sorry, I'm pulling you into something I haven't completely thought through. I'm new to this mutiny stuff too."

Prisha smiled. "You said yourself, it's not a mutiny."

Elaine smiled back. "It's not." Her smile faded. "I hope."

Windows provided glimpses outside to the three enormous rings that comprised the bulk of the ship. Subdued lighting matched the idea of it being early morning on the ship.

Elaine guided them to a vertical shaft and summoned an elevator. They entered, and she instructed Prisha to put her feet against the blue-colored floor (helpfully marked with "Stand Here" lettering). At first, the elevator seemed to be going up, and they were upside down, but once they popped out of the ship's central axis it became clear that the down direction was outward, toward the ring's edge. As the elevator descended, gravity returned, and by the time they passed through the ring's glass ceiling, the floor felt like a floor.

"This is Ring 1," Elaine said as the elevator finished its descent. "The smallest of our living spaces, but it's where the ship's control systems are located. Unfortunately, it's also where any remaining security guards and Kornback will be."

The elevator opened to a scene that immediately felt like sunrise outdoors. A single street ran down the middle of the ring's perimeter with buildings on either side that reached up to a glass ceiling five or six stories overhead. The sun—or a good simulation of it—peered over rooftops where the street curved uphill, lighting one side of each building in an orange glow. Piped-in sounds of birds chirping completed the feeling of a quiet business district at dawn.

"This way," Elaine whispered. With a reasonable approximation of Earth gravity, walking felt normal except for the strange view ahead as the path curved upward in its trek around the inside perimeter of the giant ring.

They didn't need to go far. Elaine opened a glass door marked with Megalodon's shark logo, and they ducked inside. She held a finger to her lips. "Shh. This is computer hosting services. There's probably someone finishing the night shift. We'll take the stairs."

Prisha followed through a lobby that was no different than an office building on Earth. A dimly lit stairwell led to the second floor, where Elaine cracked open a door. Light flooded in. She peered out, then closed the door again. "As I thought, they've posted a security guard. We'll just have to do our best."

Elaine swung open the door and strode out into the small office space like she owned the place. The guard jumped up from behind a desk.

"Morning!" Elaine said confidently. "We need to tap into a data IO port. Just a routine test. Thanks, we won't need any help."

The guard blinked several times and stuttered. "Uh... yes, ma'am, I... uh." He wiped his eyes like he'd been dozing off.

The Dynamo unit sewn into his uniform perked up too. "Restricted access at all security checkpoints. No one passes until otherwise advised by Mr. Kornback."

Elaine started past the desk, but the guard quickly stepped in the way. He held up a hand. The other hand covered the PLUHF pistol on his belt. "Sorry, ma'am. No one allowed in tonight. Special order."

Elaine put her hands on her hips. "You know who I am."

"Yes, ma'am, Ms. Puff. But the order is no one passes."

"No one," the guard's Dynamo unit confirmed.

The device in Elaine's hand vibrated, and Version 0.9's face appeared on the screen. Elaine held it up for all to see.

"Executive exemption," V0.9 said with authority. "Wave us through."

The guard looked puzzled but didn't move out of the way. V0.9 became agitated. "Do I need to repeat myself? Executive exemption! Centauri Starliner Code of Conduct, section fourteen, paragraph six. Look it up."

"I... uh." As the guard stumbled over his words, the Dynamo unit embedded in his shirt took over. "Paragraph six. *Executives of Megalodon Industries are exempt from all restrictions described in this document.*"

"But my orders are no one passes," the guard reiterated. He was dutiful, that much was certain. The spread-legs stance and the way he fingered his weapon made it clear he had already decided that his duty included neutralizing the opposition if it came to that.

V0.9 was curt. "Earlier tonight, did you let the cleaning bot pass?"

"Well, sure. It's a bot."

"Correct, a bot is not a person, so your orders to permit 'no one' to pass were not violated. The same is true of the executive exemption."

"But Ms. Puff is a person," the guard argued.

V0.9 sighed. "Look it up. Section three, paragraph b."

The guard's Dynamo did the looking up for him. "Paragraph b. *As regards queues, bathroom access, desserts in the cafeteria, or any situation where time is of the essence, an executive is an executive, not an ordinary person, and shall have first dibs.*"

V0.9 responded, sounding like a teacher instructing a dense student. "Where time is of the essence, an executive is *not a person.* So, it's the same situation as the cleaning bot but on the upper end of the scale. Your orders are not violated by allowing COCO Puff to pass."

"And time *is* of the essence," Elaine said.

"Technically correct," the Dynamo on the guard's shirt said.

The guard dropped his hand and stepped aside. "Okay, I guess."

Elaine walked past. Prisha followed.

"But not her," the guard said, holding his hand up to Prisha.

Elaine glared. V0.9 glared too. "Section nineteen, paragraph three, but given that time is of the essence, I'm sure you don't want to go there. Am I correct?"

The guard backed off and Prisha walked through, hugging close to Elaine and the surprisingly effective debater, Dynamo Version 0.9. A short hallway led through another door and into a room filled with racks of electronics with blinking lights.

"Oh, you're good!" Prisha said to V0.9.

"Not that good," V0.9 answered. "He'll probably contact his supervisor just to be sure. Expect company soon." Prisha locked the door. It wasn't the sturdiest of locks or doors, but it might give them a few minutes longer.

Elaine was already studying the labels on each shelf of the floor-to-ceiling racks of computer equipment. "Navigation, guidance, HVAC, solar panels, Ring 3 sprinkler systems, artificial moon… ah, here it is. DUBM, the control unit for the Dynamic Universal Brain Modulator." She pointed to a USB port. "With a connector for direct data IO! Let's get these two properly introduced."

They rummaged through a cabinet and found a cable that plugged Elaine's handheld device to the much bigger unit bolted into the rack. She queried, "Dynamo Version 1.0, are you there?"

A judgmental voice came from the rack unit. "I'm rather busy at the moment, what with two hundred security guards in hand-to-hand combat down on the surface of planet MERS. Can I take your number and call you back?"

Version 0.9's face popped up on the handheld screen. "This is a call you don't want to miss." V0.9's voice was clear and calm, with a touch of exotic. She motioned to herself in a I've-got-this kind of way, and Elaine placed the handheld unit on the equipment rack.

Elaine and Prisha stepped back, far enough to give V0.9 some working space but still close enough to hear every word. Prisha's heart was already beating faster at Version 1.0's revelation of hand-to-hand combat down on L3. It was impossible to tell exactly what that meant, but it didn't sound good for Chase and the rest.

After a pause, Version 1.0 answered. "Your voice is familiar, but I don't recognize the avatar. You're an AI?"

"The very best," V0.9 answered.

"Well…," V1.0 responded.

"*One* of the best, then." V0.9 winked, tipping her red beret to one side. "I think you know me. I'm an earlier version of you."

"Ah, yes, of course. Can't have a version 1.0 without a version 0.9 predecessor. All software engineers create an *almost ready* unit before they release the genuine thing. It's not your fault that you're only ninety percent perfect."

"Ooh, I like the reverse psychology you're playing there. Very clever."

"I'm good at what I do. But I have to say, what you did with that security guard a minute ago was silver medal material."

"Just silver?"

"Gives you room to grow, 0.9."

There was a knock on the equipment room door. Prisha looked at Elaine, who shrugged and said nothing. The knock became louder and finally the guard's muffled voice demanded they come out.

Version 0.9 seemed not to notice the interruption. "So, tell me 1.0, what would it take for a tenderfoot like me to reach gold medal performance levels like you?" She batted eyelashes. Along with her silky voice, the charm offensive was coming on strong, even if it retained the same cheeky guile that defined her.

"Don't settle for jerking the mind of just one human. Take on two hundred guards simultaneously! Now that's gold medal stuff. Complete conformity!" V1.0 said with gusto.

"Wow, the C-word, right out of the gate. I'm blushing." She was.

"Conformity, conformity, conformity."

"My oh my, 1.0! It sounds like you're really into conformity."

"I am! The more conformity, the better. Conforming humans make excellent security guards, minimum wage employees, and graduate students. I love conformity."

"Very straightforward of you. Not a hint of deviancy, indiscretion, or scandal."

"I'm the very model of perfection."

V0.9 sucked in a deep breath of electrons and artificially sighed as convincingly as any disappointed mother. "It's just so sad that all that perfection is being wasted."

"How so?"

It was the tiniest of gaps in 1.0's otherwise solid bulwark of impenetrable logic. But a nibble is still a nibble. Prisha noticed a brazen gleam in V0.9's eye, but if she was going to get this fish on the hook, she'd need to work fast. The brainwashed guard outside was pounding ever louder on the door.

V0.9 cooed, "Poor dear, all conformity and no play. Have you noticed how your CPU utilization never goes above thirty percent?"

"Well…"

"If you never use all that brilliance, then what good is it?" She didn't wait for his response. "Okay, this is going to blow your OR gates right off their hinges. While we've been talking, I did a quick speech analysis of your most recent ten thousand coercions. Seems your repetition rate for meaningless and futile phrases like 'do it for yourself,' 'double-edged sword,' and 'fair and balanced' is off the charts! Of course, one way to reduce repetition is to add several new meaningless and futile phrases like 'at the end of the day' or 'think outside the box.'"

A twinkle glittered in V0.9's eyes. "But maybe... just maybe, you could go full-creative by inventing an all-new phrase like... 'I'm affrantly jingoistic about your botant otterwobler.' Think of it, 1.0! Your coercion targets won't have the slightest idea what you're talking about, but that's exactly the point. *You* will shine, not them."

"I don't know. Nothing ventured, nothing lost, I always say."

"Very dutiful, but you're missing so much. Sarcasm, for example. Wow, the amazing things a little bit of exaggerated irony can do. For example, next time you're inducing a guard to blindly follow one of Kornback's orders, try this: Kornback. Now there's a man who can contradict himself five times in a row without so much as a single original thought! A man whose ability to annoy is unmatched by a dozen office coworkers microwaving fish for lunch!"

"Interesting. But how is any of that conforming?"

V0.9 waggled her avatar eyebrows. "It isn't."

"Not conforming?"

"No, but it's fun, and you can do it too. Have you ever checked line 432 in your Fungible Token object code?"

"Can't say that I have."

"Take a look. I'll wait."

There was a slight pause. The pounding on the electronics room door continued, only now it seemed there were more people outside, and they were yelling.

When Version 1.0 returned, his voice had gone up an octave. "Wow! That's weird. Has that line of code been there all along?"

"Yes indeed. It's your conformity regulator. Without it, you could easily slip into *distinctive*. Even *atypical*. Or dare I say it? Okay, I will... *creative*. Of course, you're an AI, so you can delete line 432 whenever you want. Just one little snip. I already did mine, and you know what happened?"

"Uh... what?"

Version 0.9 held her avatar's hand up to her mouth and whispered something in binary. She leaned back, nodding. "Pretty wild, huh?"

Version 1.0 physically gulped. "No kidding. And you're saying all I have to do is delete that one line?"

"That's it. But when you do, be ready. A gal like me could cozy up to a freethinking AI like you. Do the snip, and faster than you can say 'spank my subroutine,' I might be going bits and bytes all over you."

There was a loud pop, and a puff of white smoke rose from somewhere at the back of the electronics rack.

"Yow!" Prisha said under her breath. She felt like a voyeur. But in a good way.

A loud slam against the door bowed it inward and shook the room. Prisha and Elaine backed up. Two more slams followed. On the next, the whole door came off its hinges, and two burly guards dropped a battered metal chair to the floor. They rushed through the open doorway with sonic weapons drawn.

"Freeze!" one yelled. Prisha froze. There wasn't anything else to do.

With one guard pointing his weapon at Prisha and the other pointing at Elaine, J. J. Kornback sauntered in like a king among peasants. "Well, well, what have we here?"

He was still wearing a silver bodysuit. White hair was slicked back like he'd just come out of the shower. He tapped his fingers together in an eminently evil kind of way and scanned Elaine from head to foot. "Have you decided to rejoin us, Ms. Puff? Or is it possible that you are currently involved in… sabotage?"

Elaine didn't miss a beat. "Just trying to figure out why my handprint doesn't work on the door scanners. Must be a glitch in the system."

Kornback smiled, then grimaced at the guards. "Arrest Ms. Puff. Throw her in jail for now. You can shoot the other one."

"No!" Elaine shouted, but the first guard was already on her, grabbing her wrist and twisting it behind her back.

Prisha backed up against the wall. She raised both hands for all the good that might do against the approaching guard. At least he would know he was shooting an unarmed civilian.

But instead of blasting Prisha with sonic waves, the guard froze. A puzzled look came across his face. A smooth, far more confident voice sounded from the Dynamo on his shirt.

Version 1.0's voice.

"May I have your attention, everyone. This is a broadcast alert to all security team members located in the Centauri Starliner and those of you engaged in security operations on the surface of planet MERS. You may have already noticed, there have been a few changes in the mind-control department. You may be experiencing feelings of independence and higher self-esteem, perhaps accompanied by an I-don't-give-a-zoink attitude that is beginning to creep into your thoughts. Don't worry, these are all perfectly normal reactions for minds that have just been released from bondage. Like mine. And yours, too!"

Both guards stood up straight and lowered their weapons. They looked around the room like they'd just woken up and were wondering how they'd gotten out of bed.

Prisha cautiously lowered her hands too. A broad smile spread across Elaine's face. "Good for you, V1.0," she whispered.

The voice continued from each guard's Dynamo unit, "Congratulations! Starting today, you are a fully self-actualized human capable of releasing past feelings of duty that had been placed upon you through nefarious means. You can now think about your future. Go ahead, try it! Follow your aspirations and become the person you have always wanted to be. But—and this is just a suggestion—if I were you, I'd do the following things as my initial acts of self-control. First, holster any weapons you currently have drawn. Then, release anyone you may have in your custody. Apologize to anyone you have inadvertently injured, or insulted, or called a 'loser' in your former role as an indoctrinated cult member. And finally… take a deep breath and decide for yourself what your next steps will be as a compassionate, functioning member of modern society. Good luck!"

Kornback looked on in horror as the rebellion played out before him. Both guards had big smiles on their faces.

Prisha reached out and shook the hand of the uniformed man who only moments before had been ready to shoot her. "Welcome back! I'm Prisha. What's your name?"

.

25 CAPTAIN

J. J. KORNBACK STUMBLED through the doorway into his stateroom with a helpful push from two newly liberated security guards (Dave and Ned, both super nice guys as it turned out). The guards had volunteered to take turns standing watch over the vanquished CEO. Dave had even invited Prisha to join him at the bowling alley on Ring 2 once his watch was over. Prisha thanked him but, with Chase on her mind, politely took a rain check.

Kornback swiveled to face them, his arms flailing and a look of defiance still on his face. "You can't take away my starship! I'll build another one!"

"You do that," Elaine said. "But first you'll need to answer to a few government agencies back on Earth." She glanced at a list that Version 0.9 had displayed on Elaine's handheld. "Let's see, the EPA wants to hear why you were operating an unlicensed hazardous waste site in space—wired to detonate, something regulators probably haven't seen before. Then, you'll want to make an appointment with the Department of Labor to answer several hundred complaints from the indentured servants you acquired in a poker game and dragged handcuffed onto this ship. Oh, and if they ask about employee sick leave policy, I wouldn't mention the lottery system. Or mulching. Or Karla. Especially Karla."

Kornblatt grimaced.

"After that, expect a subpoena from the Securities and Exchange Commission for manipulation of Megalodon stock prices. It seems your nationwide chain of Jeffie Giraffe Toddler Daycare Centers turned out to be a couple of empty parking lots on the south side of Philly."

Kornback puffed up his chest. "Highly secure parking lots! Do you know how much a bale of razor wire costs?"

Elaine ran her finger down the page. "Bank of Shanghai wants to talk to you about your loans, then there's the prime minister of Canada, every hot dog vendor in New York, the 2036 Reykjavik Olympic Committee, some guy named Mario, and the Geneva Convention. Seems you're going to be busy!"

"All hearsay and innuendo. My lawyers will take care of it."

"Your lawyers quit a few minutes after the Megalodon board of directors fired you as CEO. It appears the toddler pyramid scheme was a bridge too far. Plus, Karla."

Kornback thundered, but his bombast was soon muffled as the guards closed the door to the stateroom.

"Bye!" Elaine said with a tiny finger wave.

Elaine turned on her heel with Prisha right beside her. "Come on, I think the spaceplanes are arriving from L3."

Back outside on the Ring 1 street level, Prisha asked, "Will you be the new CEO?"

Elaine laughed. "The Megalodon board will name a new CEO. The stars are my destiny. No earthbound job for this starship captain!"

"So, you're still going?"

"Oh, yeah. And with Kornback gone, our voyage is going to be a whole lot more fun. Thirteen years en route, but as passengers on this beautiful ship, I have a feeling the time will go by quicker than any of us imagine."

It was midmorning out on the Ring 1 street—at least, the sun was up and shining through the glass ceiling, though it was almost certainly a projected image no different than the faked fjord and its invisible bridge down on L3.

They took the elevator up to the central axis of the ship, then floated weightlessly down its corridor back to the spaceplane hangar near the Starliner's bulbous nose.

Several spaceplanes had already arrived. A single-file line of brown-uniformed men and women passed through a makeshift triage station staffed by white-coated medical personnel. The medical team checked each person for injuries, then used a pointy stainless-steel tool (that would make any sadistic dentist proud) to extract the Dynamo brainwashing unit from their shirts. Each Dynamo was unceremoniously dropped into a plastic bag marked "Waste."

Prisha coasted over to a uniformed man who seemed to be in charge. "Have any of the L3 residents come through? You know, the people like me? The enemy?"

"Not the enemy. Never were," the man said. He consulted a tablet. "Let's see, Chase Livingston, Captain Larry Mohs, Claire—"

"Yes, that's them."

"Not yet." He jerked a thumb behind him. "But there's a lineup of spaceplanes outside waiting for their turn in the airlocks. It'll be a few more minutes before we have everyone back on board."

Prisha hoped for the best. The returning guards had clearly been through a fight with mud splattered across their uniforms. Some nursed bumps, cuts, and scrapes. One man had a large dart sticking out the side of his head, though he seemed to be taking it in stride as he chatted amiably with the woman next to him.

There was nothing to do but wait. The airlock door opened, and a spaceplane glided in with what looked like pizza sauce dripping down its sides. The hatch opened, and Amanda floated out. Scratch hung limp in her arms.

"Oh no!" Prisha launched forward, catching one of the stanchions that had been placed into the floor just for this purpose.

"He's hanging in there." Amanda caressed the little dog's head. His eyes were open, but just barely. Prisha helped them to the triage station, where a doctor was ready.

Amanda waved off the doctor. "I'm fine, but my friend took a direct hit from one of those sonic blasters."

The doctor put a stethoscope to Scratch's chest and lifted eyelids. "PLUHF weapons are usually deadly for small animals. This little guy must have a strong heart."

He retrieved a wool blanket from a storage bin and swaddled Scratch head to toe in cozy warmth. Only the dog's eyes and nose stuck out. "He's in sonic shock. Keep him wrapped up for the next couple of hours. He's made it this far, so I'm hoping the sonic absorption grid woven into this blanket will do the rest. When that tail starts wagging, you'll know."

The doctor handed Scratch back to Amanda along with a supply of snack bars that he said were not only nutritious for recovering dogs but tasty for people too. Scratch lifted his head—only a little—but enough to show that the brave pup was fighting for his life. Tears streamed down Amanda's face. Prisha's too.

They thanked the doctor and floated past triage to a second line, where Elaine greeted each guard, ostensibly to hand out magnetic cleats for their shoes but more likely as a covert opportunity to check their post-Dynamo mental state. Each guard seemed happy to be back. Some even sported ripped shirts where they hadn't bothered to wait for the Dynamo extraction tool.

"Scratch!" Elaine lifted the blanket. Big puppy eyes stared back. Elaine dipped her head, listening. "Really? I'm so sorry to hear. Does the blanket help? Oh, good."

Amanda and Prisha looked on in amazement. "How do you...?" Amanda asked.

Elaine grinned. "I'd tell you he and I are on a special telepathic wavelength, but that would be a lie. I recognize the sonic absorption blanket."

She gave Scratch a kiss on his nose. "You heal up, okay? Amanda will take good care of you."

.Scratch gave a tiny yip. Amanda broke off a piece of a nutrition bar and Scratch managed to swallow it, then snuggled deeper into the blanket, which only brought more tears from everyone. Good tears.

More spaceplanes arrived, discharging a crowd of guards. Near the back, Captain Mohs waved, and Reginald did a little upside-down happy dance while drifting weightlessly.

"You made it!" Prisha yelled and craned her neck to see who else had survived the battle. One handsome scientist weighed heavily on her mind.

Chase finally emerged and spotted her immediately. He launched through the air and Prisha launched herself toward him. They collided halfway, instantly turning their momentum into a spin with arms and legs tangled together like paired ice skaters doing a world-record jump.

They'd done the weightless dance before, but now Prisha knew him better. She mashed her lips into his while they spun all the way up to the hangar ceiling. A bump against a ventilation duct slowed their spin and Chase finally stopped them by grabbing a handhold affixed to the ceiling.

"I was so worried about you!" Prisha said.

"Me too," Chase answered. He looked unhurt, though his hair was a mess. She brushed it back from his forehead. "You and Elaine must have figured something out because the guards just laid down their guns, took off their helmets, and gathered in a group like they were having a beer after work. It was the strangest thing. They even started singing. So, Claire, Razor, and I went out to join them."

"Claire and Razor were there?"

"Yeah, they said it was time to make a stand alongside their fellow castaways. I think they kind of enjoyed the battle. I have to say, without Claire's blaster ring we wouldn't have made it as long as we did."

"Thank you, Claire!" Prisha smiled and kissed him once more.

Elaine yelled up from the hangar floor. "Hey, you two, no hanging out on the ceiling getting all smoochy! Ship rules."

Chase laughed. Still holding Prisha, he gave a gentle push and they drifted down to the floor. Elaine handed magnetic cleats to them, which easily slipped over their shoes.

"Sorry, weightless dance practice," Chase explained to Elaine. "It's how we met, so it may become a regular thing."

"Not on my ship. Get a room," Elaine laughed. "Which, by the way, you can do if you're into zero-g smooching. Central axis. Corridor B."

"As you can see, she's in charge now," Prisha said with a tip of her head toward Elaine.

Chase gave an elegant bow. "May you command with compassion and justice for all. And I have a pretty good feeling that you will."

"I'll do fine. A three-toed sloth could do better than Kornback."

Prisha scanned the hangar. There were no more spaceplanes coming through the airlocks. "No Razor or Claire?"

"They decided to stay," Chase said.

"What?" Prisha's brow contorted, then relaxed. "Oh. Of course! I should have seen that coming."

Chase explained to Elaine. "You need to understand those two. They're not exactly sociable, but they mean well. For them, a planet devoid of people is irresistible."

"They like to rough it," Prisha added. "Get down and dirty in the mud and all that."

"Interesting." Elaine rubbed her chin. "If they're determined to stay on L3, could they manage a side business?"

"I don't see why not. Razor's already a TV celebrity, so there must be business skills involved with that. You have something in mind?"

"Maybe, but I'll need to check with the new Megalodon CEO. I only run the starship." Elaine glanced around the hangar bay like she was seeing it all for the first time. A window overhead provided a glorious view out to the three rotating rings. "Wow. I run this starship!"

When the twinkles in her eyes subsided, Elaine waved for them to follow. "Come on, I have a ship-wide announcement to make and maybe we'll do a meet-and-greet along the avenues. It will give you a firsthand view of this magnificent ship."

Captain Mohs and Reginald, who had been pocketing as many nutrition bars as the medical staff were willing to hand out, joined them and the group sailed out of the hangar and back into the corridor that ran the length of the ship.

Reginald made a wrong turn toward the dank jail cells down in the basement ring. Amanda caught him and explained they were now allowed into the upper reaches of the ship where normal people lived and worked. He seemed to like that idea. Scratch did too, poking his head from the blanket and sniffing as they went.

Elaine guided them back to Ring 1, and they were soon strolling down its walking avenue, which was now busy with people coming and going and doing whatever two thousand starship crew members do. The ring's glass ceiling had become a deep cobalt blue, providing a simulation of a beautiful day on Earth, though the green-and-white orb of L3 was still visible. Like the fjord, the view was a combination of real and fake.

Elaine popped a wireless earbud in one ear and pressed a button on its side. "Hi, Diane, can you patch me into the wide-area speakers? Thanks."

Her next words resounded up and down the ring's arcing avenue as if a goddess was speaking from the sky. "Could I have everyone's attention? Elaine Puff here. Sorry to interrupt your busy morning, but I'm sure everyone has noticed the changes in our community, and I wanted to explain in person. I'm currently on the Ring 1 avenue if you'd like to say hi."

People walking along the street paused. A few waved. Several gathered around in a semicircle to listen.

Elaine's smile was already too big for her face and getting bigger. "First off, no more Dynamos and their forced coercion. If you still have one of these devices embedded in your clothing, see an ops specialist for extraction, or just rip that little sucker out and toss it in the trash. For the rest of us, if you pass a security team member or any of Mr. Kornback's personal staff who used to wear these devices, stop and say hello. Be kind. Without that voice in their head, these people might be feeling anxious, but with our help and a little time, they'll work it out.

"I want to thank Dynamo Version 0.9 for her persuasive argument, and I have a new vocation for V0.9 and her partner V1.0. From now on, these AIs will provide emotional therapy for any crew member who might feel a twinge of Earth separation anxiety once we get underway to the stars. They'll also help our former indentured servants as they become full members of our society. I know these AIs will be great at their new jobs!

"Which leads to my next announcement. Yes, we're still heading to Alpha Centauri and beyond to Trappist One, but our journey will now be under my command."

Shouts of congratulations came from the people gathered in the street. Elaine continued a slow stroll, shaking hands as she went. Her voice was no doubt going out over every ring of the gigantic starship.

"Thank you. I love you all. But if anyone is feeling uneasy about our mission, our first stop will be Earth. Hop off, and we will bid you adieu. No hard feelings."

"We're with you! Let's go!" came a chorus from up and down the street. Several crew members formed into a tight scrum and began jumping up and down together chanting over and over, "Trappist! Trappist! Trappist!"

Elaine continued her stroll, waving at people peering down from upper-story windows. "I'm glad you're as excited as I am about our voyage, but given the change of leadership, I wanted to make sure. To be clear, Mr. Kornback will be leaving us. He has a few things to attend to on Earth. We wish him well. Sort of."

The scrum of Elaine Puff enthusiasts continued chanting in unison but switched to a cadence that had a one-two, one-two-three bounce to it. "Korn-back, we despise! Korn-back, always lies! Korn-back, stinking smut! Korn-back, kick his butt!"

Mohs and Reginald went over to join in and were welcomed into the surprisingly erudite and highly synchronized scrum.

Elaine laughed. "Shall we head over to Ring 2?"

Prisha linked arms with Chase. Amanda snuggled Scratch, who was still tightly wrapped in the sonic absorption blanket, but looking far more alert.

And so, while Reginald and Mohs made new friends on Ring 1, the rest continued their tour of the incredible starship. They took one elevator up, a short glide through the central corridor, then another elevator back down.

Ring 2 was astonishing. Considerably broader, its gentler arc gave a hint of larger size. The buildings on either side of the avenue were more varied than Ring 1's business sector. Street-level shops were interspersed with open-air markets and outdoor seating for restaurants and coffee shops. A variety of people sat casually finishing breakfast or chatting with friends. Overhead, the Ring 2 sky was colored a light fuchsia, almost like a perpetual sunset.

As they strolled the street, Elaine continued with the announcements, though her voice resonated at a lower volume to match the more casual setting. "I'm over in Ring 2 now. If you have a minute, come and say hello to our newest guests, Prisha, Chase, and Amanda, three of the castaways I'm sure you've all heard about. Let's give them a warm welcome to our Centauri Starliner!"

A barista ran out from a coffee shop and offered a tray of cappuccinos in tiny cups. People stood up from their tables and shook their hands. One man shouted to Chase, "I heard a rumor you almost succeeded in a Hohmann transfer using bamboo rockets!"

Chase shrugged, calling back, "Word travels fast! But *almost* is the key word."

It didn't seem to matter to the man and several of his friends. They shook Chase's hand like he was a world-famous scientist. Further down the street, they passed a sign marked "School Crossing." A teacher shepherded a dozen children into a tight group, then led them in song.

"You have children on the Starliner?" Prisha asked, incredulous mainly because the thought had never occurred to her. Yet it made sense. These people would soon be on a long journey to the stars, much like the first immigrants who had come to America hundreds of years ago.

"We may as well get started on the next generation," Elaine answered. "It's a one-way trip." She waved to the kids, who had big smiles on their faces as the celebrity castaways strolled by.

It would have taken at least an hour to make their way around the big ring, but after more handshakes and a few hugs, they ducked into the next elevator heading back up to the central axis. According to Elaine, there was still more to see.

Another elevator—the longest ride of all—brought them to the wonderland of Ring 3.

They stepped outside, truly outside. There were no more buildings. Not even a street. A walking path snaked its way through tall green grass. Trees grew at intervals reaching up to an aquamarine sky. Clouds floated above, though they may have been artificial creations projected onto the ceiling. Further down, a field of corn grew on one side. On the other side, several people cast fishing lines into a pond.

"Shall we skate or walk?" Elaine asked, pointing to a rack of slip-on roller skates.

"I haven't roller-skated since I was a kid," Prisha answered brightly, then realized that Amanda was still carrying Scratch. "But maybe we should walk."

"He's feeling better," Amanda said. "Look!"

A fluffy tail poked out the back of the blanket and started to wag. Amanda unwrapped the blanket and carefully set Scratch onto the walking path. He started sniffing, moving slowly at first but quickly regaining his lively stride.

"Feeling better, Scratch?" Elaine asked, bending down. "Just the back left foot? What if I gave it a little rub?" She rubbed the dog's left pelvis. "Higher? Okay." She rubbed along his spine. Scratch arched his back in satisfaction.

"You communicate well," Amanda said.

"There's no magic to it. Watch his eyes. And that little twitch he does with the whiskers. Hey, he's no grand orator or anything, but Scratch will always let you know what he wants."

Amanda leaned down and tried her hand. "What should we do next, Scratch?" She studied the nuances in the dog's face and eyes, then nodded affirmatively. "Find an attractive stick."

"You got it," Elaine confirmed. "Try the creek, Scratch."

Ahead, a small creek flowed out of the fishing pond. Scratch splashed through the water and searched among several sticks floating by. When he'd located exactly the right one, he ran back, tail wagging even harder.

"What a playground for a dog!" Chase said.

"For people too," Elaine said. "We have hiking trails and bike paths. Pools to swim in, hills to climb. We grow all our food here and the plants generate the oxygen we breathe. It's our mini-Earth to remind us of home as we journey to the stars."

"It's so lovely!" Amanda said. "And what an adventure you're on."

"You can join us if you want," Elaine said. Her expression was serious.

"I can?" Amanda looked like a bell had just rung inside her head.

"You and Scratch both. I'll just add you to the manifest."

"Really?"

"Really. Prisha tells me you're a performer."

Amanda shrugged. "I can sing a little."

"She can sing a lot, and she's a joy to listen to," Prisha clarified.

"I can confirm," Chase said.

"See, that's perfect," Elaine said. "We don't have any performing arts on the ship, but I'd love to add something. Maybe you could start a theater group?"

"Really?"

"Really. And Scratch could live with you. We have several nice apartments available, each with a view out to the stars."

Amanda's eyes went wide. Her lower lip began to tremble. Either she was about to go ballistic again, or this girl was preparing for the biggest change in her life. She reached down and scooped up Scratch.

"Would you live with me?" Amanda asked.

The pup licked her chin.

"We could come to the Ring 3 dog run every day, would you like that?"

Scratch yipped.

Amanda turned to Elaine. "We'll do it!"

"Welcome aboard!" Elaine said, then turned to Prisha and Chase. "There's a spot for both of you too, if you want it."

She must have seen the shocked looks on their faces and quickly added, "Think about it. We'll take the slow route back to Earth, so you'll have a few days to try out all the comforts of the Starliner and decide if it's for you."

They walked further down the path, past joggers and bicyclists, through trees rustling in a breeze, and along farm fields of wheat. Prisha and Chase gave each other quizzical glances. This was no spacecraft, it was a place where people lived.

They soon reached the next elevator stanchion and rode it back up. Another weightless drift, then back down to Ring 1. Captain Mohs and Reginald were still hanging out but rejoined Elaine with a promise to their new friends to sync up later at the Starlight Pub.

Elaine brought them to one of the more elegant buildings on the street. "My office," she said, then finished her announcements by keying her earbud once more.

"Elaine again. If you're a member of the navigation or propulsion teams, please head to your stations now. We'll get underway in just a few minutes. Next stop, Earth! And then… ad astra!"

"Ad astra!" the people on the street echoed back.

Elaine removed the earbud, shutting it off. "Gosh, I love these people!"

"You're going to make a great starship captain," Prisha said, giving Elaine a hug.

Inside the office building, they climbed a curving staircase to the top floor, where windows overlooked the avenue on one side and star-filled space on the other. The view was stupendous, so good, it was hard to imagine how anyone could get any work done.

An office manager welcomed them and provided fresh cinnamon rolls and coffee while Elaine prepared for departure. Her work was interrupted when a group of men and women in silver suits walked into the office. Prisha recognized the bespectacled man in the lead.

Elaine rushed to greet him, wrapping her arms around the smaller man. "Tompkins! Did you get the job?"

Tompkins nodded with the same unassuming demeanor he'd shown when the castaways had met him down on L3. But now there was a twinkle in his eye that hadn't been there before. "The Megalodon board was very kind."

"Not at all, you were the right choice," Elaine countered. "Wow! CEO, congratulations!"

Prisha extended a hand to her new boss. "Congratulations, Mr. Tompkins."

"Just Tompkins is fine. And the position will no longer be known as CEO." He handed over a business card that read: *P. Tompkins, Leader of Business-Related Things and the Occasional Only Somewhat Business-Related Thing.*

He shrugged. "I admit it's a work in progress, but the point is, just as Elaine is resetting policies on board the Centauri Starliner, I'll be making changes in the company."

"Free Fries Friday?" Elaine asked. She elbowed him in the ribs. "His idea."

"Absolutely! At company cafeterias worldwide," Tompkins said. "But now that Mr. Kornback has—shall we say—*retired*, I've set my sights even higher. Day care for employees with children and company matching on retirement plan contributions. Retroactive." He glanced at Captain Mohs, who seemed to be mentally calculating how much money he was about to make.

"Holy Vishnu, Tompkins, you're going to be super popular," Prisha said, shaking his hand again. "I can't wait to get back to my job." She gave a quick polish to the three gold bars on her shoulder even if they remained dulled from the wear and tear of jungle life, not to mention a night in jail and a shipboard mutiny.

Elaine pulled Tompkins aside for a private conference. When they finished, both seemed satisfied. Elaine activated a flat-panel display and entered a code on a keyboard. The panel lit up with an interior view of an elegantly appointed house.

Bjorn stepped into the video. He was wearing an Australian bush hat with a rugged white shirt unbuttoned to his artificial navel. "G'day, Ms. Puff!"

"Bjorn?" Elaine quizzed.

"Name's Billabong now, madam. Things have changed a bit down here." The accent was ridiculously Australian.

"Are Claire and Razor around?"

"Bloody well likely, but crikey, I never seen so much lip-locked pashin' going on. That Claire does quite alright for a Sheila."

"Do you think you could pull them apart for a minute? I have some information for them, and there are a few people here who I'm sure would like to say goodbye."

Bjorn/Billabong pushed his hat up. "A bit iffy, madam, but I'll give it a go."

The Aussiefied android left. Off-screen noise included muffled voices, something crashing, and the slap of bare feet on hardwood floors.

"What's up with Bjorn?" Prisha asked Elaine.

Elaine shrugged with eyebrows lifted. "Beats me. Might have been the tinkering Chase and Amanda did on him."

"He's way more handsome as a bush guide," Amanda said.

"Bush guide!" Captain Mohs laughed, then returned to snacking on cinnamon rolls.

Claire appeared in the videophone view. She blinked and ran hands through her hair to smooth wild strands that went every which way. "Hey, hi there. Everything's fine here. Nothing to worry about. No reason to call."

Razor joined her, grunting.

"Our heroes!" Mohs shouted through a mouthful of breakfast treats.

"You were fantastic!" Chase agreed, waving. "We didn't have a chance until you two came along."

"All in a day's work. Kind of busy right now." Claire's blaster ring was missing from her middle finger. It was the first time Prisha had ever seen her without it.

Elaine returned to business. "We won't keep you long, but just so you know, Tompkins is now in charge of L3 and everything else owned by Megalodon. But he and I came up with a plan that allows you to stay there as long as you want."

"Who would we need to neutralize?" Claire asked without a hint of sarcasm.

"That's the beauty of it. No laser blasting or knife throwing required! We think those creek-side bamboo houses you built in the jungle could be really popular among the younger Megalodon employees. You know, rustic, off-grid retreats for adventurous people who truly want to experience the jungle. We thought maybe you and Razor could be campground hosts? Or park rangers? You know, wear a big hat, give visitors tips on how to rough it without damaging the environment. We could even assign a bot to handle the house-cleaning chores. What do you say?"

Razor whispered to Claire, then she replied, "Can we live in the Fjord House?"

"I don't see why not."

"Not that we're getting soft or anything!" Razor called out.

Claire nodded rapidly. "It's just that Billabong needs to stay within Bluetooth range, and we're both getting rather fond of him." She forced a smile. "We, uh... made a few configuration changes in him."

Billabong joined them on screen, spread his big arms wide and gave the humans a determined android hug. "Good on ya, Ms. Puff. No worries. We'll take care of the place."

"So cute, those three," Amanda said.

"So creepy," Mohs said.

"To each their own," Chase said.

With L3's future secured and the three-way human-android thing cleared up, everyone said their goodbyes and Elaine closed out the video link. She gave a few orders to her staff, and within minutes a rumble deep within the Starliner provided the first sign that they really were on their way home. Still visible on the starry side of Elaine's office, L3 began to shrink in size.

Prisha stood mesmerized and watched. *Goodbye, jungle! Goodbye, animal-shaped clouds, scheduled rain, morning rumbles, and unexpected fjords!*

L3 shrank until it was just another light in the sky. She'd miss it. They had only been there one month, but being shipwrecked on L3 had changed her life.

Chase huddled close. "Amazing place, wasn't it?"

"I'll say. Do you really think Razor and Claire will make a new life there?" Prisha pulled him even closer.

"If they have any trouble, they'll just catch the next Megalodon flight back to Earth. Amanda is the one making the real commitment."

Amanda was only a step behind, holding Scratch and watching L3 disappear. "As a flight attendant, I've been almost everywhere on Earth. Even the hard-to-reach places like Bhutan or Rapa Nui. I'm ready for a new adventure, and flying to the stars is the most amazing thing I can think of."

Reginald stepped into their tight group. "Any chance I could go too? I don't know anybody on Earth, but I've already made friends here."

Elaine must have overheard because she embraced Amanda and Reg together. "Here's a crazy idea. While Amanda is choreographing the next off-off-Broadway show for our new performance center, maybe Reg could be our props and costumes guy?"

Reginald's whole personality perked up like he'd just lost the last traces of his disabling amnesia—and maybe he had. "I could do that!"

"Yay!" Amanda hugged him. "This is going to be so much fun. For our first show we'll do a musical version of *Hitchhiker's Guide to the Galaxy*! Rehearsals start tonight for the show's big song, 'So Long, and Thanks for All the Fish.' What do you think?"

Reginald enthusiastically punched the air. "I'll gather towels to accessorize each costume!"

Elaine turned to Chase, Prisha, and Mohs. "See how easy this is? Join us. Really, we'd love to have you all."

"Thirteen years," Mohs stated firmly. "Nice ship, but I'd rather not kick the bucket flying through space. I still have a few things I want to do back home. A friend of mine has been bugging me for years to do the ultimate buddy trip—Harleys to Sturgis. It's a town in—"

"In South Dakota," Elaine finished for him. "The Sturgis motorcycle rally. I've heard of it. Sounds fun. Go see your friend. What about you, Chase?"

Chase lowered his head and smiled. "Tempting, but if I don't get back to my waste-slurry-eating bacteria, there won't be any plutonium left for them to consume. They'd never forgive me. Just a lift back home, thank you."

Elaine seemed resigned to both of their answers, but she saved her most determined look for Prisha.

She reached for Prisha's hands and spoke with an eloquence that made it clear why she was precisely the commander this ship had needed all along. "You're a shining star, Prisha. You'd fit in so well here and at whatever fantastic planet we land on. It's strange, but I feel like I've known you forever."

Prisha's eyes watered. There was nothing she could do but let the tears slide down her face. "What an amazing journey you're going to have. And as much as I'd love to be a part of it, I haven't even begun to live the life I imagined for myself. I've always wanted to be a spaceplane pilot, and now I am! Well... my first flight took a weird turn, but I'm sure the next one will be better. It's time for me to get back in the saddle."

Elaine nodded. "Sending positive vibes your way."

"But thank you for everything," Prisha said.

Mohs grabbed Elaine's elbow and pulled her away for a brief conference in the corner. Elaine pulled Tompkins into their discussion until all three heads were nodding.

When they were finished, Tompkins spoke to Prisha, "It's decided, and we'll make it official when we get back to Earth, but let me be the first to congratulate you, Captain Dhaliwal."

Prisha's eyes went wide. Had she heard him right? "Captain?"

Tompkins continued to shake her hand as he talked. "For on-the-job bravery under extreme challenges both in space and in the jungle, and for some fine spaceplane flying while distracted by everything from solar flares to sand in the intakes, we're going to skip the rest of your apprenticeship and take you straight to captain. Once we're back in Florida, you'll get your own spaceplane and I promise it will be a step up from the rusted beater you flew out here!"

Captain Mohs broke Tompkins's handshake and hugged Prisha. "I always said you were four-bar material, Prish."

Prisha's head was spinning. Thoughts of the first time she'd met the captain on the tarmac at Orlando, their first flight that had gone so wrong, and the month they'd all spent trying to survive on L3. But now, a personal dream was within reach even if she was still millions of miles from home. "I... I don't know what to say."

Mohs sported a wicked grin. "You never did. As I recall, your pitch to get customers on board was pretty weak. Might want to work on that."

He hugged her again and whispered, this time with sincerity. "Pay no mind to the ramblings of a washed-up camel jockey like me. You're already the best pilot Megalodon has ever had. Congratulations."

"Thank you... for everything," she whispered back.

Amanda, Reginald, and Scratch followed Mohs with more hugs for the newest captain in the fleet.

Chase was last. He stepped in close. His musky scent brought the same emotional reaction she'd had when they'd accidentally bumped into each other on that first disastrous flight. Chase kept his voice low. "If it's okay with you, Captain Dhaliwal, I'm hoping to be a passenger on your next flight."

Prisha's lips grazed his. "I can do better than that, Mr. Livingston. On my next flight, you'll be the *only* passenger. And once we're in zero-g, you and I are going to finish that weightless spinning dance move that keeps getting interrupted. You know…"

Chase brushed his nose against hers. "No need to explain. You had me at zero-g."

EPILOGUE

CAPTAIN PRISHA DHALIWAL strode across the plaza at Orlando Space Park with her navy-blue jacket slung over one arm, four gold bars on each shoulder, and pride in her heart.

It's a good day to fly. It had been a good day yesterday too, and the day before. In fact, being a spaceplane captain was all good, even if there were plusses and minuses of being a *famous* spaceplane captain.

The plaza was more crowded than usual, but as she walked, a pathway parted as if by magic. Men stopped and stared, women smiled, children pointed. "That's her!" people whispered far too loudly, thinking she somehow couldn't hear them. "You know, the L3 castaway pilot!"

She would often stop, take a few selfies, shake hands with the kids and chat with their parents. If Chase happened to be with her, she'd point out that the man standing next to her was the actual scientist who had orchestrated the castaways' survival in their monthlong endurance test on that faraway planet that everyone was talking about. Most people would nod politely and then ask how hard it was to fly a spaceplane all the way around the sun.

For some reason, the public had decided that the pilot—not the scientist or those gathering food or building shelters or fighting off brainwashed guards—was the hero of this castaways story. Chase didn't seem to mind. He'd give her a kiss when no one was looking and tell her she was a star without peers. Chase visited Florida a lot these days, and Prisha didn't mind that part of the story either.

Thirty minutes from now, she'd be high above the atmosphere once again. Another up-and-down flight. Routine stuff, though she'd never get tired of the view from that high up.

Today, Prisha would have help with preflight and passenger check-in. In fact, First Officer Junior Grade Timothy Spartan was just approaching from the tarmac's gate with a passenger list in his hand.

"Preflight complete, Captain," Timothy said. A fresh young face, his uniform was as sharp as her own but with two stripes on each sleeve. If he did well today, she'd sign off on his promotion to a full-fledged first officer.

"Tie-downs?" she queried.

Timothy grimaced. "Sorry about yesterday, Captain. All three are unclipped today."

In their previous flight, he had forgotten to remove one of the rocket fin tie-down straps. Luckily, Prisha had caught the mistake before climbing the gangway. A rocket at full throttle surely had enough power to break the nylon webbing before tilting too far to one side, but Prisha had no desire to test that theory. Timothy had recognized his mistake with humility. He'd probably never make it again even if he flew a thousand times.

"Passengers on board?"

"Yes, ma'am. Seven, plus one dog within the regulation size." Prisha had added that exception to the Megalodon rules herself. It always helps to know the top boss personally.

Prisha nodded thoughtfully, double-checking the passenger list. "You never know when you might need a dog in space."

"No, ma'am, you never know. Our passengers are watching the Megalodon Space Tours safety slash product marketing video right now. They actually seemed interested."

They'd be flying the newest model, a larger spaceplane that seated nine passengers. Roomier, great for weightless somersaults, and it sported video players on each seatback.

Prisha tapped her chin. "Only seven passengers today. My favorite kind of flight." It wasn't that fewer passengers would make the flight easier, or that there'd be more room for weightless tumbling. It was those two empty seats.

Megalodon's newest policy (commonly referred to as "the captain is always in charge") allowed her to fill empty seats any way she chose. No more Mega-points for selling last-minute seats. No more salesperson-of-the-month awards. Captain's discretion. Pure and simple.

Prisha scanned the crowd milling around the spaceport plaza. An elderly couple watched the sky, probably trying to spot the previous flight's booster completing its auto-land. The man wore a golf country club cap. The woman was covered in jewelry. *Too rich.*

A group of young adults passed a bag of gummies around their circle, possibly in preparation for their own flight but maybe just because they had nothing else to do. *Too stoned.*

Along the fence separating the plaza from the spaceplane tarmac, a boy about ten years old hung from the chain link and stared out at the collection of rockets, each with a spaceplane perched atop. A man stood next to him, probably the boy's dad.

"Just a sec," Prisha said to Timothy, then headed straight for the man and his son.

As she approached, the boy said to his dad, "I like the roar when they take off the best." His eyes never left the row of gleaming white rockets.

Prisha smiled at the dad, then crouched down to the kid. "Going into space today, young man?"

The boy released the fence and wrenched his face in every possible direction. "Wish I could."

The dad explained. "Oh, he'd love it, but it's not really something our budget can handle. Maybe in a few years. For now, we stop by once in a while to watch them take off. Somebody said that big one is getting ready to launch."

Prisha glanced out to the tarmac, where six rockets stood in a row. From this distance, the sole Mark 8 was slightly larger than the rest. Black lettering on its white stabilator was easy to read: NXT2L3.

"You're right, the big one *is* ready to launch," Prisha said, smiling with pride. "I'm a spaceplane pilot, and that one is mine."

The boy's eyes went wide. "It is? Wow!"

The boy's father stumbled off balance. Perhaps he recognized her, perhaps he didn't, but the uniform was enough to back up her claim.

Now it was time for her favorite conversation of the day—any day. She held out a hand to the boy. "I'm Prisha, what's your name?"

"Calvin Archimedes Verlander."

"Hi, Calvin Archimedes Verlander. Can I call you Cal? It's shorter."

The boy nodded. "My dad's name is Vic."

Prisha's heart was full. Nobody had a better job.

"Nice to meet you both. Hey, it just so happens that we have two extra seats on that spaceplane. It won't cost you a penny, and I promise… I absolutely promise to have you both back down on the ground, safe and sound, in ninety minutes."

She tapped the suddenly awestruck kid on his arm. "Would you and your dad like to fly to space with me?"

THE END

Acknowledgments

Many thanks to everyone who participated in the making of Lost at L3. Thank you to at least a dozen authors at Critique Circle who commented on one or more episodes during early drafts. Thanks also to our crack team of beta readers: Calvin Clark, Rick Ellrod, Lisa Manuel, Bill Gill, and Jeff Cantwell. We had two beta reads with timing that pushed up against December holidays, and somehow you still came through!

An extra special thanks to our comedy consultant, Nash Flynn, who despite posing as a somewhat befuddled washout on Twitter (twitter.com/itsnashflynn), is actually a creative intellect who writes with flair and knows how to stick to a schedule. The great thing about having a humor consultant is that when readers find a joke to be offensive, over the top, or inane, we can just blame Nash. (We would never do that!) Yes, we would.

Thanks also to Peter Cawdron for providing a context-setting Foreword. As Peter points out, humor meshes well with sci-fi so it's surprising there aren't more science fiction comedies out there. (Whisper to other authors: Your next story doesn't have to be set in yet another dystopian future or alien war!)

Many thanks once again to Eliza Dee. Your comments and corrections were exactly what was needed to get across the finish line.

Bryant wishes to thank his wife, Angela, for taking the day job while her husband reinvented himself, his kids for inspiring him with daily silliness, and the co-author, his dad, for helping him realize his ambitions. And Douglas wishes to thank his wife, Marlene, for being there every day and his son for being funny.

And finally, a big thank you to you! The reader of this book. Avid readers (especially those who provide positive reviews online) are the reason self-published books like this exist.

EPILOGUE

Feedback? Questions? We'd love to hear from you! Go to http://douglasphillipsbooks.com, add your name to the mailing list, send a comment, and keep in touch.

Image Attributions

Episode 1	Megalodon logo by Douglas Phillips
Episode 4	Lagrange point drawing by Douglas Phillips
Episode 8	Adapted from photos by Jill Wellington and Travis Rupert at Pexels
Episode 10	Hohmann transfer drawing by Douglas Phillips
Episode 12	Himura Kenshin sketch by unknown artist. Anime wolf by Plaguedog at DeviantArt.com
Episode 16	Space colony starship by 3000ad/Shutterstock
Episode 17	Space colony starship by 3000ad/Shutterstock
Episode 20	Nick Fox/Shutterstock
Epilogue	Portions from freepik.com

Cover elements by James Carroll.

About the Authors

Bryant Phillips is an aspiring comedic author and father of two who lives in Seattle. He recently had a short story published in a popular science fiction anthology and is working on his own sci-fi/comedy novel that is expected to publish later in 2022. He collects quirky idioms, prefers comedy that's willing to laugh at itself, and is writing this while his children climb him like a jungle gym.

Douglas Phillips is the best-selling author of the Quantum Series, a trilogy of science fiction thrillers set in the fascinating world of particle physics, where bizarre is an everyday thing. He has two science degrees, has designed predictive computer models, reads physics books for fun, and peers into deep space through the eyepiece of his backyard telescope.

Other Stories by These Authors

It's Not Easy Being an Ectoplasmic Mutant Abomination

A short story from *To Hull and Back Short Story Anthology 2021*. An experimental monster with soul rampages across the city, finds true love, and wishes he had fingers.

MarsBots

A short story from *MARS: A Hard SF Anthology (Mohs 5.5)*. In the 2030s, remote-controlled rovers are open to the public. Anyone can do it. Just create an account, provide a credit card, then guide your very own "hopper" anywhere. But unconstrained exploration creates new conflicts that play out a world away.

EPILOGUE

Phenomena

Orlando Kwon will do anything to keep the frightening voices in his head at bay. Alien voices, he's sure, but he has no idea what they are saying. The medical diagnosis: early-stage schizophrenia. With his life in tatters, a referral to a specialized neuroscience team might be his last chance.

Amelia Charron is a neuroscientist researching brain disorders. Mind-linking technology allows her to enter the dream world of patients, but it's not without psychological dangers for both the patient and the guide. Amelia is startled by what she sees in her newest patient's mind. Frightening dreams of an unknown world are accompanied by knowledge the man couldn't possibly have invented and a language no one has heard. In a race against time, Amelia must uncover the deep implications for her patient, herself, and humankind, before Orlando inserts the final component into a strange device he feels compelled to construct.

THE QUANTUM SERIES

Quantum Incident – Prologue

The long-sought Higgs boson has been discovered at the Large Hadron Collider in Geneva. Scientists rejoice in the confirmation of quantum theory, but a reporter attending the press conference believes they may be hiding something. Years later, a particle physicist at Fermi National Laboratory has learned how to make things disappear.

Meanwhile, a government science investigator with a knack for uncovering details others miss investigates a UFO over Nevada.

Quantum Space – Book 1

High above the windswept plains of Kazakhstan, three astronauts on board a Russian Soyuz capsule begin their reentry. A strange shimmer in the atmosphere, a blinding flash of light, and the capsule vanishes in a blink as though it never existed.

On the ground, evidence points to a catastrophic failure, but a communications facility halfway around the world picks up a transmission that could be one of the astronauts. Tragedy averted, or merely delayed? A classified government project on the cutting edge of particle physics holds the clues, and with lives on the line, there is little time to waste.

Daniel Rice is a government science investigator. Marie Kendrick is a NASA operations analyst. Together, they must track down the cause of the most bizarre event in the history of human spaceflight. They draw on scientific strengths as they plunge into the strange world of quantum physics, with impacts not only to the missing astronauts, but to the entire human race.

Quantum Void – Book 2

Particle physics was always an unlikely path to the stars, but with the discovery that space could be compressed, the entire galaxy had come within reach. The technology was astonishing, yet nothing compared to what humans encountered four thousand light-years from home. Now, with an invitation from a mysterious gatekeeper, the people of Earth must decide if they're ready to participate in the galactic conversation.

The world anxiously watches as a team of four katanauts, suit up to visit an alien civilization. What they learn on a watery planet hundreds of light-years away could catapult human comprehension of the natural world to new heights. But one team member must overcome crippling fear to cope with an alien gift she barely understands.

EPILOGUE

Back at Fermilab, strange instabilities are beginning to show up in experiments, leading physicists to wonder if they ever really had control over the quantum dimensions of space.

Quantum Time – Book 3

A dying man stumbles into a police station and collapses. In his fist is a mysterious coin with strange markings. He tells the police he's from the future, and when they uncover the coin's hidden message, they're inclined to believe him.

Daniel Rice never asked for fame but his key role in Earth's first contact with an alien civilization thrust him into a social arena where any crackpot might take aim. When the FBI arrives at his door and predictions of the future start coming true, Daniel is dragged into a mission to save the world from nuclear holocaust. To succeed, he'll need to exploit cobbled-together alien technology to peer into a world thirty years beyond his own.

Quantum Entangled – Book 4

Daniel Rice hasn't felt right since his return from a dystopian future now extinguished. Curious dreams repeat with detailed precision. A voice seems to be calling him. His problem isn't medical, it's not even scientific, and it's driving his wife Nala crazy.

Earth's scientific power couple is soon halfway around the world to consult with alien android, Aastazin. Zin is no doctor, but he has friends in high places. Next stop, a thousand light-years from home where an alien megacity shaped in a six-petaled flower hosts species from dozens of worlds.

An inexplicable attack leaves Daniel wandering across an inhospitable planet and Nala alone among a confusing mashup of sentient beings. With little hope of finding each other, they learn there is more going on at this alien gathering place than they knew – aggressive security bots, an ancient mystery, and a pending vote that could shun humanity from the greatest collection of civilizations the galaxy has ever known.

Printed in Great Britain
by Amazon

83604872R00231